RISE OF DAAN
(CHRONICLES OF DAAN: BOOK 1)

By

D. Ward Cornell

Dedicated to my family and friends who have been supportive through this adventure, especially those that have been willing to read the manuscripts and give me feedback.

Thank you all for your support and encouragement.

Special thanks to the members of my pre-readers program, your feedback is valued more than you can know.

Extra special thanks to Theresa Holmes whose feedback makes every story come alive.

TABLE OF CONTENTS

PROLOG

I was born on a Protected World. You'd think that would be a good thing, but in truth, not so much. You see, a protected world is a sentry world. One located along the edge of human space, there to sound the alarm if there's an alien invasion. A world that is marginally habitable, so unlikely to be a target, yet well connected to the rest of humanity, so able to sound the alarm.

And that's the real problem. Marginally habitable worlds can't support a significant population. And for the few of us that live here, it's difficult to scrape out a living.

It's not like there are no benefits, though. Because of their unique role, protected worlds have the fastest, most reliable network access in the Confederation. All essential services available online are ours for free. I got to attend the best online schools as a kid, and I'm currently studying in the online Electrical Engineering program at the Faraday Institute on New London. It is truly one of the best programs in existence. Few students on the central worlds get to do their studies there. But growing up in a place this isolated, where opportunities are so limited... It's hard to describe how difficult it is.

You might ask why anyone would want to live in such a place. I ask that question all the time. The short answer is that these worlds were given away to anyone that had the means to claim and settle them. A lot of adventurers couldn't resist the opportunity. My grandfather, six generations back, was one of those people.

His name was Jared Daan. He was a rugged individualist who struggled under the boot of government oppression. He leaped at the possibility of escape, of becoming the king of his own world. And, as the idea took hold, he decided he wanted a big one.

He filed a claim for a world that was 1.2 times the diameter of the Earth, the largest one available. When his claim was granted, he named the planet Jaredaan in honor of himself. These days, most people just call it Daan.

Daan is cold and dry. It's located at the far edge of the habitable zone in this system. Its only water comes from the great ice fields at the north and south poles. Despite the cold, most of us live near the north pole. It's the warmer of the two and has the most easily accessible water. There's a narrow green zone near the equator that turned green for the first time a hundred plus years ago. My great uncle Herold Daan came up with a scheme to move ice from the poles

1

to the equator. The family granted him a large swath of land along the equator as an incentive to build the system. He spent most of his life doing it. The only green on the planet now belongs to his children.

Most of the rest of the world is desert. It's cold, dry, and barren. Forgive me if I mentioned that already, but for the uninitiated, its more cold, dry, and barren than you can probably imagine.

You might wonder how we survive here. The answer is simple. There are massive deposits of precious metals near the north pole. This was known at the time my ancestor claimed our world. The major mining consortiums also knew of these deposits. They deemed them unprofitable to mine because they were too deep in the ground, and in too deep a gravity well.

They were mostly right. What they failed to understand was the strength of our planet's magnetic field and the magnitude of charged particles in our air. My ancestor was an electrical engineer, apparently an incredibly good one. He came up with a scheme to harness the electricity in the air. It powers our town, the mines, and the rail gun we use to launch our metals into orbit. The metal trade is what powers our economy.

One of the few benefits of being a 'protected world' is that we are guaranteed duty-free trade with every planet in the Confederation. Even though we are far from the nearest populated world, we are one of the lowest cost providers of high-end raw metal for use in space in this sector. We are completely free of taxes and have more or less free access to space because of my ancestor's cleverness.

There are many stories about my ancestral grandfather. He was apparently quite a character, eccentric as well. Many of his sayings are built deeply into our culture, and most involve the number six. Spend a day in town and you're likely to hear them. 'Better to do one thing well than six things poorly.' Or 'better to have six good days than one good week.'

Of his many sayings, there's the one my mother quotes all the time. 'The sixth son of the sixth generation will stand above them all.'

Well, it turns out that I'm the sixth son of the sixth generation. My father and his five forefathers were the eldest sons of eldest sons from the great Jared Daan. I was my father's sixth son. My parents gave me the name of my ancestor, Jared Daan. I'm the first to bear that name since the great man passed. My mother says I'm destined for greatness. I think that's crazy talk. But my five brothers hate me for it.

CHAPTER 1: CELEBRATION

I come from a big family. Mother, father and six sons; eight of us in total. I've read in history books that colony worlds tend to have large families. Their authors claim that large families were needed to work the land. Children were cheap seasonal laborers, so the more kids, the more economically successful the family would be. It sounds like a reasonable explanation, but it surely doesn't apply here. Our family of eight is one of the largest. Most families only have two kids. Three is considered large.

You might ask why. In some sense the answer's obvious. We live on a marginally habitable world. On worlds like ours, the biggest shortage is food. And unlike the agricultural worlds in the history books, there's little work here that kids can actually do. So generally speaking, large families here are less prosperous. Ours is probably the only large family that's not on assistance.

That's kind of what makes today so crazy. It's my birthday. I've reached my majority, been granted my rights under the colony's charter, and Mom and Dad are throwing me a big party. I'm sixteen years old today.

"Jared? Could you come here for a second, sweetie?"

That's my Mom. Whenever she wants me to do something, she tacks a 'sweetie' on the end. It's always my first clue that she's going to ask me to do something I don't want to do.

"Coming."

I've got to give her credit. She's making more or less all the food for this party. She's rented the community party hall on the second level. My dad and five brothers are up there now getting things set up. My second-oldest brother, Jonah, is even helping. His wife Esther is here in our apartment, helping Mom get ready.

"Hey, Mom. What do you need?"

"Hi Sweetie. Could you run up to the garden for me? I need a bunch of carrots. I forgot to pick them up yesterday.

"Sure Mom. I'll be back in a few minutes."

ESCALATOR UP TO LEVEL ONE

Our town is named Jaredstown in honor of our founder. There aren't that many places like it. It's located near the north pole and is 3,500 feet underground. The garden is on the top level, level one. Our home is on level three. There are three ways to get up to level one: the elevator, the escalator, and the stairs. I've suffered a little elevator-phobia since the incident last year, so I'm opting for the escalator today. The top 24 levels of our town are connected by escalator. The escalator shaft is isolated from each floor by a pair of double doors. You enter the escalator lobby by coming through the outer doors, then enter the escalator shaft itself by coming through another set of inner doors. This system helps mitigate the flow of heat from floor to floor. The escalators aren't as popular as the elevators, so I make the trip quickly.

THE GARDEN, LEVEL ONE

Level One is where all the surface feeds come down. The feed of consequence for the garden is the light pipes. The garden uses air, water and electricity of course, but plants and animals both do better when there's natural light available.

Level One is the coolest level in town because of its proximity to the surface. It gets increasingly warmer as you go down. Down at the lowest mining levels, about 6,000 feet down, it's just plain hot. I don't see how people can work down there.

Coming out of the escalator lobby, I turn left toward the garden. It's at the end of a long access way. The power company, where I hope to get my first paying job, is at the other end.

The entrance to the garden is through a pair of glass doors. The doors are closed, as most doors in the colony are, to control air flow. On the other side of the doors is the reception area where customers can pick up orders they've placed.

As I walk in, I see that Nana is on duty.

"Well, if it isn't the birthday boy himself."

"Hi, Nana."

I've been sweet on Nana for years, but she's 18 and I don't have a chance. Still, she's pleasant to think about.

"I have your carrots." She holds up a basket with carrots in it, then sets the basket on the counter. "I'm coming to your party."

That's probably the best news I'll get today.

"Good." I can feel a big goofy smile spreading across my face. "I look forward to seeing you there."

I'm back in the hallway, heading toward the escalator. I have to pass the elevator to get there. It's on the right, so I walk close to the left wall. Elevators creep me out.

As I think I mentioned earlier, I have five brothers that hate me. The two oldest, Aaron and Jonah, have both moved out. Aaron works in the mine. He's apparently quite good at it. He has a cheap place on a lower level that's closer to his friends. Jonah is married and has a couple kids of his own. For the most part these two don't bother me that much anymore. But I still do my best to keep a distance.

The other three, Asher, Seth, and Jude are a different story. They still live at home and take every opportunity to mess with me. Mom clamped down on them after the incident with the elevator that nearly killed me. But they still get in every dig they can.

So, about the elevator incident. Seth, who has a real knack for mechanical things, got the elevator to stop one story below the level our home is on, even though the electronics showed it as arriving on our level. Jude, pretending to be nice to me, offered to take me to the movies, seven levels below. I was standing with my back to the elevator door talking with Jude when the doors slid open. Jude stepped toward the door, saying something like, "We need to hurry. The movie's about to start."

I turned and stepped into oblivion. Thankfully, there was an old fiberboard landing I managed to grab. It was rotten and it broke when I grabbed it, but it slowed my fall. I woke up two days later in the hospital.

Seth and Jude were arrested, which they'd apparently expected. Because shortly after arriving at the jail, witness after witness came in to tell the cops that the brothers were not there at the time of the incident. They'd rounded up enough liars to get them off the hook.

As I said before, my brothers hate me.

ESCALATOR TO LEVEL 3

I enter the escalator shaft and start down. I'm maybe a quarter of the way to Level 2 when there's a sudden pressure drop and music floods up from below. Several people have apparently just come into the shaft. The music sounds like the band warming up for the party. Just as suddenly the music drops, pressure increases, and I hear the voices of the new entrants. By the sound of it, two are going down,

5

one is about to come up. The one coming up steps into view and its Asher. A smile spreads across his face.

"Well, if it isn't the little Runt."

The up and down escalators are about 2 feet apart from each other. He will pass me on the left, so I scootch over to the right as far as I can without scraping against the wall.

As we pass, he leans way over into my side. "Hey, I've got a present for you." I see the fist coming but have no place to go. Red hot pain explodes in my left shoulder. My head hits the wall, seriously scraping my ear. And the carrots go flying.

"Happy Birthday, pissant. Hopefully, this one will be the last."

That's the kind of crap I get all the time.

I scurry to collect the carrots before they get ground up at the bottom of the escalator.

HOME

When I get home, Mom takes one look and knows something happened.

"Why's your ear bleeding? And what happened to these carrots? Did you fall?"

"No. Asher punched me. My head hit the wall of the escalator and I dropped the carrots. He said it was my birthday present."

"Oh, sweetie. I'm so sorry. I'll have your father speak with him."

I can't tell you how many times I've heard that line. I love my Dad. He's a genuinely nice guy, my mentor. But he's not a disciplinarian. If he's the one in charge, nothing will happen.

...

There are still a couple hours before the party, so I head back to my room to work on my project.

One of the miracles of the modern Confederation is that the worlds are all connected by what's become known as the exo-net, the internet of interworld communications. It has truly allowed remote places like Daan to have access to first-class education and training. My entire formal education has been done remotely, using online training materials and course work. It allows reasonably smart and motivated people like me to get education that's almost as good as the best universities, and to do it at my own pace.

I have one course left to complete and I need to get it done quickly. My dream job, engineer with the power company, is about to open up. Dad's friend and colleague Levi Grayson is retiring at the end of the month. There are three other candidates for the position, none of whom are very good. The company wants to hire me. But I need to have finished my power engineering degree to be eligible.

At the university, where this course is taught live, it takes 12 weeks. When I started the course, I only had 26 days to finish before Mr. Grayson's retirement. I'm done except for the project and I have 5 days left.

My project is kind of cool. It's a bit of an adaptation of my ancestor's technology for energy capture, but for personal use. My ancestor's big idea was to use huge arrays of carbon nanotubes to capture lightning bolts. Configured as a capacitor, nanotube arrays can hold almost as much power as a regular battery of the same size. Well, maybe a battery of half the size.

But that's only half of what he did. He added nanotube thyristors to the entry and exit points of the array. Ah, sorry about that. Not that many people know what a thyristor is. They've been around forever, but only people into electrical power have ever heard of them. Thyristors are devices that allow one-way current flow, the direction and duration of which can be controlled electronically. They were discovered in the semiconductor days of prehistory. Now they're made from nanotubes. My ancestor's big idea was to combine types that are useful for short-term energy storage with the types used in control circuits.

Why hadn't anyone else figured this out? Well, I'm sure they did, but to what end? This is one of those things that's only a competitive solution in super-high current flow applications, like capturing lightning strikes.

But back to my school project, my device is a capacitor made from nanotubes, both types. I can store enough energy in a 1-inch cube to power most personal electronics for a couple days. It can be charged from any source. Anything from electrostatic shocks, like you get when shuffling your feed on the carpet, to just plugging it in the wall. But, unlike regular batteries that take hours to charge, these can charge more or less instantly given the right power source, two minutes max with standard Confederation household power distribution. Plug it in, come back two minutes later, and bingo! A full charge.

I plan to finish the design this afternoon, well probably tonight, given the party this afternoon. Tomorrow, I'll fabricate one. Dad has access to everything I need. The next day, I'll file my project.

PARTY

Commotion in the kitchen breaks my concentration. Looking at the clock, I see that the party's going to start in a few minutes. The last two hours seemed to have just vanished.

I save my work, jot down a note on where to restart tonight, then get up to go see what's going on.

"Hey, Mom. Need any help?"

She smiles at me. "No, sweetie. We've got it covered. Your dad, Jonah, and Esther just took the last of the food and supplies up, all but this cart. I can push it up myself unless you want to go up the elevator with me."

The thought of the elevator makes my blood pressure spike.

Mom shakes her head. "You know you're going to have to come to terms with the accident someday. They won't give you the power job if you won't take the elevator to the surface."

I deflate a bit. "OK. I'll go with you."

She smiles. "Good." I get a hug and kiss on the top of my head.

"Hurry up and change, we need to leave."

...

As the elevator doors open, I can hear the music and a lot of noise. It seems the party is well underway. I push the cart slowly in the direction of the sound, Mom coaxing me to go a little faster. As we round the last corner, I see that the doors to the community party hall have been propped open and there must be a hundred people inside. The band is playing some kind of swing music and people are already up dancing.

"Over here."

I turn and see my father talking with Mr. Grayson, the older man whose job I'm going to be taking. They each have a pint of beer in their hand.

I redirect the cart toward Dad as he steps toward me.

"I can take that from here."

Dad hands me his beer, and he takes the cart. I'm waiting for the standard admonishment not to drink any.

"You're 16 today. So, you can take a sip if you'd like. Just take it easy."

I'm flabbergasted. The legal drinking age is 16, but I didn't expect my father to suggest that I have a drink.

"Jared, congratulations."

It's Mr. Grayson. I shift the beer to my left hand, quickly wiping my right hand off on my dress trousers, then shake his outstretched hand.

"Thank you, sir."

He laughs. "I hear you're going to be working at the company starting a week from Monday."

"That's the plan." I smile at the thought of working for the power company. It really excites me.

I get a massive slap on the back. One so hard, it nearly knocks the wind out of me. Beer sloshes out of the glass, but thankfully I don't drop it. "So, the baby of the family finally comes of age. Congratulations, kiddo.

"Hi, Mr. Grayson. Good to see you."

"Hello, Seth."

I can tell Mr. Grayson doesn't approve of Seth's antics. He turns and points to the other end of the party hall.

"The beer is over there."

My eyes follow in the direction he's pointing, where I see my dad talking quietly with the police chief. Although they are calm and quiet, I can tell my dad is a bit upset.

"Don't worry, it's nothing."

I look at Mr. Grayson questioningly.

"There was a minor incident at the company the other day. It's nothing to worry about."

"Hi, Jared."

I turn to see Nana, who's just come in through the door. She's wearing tight jeans and a tailored blouse with the top two buttons undone. I feel like I'm going to swoon.

I manage to choke out a "Hi, Nana."

She steps up and gives me a big hug.

I want to hug her back but am afraid of spilling the beer on her.

Releasing me, she says, "I see you already have a beer."

"No, just holding it for my Dad."

"Hello, Nana." The voice is my Dad's. He's apparently come back.

"Hi, Mr. Daan."

He smiles at Nana, then says to me, "I'll take that. Why don't you show Nana where the bar is?"

Nana smiles. "Lead the way."

As we step away, I hear Mr. Grayson speaking in a low voice.

"How did it go?"

"They want to..."

I didn't get the last couple words, but it sounded like he was saying the police wanted to go 'top side' to check something out.

...

Approaching the bar, Nana asks, "Are you going to have something?"

"I suppose I ought to."

Nana laughs. "Jared, you're so innocent."

I wonder how I should take that, then am distracted by a commotion over by the beer. A guy, someone I don't know but has the look of a miner, is having cross words with my older brother Aaron. I can see that Aaron is really pissed and wants to clobber the guy, who makes the mistake of pushing him.

"Enough of that!" My mom's voice cuts above the sound of the band and everyone turns to look at the two she's pointing at.

Police Chief Darren Hill walks over toward the two.

"Is there a problem here, gentlemen?"

I can tell that Aaron's fuming but have no idea why. Then I notice the concerned look on Nana's face.

She sees me looking at her and whispers, "That's my brother, Lucas. He told me there was some issue down in the mine. It appears that Aaron is involved somehow."

She points back at the two of them. Apparently, the Chief was persuasive. Aaron and Lucas are shaking hands.

"Come on." The Chief and Lucas head toward the door. I notice Asher inconspicuously trailing along some distance back, my mom smiling as they leave.

"Jared, I'm sorry. But I think I need to go. Lucas..." Nana shakes her head.

I can tell she's upset.

"Happy Birthday." The words spill out just before she kisses me on the cheek.

I notice my mom's smile turn into a frown when she sees Nana kiss me.

Nana turns to follow Lucas and the Chief out. I just want to cry but shake the whole thing off. She's out of my league. No sense getting wound up about it. I still have work to do tonight.

I see Mom's smile return as Nana scoots out the door.

THE THIRD AGE OF MAN

I ended up leaving the party early. It lost its sizzle when Nana left. But most of the melancholy wore off as I powered through the rest of my design.

I hit the sack once my work was saved, but here I lay, my mind pondering the fact that I came of age today. I'm sure our founder would find delight in it. The sixth son of the sixth generation turning 16 on the first day of the sixth month of 7266 TA. In case you're wondering, 7266 TA means 7,266th year of the Third Age of Man.

Historians have divided the history of mankind into three ages. The first age was that period of time that humans were on Earth, from the dawn of civilization until the cosmic cataclysm that destroyed the Earth in 3123 AD. That year ultimately became year one of the second age (1 SA). The second age ran until the completion of the Great Alien War in 4451 SA. The war claimed the lives of nearly half of all humanity. The day the last alien was sent to meet its maker, the human worlds celebrated, and the Third Age began.

It gives me pause to think. What will be the event that marks the dawn of the fourth age? I hope that day comes well after I'm gone. I can't imagine living with the fear of an approaching black hole, the way the people did at the end of the first age. Or living with the terror of sudden death falling from the skies as they did at the end of the second age.

I wonder if everyone has thoughts like this, worries for the future, when they come of age.

CHAPTER 2: COMMERCE

My project got filed on time. The professor that handles remote students wrote me a very polite note. In it he expressed his intent to give me an A in the class and to approve a preliminary certificate of completion for my degree. But the degree itself would be held until he received a prototype of my project and could validate its performance. I hadn't anticipated the last part. It would take months for a prototype to get to him 'through the mail.'

Dad had tested my prototype and was really impressed by it. He was willing to give me the Power Systems Engineering job based on the preliminary certificate and his personal evaluation of the project. But he made it clear that my job would be at risk if anyone challenged his authority to accept a preliminary certificate. So, his suggestion was that I create 'private' replicator specifications. I could send those to the professor along with the funds for a local replication at the professor's end.

It made sense to me, so I did it. I also filed for a patent on the design and on the replicator specs. On a lark, I also created a producer's account with the big interstellar, online sales company 'Jungle.'

It took three days, but Jungle confirmed that they could produce my device on all the major worlds. I accepted their offer. They got 2x the production cost on every unit sold. I got one credit. My payments would come 90-days in arrears, that is, 90-days after they'd shipped my product. My credits would be automatically deposited in my bank account.

Dad loaned me the 10 credits I'd need to send a 'free' copy to my professor. If he tested it in the next two days, I'd be done, degree in hand, power engineering job snagged.

Well, it didn't quite work out that way. The professor lives in a place as remote as I do. The prototype I'd paid 10 credits to get to him, ended up costing 18 credits with tax and shipping, and he wouldn't get it for a month. Dad would have to risk his job to take me on the preliminary certificate. It was the worst day of my life.

SALES

Somewhat unexpectedly, I got a message from Jungle today. Their New Products team really likes my Personal Power Pack. Over 4,000 units sold the first week and they want to run a promotion on the product. The promotion would cost me 2,000 credits. If I authorize the promotion, they would take the money directly from my bank account. The problem, of course, is that I don't have 2,000 credits. So, I don't reply. It's kind of ironic when you think about it. They've already brought in over 40,000 credits on sales of my product. They owe me over 4,000 credits, yet they want me to pay them in advance for this promotion.

"Dad, can I ask you about something?"

He looks at me as if I'm asking him to give me "the Talk."

"It's about a message I got from Jungle this morning."

"Really? What did they message you about?"

"My product is selling really well. They want to do a promotion on it."

"How well is it selling?"

"Over 4,000 the first week."

Dad is clearly shocked by the number. "That's really good. What kind of promotion do they want to do?"

"Their New Products team chooses hot new products to feature. Featured products are placed on more or less every page that's delivered showing a related product."

"Sounds like a great idea. Did you agree to it?"

"They want 2,000 credits, in advance."

"But you've already earned more than that."

"Which they will send to me in three months."

Dad seems to ponder that for a few minutes.

"Hardly seems fair. Do you want to do it?"

"Yes. I don't mind plowing some money back in. But I don't have the money, so end of story."

"Let me talk to your mom, see what we can do. If your product continues to sell, you're going to be the one making the money."

CURRENCY

Currency on Jaredaan is different than in most other places. As a protected world, we are barred from using the Confederation Credit as our planetary currency. We are required to have one of our own. The Confederation's stated reason for this is straight forward. We are privately owned worlds, aligned with the Confederation, but not members of the Confederation itself. Their real reason is that most protected worlds are net importing economies, ones with a tendency toward bankruptcy. Separate currencies reduce the likelihood the Confederation will have to bail out poorly run private worlds.

Where most protected worlds do not like this arrangement, our founder loved it. Why? Our economy was going to be driven by the metal trade and would be a net export economy, not a net import economy. Our currency would tend to become more valuable over time. He figured that he could fund our government on the spread, if he created a Jaredaan credit and locked its value to the Confederation credit.

This is invisible to most people here and most wouldn't understand it if they knew about it. But it matters to me. I'm being paid by Jungle in Confederation credits. That allows me to hold those funds on-world or off-world. And if there's ever an adverse event that restricts metal trade, I will still have funds to buy things off world.

RETIREMENT

Levi Grayson, the older man I spoke with at the party, has the power engineering job I want. The reason that job is becoming available is because Mr. Grayson is retiring. Retirement is a relatively new thing in Jaredstown. Historically, people worked until they dropped or became disabled. Makes sense, kind of. A small colony really cannot support very many people who aren't contributing.

But that started changing over the last couple years. Our population has swollen to nearly 10,000. We now have more people of working age than jobs. The logic is simple. It's counterproductive to have older people, struggling to remain productive, taking jobs from younger ones, who are just going to get in trouble if they have nothing productive to do.

I could never get away with saying that on one of the big planets, but it's a simple and obvious truth in a small colony that's light years from any other humans.

The town council has been pondering this change for years. The new rules went into place last year. No one is being forced out of their job. But starting at age 70, they're paid the standard rate for their job class whether they work or not. Mr. Grayson is 72 and the arthritis in his hands and back has finally gotten the better of him.

I had the chance to work with him a lot during school breaks. He wanted me to have his job, so is holding on another month until my certificate of completion is finally official.

SCANDAL

It's the first Sunday of the month. Aaron is due for dinner shortly. Once again, Asher has failed to bring all the groceries and I'm the one being dispatched to the Garden to pick up the missing lettuce. It really pisses me off that Asher doesn't bring all the stuff that's been ordered, then takes off with some friends before mom has confirmed the delivery.

But my spirits rise as I come into the Garden's reception area and see Nana.

"Hi Jared. I'm glad you came."

She hands me the bag.

"It was sitting right here for Asher to take, but he missed it. I'm sure he'd be blaming me if he were the one sent back. He's really turned into a jerk."

It bothers me that my stupid brother is treating someone as sweet as Nana so poorly.

"He hasn't hit you or something, has he?"

"No, he's just been mean. I spent an hour putting together an order for someone this week that he spilled on the floor. It was like the perfect set up. Everyone thought it was an accident, but I know he did it intentionally."

"Sorry to hear that. I'll see if Mom will let me do more of the pickups." I cannot believe I just said that. But the smile I get in return... Maybe this is a good idea.

...

As I get off the escalator, I see Aaron coming up from below.

"Hey punk. I see you got stuck with the grocery run again."

He always baits me like this, but I think I'm finally learning not to take the bait.

"Hey Aaron." I smile. "Good to see you. Mom's going to be happy that you've come. She really looks forward to the evenings you join us for dinner."

He seems confused about how to reply.

We walk together in silence for a few minutes and I can tell something's bothering him.

"So how are things? Still enjoying the mining work?"

15

"Love mining. I get great satisfaction from ripping metal out of the ground. But things are a bit messed up down there right now."

I think this is the most civil conversation we've ever had.

"How so?"

He gives me a look that doesn't seem very friendly.

"What's it to you?"

"Sorry, didn't mean to pry."

He looks puzzled again.

"What? You growing up or something?"

"It happens. I finished my power program a week ago."

"No kidding? But in truth, I'm not that surprised. You were always the smart one."

I can't believe what I'm hearing.

Aaron opens the door. "Mom, we're home."

...

"I hear there's been a problem down in the mine."

Mom gives Dad the furry eyeball. I don't think she wanted him asking Aaron about the scandal.

"Yeah." Aaron sticks some more potatoes in his mouth. He obviously doesn't want to talk about it.

"You weren't involved in it were you?"

Fire flares in Aaron's eyes as if he wants to punch Dad.

"No, not really."

"Aaron, if you were involved, you have to come clean about it."

I can see that Aaron is struggling with this. Part of him wants to come clean; the other part wants to run.

Mom puts her hand on his. "Sweetie, you need to tell us if you were."

Seems I'm not the only one that gets the 'Sweetie' treatment.

"I was there. I didn't know what was happening."

It looks like Aaron is about to break down crying.

"They brought in two carts. That happens a lot. At least once a week we hit a vein rich enough that we need two carts. What I didn't know is that they were going to steal one.

"The security cameras show me loading the cart. I spend 50% of my time loading carts. It's far from incriminating that I'm the one loading it."

He pounds his fist on the table as he says the words. Everything on the table jumps. So do I.

"Do you know what evidence they have against you?"

Dad asks this very compassionately.

"All I've been shown is the clip of me loading the cart. But I know nothing about this. I don't know who the culprits are. I don't know where the material went. I was just the guy on that shift that day. Showing up for work on time and doing what I do best."

"Have they filed charges against you?"

"Not yet. I've been questioned several times, but I have no answers. I didn't even know the cart had been jacked until they started asking me about it."

"OK. I'm sure this will work out. We're here for you no matter what happens."

"Thanks, Dad."

...

What a strange evening. First the conversation in the hallway on the way back from the escalator. Then the confession about the goings on in the mine. He even gave me a hug as he left. I feel bad for the guy.

This type of event is something else about living on a colony world instead of a normal civilization. Criminal justice is simply different. On colony worlds, we cannot lose people. There's no capital punishment; well there is but we don't call it that. For the most part there's not even jail. We're all stuck here, captives of the planet so to speak.

What we have instead are prison camps. Well, prison camp actually. It's on the equator, on the south shore of the lake fed by the polar ice transport system my great uncle built. They taught us about it in elementary school. It's not a very nice place. Hot during the day, cold at night. Infested with all kinds of biting and stinging things. It even has poisonous frogs and snakes.

All of our real agriculture comes from the green zone. But the prison camp is where the sugar cane is grown. Prison camp sentences run from 1 year to life, depending on the offense. As compared to normal civilization, sentences here would be considered extreme.

Murder is rare, but when it happens there's only one sentence. Banishment. You are taken to the surface and left there.

Theft of the magnitude that happened in the mine will probably result in a life sentence for anyone directly involved. If the council should decide that Aaron was a willing participant, he'll probably get 5 years. In truth, Aaron isn't smart enough to have been the ringleader and the council knows it. But the thought of even one year in the prison camp sends a shiver down my spine.

GOVERNMENT

The protected world statutes allow a lot of flexibility in terms of how the protected worlds govern themselves. The only real bounds are imposed by the trade agreements, which functionally ban slavery and other egregious forms of human suppression.

Most protected worlds are run commune style. Jaredaan is different. Each of our major population centers—Jaredstown, Ashcrag, Heroldstown and the space station—has an elected mayor, police force, and other governmental functions. These are organized as each community sees fit and funded by the communities they serve.

The planet as a whole is governed by a Board of Elders. The number of elders on the board has changed over time, but there are currently seven. An elder's term is seven years and elders are barred from having consecutive terms. Elders must have a direct patriarchal link back to the founder, meaning their father and all his forefathers must be a son of the founder. Women can and do serve, subject to the paternity rule.

Every eligible citizen on the planet has a priority number for serving. Mine is six, which is relatively high. Every year an existing elder rotates off and a new one rotates on. The new one is chosen by the sitting elders, based on priority and other criteria not disclosed to the public. My father will be rotating on this year. It will be his first term as an elder. As a direct first-son link to the founder, his priority level is one. Every priority one in history has served. He's turned it down several times, but the elders pressured him into it this year.

Uncle Walter will get the top job this year. It will be the last year of his second term. He's not very well liked. My dad is one of the few that get along with him. I think that's how they twisted his arm. The other elders wanted someone that could buffer Walter's harsher tendencies.

PROMOTION

To my surprise, Mom and Dad offer to loan me the 2,000 credits for the promotion with Jungle. They are charging me 500 credits for the three-month loan. That's a big price to pay, but they're probably just going to spend it on me anyway. Mom jokes that they needed to charge me something since they would be covering the cost of converting their 2,000 Jaredaan credits to 2,000 Confederation credits. I laugh at that since the conversion cost is 1%, totaling 20 credits.

Jungle was less than happy that I took so long getting back to them. But they are still anxious to get my Personal Power Pack into next week's Featured Products list. Sales in week two were a little less than in week one, but at this point I'm up nearly 8,000 credits. If sales continue at this rate, I'll be making more money from Personal Power Packs than from my engineering job.

POWER ENGINEER

The Power Company and Town Council approved me to start working. I will be an assistant to Mr. Grayson until I get my Power Engineering diploma, then will be promoted to Power Engineer 1 when Mr. Grayson retires.

Today is my first day. Dad took me in this morning. He was even gracious enough to take the escalator up to Level One. We went in and he took me to the Personnel desk to get the appropriate paperwork done. Now I'm waiting for Mr. Grayson to come get me and take me to the Engineering Office.

"Jared, so good to see you. Welcome."

"Mr. Grayson, thanks for coming to get me. I've been looking forward to today for a long time."

We start off down the hall.

"Jared. When here in the office, you should call me Levi. Everyone in the company treats everyone else like family, first name only."

I knew this, but really didn't get it until just now.

Apparently, my silence on the matter amuses him.

"I used to be young once. I still remember coming into the office that first time. I was about your age. A little older, but still shy. When my first boss told me I needed to address him by his first name, I wasn't sure I could do it."

"Thank you for sharing that, Levi. I hope I live long enough to give the same talk to some kid 50 years from now."

He laughs and slaps me on the back. "That's the spirit."

...

Day two on the job and I'm going to the surface. I went up once before when I was a kid. The long elevator ride and the sight of snow and ice still stick in my memory. It will be curious to see if those memories resemble what's up there at all.

But today will be much different than that day in school. Today, I'll be going outside. It's the first time. And it's dangerous. A storm came through last night, dumping a lot of snow. We collected over 100 lightning bolts, completely filling both our capacitors and our longer-term storage facilities. But one of the units did not switch off in time. It took additional lightning strikes.

The units are designed to handle multiple strikes in the same storm. They're also designed to take one, maybe two, additional strikes when they've reached nominal capacity. But when their absorption capability is saturated, the units can be damaged. Any energy collected after the units are full can cause damage, because the power has no place to go and turns into heat.

The higher ups had inspected the unit with remote cameras. By all appearances only the control unit was damaged. But someone would have to go up, inspect it and repair anything that was actually broken. Mr. Grayson, I mean Levi, lost his certification for surface work last year. So, I'm accompanying my Dad, who is a senior engineer. As a newbie, I'm not certified yet. I'm going up on a training permit.

...

It's freezing cold in the elevator lobby. According to the thermometer, it's -10° C in here, -60° C outside. There's also a lot of snow blowing around.

"Let's put on the extreme cold gear first. Without those gloves, you're at risk of your hands freezing to the other gear we need to get."

I already know this. It's part of every training video I've had to watch over the years.

"Thanks for the reminder, Dad."

We help each other get into the cold weather outfits and check each other's seals. The gear itself is surprisingly thin. It's made from the same insulating material they use in space gear.

We check the power packs to make sure they're charged, then attach them to our belts. Again, we check each other to make sure the power pack is secure. Lastly, we put on our helmets. As soon as the helmet is on, a small air circulation fan starts blowing. The fan serves two purposes. Its primary purpose is to keep the air inside from getting stale. The surface atmosphere is breathable in terms of its composition, but it's so cold it will freeze our lungs. So, the suit has an air exchanger that pumps out the old air and sucks in new air in a way that warms it enough to be safe. The fan then assures that the air circulates up to our faces where we breathe it.

The fan's secondary purpose is to equalize the temperature inside the suit and help the face plate stay clear. If your face plate frosts over on the inside, then you're in trouble.

Now suited up, we head over to the garage. The garage is heated to 5° C. Our snow crawlers are in the garage as is the equipment and replacement parts we'll be using today. We load the parts into the snow crawler, then get in ourselves.

To protect the garage, the snow crawler has to pass through an air lock to get out. Dad's driving and uses the door controls to open the inner door of the airlock. We drive in and he shuts the inner door.

"Ready?" He smiles over at me. "I'm about to open the outer door."

"Let's do it."

The outer door starts to open, making a lot of noise, then it stops.

"Looks like we have a snow drift blocking the door. It happens now and again, but it's not all that common."

Dad looks a little concerned.

"Let's go get the snow blowers. I'll take the left side you take the right."

Our snow blowers are just what the name implies, machines that blow snow. Somewhere, I don't actually know where, there are some huge fans. They feed two hoses located in the airlock. The hoses are big, like a firehose. They may actually be firehoses.

When the system is fired up the hoses are pressurized to 25 psi. When we ultimately open them up, the fans will go into high gear and the pressure will increase. Holding onto a hose with that much air coming out, would be like holding onto a jet engine, something you seriously don't want to do. Our hoses are mounted on sturdy carts that can handle all the thrust that will come out of the hoses.

On either side of the main outer door there are little metal portholes that are latched shut. Dad raises his cart up to the top porthole, about 20 ft up and unlatches it. Some wind and snow blow in, but the porthole is basically clear.

The next porthole is 2 feet lower. I get to the one on my side first and open it.

"Clear."

"I've got the next one."

Seeing that I was getting the 18-foot porthole, Dad goes directly to the one at 16 feet. "I bet the next one is the one we want."

I open the 14-foot porthole. "It's blocked."

Dad opens his 14-foot. "Blocked on this side too."

We both attach our hose to our porthole.

"This shouldn't take long. Let's give it a two second burst."

I double check my controls to make sure I know how to do that. "OK. Ready on your go."

"Three, two, one, go."

We both trigger the burst of air and the exterior door rattles.

"I can see more of the drift now. Let's do a five second burst at the 10-foot porthole."

We do blasts at 10 feet, 6 feet, then 2 feet, and the outside door opens without a hitch. I'm stunned by what I see. Much of the snow we've blown away is still suspended in the air. Millions of little ice crystals glistening in the weak sunlight.

"This is incredible!"

Dad smiles. He remembers it's my first time outside, first time to see a spectacle like the one playing out in front of us as the air moves.

"I wish we had cameras built into these suits. Very few people ever get to see this."

Dad seems to be enjoying the moment of peace, then snaps out of it. "Let's go. We have a power unit to fix before the weather turns."

Ten minutes later we're at the unit that needs repair. Dad's the first one out.

"Yep. The flow controller is burnt out. I also see carbon deposits on the channel generator. That needs to be fixed as well. Can you start on the flow controller? Pull it out, put the new one in?"

"I've got it."

I can tell Dad likes being out here with me.

"I'm going to do a more detailed inspection of the unit. We're here, so might as well fix everything we can."

One of the issues with operating equipment like this in the cold is the cold itself. Any moisture at all on the bolts causes them to freeze in place. The metal itself contracts. Anything that might be flexible at room temperature isn't flexible out here. The phenomenon is fighting me right now. At room temperature the swap I'm doing would only take a couple minutes. I still haven't got the first bolt off. It's frozen in place and the torque wrench I'm using is coming up against the pressure limit of this bolt at -60° C. I back off on the pressure.

"Hey Dad. Any tips on getting this bolt off? According to the torque wrench, I'm at the pressure limit for this bolt type."

"Simple solution. There's a hand torch in the snow crawler. A one or two second blast will loosen it if the nut is over-compressed. Be careful with it. The nanotubes are flammable."

Three minutes later, bolt one is off. Another couple minutes and bolts two and three are off. But bolt four is not budging.

"I got three of the four, but the last one is not giving it up."

"Give me a minute."

Dad finishes his inspection of the unit, then emerges from around the other side shaking his head. "This unit is on its last legs. There's a stress fracture with carbon scarring on the other side. More carbon scarring on the channel generator than I saw at first."

The channel generator is the part of the system that attracts the lightning bolts. Lightning is basically just a static discharge caused by the charge imbalances between the clouds and ground. Lightning can also go between the clouds, but we don't try to catch those.

When the static charge reaches a certain point, it starts ionizing the air, which makes the air conductive. When an ionized path extends far enough between cloud and ground, a conductive channel is formed, and the charge jumps through the channel connecting the circuit.

Most of the time the channel starts up in the cloud reaching down to the ground. The trick my ancestor discovered was to create a channel at ground level and project it toward the cloud. There are sensors that detect which clouds have the strongest charges. When a charged cloud is in the right position, the unit fires a stream of ionized particles at the cloud.

It usually won't do that until the cloud has started to emit its own ionized particles, referred to as lightning leaders. The two streams of ions are attracted to one another, and when they connect, BAM! The cloud's charge flows down through the channel into our nanotube capacitor.

Each lightning strike has about 300 kilowatt-hours of electrical power. You don't have to catch all that many of them to power the colony for a month.

Coming back to the moment, I see that Dad's wrestling with bolt four also.

SNAP!

"Ah, I broke it." Dad's anguish is clear as he spits out a series of expletives. Something that's unusual for him.

After a bit of stomping around, he looks up at me. "I'm going to need to call this one in. See if you can lift the controller out, then check to see if any pieces have fallen in. But be careful. The unit has been discharged, but there is undoubtedly some charge in some of the nanotube cells. You don't want to mess with that."

23

He stomps off to the snow crawler and gets inside.

Extracting the controller is easy now that the bolts are off. But one look inside answers the question about the state of this unit. Dozens of the nanotube cells have ruptured. Some apparently caught fire and burned up. This unit is a total loss.

CHAPTER 3: TENSION

In the excitement of the new job, I'd forgotten about my Personal Power Pack product. On logging in, I'm shocked by what I see. Sales during the first week of the promotion were 12,000 units. Total units sold in the first three weeks... 20,000 units. If sales continue at this rate, I'll make over 25,000 credits this month. My annual salary as an engineering assistant is only 30,000. And it will only increase to 36,000 when I get my certification and am made an Engineer.

While checking my messages, I see that Jungle is sending me more promotion offers, some with price tags as high as 20,000 credits. I don't know what these guys are smoking, but it's not going to be my credits. 20,000! What a ridiculous number to throw at a kid with 100 credits in his bank account and a note for 2,000 due in 10 weeks!

I suddenly start laughing, the humor in the situation finally registering. If this continues for another year, I'll be one of the wealthiest people on the planet.

"What so funny, sweetie?" It's Mom.

"I just got another message from Jungle. They're offering me more promotion options. Their recommended option is 5,000 credits. Can you imagine such a thing?"

"That's ridiculous. Did your last promotion generate any sales?"

I'm about to answer when I realize for the first time that this might end up being a problem. Everyone's heard of overnight Jungle millionaires and it isn't something well thought of on Jaredaan.

"That bad?"

"No. Not bad at all. I actually sold a lot."

"What do you mean, a lot?"

This is dangerous water. I can feel it. But lying to my mom really isn't an option.

"Around 12,000 units sold during the promotion."

"How many sold before that?"

"The previous two weeks sold a total of about 8,000."

"So, you've made 20,000 credits in the last three weeks?"

"Less 2,000 for the promotion."

I can tell this isn't sitting well with Mom.

"But you haven't seen a penny of it yet?"

"No. Ten more weeks until the first payment. And you'll get most of that."

"That's still a lot of money. You should keep this to yourself. People aren't going to like it."

INSULTS

Word of the power unit failure got out. Most people don't care. It's been years since the colony had a power shortage. But a few of the old timers are worried. The last time we were short of power things got pretty bad. And it started the same way, a unit blew because it was old and undermaintained. This unit was certainly old, but it isn't clear to me that it's been undermaintained.

Nonetheless, Asher has suddenly become an expert on the topic. He's more than happy to tell anyone who'll listen that the failure was my fault. He's an expert. He has his diploma. I'm only 16 and don't even have a diploma, yet I've been hired because I'm my father's favorite.

This is the kind of stuff that makes me crazy. I worked hard. I earned my degree by the time I was 16. Asher is a lazy sloth with no sense of ambition. Seth and Jude aren't much better, but for now seem satisfied to let Asher be my principal tormentor.

THE GREAT ALIEN WAR

A new documentary on the Great Alien War (GAW) came out recently. I stumbled over it while checking my Jungle account earlier and decided to watch it.

I knew, but had lost track of the fact, that the GAW is what motivated the creation of the Protected Worlds program.

The aliens came from the Perseus Arm of the galaxy, from Earth's perspective the next arm out from the core. They came across the void to enter the Orion-Cygnus arm along the outer edge. The human core worlds were, and are, mostly located along the inner edge of the Orion-Cygnus Arm.

The aliens became aware of humanity shortly after arriving in our arm. Humans had been sending radio, and other communications, into space for thousands of years at that point. So, the aliens had no trouble figuring out where we were and what our vulnerabilities would be. They took their time, built a huge war machine, then descended on us. We didn't become aware of them until the day they

26

captured our first world. In a week, they'd captured three, then they paused. They had a lot of food to process.

The pause is what saved us. It only lasted a month, but by then we'd found weapons that would be effective against them and their ships. It took a long time and cost half of humanity, but we won.

In the aftermath of the war, our government and its scientists came to two major conclusions. The first was that humanity was too concentrated, more of us would have survived if we'd been more spread out. The second was that we needed some sort of early warning system, maybe planets with too small a population to be a target, but with the ability to sound the alarm early.

I'm told the original drafts of the law referred to a planet like ours as a *Protective* World. Some bright legislator apparently thought it would be an easier sell if they called it a *Protected* World. I don't know if the story is true, but I like the theory.

Anyway, I watched the documentary and was reminded how gross the aliens were. The best analogy I can think of is like humanoid ants. There were millions of strong workers that served just a few kings and queens. The workers were kind of human-like. They stood about a meter and a half tall. They had four-digit hands and feet. The hands had opposable thumbs that allowed them to grasp. The feet had opposable big toes, which allowed them to grasp as well. Their torsos were muscular and sturdy. But that's where any similarity ended.

Most of their body was covered in armor-like scales. They had tiny heads, which seems to go hand-in-hand with their automaton-like behavior. And they were genderless, unable to reproduce.

In contrast, the kings and queens were gigantic. Everything about them was big. Hands, feet, head, genitalia... everything. And they had gross doughy skin, no scales, and never wore clothes.

They also had absolute control. Scientists say that both kings and queens were telepathic and could carry on complex communications simultaneously with multiple parties. They also had powerful pheromones that completely enslaved their workers. Waves of them would come. They had no fear, felt no pain. Nothing stopped them. Their scales stopped most firearms. They just came and came. A sea of scales ready to consume anything in its path.

I know I'm going to have a bad dream featuring scales tonight.

As the movie finishes, another screen comes up. On it is the familiar visage of Melvin Harsoal, the famous historian. I know of him from my ancient history class in high school. I took the course on the exo-net. The online school used a series of videos that the professor narrated. In almost all of them he toured the places he was talking about. I never heard anyone who made history sound more real.

He was a kind grandfatherly old man that I loved. Sadly, the image is titled, *In Memory of Melvin Harsoal, teacher and beloved friend*.

DATE

It had been a long day. Dad and I spent the day working on another unit that had been acting up. The more I see of the lightning capture units, the more I sympathize with the old timers who are worried. Every unit I've seen has carbon scoring, which seems to be the beginning of the end for them. Dad and I are trying to get ahead of it. We were up top every day this week, and it's left me feeling tired and discouraged.

"Have a good weekend, Janet." I smile and wave as I leave. Janet is the evening receptionist.

As I make my way toward the escalator, I see someone coming the other direction. Still too far away to make out who, but I think it might be Nana, so I hasten my step.

"Hey Jared." She waves at me. It's definitely Nana, but I'm still struggling to see her. The bright surface sun has affected my eyes. A funny thought, that. Our sun is not very bright. But the snow seems to magnify it.

"Hey Nana. You headed home?" She lives on a lower level. She's on her own now and the Garden doesn't pay well enough to snag an apartment on one of the higher levels.

"Yep. Just finished my shift. Aren't you supposed to be done earlier than this?"

She stops at the top of the escalator, seemingly reluctant to go down.

"I've been doing work up on the surface this week. It's hard to get a good day's work done up there without running late down here."

"Rumors about the power units on the surface aren't good. Is there any truth to them?"

I let the question sit for a minute.

"I don't know. What rumors are you hearing?"

"Asher has been saying nasty things. He seems to think you're in over your head."

I get a good laugh out of that.

"Asher has no idea what he's talking about. If you assume the opposite of what he says, you'll get closer to the truth."

"You two are still at each other?"

The comment really hurts. I don't think well of Asher, but I rarely say anything negative about him.

"I think it's mostly him being angry about me working on the surface while he works in the Garden. He really hates the Garden, which is hard for me to understand. I enjoy the Garden. I'm an engineer by nature but wouldn't mind working in the garden if there were no engineering work."

"Have you ever thought about giving him your job?"

I start laughing. "Then we would definitely have power problems."

She laughs along.

I note that we're still outside the escalator lobby on the top floor, and she's suddenly looking at me shyly.

"Would you ask me out tonight?" She blurts out.

"You mean like on a date?" Oh my god. Can't believe I just said that. "I mean…" the words hang there as I stutter. She seems to wilt.

"Nana? Would you go on a date with me tonight?"

Hallelujah! I finally got the words out.

"Are you sure you want to go out with me?"

"Nana, I've had a crush on you for years. Of course, I want to go out with you. Just never thought you'd go with me."

She smiles sweetly. "Dinner and putt-putt on level 10?"

"Sure. Is there a place you'd like to eat?"

She pulls out her communicator, messes with it a bit, then shows me the place.

"OK." The place seems reasonable to me, will probably seem even more reasonable when I finally get my first payment from Jungle.

She holds out her communicator to bump against mine and the place shows up.

"I need to take a shower, get the grit off me. Meet me there at 7:00."

I smile. "7:00 it is. I need a shower too. It might be 60 below on the surface, but it's hot in those suits."

"Great. See you there."

There's a ding and people start getting off the elevator.

"I'm going to try to catch that." She calls out, running down the hall toward the elevator.

Me? I'm sticking with the escalator.

...

Back at home, Mom seems happy that I'm going out tonight. I know she wants me to be getting out more. "You need more than just work," she says.

Out of the shower, I still have a few more minutes, so I check my Jungle account. The week won't close until midnight, but I'm curious to see what's sold this week. 14,000 units. I really struggle to believe it's true.

I just got my first paycheck today. 1,000 credits. It's the first time I've ever had money of my own and I'm feeling a bit flush. But my account with Jungle has accumulated 34,000 credits in just four weeks. I can't let anyone find out about this.

LEVEL TEN

Level 10 is the level Jude was taking me to the day of the elevator incident. I used to go down there fairly often, maybe once or twice a month. It's the entertainment level. But I haven't been back there since the 'accident' and I feel my blood pressure rise as I exit the level 10 escalator lobby.

I haven't been to this restaurant before, so have my head in my communicator when I hear a voice I'd rather not be hearing.

"Hey, what's the kid doing out on his own?"

It's Aaron.

"Hi Aaron. I'm meeting a friend for dinner. What are you up to?"

"Same. I heard you started working."

"I did. Got my first paycheck today."

"Congratulations. That's a big deal. Do you have time for a drink? I'll buy."

I really can't believe we're having this conversation. I've wanted to make peace with my brothers for a long time, but I'm about to be late for my first date.

"Ah... I'd really like to. Really. But I'm late. Tomorrow?"

I can tell he's insulted that I'm not dropping everything to have a drink with him right now. But it looks like I'm going to get away with it.

"Sure, tomorrow will be great. I'll message you."

He turns and heads off to wherever he's going. There's a lightness to his step I haven't seen before. Something good must be happening for him. I'm glad.

I finally get to the restaurant and see Nana waiting nervously out front.

30

"Hi. Sorry I'm late." I say this as humbly as I can. "I ran into Aaron on the way over. He actually asked me out for a drink."

"He's older, right?"

"14 years. Always used to pick on me. This is twice in a row that he's been nice to me."

"I'm glad. Want to go in?"

We go in and grab seats. A waiter comes, brings some water, and drops some menus on the table.

"What's good?" I'm realizing as I look at the menu that this may be my first time actually eating in a real restaurant. I don't recognize a lot of the things on the menu.

I think Nana senses my discomfort but I'm not sure. I'm so out of my league.

"I think you'll like the braised shank, with carrots and potatoes."

I have no idea what a braised shank is, but don't really care. Nana is smiling at me.

...

I wake, and for the life of me, can't figure out where I am. I feel a touch on my belly and almost jump out of bed.

"Someone is touchy in the morning."

Nana? I turn to look and there she is. This must be a dream.

"Seems someone had a little too much to drink last night."

Slowly it comes back. Dinner. Shanks? Red wine?

"Struggling to remember?" She smiles brightly at me.

I'm stricken with guilt, even though I don't know what I've done.

"It's the sweet red wine. I'm feeling guilty for having given it to you. Was it your first time?"

I'm struggling to understand the question, then it sinks in.

"Yes. First time for sweet red wine."

"Is that all?"

I hate questions like that.

"I think so. Maybe?"

She laughs. "You are so innocent." Then shakes her head. "I like you Jared. I really do. But you're obviously not ready."

She pops up out of bed and runs into the bathroom. It's the first time I've seen female parts in the flesh, and I'm stricken with desire. I can't believe that I've blown it.

Minutes later she's back and dressed.

"Come on. You need to get out of here. There's still a chance you can get out without being noticed."

31

Heart heavy, I get up, get dressed and head for home.

DRINKS

Surprisingly, Aaron called. We'd be doing drinks at 6:00. He'd picked a place near the restaurant where I had dinner with Nana last night.

Mom is a little pissed that I'm going to be out two nights in a row, but she doesn't seem to have caught on to the fact I was out all-night last night. She tends to sleep in until 9:00 on Saturdays, and I got home well before that.

I take the escalator down to Level 10 again. Strange that the elevator to the surface doesn't seem to bother me, because the elevator to Level 10 still seems out of my reach.

I meet up with Aaron. His first statement is, "Who were you seeing last night?"

When I don't answer immediately, he bursts out laughing. "Baby brother, if you'd told me it was some guy, I would have believed you. But the silence is sure indictment that it must have been some fine piece of..."

"Aaron, please don't say it."

He looks at me with sympathy. "You must really have it for her. Condolences."

It's such a strange response that I don't know how to take it. "Jared, you're so innocent. My heart breaks for you."

His comment is so unexpected. I have no idea how to respond.

"Jared, this is a tiny colony. Everybody is in everyone else's business. I don't know who's captured your heart. But I guarantee you someone does. And when they out you, you're going to be in a world of hurt."

I sense that he knows something about where I was last night. But I have no idea how he would have found out.

HOME

I used to think I was the smart one. That was then. This is now.

Mom forgave me for being out two nights in a row. Asher, Seth, and Jude have been unusually quiet about it, but more than once I've caught them snickering behind my back. I used to think of these guys as the three stooges, idiots who had no idea what was actually going on. They certainly don't know anything about the technologies that make our life possible, or the very fragile economy that supports their existence. But the events of the last couple days leave me wondering who the stooge really is.

A quick check in with Jungle shows that another thousand units were sold by the end of the week last week. Another 4,000 sold today. 39,000 total. I am now the wealthiest member of this narrow slice of the Daan family. The belief that I have money gives me the courage to call Nana and ask her out for real tonight.

She accepts.

A quick check of my bank account shows that dinner Friday night cost me a little over 300 credits, which leaves me about 700 credits to get through the next two weeks.

LEVEL TWELVE

Now that I know where Nana's place is, she lets me come pick her up.

"Hey." I smile at her, almost cringing at the pathetic greeting.

"Hey." She answers back with a teasing smile.

I've had a crush on this girl so long that it never occurs to me that she's making fun of me.

"Any idea where you'd like to go?"

Her look makes me realize that's not what she was expecting to hear.

"Jared." She looks me straight in the eye. "When you ask someone out, you're the one that's expected to pick the location. You're supposed to be dazzling me."

Those words send my mind to a place that I know it shouldn't go, but I can't help myself.

"Have you ever been to the surface?"

She looks at me astonished. "No."

"Want to go?"

"Are you serious?"

I need to stop this. I could lose my job if I take her up there. Instead, I smile. "Of course, I can."

"What? You have a pass card for the elevator to the surface?"

I pop my wallet out, pull out the pass card and smile.

She stands there looking at the card, clearly surprised that a trip to the surface is a possibility. Then a smile blooms.

"Maybe someday, but not tonight. I know a place that has live music. Want to give it a try?"

I'm all smiles. "Would love to."

Once again, I wake in Nana's bed. But this time I remember what happened the night before and am hoping for a little more when Nana wakes up.

She actually taught me to dance last night. It was fun. That, plus a little alcohol, made us anxious to get back to her place. If memory serves correctly, clothes were shed as soon as the front door was closed.

Nana stirs, pulls me closer, and after a little more play, we fall fast asleep again.

Nana shakes me awake. She's clearly upset.

"I think Lucas is here." She whispers.

She actually looks scared.

"He has a key. I didn't have enough money, so he co-signed my lease and insisted on having one. He crashes here sometimes when he's drunk."

Looking at the clock I see it's a little after 5:00 AM.

I hear retching in the bathroom.

A minute later, Lucas walks into the room.

"So, who's banging my little sister?"

"Get out!" Nana screams, then starts crying.

He puts his hands up in surrender, a cruel smile forming on his face. "OK. We can talk about this later."

He steps out of the bedroom. Out in the living room we hear him shuffle through some things, then the door slams.

Nana is crying big time.

"Hey, he's gone now. It's OK."

She shakes her head and curls into a ball.

I put my arms around her, feeling her tremble.

"It's all right." I whisper. Again, I feel like I'm in way over my head.

After a while she quiets down.

"You should probably go."

"What? I can't go while you're like this?"

She turns to look at me and smiles compassionately. "Jared, you're so sweet. I'm glad I got to be with you. But I don't think you should come down here again until things settle a little."

Her words burn through me like a knife in my heart.

"Come on, get yourself put together, then go. You may still get home before your family finds out."

She gently pushes me out of bed.

I'm crushed, completely crushed. I quickly locate my clothes, which were scattered across the living room, then get dressed and leave without another word. Once in the escalator shaft, I plop to the floor and weep.

CHAPTER 4: ENTRAPMENT

It's been three weeks since that terrible morning at Nana's, and I've been in a deep funk. The joy of being with her, followed by the crushing rejection of being thrown out, has left me empty. I've called several times, but no answer. I've stopped by the garden a couple times, but she hasn't been there. The person on duty suggested I should stop coming by looking for her.

Word of me being caught in bed with Nana has spread far and wide. My brothers rib me about it mercilessly. My Dad has been surprisingly compassionate about it but is getting tired of my sulking. But the relationship with my mother has become very chilly, something I haven't experienced before.

But I don't understand why. I'm of age. Sex is not exactly a forbidden thing. Very few people get married until there's a baby on the way. Why is it such a big deal that I got caught at Nana's?

SURFACE

My diploma came a few days ago, so I'm now on full time as a Junior Engineer. My surface access status now allows me to ride the elevator up to the surface facilities on my own, although I've never done so. I still need a senior engineer with me to actually go outside. Most days, I go up with Dad. On days he doesn't have the duty I go up with our other Senior Engineer, a fellow named Rylan Graham, who goes by Rye.

Rye's more of a divide and conquer guy than a teamwork guy. When I come up with Dad, we'll spend most of our time working together on one unit, then move on to the next. When I go up with Rye, I take one, he takes the other. Safety rules require a minimum of two people at a time on the surface. But more than once Rye has bailed on me, leaving when he's done and not telling me.

Dad says I need to report this, but I haven't. Today is one of those days. I have no idea when he left, but his snow crawler is back in its garage, so he must have gone back down.

I'm really close to having this unit, #12, completely refurbished. Storms are supposed to settle in later this week, so I plan to stay up here as close to sunset as I can in the hopes of getting it done.

...

It's done! As I bolt the final panel in place, my communicator sounds. It's built into my suit. I only need to push a button on the back of my glove to answer.

"Hi, this is Jared."

"Jared, where are you? You haven't clocked out and your snow crawler isn't in the garage."

It's Dad.

"Just finishing up. I think I have unit #12 ready to go back online."

"You need to hurry. It's dusk and there's a storm closing in. I'm turning on the light above your garage. Visibility drops to nothing once the wind starts blowing."

"I'll be down in a minute."

As I cut the connection, I look up at the sky. Relatively clear, but dark. It's later than I realized. I finish buttoning up the unit, then get back in the snow crawler and head off for the garage. As I'm turning around, I see clouds on the western horizon. Then a lightning bolt. I need to hurry.

The trip back to the garage is longer than I remembered. The winds have been picking up and the air is filling with ice crystals stirred up by the wind. My headlights are starting to white out the area around me, and for the first time, I'm starting to get a little scared about being up here.

I have to stop. I can't see and don't want to risk hitting one of the units. As panic starts to set in, my training kicks in.

"Turn off the headlights." I say to myself out loud.

As soon as the headlights are off, I can see the light from the garage, it's only 100 feet away. It's bright enough I can see my way there.

Ten minutes later, I'm exiting the airlock. I'm back safe, but I cut it way too close. The garage is closed, airlock sealed. I quickly hang the cold suit in its closet and put on the heavy wool sweater I bring up with me each day.

As I walk into the elevator lobby, there's a ding. Someone has come up! The door opens and Dad comes racing out in a panic.

I put up my hands. "It's OK. I'm back. I lost track of time, but I'm back, none the worse for wear."

Dad's panic turns to anger. "What the hell were you doing out there on your own! You know it's against the rules!"

The anger quickly morphs into relief. He throws his arms around me, pulling me into a tight bear hug."

I can feel him trembling.

"God, I thought I lost you."

He holds me like that for a while, then lets me go, wiping tears from his eyes. "Come on, let's go down. It's cold up here."

SUSPENSION

Surface work is only allowed from an hour after sunup until an hour before sunset. The specific times are posted every day.

There are further restrictions on exposure. Surface work is limited to six hours per day. More than that is risky because of dehydration. You can't eat or drink while in the suit. It's never warm enough on the surface to open your faceplate for a sip of water.

It's also prohibited to be on the surface alone, or when there is a weather alert.

When Rye and I went out the other day, we went out about 5 minutes early. In fact, all surface workers tend to go out a few minutes early if the weather is clear. No one ever calls us on it.

But in my effort to get unit #12 back online, I stayed out two hours past the sunset cutoff, twelve and a half hours in total, the last thirty minutes of which was under a weather alert.

If I had realized the time or weather alert was there, I would have come in sooner. But I didn't know. Dad usually tracks that stuff. I just lost track.

In retrospect, it's easy to understand Dad's panic. I actually feel really guilty about it.

Anyway, I was written up for being on the surface alone, after the formal cut off, during a weather alert, for more than twice the safe exposure time.

The company safety board called me in for a hearing. The condemnation went on and on, long enough that I thought they were going to fire me. Instead, I got a one-week suspension without pay and a written warning. The warning made it clear I would be terminated if there was another violation.

The first day home, I mostly stayed in my room moping. I was completely broke at this point, had lost Nana, and now didn't have any work. The combination of grief over Nana and guilt about work was paralyzing.

...

It's now Day 2 of my suspension. I decide to check on my Jungle account. It's been several weeks since I've checked. It takes a while to understand what I'm seeing. 91,000 units sold. Over 1,000 five-star reviews.

Checking my message queue, I see promotional offer after promotional offer. The last one catches my eye.

The price tag is 10,000 credits. My product will get premium placement and be placed in stock at forward shipping locations. Shipping on worlds with local stock will be free with three-day delivery.

Blah, blah, blah. Then the line that catches my eye.

As a vendor with over 50,000 credits in scheduled payments, you can finance your promotion from your scheduled payment account for a 10% premium on the promotion cost.

I have to read it several times to believe it. They expect that this promotion will increase sales by 25% over the next two weeks, the term of the promotion. And I can pay for it with 11,000 credits from my scheduled payments.

I accept the deal. Another message pops up a few minutes later. It's a product suggestion. I've never heard of such a thing. They've sent me 'specs' for a product their research team thinks will be a best seller. Rectangular, 2 inches wide, four inches long, half an inch high with 100 kilowatt-hour capacity. There's some mealy mouth language at the end saying they take no responsibility for the accuracy of their demand estimate, or for the specific specifications.

I read that to mean I can design and submit any product I want, just as I can on any other day. But the one they sent me, is their best guess at what will be most successful.

Well, with nothing else to do this week, why not!

SUBMISSION

Strange thing. It took me an hour or so to get back into the design of my Personal Power Pack. When I did, I found numerous design flaws. There's something about the reconditioning of Unit 12 that made the technology more real to me, more alive, more potent, more organic.

Sorry for all the more's, but I think I've come to understand our nanotube power storage systems at a level comparable to my ancestor. As much as I'd like to redo the original, I have the sense not to. Instead, I've created the new one Jungle thinks will sell.

I file the patent and wait three days for confirmation of the filing. I then file a new design with Jungle. I use their specs in the product description, but submit a design that far exceeds it.

POWER TECHNOLOGIES

My degree is in Power Engineering. My specialty is lightning capture. But to get my degree, I had to study all types of electrical power generation, distribution, and storage technologies. I got top marks in all those, but in truth never understood them as well. That made me something of an oddity in school. Jaredaan is one of the very few places that has commercial lightning capture systems. It's one of those niche technologies that aren't even covered in the required curriculum. Most of my courses were actually about the main line technologies: fusion and antimatter.

Almost all major population centers have antimatter power generation. Smaller locales with populations of 100 million or less are more likely to have fusion systems. Most peaking or voltage support generation is synth-gas, in densely populated areas, or ethanol, in rural agricultural areas. Wind and solar photovoltaics are also popular in less densely populated areas.

Every one of these systems is a 'lowest' cost system, in terms of credits per kilowatt. What separates them and gives them a niche is the amount of power required. For example, if your city needs 100 terawatts, that's 100 billion kilowatts, you put in an antimatter system. The fuel/generator system costs about 1 trillion credits to build, but the fuel is only 0.01 credits per kilowatt and the capital cost is only 10 credits per kilowatt, which is cheap.

Jaredstown with its 10,000 people only needs something like 1 gigawatt. An antimatter system here would be totally farcical. In contrast, it's the perfect size for lightning capture, which has no fuel cost and only costs 10 credits per kilowatt to build.

Our space station and two space ports each have a small fusion system. I have the technical qualification to work in each of these places, but absolutely no interest.

RETURN

The week-long suspension is up. I return to the office and get the oddest greeting. Unit #12 is back up. It was put in service the same day I got put on leave. Over the last week, it's had the highest performance rating of all our units. Everyone seems happy the unit is online and appreciative that I sorted out the underlying problem. But a gloom hangs over the company. And most everyone diverts their eyes after greeting me the day I return.

Shortly after checking in and confirming I'm back on the pay roll, I find out that my surface access has been locked out. I'm welcome in the office, welcome to review and comment on the various engineering change orders (i.e., upgrades and fixes) that have been proposed in my absence, but my surface privileges have been revoked.

The paperwork and moronic change order reviews is soul crushing. I need to go back to work, not babysit the morons! Ah... I better not say that out loud.

JUNGLE

Another week of mind numbingly non-work goes by. Our power system is getting weaker by the day. But I'm being held on the sidelines, reviewing proposals that will make it worse. But Jungle comes back with a product approval. They like the new product. They still get 2x manufacturing cost, but I now get 2 credits per unit. They're throwing in a free promotion. They disguised it as a competition award or something like that, but on day 1 ten thousand units go out and I'm up another 20,000 credits. Any other time in my life, I would have been worried about the numbers. But in the wake of all the rejection sent my way of recent, I cling to the success of my products as if they were my lifeline.

...

Today is the day! I'm expecting 9,000 credits to show up from Jungle today. My product started selling in the middle of the calendar month that's paying out today. I earned a total of 20,000 credits by the end of that month. The promotion I recently launched, cost 10,000 credits, plus a 10% premium because it was paid from my scheduled payments, not with cash.

Checking my bank account, I see that 9,000 credits were deposited I quickly pull a draft to transfer 2,500 to Mom and Dad: 2,000 for the loan, 500 in interest. Looking at what's left I chuckle. The loan is paid off, and I still have the equivalent of two-month's pay from the power company in my account.

LEVEL ONE

Another stupid day at the office. I leave on the early side and head for home. The world's been closing in on me and I need to go hide in my room.

My products are selling like crazy on Jungle. I'm making over 5,000 credits a day at this point. Maybe I should quit this job and get my own apartment, so I never need to see my brothers again.

As I approach the escalator shaft, I hear a voice.

"Jared!"

My heart melts. I look up and see Nana running my way.

"Jared, I'm so sorry."

She wraps her arms around me, clinging tightly.

I return the hug, clinging to her as if my life depended upon it. I can't help myself. I love this woman.

"Come home with me. I've missed you."

I know this is the wrong thing to do. But I'm once again hopelessly smitten.

"I've missed you." The words slip past my lips.

"Come on." She drags me toward the elevator. An alarm sounds in the back of my mind, but I can't process it. The only thing going through my mind is... Well. I probably shouldn't say.

A harrowing ride down the elevator, the short walk to her apartment, and the rapid shedding of clothes, then I'm home! I'm finally home again!

I fall into a deep and peaceful sleep. Little do I know that this will be the last peaceful sleep I'll experience for a very long time.

LEVEL TWELVE

I wake early, Nana's warmth next to me. I hear her tender breathing. Her heart beats gently beneath my hand. It's like I've died and gone to heaven.

I fall back asleep.

...

There's a pounding on the door. It startles us both awake. The thought goes through my mind. *Not again*.

Indeed, not again. This time a lot worse.

The noise at the door gets louder.

Nana looks at me with sad eyes. "Sorry." Then buries her head in her pillow.

There's a shattering sound. Someone's apparently kicked in the door. And once again, all my clothes are on the living room floor.

"Jared Daan!" A voice calls out.

It sounds like the police chief, which is utterly befuddling.

I grab a towel and dash out in the hope of gathering my clothes in time. Instead, I'm hit with a taser.

"Jared Daan. You are under arrest for solicitation, vandalism, and grand larceny. You have the right to remain silent. Anything you say will undoubtedly be used against you."

My paralyzed body lays on the floor shaking as two police officers drag Nana's naked body out of the bedroom. Through the open door, I see Asher and Nana's brother Lucas smirking at me.

What the bloody hell!

CHAPTER 5: TRIAL

We arrive at the police station. Dad is waiting there for me. I've never seen him so cross. I have no idea what this is about, and no one has told me anything. But Lucas' and Asher's presence outside Nana's apartment was suspicious.

The taser paralysis has been wearing off. I'm buck naked and still have little control over my body. I was wheeled here on a gurney, covered by a blanket. Nana apparently got the same treatment. I can't move, so can't know for sure, but think she's on a gurney right behind me.

"Take her back to be examined." It's the police chief's voice, but I don't know who he was speaking to.

"We found him at her apartment." It's Chief Hill again, this time he's talking to Dad. I know because I see my Dad shake his head, then turn and glare at me.

"Given the condition we found them in, it's unambiguous, but the woman will be checked for semen. A quick blood check from him will tell us everything we need on that charge."

Dad is really glaring at me, but I don't get it. I can take up with a woman if I want. There's no law against that.

"On the other matter, I think we have the evidence we need in his wallet."

What other matter? What evidence could there possibly be in my wallet?

Dad shakes his head. I can tell he's on the verge of tears.

Dad takes a deep breath, then says to the Chief. "I won't post bail. He may have the funds, but you'll have to ask him. I don't think I know my son anymore."

"Understood." The chief says to Dad very compassionately.

Dad turns to go, then stops and looks to me.

"I'm very disappointed in you Jared. I thought you would turn into something, but I guess the fast road was too tempting. Your mother will be crushed."

I'm getting enough strength back that I manage to get a "What?" out. But he just shakes his head, turns his back, and walks out.

"OK, Jared. We need some blood and fingerprints once you're locked away in a cell. We'll get you some prison garb. You'll be arraigned in the morning."

I'm totally flabbergasted. I feel a tear roll down my cheek. I may be paralyzed, but the tear ducts apparently still work.

ARRAIGNMENT

I'm cuffed and put in leg irons. The purple prison clothes are made of an uncomfortable rough material that makes me itch. With the cuffs and leg irons on I can't scratch anything, and the itch is driving me crazy. But this whole thing is crazy. I have no idea why I'm here or what I'm accused of.

I've been assigned a public defender for the arraignment. Her name is Felicity Gall. She seems to be as unhappy about being stuck with me as I am with her.

We are led into a courtroom and seated at the defendant's table.

She whispers to me, "The charges against you are very serious. They wouldn't be giving us a private hearing like this if it wasn't.

"This is a simple procedural hearing. They are going to read the charges. Then we will enter a Not Guilty plea.

"If you remember nothing else, remember this. Do not respond to anything they say today. No matter what it is, do not respond!

"I have a hard time believing these charges are true, so expect to be shocked. But this is not the venue to defend yourself. It is simply them telling you what you are being charged with.

"Understood?"

I nod my head. I can't believe what's happening.

...

The first charge shocks me to the core. They say Nana is a prostitute and I'm charged with soliciting her services. I am so dumbfounded by this, I can't breathe.

HOSPITAL

Apparently, I passed out after the first charge was read. No one was expecting that. I was standing in front of the judge, who was reading the charges, hands in cuffs and ankles in leg irons. No one was there to catch me, and my head hit the marble floor hard enough to give me a concussion.

I will be in the hospital for several days, so the arraignment was rescheduled for next week. The judge agreed to allow my lawyer to read the charges and work with me to start building a defense. Apparently, this isn't usually true, but it is the first time that anyone has heard of a suspect being seriously injured because they passed out in shock during an arraignment. The judge apparently thinks it would be better for me to hear the rest of them before I come back in.

The session with the lawyer starts poorly.

"Yes. I had sex with Nana. She's my girlfriend."

"Jared, that line won't work. You don't pay your girlfriend to spend an evening with you."

"I didn't pay her. Usually, we go out to dinner first, which I pay for. But I don't pay her.

"Why do they think Nana is a prostitute?"

She rolls her eyes. "Are you saying you didn't know?"

That line craters me. I must really be a stooge. I lay back and shut my eyes. Will someone just shoot me?

I don't respond to anything else she says, and she eventually packs up and leaves.

...

Guests are also being allowed to visit me in the hospital. I'm chained to the bed and there's a guard posted at the door. But no one's come until now.

Surprisingly, Aaron comes to visit. He enters, head held low.

"I've come to say I'm sorry. I didn't realize you didn't know about Nana. When her mother passed, they gave her a place in public housing on one of the lower levels. Lucas wouldn't help her. Working in the garden, she doesn't make enough to get an apartment of her own. Lucas offered to get her an apartment on the 12th level, if she'd sleep with some of his 'friends' two nights a week. The ones he proposed were ones she'd been with before, so she went with it.

"Now, of course, she's trapped. He's her pimp. I try to see her every week or two. Ash, Seth, and Jude have all been with her. I knew you liked her, so hired her to take you home with her that first time. I can't believe you drank so much sweet red wine that you passed out without getting any.

"I think that's why she saw you the second time. She'd already been paid. But the second time went to hell when Lucas caught you with her. He told me he riffled through your stuff before leaving and 'took his payment.' I'm not sure who paid her to seduce you the night of the arrest.

"By the way, it's prostitution if she offers to sleep with you for money. It's solicitation if you offer to pay her to sleep with you. It's not that way everywhere, but that's the law in Jaredstown. Great grand pop apparently had a thing for women and wanted the rules on this matter to be clear.

"Anyway, sorry. I wanted to give you a nice birthday present. It kind of backfired."

"Is that why Mom has been so mad at me?"

Aaron stares at me for a while. "I really shouldn't tell you this." He shakes his head a couple times as if trying to stop himself.

"Nana's mother did the same thing after her husband died. Dad visited her once. He'd had a big fight about something with Mom. Mom almost left him. You were the last of her men who hadn't visited that family."

"Do you know anything about the other charges?"

"Yes. You've been framed. But I don't know enough to get you off the hook."

"Asher, Seth and Jude are in on it aren't they?"

"Ash and Seth for sure. I'm not sure about Jude, but maybe."

...

Everyone used to say I was so innocent. For the first time I get it, truly get it. A deep, deep depression sets in. I fall asleep, hoping never to wake up again, but am tormented by dreams.

Nana: "I like you Jared. I really do. But you're obviously not ready."

Aaron: "You must really have it for her. Condolences."

Nana with very sad eyes: "Sorry."

I am the stupidest human ever born.

CASE

The shock of what's happening has worn off a bit. The injustice of it hasn't. Nonetheless, my rational brain now understands what's happened. And the evidence planted against me is overwhelming. My brothers are predatory geniuses.

The specific charges against me are a.) stealing raw gold ore from the mine, and b.) damaging Unit #3 in a failed attempt to dispose of the evidence. The charge related to solicitation is being tried separately, even though my relationship with Nana enabled my brothers to frame me.

It sounds farfetched, but the evidence is damning.

47

My guess, based on the evidence I've been shown, is that Seth found out about the gold strike at the mine. Gold is not one of the things we mine there, but we do find the odd vein now and again. Seth, with all his mechanical skills, is on the team that does that kind of specialty mining. He wasn't one of the people directly involved with exploiting the vein, but he was the one that scheduled two carts to be delivered the day Aaron was loading. And he would have had access to the carts after they were loaded. This aspect of their case is weak. I've never been down in the mines and the only evidence they have against me is some DNA and fingerprints found on the cart. It sounds damning, but the cart was found on the surface and there would have been plenty of time to plant DNA and/or fingerprints.

Anyway, they took the cart somewhere, cracked up the rock and scraped out the gold. They then took the cart with scrap rock to the surface where they attempted to dump it behind Unit #3. There's a gully back there. Anything heavy like rock that falls in will get buried in the snow after a couple days and eventually make its way to the bottom.

Unfortunately, the culprit apparently lost control of the cart, and damaged Unit #3.

The cart and a lot of rock was recovered. Experts confirmed that the rock came from the mine and would have held between 5 and 25 kilograms of gold.

The police asked me a lot of questions about this, but I have no idea where these guys would have crushed the rock and scraped the gold out. I know nothing. I also know nothing about where they might have done it. The police asked me if I did it here, or there—they named several places, all apparently in the mine. I'd never heard of any of them.

So how did they pin this on me?

Nana provided the perfect diversion, twice in fact. Lucas apparently helped himself to my surface pass card the morning he broke in on us in her apartment. That's what allowed the culprits to get to the surface. I never knew the card was missing, so assume they ripped it (i.e., made an illegal copy). Seth has the skill and equipment to do that.

The last night I was with Nana, I'd apparently left the office without clocking out. She was waiting for me near the office and we disappeared down to her place without being seen by anyone who would recognize me. That had to have been part of their plan, because within minutes of me leaving, one of them, dressed in my wool sweater, went up to the surface with the cart. Perfect timing.

His face was covered, but it was my sweater. Security video shows the culprit, allegedly me, in my sweater, 'my' jeans, with my gait, going up to the surface, then going behind a screen to put on my cold suit. He exited the garage on my snow crawler, pulling the cart behind. They have video of the cart going in the direction of Unit #3. But there is no video coverage at the unit itself. My guess is that Asher is the one that did this. He has the training and knowledge of the operation. But I don't think he's ever been outside before, so it was a gutsy move.

By the way, Unit #3 is the one Dad and I attempted to repair the first day I went up. It was toast, but over time Rye and I had coaxed it back to life. It finally went back online a week before my suspension.

But, back to the evidence... The pièce de resistance in this framing operation was a couple flakes of gold found behind my desk at home.

The irony is that I doubt they looked behind Seth's or Jude's desks for gold flakes or scrubbed my cold suit for Asher's DNA.

I've been asked several times, if Aaron was my partner in the mine. Since I'm claiming innocence, I'm saying no. I have to. But I do know that poor Aaron is still a suspect and still doesn't know that the material he loaded into the cart that day had high concentrations of gold in it.

PUBLIC DEFENDER

I'm sure enough about who did this and how they did it, that I want to fight the case. The lawyer I've been assigned doesn't like the idea.

She agrees that their case about me being part of the ore theft is weak. She also acknowledges that Nana has given a deposition saying I was with her all night, which would be a good alibi.

But she thinks Nana can be flipped. She has been arrested several times. And the prosecutor is going back and forth about which of us to charge. I don't see how they can make that stick without evidence of payment. She says evidence like that is easy to fabricate.

Discussion of Nana has me in a funk again, and my lawyer is tearing down my confidence in our justice system. We don't need to decide yet, but she promises to try for a light plea deal.

BETRAYAL

Nana flipped today. She's now saying I came to her place uninvited at two AM. I appeared to be freezing, so she let me in to warm me up.

She's says I paid her 100 credits and has cash with my fingerprints on it. I am well and truly screwed.

PLEA DEAL

The prosecutor is going for 20 years in the prison camp. He'll drop it to 5 years if I plead out. My lawyer thinks he's worried about the fact they haven't found the gold. They've searched my room and office. Our house, Aaron's apartment, and Nana's too. And the entire interior of the power company's surface operations.

If they can't prove there's been an actual theft, then all they can get me on is damaging the unit. She thinks a jury will buy that there's been a theft, but it will cost the prosecutor his job if he pushes for a conviction and can't get one.

She wants to make a counteroffer, plead guilty on all counts in exchange for a 5-year sentence with eligibility for early release on good behavior after 1 year. She presents me with a document to sign. She thinks he'll take it. If I sign now.

This is so unfair. I'm the victim, as I have been since the day I was born. My brothers have won. Maybe life with crawly poisonous things will be a better life than the one I've had here.

CHAPTER 6: TRANSPORTATION

Today is the day and another element of my new life snaps into focus. All of my assets are being seized. Everything. My computer, my clothes, my bank account... Even my toothbrush. I'm being sent to the equator, some 8,000 km away with nothing but the shoes, clothes, and blanket issued to me in the jail.

One of the guys there was even ribbing me about the trip down, saying there's only a 90% chance of surviving the trip. I don't really believe him but doubt there's a 100% chance of surviving it either.

People have been lining up outside the jail for a while. I've only seen this happen once, that's how few people get convicted of crimes this severe, but I will be marched down the access ways in my purple jumpsuit, with my hands cuffed behind my back, my ankles in leg irons, and two cops, whose job it is to hold me up and keep me moving. I think the idea is to humiliate the condemned and scare the kids into behaving themselves.

But as an innocent, being walked out to the transportation hub, I realize that this is when the bad guys get proof positive assurance that they got away with it. I wonder how long it's going to be before Asher ends up at the prison camp with me. He is no doubt emboldened at this point.

And I think about the town. Asher got my job. It's hard to imagine the town's power will be up that much longer. As we step out of the jail and start the mile-long crawl, I see Nana. She locks eyes with me. She's obviously been crying. My heart still beats for her. With all the money I'd be making if this hadn't happened, we could have had a good life together. I smile at her, then look away. I don't need any more of that.

It takes a while, but we finally make it to the elevator. The tunnel to the space port is on level 2, the one where my birthday party was held. It's a short uneventful ride up. The thought makes me smile. With any luck I will never see that elevator again. The doors open and the family is there. This is where the family gets to say goodbye. To my surprise, everyone is there. Dad seems to be the one that's most upset. I think he's figured out that I'm innocent.

He comes to hug me. The cops stop him, then give in. It's like that night I was out on the surface too long. Only this time, he really has lost me. My mother is very stoic. She doesn't approach. She's nowhere near believing I'm innocent or forgiving me.

Aaron's like Dad. He knows I didn't do it. Knows he had a role in setting me up. I know it was unintentional, but the guilt is obviously eating at him. He weeps as he hugs me and keeps whispering sorry.

The three stooges, or maybe I should call them the three criminal master minds, mostly gawk. But Asher can't let it be.

"Finally getting what you deserve."

"Spend the gold quickly Ash, they will eventually figure out that you did it."

I see fear pass across his eyes, then the retort. "Well, if you tell me where it is, maybe I will."

"Look under your bed, idiot."

The cops have had enough of this and whisk me past the area boxed off for the family. I hear my mother say, "I knew I should have stopped at five."

The comment hurts, but then I realize she had a lot to do with this. The real reason the sibling rivalry in our family got so far out of hand was her constant chant about the sixth son of the sixth generation. Bullshit from day 1. And here I am, paying the price for her excess.

One of the cops says, "It's never easy, the family farewell. Your father and brother clearly believe you. You should have fought it."

I look at him strangely. "What? And get twenty years!"

"Maybe, maybe not. Very few people make it to 5 years down there. Only a handful have ever come home, and they weren't the same when they got back."

I lock my eyes straight ahead and keep plodding along. I can't take any more of this cheery banter.

RAILWAY

The railway connects Jaredstown with the small mining town of Ashcrag. It was the second settlement the founders built on the planet. It's the one that has the majority of the precious metals the surveyors discovered years ago. They have gold, platinum, silver, copper, and titanium. Their output is a fraction of ours, but revenue nearly half.

The town is comparatively small because building conditions are not as good there. They don't have as much solid bedrock.

The space port, where we're going, is in between. Most of the traffic on the rail line is raw metal, heading to the space port to be launched into space. But the same railguns that launch the metals also launch the weekly shuttle between operations here in the north and Heroldstown on the equator.

I've seen videos of the shuttle in operation, but never actually met anyone that had taken it. Apparently, it's not for the weak of heart. The shuttle is basically a glider with a small amount of compressed gas that can be used as thrust in an emergency.

I've not heard of a shuttle crashing. But I have heard of people dying from heart attack or stroke because they can't take the g-Force of launch.

Yet another interesting experience to look forward to.

...

We finally reach the train. At the end, I see the special car made for transporting prisoners. It has three compartments separated by inch-thick plexiglass.

I go in the center compartment. One of the cops will take the front, the other will take the rear. The conductor opens the door to my compartment. The leg irons make it impossible to step up high enough to get in, so the cops have to lift me up.

The leg irons are bolted to a bar along the floor of the compartment. The chains around my waist are bolted to the seat. My cuffs are adjusted so that I have one hand cuffed to each side of the compartment. It gives me a little more movement. I think the purpose is to allow me to steady myself when we go around curves.

I'm told that the train will leave as soon as we're aboard. I'm sure that's for the benefit of the cops, not me. I'm just along for the ride. I go where I'm told to go. Eat when I'm told to eat. Sleep when I'm told to sleep. I have no liberty. I'm a piece of property at this point, a machine that they're going to put to work on a very dangerous plantation where actual humans fear to tread.

The conductor shuts and locks the doors, then whistles for the train to depart.

His last words are, "The trip is about 100 km and will take a little over 2 hours. Good luck."

SPACE PORT

We arrive at the space port. Our car is decoupled and towed to another area where we can disembark. The rest of the train moves away. Apparently, we are, well I am, the only real passenger today. I wonder if I'm the only one headed down south. It seems an incredible waste. I'm just one person. Well, I used to be one person, now I'm just one piece of property. The sanity of this is a bit puzzling to me. If there's anything our great ancestor treasured, it was thought and intelligence. The same is true for our current leaders. So, there must be other stuff that's going down south, otherwise they'd be taking me to the local pen.

That raises the thought, *Is there a pen here?*

It no sooner passes through my mind than I know there must be. Humans, all humans, periodically do something really stupid. Something that requires them to be put in isolation until they regain their minds. I'm sure the preponderance of those stupid things happen somewhere private where no one ever needs to know. But the thought stands. They must have a pen here. It'll be interesting to see where they take me.

It occurs to me that I need to pay attention. Everything going on around me is inevitably inefficient. I don't mean that from the perspective of the prisoner. I mean that from the perspective of the upstanding citizen that I am, whether anyone recognizes it or not.

The camp may kill me. But, if it doesn't, I will return to society. I hope never to grace my presence on Jaredstown again. It's a cursed place that needs to freeze to death. Who knows, with Seth at the helm, it certainly seems possible.

A deep breath. I need to calm myself. There are cursed people in Jaredstown, ones that would serve society better if frozen as statues on the surface. But the majority, the vast majority, are just fellow humans trying to find their way to tomorrow.

...

The two cops handling me seem more relaxed here. I can imagine several reasons why that might be. But the scientist in me needs to watch and wait. My perspective on human life has been proven to be uselessly narrow. If I'm to survive this trial, and eventually grow to make a difference, I need to understand the things going on around me, including the street savvy that my brothers developed. But I need to do so without losing my soul the way they did.

"We're here." One of the cops announces. For the first time I actually look at him. His name tag reads 'Max Baker.'

"Thanks, Max."

My comment seems to startle him. More proof that if I'm to survive this, if I'm to have a positive impact on our world, I need to approach things differently. I need to become very aware of the people around me.

He looks at me, then says conspiratorially, "We know who the real culprit is. Sorry this got hung on you. Don't worry. He will have his comeuppance soon. Word's been sent ahead to go light on you."

He comes closer. "The rules require us to take the leg irons off before you board. If you promise not to kick me or run, I'll take them off now. There's no way out of here. There are people nearby who will taser you if you act out."

I notice that Max's partner, Henry Salamone, is standing back with a glint in his eye. They probably have a bet between them about whether I'll act up or not.

"You have my word, Max."

The leg irons come off and I extend my hand to shake. The chains that replaced the cuffs on the train restrict my movement, but the hand reaches out toward him far enough for its intent to be clear.

After a minute of eyes darting back and forth between my eyes and my hand, he reaches out to shake.

Henry seems disappointed by the civility.

Then unexpectedly, Max says, "I always thought you'd be the one."

He steps back as two guards from the prison camp enter the waiting area.

"Come on. We need to get you aboard quickly or we're going to lose our launch slot."

I turn to the speaker who has no name tag and nod my head in submission. They grab me roughly. It's irksome, but I get it. They need to establish their superiority. I nod to Max, then smile at the new guards. "Lead the way."

SHUTTLE

As we approach the shuttle, I realize it looks a lot like the commercial suborbital space-liners you see on other worlds. It's smaller than the pictures make it appear. It's maybe 30 meters long, with short, thin swept wings on either side and a shallow rear stabilizer on the back. The big difference is the absence of engines.

Ahead of us, I see a small passenger lobby with several people in it. But as we approach, the guards steer me towards the shuttle. Apparently, we're going to be boarding first.

There are steps up to the entry hatch, which explains the removal of the leg irons. We climb the stairs, then enter the hatch. A less-than-friendly flight attendant points to the compartment in the back.

The lead guard puts his hand on my back, indicating he wants me to go in first. I have to stoop. The ceiling is less than two meters from the floor.

As we make our way back, I note the interior configuration of the plane. There are two narrow seats on the left of the aisle, one on the right. The shuttle has 9 rows, the back three of which are blocked off with thick plexiglass.

"You get the window seat on the left in the middle row."

I nod my head in acknowledgement.

When I get to the row in question, I start to squeeze in.

"Hold there for a second."

The lead guard, who is the first one behind me slides into the two seats behind mine.

"We need to cuff you to the wall and to the arm rest on this side."

I hold still passively, letting him move me however he needs to. I hear a snap and see the chain that restrains arm movement has been locked in place along the wall. A second snap confirms the chain around my waist is secured there as well.

"OK. Sit down in the window seat."

I sit. It's a tight squeeze, but the seat back is soft, filled with a gel or something.

"Watch out, I'm lowering the divider."

I scooch up against the window and a plexiglass divider comes down, locking me in place. It's tight and I have a momentary spike of claustrophobia, which thankfully fades away as I settle into place.

The door to our little cabin closes and the normal passengers start filing in. Most give me a good eyeballing. But I don't detect any open hostility.

The lead guard takes the seat behind me. His partner takes the seat across the aisle from me. The empty row in front must be for the comfort of the regular passengers. I get that. If I were one of them, I wouldn't want to get too close to the guy in this seat.

...

The hatch at the front just closed, everyone is strapped in, and the shuttle starts to move. It takes a second to realize that the shuttle itself isn't exactly moving. It's still sitting stationary on a platform that is moving the shuttle toward the wall in front of us. From my perspective it looks like we're about to hit the wall, then I notice a slit in the wall that the wings will fit into.

The screen mounted in the seat in front of me lights up and a video starts playing. It reviews a bunch of relatively obvious safety things, then starts showing what's actually going on. The shuttle is being inserted into a launch tube. The main tube's cross section looks exactly like the shuttle's cross section but ever so slightly larger. On looking out the window, I see the front edge of the wing sliding into the tube as the wall inches closer and closer to me. When my window passes into the tube, I'm shocked at how little space there is between the shuttle and the tube.

I get another little spike of claustrophobia.

The pilot comes on to make an announcement.

"In a moment, you will feel a jolt as the magnetic fields engage us. Once that happens, the platform that carried us in will withdraw, and the rear tube hatch will close. We will sit that way for about 5 minutes as the big pumps remove the air surrounding our spaceplane."

A count down timer starts on the screen in front of me.

When it gets down to 10 seconds, the pilot comes on again.

"Shortly after the timer finishes counting down you will feel another jolt as the forward hatch to the holding area opens."

I see controls on the screen. Thankfully, the chains binding me to the shuttle have enough give that I can reach them. I activate a video that shows how the system works.

We are in a skintight, evacuated tube that's 312.5 kilometers long. It runs up through one of the tallest mountains on the planet. We will be magnetically accelerated through the tube at just less than 4 gravities for 125 seconds. That will give us a speed of 5,000 meters per second when we exit the tube near the mountain's summit. The exit is at an altitude of 32,500 meters where the air is very thin, less than 0.5% of ground level. When we're close to the end of the tunnel, airlocks close to the tunnels base will be opened, pumping air in behind us.

Seconds before we reach the end of the tube, its forward hatch will open. Thin air will rush down to greet us. But the much higher-pressure air rushing in behind will propel us out into the upper atmosphere. For the next 8 minutes, our momentum will propel us up to a peak altitude of 55,000 meters, at which point we will start our descent. The semi-ballistic flight will continue for another 10 minutes.

Once the air gets thick enough, the shuttle will glide down to the space port in Heroldstown.

There's a note clarifying the term "semi-ballistic." The shuttle is equipped with a small grav drive that reduces gravitational pull on the shuttle for the 18 minutes that it's above the atmosphere. Flight is ballistic other than for the offset gravitational pull. Curious.

Another countdown timer pops up on the screen. We are going to get slammed with 4G acceleration in 3, 2, 1... It's like a giant hand has just pushed me back in my seat. I feel my heart start to beat faster as I struggle to breathe.

As my eyes refocus, I see that a new countdown timer has started. This one shows the time remaining until the acceleration stops. Out of the corner of my eye, I see lights flashing by outside my window. They seem to be passing at a constant rate. How can that be if we're accelerating?

Duh... The lights are getting further and further apart. I wonder if these lights were the countdown timer back in the old days.

When the countdown timer finally reaches zero, several things happen in rapid succession. A huge vibration passes through the ship. It must be the pressurized air behind us giving us the final push out of the launch tube. The next is the light. Brilliant daylight floods in as there's essentially no atmosphere to block it. Next, the stomach-in-your-throat feeling of free fall hits as we settle into our ballistic course above the atmosphere.

Then lastly, I notice a slight glow along the leading edges of the wings. We are above the vast, vast majority of the atmosphere. But there's enough to start heating the wings. In fact, it's starting to get really warm in here.

As I look back toward the wings, I see the planet. Wow! We are really moving. We are far enough south already that there's no sign of snow, just barren rock. Then I notice the tinge of green along the horizon. It's so amazing, that I forget for a moment the circumstances that brought me here.

...

We're on approach. We're coming in from the north west. The lake is clearly visible, as is the ice transport system that feeds it. Surprisingly, further to the east there appears to be a large sea. That was not covered in our geography classes in school.

All along the south edge of the lake are the agricultural areas. The commercial agricultural land appears to be well organized and tidy. In contrast, the sugar cane fields along the southeastern shore of the lake seem overgrown and messy.

At the far eastern edge of the lake is the sugar refinery and ethanol distillery. Dark smoke billows up around the refinery and is blown to the northeast by the wind. It's located along the south shore of the river that carries water from the lake to the sea in the east.

I think I can see the penal colony located between the cane fields and the refinery. But there's not much there, not much to see.

The main industrial area starts to the north east of the lake and runs east along the river about as far out as the sugar refinery, south of it.

Lastly there's Heroldstown along the northwest shore of the lake. It was built to support the ice transport system and grew from there.

We're just passing over the mountains to the west of town and are now on final approach to the space port.

...

As we touch down, I realize my new life is about to begin. It's hard to believe that a month ago I was in love, had a good life, a good job, and was about to become rich. Now, I'm nothing. Absolutely nothing. My head drops, the tears flow. And I really don't care what the others think about it.

CHAPTER 7: EXILE

We landed just before sunset. But it's dark now. It's a 79-kilometer drive to the prison camp. As part of their compensation for the trip, my guards were given passes for a night in town tonight. When they drop me off at the local pen, the lead guard finally introduces himself. His name is Jesse Smith. He goes by Jess. And he kind of apologizes for dropping me off there.

"Jared, it's like this. The round trip is hard. You felt the return, imagine doing an up and back in the same day. We get a one-night pass that we can use up there or down here. Where would you use it?

"Your accommodations here are no worse than at the camp. A lot of the inmates would say they're better here. And there aren't centipedes or cane toads either. So, this is a far better place to spend your first night."

"Understood, Jess. Not a problem."

He looks at me strangely, then takes his leave. I get it. Everyone has a life. Everyone has crap they need to put up with. I'm glad he gets a night on the town. But as the local cop walks me back to my cell, I realize things here are nothing like home. There are already eight guys in a cell with four beds. They all look like street brawlers. No one would ever accuse me of that. I look like the booky geek that I am.

I'm deposited in the cell. The guard chuckles as he locks the door. "Good luck."

As soon as he exits, the mob approaches and a whole new, fresh hell begins.

HOSPITAL

I wake in intense pain. My head is killing me. The rest of my body feels like it's been sent through a woodchipper. And I really can't see anything. It doesn't feel like I have a bandage over my face, but blinking my eyes only reveals the slightest change in darkness.

I try to touch my face, but my hands are constrained. So are my feet, I think. I can't feel my right foot at all.

But my hearing is OK. It's quiet, but there's clearly a lot of activity going on nearby. I hear a cart roll by somewhere near, but it sounds like it's in another room.

My door opens. I sense someone approaching but looking in that direction only reveals the same dark cloudiness.

"Mr. Daan. I see you're awake."

The voice drives nails through my head. Whoever it is apparently sees me wince.

"What's the last thing you remember?"

I try to say, eight thugs, but I don't seem to be able to speak properly. It comes out more like a-hugs. And the effort really hurts.

"I'm going to shine a bright light in your eyes, just track it as it moves."

Things get a little brighter. I sense movement, but until the blinders come off, there's no chance I can track it.

"Pupils contract, which is good. But you're not tracking the light. That's not good."

Silence for a moment.

"I'm going to order more tests. Mr. Daan, you were beaten, nearly to death, then left in a pool of blood for five hours. We were barely able to save you.

"There was significant swelling of the brain. It has taken the feeling in your right foot and appears to have taken your vision. The larynx in your throat was damaged, as were your genitals.

"We've had you on medications to reduce the swelling and it's substantially reduced. It's a good sign you woke today. That's always the first step. Hopefully your vision and right leg will see some improvement in the next couple days.

"But if there's no improvement in a week, then there likely won't be. Either way, we can only hold inmates for two weeks, so we will do everything in our power to get you better in a week."

He slaps me on the right leg, but I don't feel much. Then he stands.

"Get better, Mr. Daan."

I hear him messing with some stuff, then leaving. I can feel my body relaxing and the pain receding. He obviously drugged me. But a new rage begins to burn as consciousness drains away.

RECOVERY

Sounds tickle my ears and I slowly crawl up from the depths. Amazingly, my head is not pounding. But a new pain replaces it, my right leg. It's like the worst case of it falling asleep that I've ever experienced. I wiggle my toes, which helps.

I can also see! A little anyway.

As my mind slowly engages, I realize that there's an alarm of some sort going off. A nurse rushes in, takes one look at me, then starts messing with the gear attached to me.

A doctor comes in while she's doing that. He looks at me and smiles. No one has said anything yet. Maybe they don't speak with sub-humans.

He confers briefly with the nurse, but I can't make out the words. Then he looks at me, the big goofy smile still in place.

"You're getting better. I was admittedly worried when I saw you yesterday. I'm sure the drugs played a role, but you are incredibly resilient. Can you see?"

"Not perfectly, but yes. I can see."

He smiles more. "And speak too, it would seem."

The doctor seems genuinely happy for me.

"You apparently tossed around a bit before waking. One of your lines came loose. In case you're wondering, that's what set off the alarm."

The nurse is still working on me. She's on the left side of the bed, the one closer to the door. The doctor moves around to the right.

"I'm going to test your reflexes."

He uncovers the right leg and touches my little toe.

"Do you feel that?"

"A little. It's all tingly, like it's gone to sleep."

He takes out his little rubber hammer and taps that magic spot on the knee, the one that makes it flex. The knee bends, but the little hammer has really sent the tingling to a whole new level.

I groan.

"Sorry about that."

I hear the nurse say, "Everything is reattached. Need me for anything else?"

She's obviously talking to the doctor.

"No. Thanks for getting here so quickly."

She smiles at him in a way that makes me think this is more than just a work relationship.

The nurse closes the door, then the doctor takes a seat.

"We took additional tests a couple hours after you fell asleep again yesterday. The brain swelling has gone down. The fact that you have sight, and feeling in your leg, implies the swelling was the cause. What's less clear is why it swelled as much as it did. You have a concussion, but only a minor crack in your skull. Have you had a concussion before?"

I want to say, "No. Not until I was taken into the government's protective care last month. Now I've had two."

But I have the good sense not to.

"Yes, a little less than a month ago. I was in the hospital for a week."

"Really? Where?"

"Jaredstown."

Understanding dawns. "Ah, sorry. I lost track of the fact you just arrived." A moment of silence.

"You're going to need to take care of your head. You came very close to death. Even a small knock on the head now might do you in. I'll include that in your discharge instructions. There's work you can do at the camp that won't put you at much risk."

Another pause.

"I work down there sometimes. It's not as bad as you probably think. No one would volunteer to go work there. But it's not the death sentence you've probably been told it is."

His words are said with kindness. But so were Jess's before they locked me in a cage with eight murderous sadists.

"At this point, I'm optimistic that your sight will return to normal, or at least close to normal. Your leg would benefit from some physical therapy. I might be able to get you a little before you're discharged.

"We scanned and scoped your larynx while you were out. It's not out of the woods yet, but if you limit speech and keep your voice low, I'd say there's a 90-plus percent chance of a full recovery.

"Your testicles are a different story. They were severely damaged. We had to go in and remove some tissue that threatened what's left. By the time you leave, it should give you minimal pain. But I'm sad to say the odds of being able to sire a child are well less than 50% at this point."

Children are the last thing on my mind at the moment. In fact, I'm not sure I'd want to bring one into this world, so I'm not that worried about it.

He stands to leave and slaps me on the leg again. It sets off another round of intense tingling, but not as bad as it was when I woke.

"Get better, Jared Daan. Your recovery has been quite remarkable. As you are, no doubt."

DRIVE

I was discharged from the hospital today. My groin still hurts enough that it's hard to walk. But that didn't stop them from cuffing me and putting the leg irons on. I can barely walk, and the bruises still haven't faded yet, but they shackle me anyway! It seems the murderous brutes in the pen aren't the only sadists in Heroldstown.

I notice that Jess is not among the guards along for this journey.

But despite the discomfort of the journey, the drive to the prison camp is incredibly interesting. I've never spent this much time on the surface, and I've never been on the surface without a cold suit. It's not exactly hot here. Maybe it could be out in the direct sunlight. But it's not cold either, 22°C.

We pass building after building as we make our way east on the north side of the lake. Some of the areas we pass appear well maintained, others not so much. But the thing that impresses me most is the space, how spread-out things are. I don't know how large Jaredstown is, but it's nothing like this. We have a total population of about 10,000 and I never found it to be all that cramped. I'm told its worse below level 26 where the escalator stops.

But here... There's 80ish kilometers of development north of the lake, and another 80 kilometers of agriculture on the south side of the lake. Yet the population of the whole region is only 3,000. It seems you could go a long time here without seeing another living soul.

Maybe I'll like that, if and when I finish my sentence.

ARRIVAL

Once over the bridge that crosses the river at the east end of the lake, the scenery changes. Other than the sugar refinery and the ethanol distillery, there's no other visible development.

Wild sugar cane grows uncontrolled near the roadway and here and there toward the East. But looking west along the south shore, it's all greenery. I've seen pictures of cultivated sugarcane. The healthy plants look like a cross between bamboo and corn. The main stalk is stiff and straight, ribbed like bamboo. The leaves are more of a cross between the two, the size of bamboo leaves, but more of the ribbing you'd expect from a corn leaf. Sugarcane also has very corn-like tassels at the top.

The stuff growing wild here has similar qualities, but the stalks slump over at the base. It doesn't look very healthy.

64

That of course changes as we pass through the gate into camp. A couple rows of beautiful specimens line the driveway to the main reception building.

The fence surrounding the camp is not in particularly good shape. It won't stop anyone who wants to get out. It's obviously something put there as a reminder that bad things will happen to you if you go any further. The hinges on the gate have rusted to the point where it's hard to believe it could be closed.

We pull up to the reception building. It's a modest two-story structure made mostly from wood. The building, the front anyway, appears to be well maintained. Four more guards come down to greet us. The four others in the van get out, leaving me chained in place.

It's comical seeing eight muscular, armed men here to escort a shortish, skinny nerd, cuffed, shackled, and barely able to walk because of the pain in his groin.

The leader of our little caravan tells one of the others that he needs to speak with the boss before they unload me. So here I sit.

Five minutes later, he comes back out and points to me.

"The boss wants to speak with him. Help him out, then bring him up. And be careful. He was seriously injured, just discharged from the hospital today."

He goes back in. The guard that locked me into the van at the hospital, opens the door. He removes the locks that hold me in place, then offers a hand to help me out. As I stand, I feel ripping in my groin. I look down and see blood. The guard catches me as I collapse, then drags me up the steps so he can lay me down on the wooden floor, not the gravel driveway. I hear one of the other guards call for the prison's medic, then my mind slips into darkness.

CAMP HOSPITAL

I wake to darkness. The first thing I notice is the noise, the night air is filled with it. Crickets chirp. Cane toads croak. Rats scuttle through the rafters. Eyes glow outside the window.

The slightest movement triggers pain, but in truth, not that much. I'm once again chained to the bed. A relatively heavy blanket covers me, which makes sense given the cold air in the room. I let the night sounds calm me and fall back asleep.

...

I wake again. Light floods in from outside. There's a lot of activity going on outside the privacy curtains.

I hear the sounds of medical staff tending to a patient on the other side of the curtain to my right. From the sound of it, the patient is female. She seems to be struggling to breathe.

I hear what I presume to be the curtain to her space slide open.

"Hi, Doc. It's Brenda again, another centipede bite. We've administered the same antihistamine as before, but it's not helping."

"Understood. Put an IV line in and start the drip. Add 50 ml of this."

I hear scribbling on a pad.

"It's a corticosteroid. It should help relieve the pulmonary inflammation."

Again, there's the sound of a curtain opening and closing. Moments later, my curtain opens.

"Mr. Daan. I'm Dr. Tomás Daan Avery. I suspect we're cousins of some sort."

He offers his hand to shake.

"Dr. Avery, a pleasure." I shake his hand.

"You've had a tough time of it my friend. I'm sorry about the treatment you received yesterday. You should not have been transported the way you were.

"We were able to clean it up and stitch it last night. You're at significant risk of infection, so I put you on an antibiotic drip."

He points at the setup attached to my arm. I hadn't noticed it until just now.

"I also got the discharge instructions from the hospital in Jaredstown and the hospital where you were treated here. The warden is less than happy with the restrictions, but after seeing your unconscious body on his front porch yesterday, he's not fighting it."

"What's my prognosis?"

"You're young and surprisingly fit for someone whose been underground your entire life, so I expect you'll be ready to start serving your term in a couple weeks. Your prospects for creating offspring are not very good, but that's a forbidden activity here and we'll have better information on your recovery by the time you leave us."

The implication that my confinement and torture don't count toward my sentence causes my blood pressure to spike. He sees the dark look on my face and smiles.

"Don't worry, it's nowhere near as bad here as you've been told. Many people choose to stay here when their sentences are complete. You'll see why once we get you out of here." He indicates the building.

The implication that I might want to be here rubs me the wrong way. But I chasten myself. There are only three population centers on our planet: Jaredstown, Ashcrag and the green zone. I will never voluntarily go back to Jaredstown and can't imagine going to a place like Ashcrag. So, my life is now in the green zone. And unless I can find my way off this miserable planet, the green zone's where I'll spend the rest of it. I struggle to believe I'd continue on in the prison camp, but I need to keep my mind open about what I'll do after I'm released.

DISCHARGE

The stay at the Camp Hospital lasted longer than anyone could have expected. I ended up getting an infection in my testicles. And, no, it's worse than it sounds.

The inflammation triggered another round of brain swelling, numbing and near blindness. The doctors tried to explain it to me. Inflammation, C-reactive protein, leukocytes... Yeah, lots of big words that have no meaning to me. But it turns out that the doctors and facilities here are good, shockingly good. It took a while to find the underlying causes, but once known, I was cured in a week.

Anyway, I'm being discharged today. In the interim, it was confirmed that my sentence here does not start until the day I am assigned a cabin. I have a lawyer assisting with the appeal. I was arrested almost exactly three months ago. I've been imprisoned, beaten, tortured, and stripped of all liberty for three months. I am sentenced here under the laws of Jaredstown. So, the appeal will be filed there. My lawyer says she expects me to win the appeal.

CABIN

I've been assigned to Cabin 129 along Black Creek. It's about 10 kilometers from headquarters and the hospital. The doctor placed work restrictions on me, so I won't be working in the field. Instead, I have one of the support roles. I'll be working kitchen and distribution, which actually doesn't sound that bad. Our cabin is one of the kitchen cabins.

It's relatively large. It houses the community dining room and the kitchen that services it. Four men and four women call this cabin home. The men are in Rooms 1 & 2 in the back-left corner of the building. Our two rooms share one full bathroom. The women have Rooms 3 & 4, located in the back-right corner of the building.

I'm in Room 1, second bed. My address within the camp is 129-1b. My roommate in bed 1 is a fellow named Alex Tanner. He's older, it's hard to discern his age, but I'm guessing 45. He's 15 years into a twenty-year sentence, and a remarkably mellow nice guy. As a general rule, the people here do not talk about what brought them here. But I have a hard time believing that he was a violent criminal at some point in his life. I haven't met the two guys next door, Hayden and Tucker, or any of the women yet.

The cabin is in halfway decent shape. According to the little brochure about the cabins that I read in the hospital, the cabins are built from wood grown, dried and milled on site. It said the floors and walls were all made with tongue and groove wood. I suppose that could be true, but a quick look at the floors and walls of our room shows lots of gaps, no tongue and groove. I've already seen cockroaches, centipedes and geckos crawling in through the gaps.

SECURITY

As I suspected, there is little security around the camp. There are random patrols that go by, but most everything here is done on the honor system. Hard to believe for a prison. But the reason is obvious, the camp is huge, over a thousand square kilometers, and there's no place to escape to. The nearest sources of food and potable water are 20-kilometers or more from the perimeter of the camp. We all have to check in with our supervisor at some point every day. We need to log our work hours every week and our supervisors need to vouch for our work product each week. We are technically in prison, but we have a remarkable amount of liberty. And the penalties for violations are severe.

The guy who previously had my bed was a constant slacker. He was eventually reported, then caught slacking. He's now serving a one-month sentence in a hot box.

What's a hot box? It's a cubic wooden box 2 meters on a side. The floor and ceiling are solid, the sides are built with boards 8-centimeters wide mounted horizontally 3 centimeters apart.

The boxes are set on stilts about a meter above the ground. There's a slot big enough for food and a 2-liter bottle of water to be delivered once a day. There's also a hole in the floor that serves as the toilet. You're put in there with the clothes you're wearing and a blanket, then sealed in. Shorter people can stand or lay down in one. Taller people can't. I'm told the stench after a couple weeks is overwhelming.

The guy who had my bed will be reintegrated into a more highly supervised portion of the camp when his time in the hot box is up. I'm told that few people risk the hot box a second time. One of my job responsibilities will be making daily deliveries to the hot boxes in this zone.

DAY 1

Today is my first day on duty. I work a split six hour shift every day, Thursday through Tuesday. In the morning after breakfast, I make my hotbox food deliveries. It's hard for me to believe, but there are 20 active hot boxes in our zone. I suspect this will be physically easy, but emotionally difficult work.

In the late afternoon, I have food prep responsibilities in our kitchen.

Last night I met the rest of the building's residents. My roommate Alex is the morning chef. He has the lead on breakfast and lunch food preparation. His counterpart, Page Ryan in Room 3a, works the dining room for the breakfast and lunch shift.

Page's roommate, Finley Nevin, has the lead chef role working the dinner shift. One of the other guys in our block, Hayden Meyer, works the dining room for the dinner shift.

The rest of us in the building, myself, Tucker Snow in room 2b, and Sophie Grant and Clare Timbral in room 4 have the fill rolls which include deliveries, food prep, clean up, dishwashing, and gofer.

...

The morning starts easy enough, Alex is up and out a little before dawn. The noise wakes me. But I have three hours before I need to report. I drift off, then wake again to the alarm.

...

When I arrive in the kitchen, I get a cross look from Alex.

"Late for your first day on the job?"

"What?" I'm flabbergasted to hear this. "My instructions say deliveries start at 9:00." I point at the clock. "It's not 9 yet."

"Yes, deliveries are supposed to start at nine, but you need to prepare them first. That takes at least an hour."

I look at him bewildered. "No one told me that."

The cross look intensifies. "Hang on."

69

He finishes up the bacon he's cutting, then comes over and checks out my instructions.

"OK. You're right. Not there, but it was supposed to be, and you still need to do the work."

I stand there looking at him. I have no idea what I'm supposed to do.

Sophie walks in and immediately realizes something's wrong.

"What's the matter?"

"Package prep wasn't included in Jared's instructions."

She looks at the clock. "Not good. I know the process and am happy to help. Let me see if Paige is OK with that. I need to get after the dishes, but maybe she'll cut me some slack."

She goes out then comes back a few seconds later smiling.

"OK rookie. Paige says I can help, but I can't do it for you."

She points at one of the cupboards lining the walls.

"There are plastic trays in there." She points to another. "Water bottles in there. Step one is pulling one tray and two, one-liter bottles for each person on your list. You can use the prep table over there. I need to use that table too. You're supposed to be done with the prep by the time I arrive, so that it's available for me. Looks like we're going to be sharing.

"Once you got the stuff, fill and seal the water bottles. Pump's over there. Go."

I start moving as fast as I can.

She laughs, then starts setting up for the dishes.

Sophie looks to be early thirties but behaves as if she's 10 years younger. She's average height, thin, and has irregular features. Something obviously happened to her at some point. That said, it's easy to see her as a friend.

While I'm scrambling, she starts filling a giant pot from the pump. It's a hand pump with good flow, but I can see it's going to take her several minutes.

I have all my stuff, but she's only half done.

"What's next?"

Her eyes dart around. "Alex, do we have today's list of foods for the hot boxes?"

Alex points to a bulletin board.

"Start fetching the items on the list." I can tell she's getting short of breath from the pump by the sound of her voice.

"I'll finish pumping if you start the list," I say with all the enthusiasm I can muster.

She looks at me oddly. "Deal."

She takes off for the bulletin board and I start pumping. The pumping takes a lot of energy.

I finish, then help Sophie lift the enormous pot onto the stove.

"This is another one of the things you're supposed to do before I get here," she says meekly. "The boxes over there have everything. One each on a tray."

She looks around, then points. "Those are the carts you need. They load into the electric vehicle you'll use. As you finish a tray, put it into one of the carts. When that's done, I'll show you were the vehicle is."

She takes off for the dining room, looking up at the clock as she does, then shaking her head. "10 minutes late starting."

I'll have to make this up to her somehow.

I grab a bottle and take it over to the pump. One stroke of the pump and I know I'm in trouble. Most of the water didn't go into the bottle, it just went down the drain.

I hear Alex snickering. I look at him. He points at a funnel. I grab the funnel and start filling. This is going to take forever.

...

I finally head off for my deliveries at 10:15. I'm incredibly frustrated. But I reign in the frustration. It's undoubtedly more frustrating for my clients than it is for me. The zone supervisor pulls up as I'm leaving. Looking in the rear-view mirror, I see him staring at me, then jotting down a note in his notebook. Great, just great.

My first stop is hotbox 2192, occupied by Waylon Clarke. Poor Waylon is the slacker that used to have my bed. The script I've been given requires me to speak with the boxes 'resident' before leaving the food.

When I show up at the box with my motorized cart, the stench is overwhelming. I have to choke back the bile rising in my throat. Nonetheless, I approach with as light and airy flair as I can.

"Hey Waylon. How's it going today?"

The wind shifts a little and the stench becomes overwhelming. I choke a bit, then vomit my breakfast up on the ground next to his box. I thought that night with the sadists when I landed was bad. This is different, but somehow worse.

I use the club that comes with the job to bang on the walls of Waylon's box, but get no reply. The administration will come after me if I bail on my duty, so I do as I'm required. I step up the first rung on the ladder leading up to his box and peer inside. The sight sends me screaming. I barf again and know I'm going to pass out, so I go to my cart, sit and put my head between my knees. Falling and hitting my head could be disastrous. One of the roving guards comes over to hassle me, but the tears dripping from my chin give him pause.

"Hey. It's OK. I'll go check." He pats me on the shoulder.

I know what he's going to find. Waylon slit his throat. I have no idea how. But the finality of it is confirmed by cockroaches and centipedes taking up residence in his mouth. Even if I live to be a thousand years old, that sight will never leave me.

CHAPTER 8: ACCEPTANCE

The last six months have changed me. For the first time in my life, I have friends, I belong. The administration hassles me now and again, but for the most part leaves me alone.

When I left the hospital three months ago, Dr. Avery scheduled me back for a checkup. That was this week. I'm only allowed to have 'elective' medical care on my day off, so I went in on Wednesday.

To our surprise, the crack in my skull is not fully healed. He's also worried about my periodic headaches. My male parts are fully healed at this point. Mutilated, but healed. It's been a while since I've had any pain there. But being reminded of this particular dysfunction is not exactly encouraging.

But the good news from the whole experience is that he's keeping my work restrictions in place another three months.

KITCHEN

My first day on the job, three months ago, was traumatic. I got written up for a late start, despite the fact I followed my instructions exactly. Then there was the trauma of finding my very first client dead and insect infested.

But since then, I've developed a very steady rhythm. I'm never late and always finish early. The engineer in me has proactively tried to find ways to improve my work process.

I got permission to try something new this shift. Last night, I pumped out the water for the bottles today. I then boiled the water last night, covered it, and let it cool. Why? Over the last several months we've had a number of people develop stomach issues more severe than typical food poisoning. The doctors eventually determined the cause to be bacteria called *Shigella Dysenteriae*.

This species of bacteria is frequently found in kitchens with deficient sanitary practices, so the administration came down hard on the kitchens. But our processes were quite good already. We tightened up a bit, but there was little more we could do. Nonetheless, the infections continued, mostly among delivery clients. Biologists were brought in. They determined that the problem was bacteria in the ground water coming out of the pumps, not the kitchen sanitization procedure in general. The issue snapped together when we found out that the cane vipers plaguing the lake area carry this bacteria.

We've been given sanitizing agents to put in the water bottles, but the stuff tastes like poison. A better solution would be to boil the water.

From a work process point of view this really streamlines my mornings. At some point in the afternoon portion of my shift, I pump out the water for tomorrow's bottles and put it on to boil. Later, I cover it and let it cool. In the morning, I dispense it into the bottles. For the delivery teams, mornings are always the more time constrained. So, the new process will improve things in three ways:

1. Providing our clients with safer water than we do now.
2. Getting rid of the bad tasting sanitizer that the clients hate.
3. Moving morning work to the afternoon.

Today is the first trial of the morning run. It ends up saving me more than half an hour.

DELIVERIES

Box deliveries have dropped off a bit since Waylon's death. It scared a lot of people, both inmates and administration. The prisoners all fear the boxes. Now they fear them more, which has tightened up prisoner behavior a bit.

But the death of a prisoner from such a brutal form of punishment has put the administration under tighter governmental scrutiny. It's been a long time since there was a death in one of the hotboxes. They're more miserable than dangerous. Anyway, the tightening of scrutiny has raised the bar for administration of disciplinary action.

At first, I was worried about that. I really know the delivery job at this point. And I like the contact it gives me with clients, even the ones in the boxes. I can't help but think I could have helped Waylon.

But back to the point, total deliveries are up despite the drop in the number of boxes. Several factors have driven the increase. One is a new government ruling that went in place last year. It prevents the prison camp from requiring retirement age people to work.

Apparently, the courts went really heavy on life sentences some years back. So, a significant fraction of the population now are lifers. In the old days, they were forced to work until they dropped or got medical release from work. And the administration got pretty good at getting sentences commuted for those no longer able to work.

Many of the prisoners at that point in their life did not want to be released. Medical care and life in general are pretty good here, once labor in the fields is taken off the plate.

Several of those getting commutations started fighting them. Two months ago, the courts issued a new ruling. Commutations would only be considered if they were initiated by the prisoner. The upshot is that our senior population is expanding about 2 people per month. That will eventually become a problem, because life expectancy in the prison camp is the highest on the planet.

It's ironic when you think about it. We were taught as kids that this place was dangerous, and you'd be lucky to survive a 5-year sentence. Yet, when truth is told, we have the longest life expectancy on the planet. It makes me wonder how much of the other stuff they taught us about our world is actually true.

...

Two retirees have been added to my delivery schedule today, Norah Castle and Ethel Barry. They live in cabin 007, a little further down Black Creek, closer to the lake. I'm told they're ancient, both over 100. I'm looking forward to meeting them.

ORIGINS

When my great grandfather first surveyed our planet, they found no native life. As they began mining, they did find microbial life. But it was never convincingly proven whether the microbes were naturally occurring or the result of human contamination.

All other life on the planet was imported and, because of the expense, the items brought were carefully selected. Vegetables and fruits were first. Over time food animals were brought. All were taken to Jaredstown in the north, so there was little contamination across the rest of the planet.

But as great uncle Herold's ice transport system got to its final stages, soil needed to be developed. Some was brought in, but it was infeasible to bring in enough to matter. Instead, fast-growing plants, growth stimulating insects, and fertilizer were imported. I never studied this in any detail in school, I was drawn to math, physics and ultimately power engineering. But what I do know is that the third generation, led by great uncle Herold, made a massive investment in terraforming. That effort included the importation of sugarcane, a plant that created an optimal mix of products to support the terraforming effort. Which products? Food, in the form of sugar and molasses, although little sugar or molasses is diverted for consumption. Energy, in the form of alcohol, created from the fermentation, then distillation of excess sugar and pulp. And soil, created by composting the massive amounts of bulk fiber produced by sugarcane. One of the big efforts in the prison camp is composting fiber. We use that new soil to continue growing the camp to the south.

But, as anyone who has walked through a sugarcane field can tell you, sugarcane comes with its own ecosystem of creatures that you simply cannot weed out during the importation process. That's how we got the cane toads, cane spiders, centipedes, and cane vipers. Their eggs were in stasis along with the cane roots that were imported.

Although all these species can be linked back to ones that evolved on Earth, they all evolved further on other planets. None of the species actually imported ever existed on Earth, only their evolutionary cousins. And once here, in a new environment, each of these species evolved rapidly to adapt. One of the biologists did a talk on the topic some weeks ago. Our cane toads and cane vipers have evolved enough in the 100 years they've been here to be classified as a separate species not found on any other world.

Cane toads are among the strangest creatures. They're born from eggs laid in shallow water. They emerge onto land when they're only about a centimeter long. They'll eat almost any insect, particularly those that feed on sugarcane. They'll also eat food scraps.

We use cane toads in our composting operations. In addition to insects, they'll eat almost any type of food that a human does, so we carefully separate out the food scraps to put in the toad pens. When the toads get large enough, they are separated out and killed, then thrown in with the fiber compost. Within hours of death, cane toads develop an overwhelming stench. Whatever's in that putridness seems to drive faster and more complete composting. I pity the prisoners that get assigned that job.

And the irony? Cane toads are poisonous. Their skin is toxic, and they have massive glands on both sides of their head that secrete poison. Lick a cane toad and you'll find yourself bleeding from every orifice within an hour.

And the ones here can grow to be huge. Few get larger than 15 – 20 centimeters. But we have seen them as large as a meter long, weighing 50 kilograms. The really big ones can blow poison out of their glands. It normally comes out as a milky fluid. But, when the big ones really push it, the fluid bubbles out and forms a mist. Inhaling too much of that will kill you.

On our world there are only two predators to control the toad population: humans and cane vipers. Anyplace in the camp that's wet and has cane toads will have cane vipers. If one of those bites you, life expectancy drops to about 2 hours. If they can pump enough medicine into you during the first hour, you've got a 50-50 chance of survival.

CABIN 007

I pull up in front of cabin 007. It's really close to the lake, which I can see from here. Something ahead moves in the tall grass startling me. Looking more closely I can see that it's an enormous cane toad. A kilometer inland, where the kitchen is, you only see cane toads at night. It's too dry for them in the day.

Surveying the area a little more closely, I see how overgrown everything is, enough that it creeps me out. I see that the ladies have done a good job of keeping the area around their cabin cleared. But everything else is jungle like.

I go to step out of my cart and immediately see that the ground is soft and wet. The lake has expanded over the years, driving moisture further inland. I'm sure this area was dry when the cabin was built.

Looking toward the lake a little more closely, I see that the marshes start another hundred meters or so down the road. The marshes are known to be infested with cane vipers.

Now I'm afraid to step out of the cart. Domestic cane viper venom kills in a matter of hours. I look to see if I can spot one. It doesn't take long to spot dozens. I also spot a lot of cane toads. What I see makes little sense. Well maybe it does. The toads hang out near the cabin. The vipers seem to hang back. In the rest of the universe, vipers like these eat the cane toads. But the longer I stay still and watch, I spot numerous giant toads near the cabin, and no vipers.

"You! Are you the new delivery boy?"

I look up and see an older woman, 50, maybe 60 years old.

"Yes."

"Well then, deliver the food. If you wait out there too much longer, you're going to become the food."

I stare at her, not knowing what to make of her or her comments. Then I notice her eyes. They're clear with none of the cloudiness of old age. Her pupils are coal black. But her irises... They must have been green at some point. Now, they're white with flecks of green.

"Oh, god. Do I need to break in another one?"

She comes stomping down the steps and approaches the cart, walking stick in hand. This one's a lot older than she puts on. I start to get out, but she points to me and says, "No!"

Her walking stick strikes out, hitting the cane viper I was about to step on.

She shakes her head. "City boy! Stay in your cart. Point to the food and I'll get it. No sense in getting another one of you killed. They really ought to give some training before they send babies like you out into the field."

I'm a bit offended. But looking down and seeing the viper below in its death froes, I point to the container with their food.

"Next time pull in closer and jump out of the cart immediately. We have protections in place on the steps and porch. You're not safe there."

As I look at her pointing, I notice she's wearing white gloves with lace around the wrists. It's so out of place that I'm frozen in confusion.

My reverie is broken as a viper falls from above. She intercepts it with her walking stick. It goes flying over toward one of the giant toads. It lands and starts coiling to strike, but the toad is gone before it does.

She grabs the trays and scampers back into the cabin.

"Sonny boy, if you expect to survive in this part of the swamp, you need to learn its ways. Now scoot. I'm too old to go all the way to the kitchen myself to get food."

The door slams shut, triggering a round of croaking from the toads. I'm totally freaked out. I do the fastest U-turn of my life and stomp on the go pedal.

What the hell have I gotten myself into now.

MEETING

I received a message from our zone supervisor this morning asking me to meet him at his office during my break between shifts. No reason was given, but I've been a model prisoner so struggle to believe that it could be disciplinary. As soon as the morning deliveries are done and kitchen cleaned, I head over.

...

I arrive and see the door ajar. I'm not sure if that's an invitation to enter or not, so I knock on the door frame so as not to accidentally open it.

"Door's open."

I push the door open and step in. It's actually the first time I've been in his office. All previous interactions have been in my building or on the road.

"Ah, Jared. Come in and close the door."

"Good afternoon, Supervisor Barnes." I say as I close the door.

"Please have a seat." He points to the chair closest to the desk.

I see that he's smiling. I think it's more amusement than happiness. Once I'm seated, he starts.

"Thanks for coming over."

I try to keep the smirk off my face. It's not like I have a choice.

"Some things have come to my attention that I wanted to talk with you about."

That's an auspicious way to start if you ask me, but I do my best to keep a neutral face.

"Your clients uniformly love you, even Ethel. And your productivity rates are the highest in your job category by quite a bit."

He pauses, as if to decide what to say next.

"We don't get very many teenagers sent to the camp. It's hard to get in enough trouble to get sentenced here when you're only 16. You're the first I've had in one of my zones. And after your first day, I was worried."

The implication my conviction and first day performance where somehow my fault causes the temper to flare, but I hold it in.

"So, how do you do it? What background do you have that enabled you to get into so much trouble before, then come here and be our most liked and productive worker?"

There's silence as he waits for a reply.

"I didn't have that much to do with the events that sent me here. I get along because my parents trained me to be courteous and helpful. And I think my performance here has to do with my engineering background. I always try to find better ways of doing things."

My answer clearly isn't what he was expecting.

"Engineering background?"

"Yes. I have a bachelor's degree in Electrical Power System Engineering from the Faraday Institute on New London. It was always my dream to work at the Electric Company in Jaredstown. My older brothers wanted that too but were never very good. I got the job a month after turning 16. They framed me for a crime they committed in order to get me out of the way."

I can see that supervisor Barnes isn't buying it and hope I don't get in trouble once again for telling the truth.

"Curious. I find that hard to believe, but that's not the reason I wanted to talk with you, so I'll leave it there."

He pauses as if wondering how to continue.

"Alex has told me about the process changes you've made in the kitchen. He thinks those have had a lot to do with the efficiency improvements in your building. Things like drawing and heating water in the afternoon, the way you fill your bottles, how you've reorganized the dishwashing operation... Your kitchen puts out more food than any of the others, has lower food-borne illness rates, is always the first to finish their shifts, and has the largest and best delivery performance in the camp. The warden wants to implement these procedures in the other zones.

"I asked Alex about it. He said you were the one responsible. Tell me how that is, what did you do?"

"The first day, I arrived a few minutes before the time stated in my instructions. My work instructions didn't include the set-up steps. So, I ended up being early, yet an hour and a half behind. There were no written instructions for my work responsibilities, so Sophie walked me through it. I could do some of her stuff faster than she could, so we swapped things around to save time.

"I wrote down the procedures for both jobs. Reviewed them with Alex and Sophie, then suggested some order of operation changes that reduce the minimum efficient completion time. Just standard engineering 101 stuff.

"I think that helped me integrate in. We learned to work collaboratively, and I enjoy working with them."

"Do you have any proof that you have a degree?"

"I did at one time. But I was stripped of everything before being shipped down here. If I had an exo-net connection, it would be easy enough to log into the Institute. But even then, I don't have any funds to pay the processing fee for confirmation. So, I guess the answer is no. I don't, but proof exists. I just don't have it."

More silence.

"OK. The warden wants to meet with us. I'll see if I can schedule that for Wednesday. Copies of your written instructions would be useful."

"Will do."

"Thanks, Jared. You've done really well here."

He gets up and opens the door. That's my cue to leave.

...

As I walk back toward my building, I hear the sonic boom created by the shuttles as they come in for a landing. This isn't the day the shuttle runs up to Jaredstown and back, so it must be a delivery from off-planet. I look up and catch a glimpse of the shuttle's reflection. Some lucky person is about to get something they've been waiting a long time to get. Lucky them.

REPAIRS

One of my background projects has been repairing the cracks in the floor and walls of our room. I'm the only one in the building that hasn't been bit by a centipede yet. I almost lost that status a couple weeks back when one was crawling up through the floor next to my foot as I was getting into bed. Alex saw it and warned me.

A really good seal is impossible, I don't have access to the right materials. But I've come up with a halfway decent kludge involving small wedges of wood driven into the larger cracks and sawdust mixed with glue rubbed into smaller ones. So far, it's been working well. Alex apparently likes it. He's actually helped me scavenge some of the materials.

INFESTATION

We've developed a bit of a toad problem at our cabin. Each cabin is elevated up off the ground. The main floor is at about chest height. The space beneath is a crawl space that gives access to the plumbing, etc.

My first inkling that we had a problem was the intensity of the croaking at night. But it never occurred to me to look under the cabin. But it came to everyone's attention last week. A group of prisoners have formed an 'Irish Dancing' club. I'd never heard of it before. It's a form of dance that involves a lot of foot stomping.

They got permission to come over to our zone to put on a short demonstration the other night. I'm not that into it, but it was a bit different and therefore interesting. It was also loud, really loud.

About 5 minutes into the demonstration there was a strange smell and one of the old timers yelled. "Toad gas, everyone out of the building."

Sure enough, one of the giant toads had taken up residence in our crawl space. The dancers' foot stomping apparently scared it big time and it blew a mother lode of poisonous gas out of its glands.

So, the administration removed the toad, right?

Wrong. A quick inspection showed that there's a plumbing issue under the building. The experts say that's what attracted the toad. There's a long, drawn-out process we have to go through to remove the toad, fix the plumbing, then reseal the crawl space. And, as long as we don't agitate the toad, it's not a threat. The current estimate is that they'll get to it in a week. Until then, we need to be quiet.

Great.

DREAMS

It was a long and unusually difficult day. You name it, it happened. A food slot in one of the hotboxes got jammed. My cart got a flat tire. Someone bumped one of the racks of completed trays, dumping them all over the floor. Then a 3-hour trip into insanity at Cabin 007.

They're my last stop on the morning portion of my shift and I've learned at this point how to safely get out of my cart to make the delivery. Well, I get to the door and Norah invites me in for a cup of tea. I make the mistake of going in, despite being so far behind schedule. Once inside, there was thing after thing they wanted me to do for them. And soon I'm worried about getting back in time to start the second part of my shift. They finally release me. They understand that being late for a shift is not an option.

Anyway, I open the door and there's a cane viper sitting on top of the rack of trays in the back of my cart. It's spotted a relatively large toad that's hopped up onto the cart's passenger seat. I've got to stop this, or the toad is going to poison my cart and there's no acceptable way to clean the cart here.

Norah hears me say, "Oh, shit." She comes to the door and starts laughing. They keep a sling shot by the front door. She grabs it and lines up a shot on the viper. As it coils to strike, she lets go and hits it, at least enough of it to knock it down onto the floor of the cart's cargo bed.

Ethel, having figured out what was going on, comes out with a fishing pole. She's tied some sort of bait on the end.

"Your turn, sonny boy. The toads love this stuff and will go for it. Just dangle it on the far side of the cart and it'll hop out."

I just about get the bait in position when another viper drops from the tree and knocks the fishing pole out of my hands. The snake lands disoriented next to the toad. Seeing the viper, the toad hops out of the cart. Ethel seems to think this is the funniest thing that's ever happened. Me, I'm more worried about the two cane vipers now in my cart.

With the toad gone, the two vipers eventually leave of their own volition. Ethel quickly checks to make sure the cart's safe, then waves me down.

As I get in, she slaps me on the back.

"Sonny boy, you need to come by more often, that's the most fun I've had in years."

...

I'm late and ought to be worried about that. But as I clear the danger zone all I can think about are these two old women. How did they live to be over 100 in a place like this?

Then the companion thought comes. How can two women so old be so spry? Something doesn't add up here.

...

It's not clear whether I'll be reported for being late. Probably not, the others covered for me. I do extra cleanup work as a thank you.

When my head finally hits the pillow, I fall asleep immediately.

...

I wake, fully conscious with unusual clarity of mind. I can see that the large toad under our cabin is dead. Vipers took it down right underneath my bed. I start drifting up, out of body. I can clearly see myself but am unable to move my body. I'm detached from it and drifting away. Curiously, I know I'm not dead, so am either having an out of body experience or hallucinating. Out of body experience seems to be the more likely, but I base that solely on the acuity of my awareness.

Up I drift, wondering whether I'll see the space station. No sooner does the thought pass through my mind than I'm there. This is really weird.

I cast my consciousness further out and find myself on New London. It's familiar. I've seen many pictures of the planet and the campus. But something is wrong here. The wrongness is terrifying, then realization snaps into place. They're dead. All dead.

I pop into an arbitrary room and am met with a sickeningly familiar sight. It's like Waylon in the hot box, insects feasting. The horror of it pops me back out into space. Every planet my attention falls upon is dead or dying.

...

"Jared! Jared! Wake up!"

I snap awake in terror. Alex has been shaking me trying to get me to wake up. I roll over the edge of the bed and barf on the floor.

"What's the matter, Jared?"

Alex looks afraid.

"The toad under the cabin is dead. Vipers got it. It apparently sprayed a lot of poison before they took it down."

Alex looks at me like I'm crazy. "How do you know that?"

"I saw it."

"What, in your dream?" The question is asked with a lot of cynicism.

The question seems to bring me back into this reality. Although I'm still certain the toad is dead.

"Yes."

There's a knock on the door. It cracks open.

"Everything all right in here?" It's Hayden from the room across the hall.

Alex answers for me. "Bad dream."

"Maybe bad food." Hayden points to the mess on the floor.

I get up. "Guess I should get after that."

Technically, we're not allowed to leave the part of the cabin where our rooms are. But it's not a rule I've ever seen enforced. I head off toward the kitchen. It's early, but there's enough light in the sky to see outside. As I go to switch on the kitchen light, I see something that freezes me in my tracks. Three vipers are slithering away from the building. Irrational certainty settles in. Those are the three that killed the toad. It was too big for them to eat, so they're heading off to find food elsewhere.

A second certainty strikes. Something terrible is happening on New London—and the other worlds I saw.

CHAPTER 9: FRIENDS

Our meeting with the warden is at 11:00. I meet Supervisor Barnes at his office at 10:00. His vehicle has both the speed and range to get us there in time. Headquarters is only ten kilometers away, but the only roads that connect are dirt and deeply potholed. Nonetheless, we'll still get there on time.

...

After 20 minutes in the waiting room, the door labeled Warden Archer Glenn opens. Several professional looking people come out followed by a tall, thin, older man, who's obviously the warden.

After the last handshake, he turns to Supervisor Barnes.

"Gavin, good to see you. Who's that you have with you?"

I'm in prison garb, so the fact that I'm a prisoner isn't in question. I'm guessing that the warden has forgotten why we're here.

The two shake hands, then 'Gavin' introduces me to the warden. It's actually the first time I've heard our supervisor's first name.

"Sir, please meet Jared Daan. Jared, this is warden Archer Glenn."

The warden gets a bit of a sour look when he hears my name but shakes my hand anyway.

We go in and take seats, then the warden starts.

"Remind me what we're here to talk about today."

"The efficiency improvements and reduced food-borne illness cases in our zone."

"Yes, yes. Very impressive. We need to get what you're doing out to the other zones. Does Jared have something to do with that?"

"Yes. He's the one behind it all. Turns out he has an engineering degree from the Faraday Institute on New London and has been re-engineering our food work processes."

He pulls a piece of folded paper from his pocket, flattens it out, and slides it across the table. I see the upside-down version but know immediately what it is. It's a validated copy of my diploma and a picture of my student ID card.

The warden looks at the paper, looks at me, then looks at the paper again.

"Well, I'll be damned."

He looks at me again and I can tell he wants to ask why I've been sent to prison camp. He undoubtedly has a copy of the verdict and sentence in his files but is now struggling to connect the dots.

"Jared, can you give me the high-level overview of the changes you've made and how you got them implemented?"

I tell him about my first day, the issue with the instructions I received, how my team rallied around me, and how we worked together to document and improve our work processes.

"Did you bring a copy of your procedures with you?"

"They're handwritten and there's only one copy. But yes, I have them."

I pull the folded documents from my pocket, flatten them, then slide them across the table.

He quickly reads through them.

"Sensible, but what did you change?"

"There's not enough time to pump and boil the water in the morning. You could always come in another hour and a half earlier, but that would leave you with a lot of dead time. Doing it in the afternoon means you can do other things while the water is boiling, and it can cool overnight.

"Along the same lines, we used to fill the bottles directly from the pump, using a funnel. It's a very inefficient process with a lot of spilt water. Filling the bottle from the spigot on the pot goes much faster, and with a minor equipment upgrade we could make it even faster.

"It's kind of the same with dish washing and sanitization, reorganizing the process so you can do something productive while the water is heating.

"Similar with delivery. Optimize the order of operations for meal preparation, then optimize the delivery route.

"It's all pretty simple. I had the advantage of being a newbie. There were no written instructions, so I had to ask a lot of questions, which led to a lot of whys and what-ifs. Once a process is documented, it's a lot easier to optimize."

"Truly amazing."

There's a moment's silence as if the warden is trying to decide something.

"What would you think about training others? With the financial pressure brought on by the retiree situation, we could use your skills a lot more productively here than in the kitchen."

"I'm thinking we could start with you training a replacement, then rotating you through the various zones to help them. Then ultimately moving you to headquarters to start reviewing and documenting other processes."

This is dangerous territory for me. I'm coming up on my early release date. If I turn this down, it might work against me. On the other hand, if I agree to do it and my appeal fails, who knows where they'll send me when they're tired of having me at headquarters.

But this whole line of reasoning is stupid. I'm a prisoner. I do what I'm told. Any illusion that I have a say is just that. An illusion.

"Sure."

POPULATION

I've been on the new job a month now. It's been interesting. I actually know a lot more about the camp now than I did before. I doubt the administration realizes how much.

There are 10 zones. They are roughly the same size, each about 15 square kilometers. Each zone is targeted to have 80 active workers. A little less than one in ten of those work in the kitchen. The smallest kitchen only has 6 workers, but that kitchen has no regular deliveries.

Although there are hot boxes in all the zones, there are only 24 active hot boxes, so prisoners sent to a hot box are for the most part locked up either here in Zone 3, or in Zone 7. So, for now only Zones 3 and 7 have people working hot box delivery.

There are 37 retirees in total. Most are in the first four zones. These are the oldest zones, brought on-line some 100 years ago. The administration has been trying to concentrate the older population here, channeling younger people out to the newer zones. If it weren't for my medical disability, I would have been sent to Zone 10, which is short field laborers. Dr. Avery still has me on disability, but I'll probably be taken off next month. Thankfully, the warden really likes my work, so I suspect that he'll keep me at headquarters.

The logistics of the last month have been interesting. For the next month, my official residence will be here in Zone 3. But I've been given an open room in one of the two room cabins closer to the lake. The newbie, a guy by the name Vince Martin, got my old room. He's older, late twenties, also on disability. By nature, he's a real street brawler. I hope I'm wrong, but I suspect he'll be sent into the field when he's released from disability, at which point he will act out, spend one or two cycles in the box, then get moved to hard labor. I really hope I'm wrong about that. But he's an angry young man with a tendency toward violence.

He's still hurting enough from injuries sustained before he moved here that his training went smoothly enough. The training trip down to cabin 007 was interesting. The ladies didn't like him very much. Ethel says the critters will get him in the first month, so there's no sense training him. I suspect she's just sad that I'm moving on to something else.

At this point, I've spent a day or two in each zone. The warden gave me a fancy vehicle like Supervisor Barnes has. He's also told all the zone supervisors to expect me to stay in their zones overnight now and again. I'm being given an unusual amount of liberty. Enough people are unhappy about it that I fear I'm once again going to get in trouble for following the instructions I've been given.

I've had one odd realization as I come to know more about the camp. The population of Jaredaan is only about 17,000. There are 837 prisoners in the camp, which is about 5% of the total population. It seems ridiculously high to me. I wonder how many prisoners actually belong here.

HEADQUARTERS

I've been called back to headquarters unexpectedly. Something's apparently happened. Supervisor Barnes is tight lipped and obviously unhappy. I'm worried.

Since I have my own vehicle, I go on my own.

At the front desk, I'm greeted by a delightful young woman, named Summer. She's about my age and obviously not a prisoner. When she smiles at me, I'm reminded of Nana. I haven't thought about her in months. It still hurts, and it's still hard to believe I fell for it. But as she said, I was so naïve, probably still am. But no sense dwelling on it.

Summer tells me that my meeting is scheduled in the large conference room on the second floor. I'm escorted up by one of the guards.

...

I enter to see the warden and my lawyer, Audrey Preston. The warden looks very unhappy. My lawyer is beaming. I'm guessing that I won my appeal.

"Jared," the warden starts. "Ms. Preston has some news to share with you."

Her smile droops a bit.

"Jared, I have both good and bad news to share with you. The good news is that your felony convictions have been overturned."

She slides a court document across the table to me.

"This document absolves you of all wrongdoing with regard to the theft of the gold ore and vacates your conviction on that charge."

She slides another one across the table.

"This one absolves you of all wrongdoing with regard to the damaged power unit and vacates your conviction on that charge as well."

"Lucas Young is being charged for stealing the ore. Your brother, Asher, has been charged with damaging the power unit.

"Asher has been fired from your old job."

She slides another document across the table.

"The power company would like you back. This is a formal offer from them. They're even giving you a raise."

Her smile is back.

"The bad news?" I have the sense that the bad news is really bad.

Her head drops. I can see she doesn't want to be the one delivering it.

"I'm sad to tell you that your father has died. He was struck by lightning while trying to rescue Asher who was outside when a storm came up."

"Asher had been looking for some of the gold that he hid on the surface. He had it on him when he was rescued. That's when he turned state's witness on Lucas."

"Does that mean Asher is not being prosecuted?"

"He pled to a lesser crime that allows him to remain free, on probation, in Jaredstown."

"And my property that was seized?"

"That's more difficult."

"How so?"

"Jaredstown took the money in your bank account, then closed it. No one knew at the time how much you had. They no longer have the means to pay it back."

"So, I own Jaredstown?"

She gives me a wry smile and shakes her head. "No. You would need to sue them to get it back. You'd undoubtedly win the case, but they won't be required to give you anything. It'd be like a legal acknowledgement that you are in the right, their only obligation would be to pay you what they could, when they could. Unfortunately, they're deeply in debt. You'd be last in line. Protected world charters are written that way because the odds of bankruptcy are so high."

"Is there a computer with an exo-net connection I can have access to? I need to check on something."

She slides hers across the table to me.

"Please give me a minute."

I quickly log into my Jungle account. There are at least a hundred messages waiting in my queue. It will take a while to get through them, but the short answer is that I have 90-days to establish an account for my payments to be deposited into. My balance. 629,312 credits.

I start laughing.

"What is it?"

"I need a new computer and a new bank account. Can you help me set one up? There are a lot of credits waiting to be deposited."

I pick up the offer from the power company and rip it up. The only thing that would possibly have brought me back to Jaredstown was my father. Now that he's gone, I renew my vow never to return.

...

It turns out that an overturned conviction is not enough to gain my immediate release. There's a process, of course. Audrey had filed all the papers a couple days ago and expects I will be released tomorrow.

I execute a power of attorney agreement allowing Audrey to set up a bank account in my name. She'll be back tomorrow to complete my release. She'll also bring my new bank documents with her.

The warden sat here through the whole thing. He wanted to talk with me once she'd left.

"Any chance I could talk you into staying on as staff? We have a relatively nice staff apartment available. You could move in today."

"I have some things I need to deal with that are relatively urgent, so need a couple days off. But I'm interested in staying, at least for a while."

"I need someone with your brains to help me find better ways to run this operation. Things are getting really tight budget-wise. Output from the mines at Jaredstown is down, which means all governmental functions are facing budget pressure. That on top of the retiree ruling is about to make the situation here much more difficult. If we can't find solutions, the quality of life for both the prisoners and staff will come crashing down."

"I'd like to help with that. Will I be able to go back to town with Audrey tomorrow? I need to buy some clothes and a car. Will I be able to keep a car here?"

"You have money for a car?"

"Yes. I have money off world that Jaredstown did not get."

"How?"

"Jungle. I have two best selling products. They owe me quite of bit, more than enough to buy a car."

"I can arrange a parking spot. You are really something, Jared Daan. Maybe the legend is true."

CABIN 007

The warden gave me a message to pass to Supervisor Barnes. I'm relieved of official work responsibilities for the rest of the day and tomorrow. He's surprised, but doesn't give me any grief.

My next stop is the kitchen. Alex and Vince give me the go ahead to do the delivery to Norah and Ethel on my own. Fifteen minutes later, I'm there.

Ethel opens the door. "Hey, sonny boy. Good to see you. It happened, didn't it?"

She motions for me to come in.

"You've got to tell us all about it. We've even got a special treat for you."

I'm shocked, but know I shouldn't be. I think I've figured out what's going on here. That's why I wanted to come see them. I'm hoping they'll come clean.

...

Ethel asks me to put the food in their kitchen. Knowing how much they like pears and cheese, I slipped a little extra of each on their trays.

"I brought you a little extra today."

"Oh, sonny boy. You're so kind to us."

I enter the kitchen and see that Norah is just pouring the tea. I also see a small plate with some food that I don't recognize and a bit of cheese. It's as if they knew what I was going to bring.

Ethel leads the way to the sitting room, where we all sit in silence a minute. Then she starts.

"Do you know how old I am?"

"No. I was told you were over 100, but I struggle to believe it."

"I'm 127, third generation. They sent me here almost exactly 100 years ago. My crime? I was your great Uncle Herold's girlfriend. They ran me off to the prison camp, when his wife, Alice, daughter of your great uncle Asher, the one that founded Ashcrag, found out he was cheating on her. First cousins marrying each other. What a stupid thing. None of the pregnancies carried to term."

"But they had five children, didn't they?"

"Alice did!" Norah starts cackling, but I'm not getting it yet.

She shakes her head. "Jared, you're so naïve. When Alice realized that Herold was firing defective seed, she started slipping out to see other suitors that might get her pregnant with a baby that might come to term. But she still liked your Uncle Herold's ministrations and didn't take kindly to the idea of him having someone else. Poor Herold never figured it out. He was a better engineer than husband. But Alice still wanted him all to herself.

"But the joke ends up being on them! They're long gone, yet here I am." More cackling.

I would never have guessed that this was where the conversation would go. But as interesting as new insights into family history might be, I need to steer this conversation in a different direction.

"It's the toads, isn't it? The mist the big ones give off."

"Knew you were the smart one."

"Do you have visions?"

"We both do, yes. But it's probably not what you think."

"No?"

"You're not actually seeing things that are happening. The mist simply gives you clarity. It lets you see things you already have the information to figure out but haven't figured out yet."

"Oh."

"What did you see?" Norah asks meekly.

"Several things. The first was the attack on the toad that had moved into the crawl space beneath our cabin. Several vipers had tracked it down. I saw that it had spewed a lot of poison as they came. Nonetheless, they ultimately killed it. But that's not the scary part." I pause, suddenly worried that if I say it out loud it will be true.

"There's a plague or something on the core worlds. In my vision, everyone on New London was dead."

"We've seen that one, too. We didn't see New London. We have no connections there, no information about the place. But we have periodic contact with Caladon, where I came from, and New Brazil, where Ethel came from.

"When you have your access to the exo-net restored, you should research it, then come back and have visions with us. Maybe we can figure out what's going on. We may be able to help."

The idea that we could help seems absolutely preposterous to me. But I've learned respect for these two. "How could we help?"

Ethel laughs. Norah joins in.

"Well."

"Jared, you can be so funny sometimes."

I don't respond. I just wait.

"Spoil sport." It's Norah. "The first answer should be obvious to you. It's what you were born to do."

I groan. Not the sixth son thing again.

"It's true, you know. Even if you won't admit it to yourself."

"But I understand your frustration. The answer is in the toads and vipers. We are younger now than we were when we discovered their secrets. Each have curative qualities. Together, I think we can figure out how to apply them."

The truth in their statements hits me with a jolt. It's almost as if I'm having another vision.

"You were absolved of all wrong-doing today, weren't you?"

The sudden change of subject catches me off guard.

"Yes. How did you know?"

They laugh at me again, but Ethel answers.

"After your second visit, the visions told us you weren't guilty. We also deduced that you expected release. The look on your face when you showed up today was the clincher."

"I'm scheduled to be released tomorrow. I'm going to head in to Heroldstown. There are some things I need to deal with. When I'm done, I'll be back. The warden has asked me to join the staff..."

"You don't need the money, do you?"

I'm surprised to be cut off that way, then realize their visions had told them I didn't need money.

"No, I just need continued access to you and our menagerie."

"I don't think you need to be on staff to get access, but good idea. It'll make things easier."

I notice that Ethel has a sly smile.

"What?"

"Such a sweet innocent boy. I suspect we aren't the only people you're interested in seeing."

The thought of Summer passes through my mind.

"No, I guess you aren't."

Several moments pass in silence.

Then Ethel asks, "Jared, are you ready?"

I struggle to understand the question but know at this point to think before I respond. I see Norah eyeing the cookies on the plate. The ones no one has touched yet. I lock eyes with her and am momentarily distracted by them. Her irises are white, like Ethel's, but have thin streaks of gray.

A few more seconds pass in silence, then my mind comes back to the cookies.

"The cookies. You don't need to wait for a toad to gas off. You've figured out how to bring the visions on at will."

"That plus." Again, it's Ethel. She lifts the plate. "Ready?"

I lock eyes with her and once again notice their strangeness. A question shoots through my mind. Could the eyes be related to the visions?

"Are you going to join me?" I ask.

"Probably best if we didn't. It's hard to know how the first time will go. It's better if we're here and sober, so we can care for you if it doesn't go well."

I stare at her some more, then reach for one of the cookies.

HEADQUARTERS

I park in front of the headquarters building knowing I'm late. The ladies didn't wake me and get me ready in time. Crazy night, but more on that later.

I enter the building's lobby and all but grind to a stop. Summer is on the front desk. Her smile captures me.

She laughs. "Jared. They're waiting for you upstairs. You better hurry."

I take off for the stairs and am halfway up before I realize that I have no escort this morning. I enter the conference room expecting to be harangued for my tardiness, but instead get a, "There he is," from the warden.

"Apologies for being late."

Surprisingly, it's Audrey, my lawyer, that replies, "Jared, you were officially cleared for release at dawn this morning, before this meeting was scheduled. But if you expect to make it in the civilian world, you need to be prompt for meetings."

"Sorry."

I can tell that my lame reply is not earning me points with my lawyer, but the warden seems more neutral. Then the insight strikes. To Audrey, I'm now a paying client, so she needs a pretext for the bill I'm about to be slammed with. To the warden, I am a much-needed employee, one whose good side he needs to be on. The residual effects of last night's adventure apparently haven't worn off yet.

"Do you have bank documents for me?"

Audrey apparently realizes that there's upside to having me on her side. "Yes. I assume you want to go into town today."

"I do."

"You can come back with me. The state's paying me to drive down and back. But once in Heroldstown, you're on the clock."

"Your rate?"

"225 credits an hour."

That's the steepest number I've ever heard. But a thought quickly follows. *You've never hired anyone, never heard their number before.*

"I need five things. Clothes, help at the bank, a computer, a car, and a place to spend the night. How much?"

She starts to say a ridiculous number, then stops mid-sentence. "Two hours. I think we can get that done in two hours. But you need to cover the expenses."

"Deal."

I turn to the warden. "Is there a way for me to reach you? My plan is to be back tomorrow. That said, this is a first for me, so no guarantees. But I really want to work here with you."

He smiles, then hands me a card. "I think you're going to need a mobile communicator also. A place will be ready for you tomorrow afternoon. Just let me know if you're going to be late."

I nod my head to him. "Thank you, sir." It's the first time I've said that honestly, from my heart, not from the compulsion of my imprisonment.

STORE

The ride back into town is as different from my ride to the prison camp as conceivable. The ride down on my arrival was slow and bumpy, pain almost every step of the way. The return is fast, pleasant. Audrey is a fountain of information and entertainment.

She parks her car in the clothing store's parking lot, then turns to me.

"The clock starts when you open the door. Fair warning, they will attempt to drag this out for hours. I'll forward you 25 credits, enough to buy you some clothes to wear into the bank. Your hotel's over there." She points to a building a couple blocks away. "It'll be an easy trip back if you want more. Ready?"

We get out of the car and by the time we get to the store's front door, I realize that I'm in the process of spending more money than I'd ever imagined I'd have.

It doesn't take long to realize that Heroldstown is not a wealthy place. We are the only customers in the store and the two salespeople seem to compete with each other to sell me something. Once Audrey announces the budget, with the finality that only a lawyer can bring, they compete to find me the best outfit that can be bought for that amount. Neither seem to even notice that I'm dressed in prison garb. Then with the clarity of a vision, I realize that Audrey has done this before. The store knows I'm being released and wants me as an ongoing customer. Then with equal clarity, I realize that this is something any free person would know instinctively. I'm so remedial.

Twenty minutes later, we emerge. I'm dressed in business casual slacks, a dress shirt in a pale color that I don't really understand, and a 'sports jacket' that Audrey seems to like. I don't understand any of it, other than the bill, which was 25 credits. Next stop is the bank.

...

We enter the bank, and someone greets us shortly after coming through the door.

"Mr. Daan. We were so sorry to hear of your wrongful conviction and sentencing. But rest assured, we will be here to protect your assets from any further assault."

I look at the 'banker' greeting us with a neutral face, but internally scoff at the transparent gratuitousness.

An hour later, I leave the bank with 625,000 credits in my account and another couple thousand in my pocket.

CAR DEALER

I've seen pictures of cars, cars of every type. But until landing in Heroldstown some months ago, I'd never been in one. Now I wanted to buy one. It was the only way I could see my existence here working. I needed a cart to get around the camp. But the only way I would be able to get out of the camp was if I have a vehicle of my own, and I was confident my plans going forward would require me to leave the camp now and again.

As we pulled into the car lot, Audrey let me know that she needed to leave in about an hour. If I could make a decision quickly, she would accompany me to the hotel. If not, then I would have to go on my own.

Before we even open the door to get out of her car, a salesman comes out to greet us.

"Welcome, my friends. How can I help you today?"

I smile at the man and offer my hand.

"Hi, I'm Jared Daan. I'm looking for an electric hover car suitable for highway or off road. It needs to be rugged."

"You're thinking about exploring outside the city limits?"

"I am. I'm curious about where the river goes and what I might find if I follow it downstream."

"Hum... I've only got two in inventory. One new, one with a lot of kilometers on it. How much were you thinking about spending?"

"I don't have a fixed amount in mind but plan to pay cash."

"Well, let me show you what I've got. We can order you anything, but best-case delivery on a custom order is three months."

He takes me to see the used vehicle first. It doesn't appear to be in particularly good shape.

"It's a bit banged up on the outside. The grav generators are in excellent condition, but the batteries only hold a two-hour charge."

"How much?"

"2,100 credits."

"New batteries?"

"They're priced by capacity. New 12-hour batteries will cost another 1,200 credits."

I'm surprised how cheap this is.

He takes me to see the new vehicle, and it's love at first sight. It's a surprisingly sporty two-seater, with an extended flatbed. It's designed for off-roading and can carry enough equipment for an extended journey. In addition to 12-hour batteries, it comes with a portable anti-matter power generator that can hold up to 10,000 hours' worth of fuel.

"This is a beautiful unit. It was custom ordered by a guy who got transferred off world before it arrived. He paid 59,000 credits for it.

We can offer it to you for 56,990 if you're interested. It was never titled to him, so is technically still new."

"Do you have electric carts?"

The question seems to deflate him.

"Sure, this way."

...

An hour later, Audrey and I head off to the hotel, her in her car, me in my new cart. I bought the new off-road hovercraft also and will be back with a check from the bank tomorrow to pick it up.

HOTEL

This is my first time in a hotel. Audrey helps get me checked in, then takes off. She agrees to meet me at the bank tomorrow at 11:00 with an invoice for her services and retainer for the coming year.

The hotel isn't much. My room is about the same size as the one I've shared with Alex the last several months. The furnishings are nicer than at the camp, but not as nice as the ones I had at home. The staff is friendly, but the service isn't exactly prompt. The best part about it is that it's in a business area, which gives me the opportunity to pick up more of the things I need.

My first stop is the 'Access' store, where I get a personal mobile communications device, an exo-net connection, and a new computer. The exo-net connection ties directly to the satellites that provide the connections off world. My own satellite link means that I can be connected anywhere in the camp or anywhere out in the wilderness. The box itself is a bit expensive but is devoid of any ongoing fees. This stop costs me another 1,100 credits.

The next stop is an outfitting shop. There I get a portable shelter and other equipment I'll need for trips out into the wilderness. Another 700 credits spent.

The last stop is at the clothes store. It's the first time I've bought clothes completely on my own. Once again, the staff compete to bring me the best items they can find. Seven complete wardrobe changes, a light jacket and two suitcases later, I leave the store. Another 850 credits spent.

VISIONS

As I settle in for the evening, my mind goes back to last night, the cookies Ethel gave me, and the visions that followed. It turns out that the ladies have been doing this for a long time. They have several techniques to leverage the psychic enhancement derived from the toads.

My vision that night back in my cabin was of the type that comes in dreams. There are two other types that come while you're awake. The first cookie I ate was a mind enhancer. There are no vision qualities to it. Instead, it's more like all of your mind is turned on, not just the fraction we normally use. In that mode you are fully under control and think about the things you choose to think about. Memory is also enhanced. I could play back memories as if I were experiencing them again for the first time.

As I felt the enhanced state coming on, the ladies started asking me questions. One of the lines of questioning had to do with the land East of the sugar mill, refinery, and ethanol facility. In school we were taught that this was barren land incapable of supporting life. What I saw during my suborbital flight was something quite different.

Ethel and Norah believe that there are people living out there near the Great Sea. Official government information does not acknowledge the existence of the sea. There are, of course, local rumors of a significant body of water, but these are denied by the government. The ladies have come to believe that most of the escapees from the camp did not die in the wilderness as the government claims. Instead, they think the escapees have formed their own communities.

Anyway, as we talked through what I saw during the descent, pushing deeper into the enhanced memories, I came to agree with them. There was no definitive proof in my memories for the existence of additional settlements. But the evidence suggested that their explanation was more likely to be true than the government's was.

After a while, they gave me another food to try. It brought on the second form of wakeful psychic enhancement. In that form, both the conscious and sub-conscious mind go into overdrive. I felt like my IQ had jumped to 200. In that mode they pressed me on several subjects. How should we go about confirming that a plague is coming? How do we use the resources here to deal with it? Is it possible that the toads and vipers have migrated downstream to a place where we would have more flexibility to pursue solutions?

Somewhere during all that discussion, I went out of body again, traveling all over the place. I picked up the odd insight here and there. But in truth, didn't learn anything of consequence.

Yet, I woke this morning knowing I needed to go exploring downstream.

BANK

I meet Audrey outside the bank. She hands me my invoice before we go in. It's only for 1,000 credits.

"I thought it would be 450 for the time yesterday and 1,000 for the retainer."

"The state paid me enough for yesterday. You still planning to get that hovercraft?"

"Yes. I really need to do some exploring beyond the city limits."

"OK. It's your money. You are possibly the wealthiest person in Heroldstown you know. Word will get out. And an identifiable vehicle like that will make you easy to spot."

"Didn't think about that. But given what they have, I'm still going with it. I don't want to get stuck without power a hundred kilometers out of town."

We enter the bank and are immediately whisked to the bank manager's office.

"Mr. Daan, so good to see you. I'm Miles Brown, the bank's general manager."

He shakes my hand, then nods to Audrey. "Ms. Preston."

He indicates seats for us.

"Thank you for calling ahead to let me know you were coming. I understand you need to make some payments?"

"Yes." I slide the two invoices across the table. "I'd also like to withdraw another 1,000 credits in cash."

"You're spending a lot of money, Jared." He gives me a concerned look.

I think it's funny that I'm Mr. Daan when depositing money, Jared when I'm withdrawing it.

"True. But it's necessary. I'm a successful entrepreneur who's been separated from my business for a while. Everything I've bought is needed to continue growing my business. A hovercraft this nice was a bit of a splurge. But I need a vehicle and the other ones in stock weren't up to the task.

"And so you aren't caught off guard, I'm also planning to purchase some equipment from off world this month. It will cost over 100,000 credits."

"I see."

It's funny how some people say 'I see' when clearly, they don't.

An assistant comes in and takes the instructions he'd scribbled out and the invoices.

"We'll have your money and checks in a few minutes. So, tell me about your business. I'd heard that you were going to be working at the prison."

"I plan to continue on at the prison, at least for a while. There's a lot I can do to help those people. Most are really decent people who stumbled into misfortune.

"But my business is personal power equipment. It's based on our founder's ideas. Those are all in the public domain now, but few people understand them the way I do. That's my advantage.

"I currently sell on Jungle. With their help, my products have become very popular."

"How long have you been doing this? You're only 17, right?"

"My first product went out just about a year ago. The second went out just before my brother framed me for his crimes. I suspect my account here will get a lot bigger over the coming year."

The statement triggers a vision that nearly knocks me out.

"Jared, are you alright?" Audrey's looking at me with genuine concern.

"Sorry. Just had a very powerful idea that stole my attention for a moment. It happens now and again."

"You really do live up to the legend, don't you?" Miles says with some wonder in his voice.

Seems there's no escaping the legend, even in Heroldstown.

RETURN

My new vehicle is a real hotrod. Hover vehicles are really designed for off-road. On a smooth highway, it's easy to go way too fast. It's the first time I've driven on a highway, the first time I've driven a high-performance vehicle. I'm lucky to have made it back alive.

The car dealer helped me tie down my new cart. A nice person at the hotel helped me secure my other supplies, and driving up to the headquarters building, I see that the warden has already marked a parking spot for me. Now it's time to go see my new apartment.

...

I walk into the headquarters building and once again see Summer at the front desk. I can't help but grin.

She smiles at me also.

"Jared, you're back." She pops up out of her chair, grabs some keys out of a drawer, then says to someone I can't see, "Larry, can you cover the front desk for a while. I need to show Jared to his new apartment."

I hear him reply but can't make out what he says. I also see that it flusters Summer a bit.

She looks at me. "Don't listen to him." Then points to my right. "I'll see you down the hall."

I head in the direction she indicated. A moment later, a door opens, and she comes out. She sees me and smiles again, then points down the hall. "We can go out the back. Your new place is close."

We exit, step down a few steps, then head down one of the paths radiating away from the headquarters building.

"Dad's giving you a really nice unit. A new hire usually wouldn't be eligible for one this nice. He obviously thinks you're going to be successful here."

For the first time my eyes lock on her name badge. Summer Glenn, the warden's daughter. Just my luck.

I'm so distracted by the thought that I almost trip over an uneven spot in the path.

"You should watch where you're going."

I look at her and she blushes. She apparently thinks I've been checking her out. I start to say something, but there are no words.

She starts laughing. "Caught you."

I want to say that I was trying to read her name badge but have the wisdom not to.

"Seems you did. So, what can you tell me about my apartment?"

My eyes alternate between hers and the path ahead. I don't want any trouble with the warden.

"It's classified as a 1-bedroom, but it has an office that could be used as a second bedroom. It's on the ground floor and has its own door to the outside. It's furnished, has a full kitchen and sitting room. It's actually nice.

"It also comes with the professional staff amenities: cart parking in front and use of the separate workout and dining areas that aren't open to the prisoner population. You're entitled to use any of the prisoner facilities, but most don't.

"I understand that you're also getting a private parking spot for a car. You have a car?"

"Yes. Brand new. Off-road hover craft. I also bought my own cart, so we can return the one I was using to the pool."

She stops. "You did what?"

I stop and turn to look at her. Apparently, I've broken some staff norm.

"I hope that's not a problem. My work will require me to spend a lot of time in the marshy areas. It's hard to keep the toads and the snakes out of the camp's open carts. I bought one for myself that's fully enclosed. It's safer."

"How can you afford that? Did your father leave you an inheritance?"

"Definitely no inheritance. Although I've never physically left the planet, all my time has functionally been spent on other worlds. I got a remote job and am paid a lot by Jaredaan standards. Most of that money has stayed off world. I've accumulated enough to live comfortably."

"But you're only 17."

For the first time I realize, I don't know how old Summer is. I assumed she was my age. But in fact, I have no idea.

"Is that a problem? I want to help out here. But I don't want to take the same risks that the prisoners are exposed to."

She starts walking again. Slowly. She looks at me. "I'm 17 too. I've lived here my entire life. I finished high school early and started working here the day I turned 16. I still live with Mom and Dad, so have essentially no expenses. I thought I was doing pretty good, but I don't have enough money to buy my own cart yet."

"It's not like it's a competition." In retrospect, I realize that was not the right thing to say.

"Life is a competition, Jared. The winners get to have some liberty, some sense of self destiny. The losers end up here. I want more in life than this place."

As I wonder how to respond, it strikes me that I never had a conversation like this with Nana. She was street wise and pleasant company. But I never sensed depth.

Summer is different. She's easy on the eyes and pleasant to be around. But she also has depth of character, independence of thought. She is her own person. And I think I really like her.

...

Once the tour of the apartment is done, Summer gives me the keys and helps me round up some laborers to get my new cart off my new hovercraft. Once that's done, I load my stuff into the cart, then unload it into my new apartment.

I have an appointment with the warden at 4:00, so still have time to set up my exo-net connection and check my Jungle account.

WARDEN'S OFFICE

"Jared, come in. I hear you bought yourself a hovercraft and an enclosed cart. Good idea, but there are restrictions on enclosed carts that you need to comply with."

"Which are?"

"I'll see to it that you get the appropriate rules. We had enclosed carts at one point. They ultimately ended up being used to smuggle too much stuff out of the camp. We eventually stopped buying them. Security needs to inspect your cart on every entry and exit. Those inspections need to be scheduled in advance."

"Ah... Wish I'd known that. The cart was not driven in. It was tied onto my hovercraft, which has already been unloaded."

"We can let it pass this time.

"Let's get the paperwork signed, then we can put you to work."

APARTMENT

On the way back to my apartment, I stop at the staff café to get dinner to go. From what I'd heard earlier, I thought the food was free. It's not, you have to pay for it. But it's cheap and they don't take cash. Instead, they scan your ID. The meal is charged to your employee account which is automatically deducted from your pay at the end of the month.

It suddenly dawns on me that they do the same thing for the apartment rent. I should have paid more attention to the documents I was signing. I wonder if the average employee makes enough to cover their rent and food. From what Summer said, it seems they don't.

It doesn't really matter to me. I make more from Jungle each day than I'm being paid per month here. But it's a pretty slimy scam if your work only covers your food, rent and health care.

I put the food in the oven, then relax for a minute. It's tempting to just be lazy, live day to day and just let life flow. That's how I got through the months of imprisonment. But it's not me. I own my life again and I have things to do.

The short-term list is easy. First, I need to get caught up on Jungle. Then I need to figure out what I can do here to buy myself more flexibility. I don't really want to spend more than a couple hours a day actually working for the warden.

The long-term list is more difficult. I need to extract as much information from the ladies as I can. I need to know everything they know about the medical impacts of the wildlife here.

I also need to spend time on the exo-net to find out what's going on out in the Confederation. Something IS going on. Ethel and Norah are certain of it. I am too. If my vision was right and the Confederation is dying, then we are in trouble. Because as much as our founder wanted us to be independent of the Confederation, we aren't. We're not even close. If the inbound shipments stop, our world will slowly die.

Then there's the item that really gnaws on me. Something is going on downstream. It's odd to be so certain about something I don't have evidence to support. But something IS going on down there, and I need to know what.

ORIGINS

As I settle into bed, my mind drifts back to yesterday's conversation with Ethel and Norah. Ethel's family came from New Brazil. Norah's came from Caladon, the same planet as our founder. Although people have emigrated here from all over the Confederation, the preponderance were from Caladon and New Brazil, which is curious to me. They're relatively far apart. And culturally different. New Brazil still has Portuguese as an official language.

For a planet to be a member of the Confederation, it must list the standard language, which we just call Standard, as its official language. A planet can have additional official languages, but few do. New Brazil is one of those that does.

When you think about it, it's amazing that the Confederation formed at all given the language rule. Humanity started leaving Earth somewhere in the middle of the third millennium AD, the years 2001 to 3000. All the original colonies were sponsored by one country or a small collection of countries.

When it was determined in the year 3012 AD, that a system of black holes would be passing through the solar system in about 100 years, the exodus began in earnest. Some countries like Brazil invested everything in one colony that took the name, New Brazil. Others, like Canada, invested in multiple. Initially, they all fought for the name New Canada. New Quebec was the first to go its own way. Eventually, the people from western Canada realized they were going to lose the battle of the name with the people from the east. And ultimately opted for the name Caladon. But history seems to have lost the details of why that name was chosen.

And why do I know all this? Our founder was from Caladon and, for a time, was a person of great consequence there. One of his many edicts required this version of history be taught in all schools on our world. He was truly a man of limitless ego.

CHAPTER 10: DEVELOPMENTS

Over the last week, Jungle has taken more of my time than I would have liked. I finally worked my way through all the messages they sent. Their new products team had sent me many promotional offers and product suggestions while I was away.

One of the product suggestions was ridiculously easy to do. So, I kicked it out and sent it to them, only to get a rejection noting that my account was locked.

When I tried to contact them to find out why. I kept getting auto reply notices saying my account was not eligible for new product team promotions. You can't apply to have things reviewed by the new products team; you have to be invited.

I was finally able to speak with someone. I tried to explain my situation, at least as best I could while leaving out the prison part. And I kept getting the 'you need to be invited' line. I finally got the person to actually look at my account. They confirmed I was locked out, then gave me the 'invited' garbage again. When I finally got them to look at my account, sales levels, etc., things changed immediately.

"You actually created one of the products they requested?"

"Yes. That's how I found out I'd been locked out."

"Oh." I hear more noise on the other end of the line. "OK. You are unlocked. I've found the message you sent and am putting it back into the system. Sorry for the inconvenience. You should hear from someone in the next 72 hours."

I guess the good news is that my products are still selling. Sales are starting to drop off, but I'm still making over 10,000 credits a week. But given my belief that the core worlds are in trouble, I want to get more products up for sale so that I make more money now. And I want to use that money to buy things that will help me survive here, if shipments from the core worlds should stop.

CANE FIELDS

Apparently, things in Jaredstown are not good. I've made no direct contact with anyone there, so don't really know this firsthand. But the warden told me that electricity production has dropped to disastrously low levels, which is driving up the demand for ethanol. Apparently, it's viable to back load it on the ice transport system. With the demand for alcohol up, so is the demand for sugar cane. So, he wants me to figure out how we can increase cane production.

Today, I'm making my first trip out into the fields. I already know this isn't going to be fun. I plan to do two inspections today. The first will be in Zone 3. They currently have the highest production rate. So, I want to learn about their process and ways they think it could be improved.

Then, assuming that I get done early enough, I'm going to go visit Zone 5. They have the second lowest production rate. Zone 10 is lower, but it's also understaffed and its output per worker is above the camp's average.

...

I pull up to Supervisor Barnes' office. His door is open, so I go in.

"Jared, good to see you."

"Gavin, it's nice to be back. The boss has briefed you?"

"Kind of. The camp needs to increase cane production. We are the highest output zone. He wants you to figure out why."

"Exactly."

"I already know why."

I smile. I'm sure he thinks he does and there's a pretty good chance he's right. But I doubt he knows it well enough to replicate elsewhere.

"Tell me." I say this as good naturedly as I can. He's a decent manager, one that I want on my side.

"We have the best, most experienced people. And our zone has the best mix of wet and dry land."

"Could you show me?"

"Sure." He points to my cart. "OK if we take yours?"

"Let's go."

Over the next four hours, we drive through the fields and around the perimeter. We stop and talk with many of the workers in the field. Most of them recognize me from my time in the community dining room. We stop back there for lunch, just as they are closing down lunch service.

"Jared, good to see you."

It's Alex and he really does look happy to see me.

"The buffet is mostly shutdown at this point, but I can heat some stew for you."

He knows that I always loved his stew with fresh baked bread.

Turning to Gavin, I start the debrief.

"Your land appears to be well maintained. I'm not an expert, but it sure looks good to me."

"Do you know why the warden has asked you to do this?"

"We need to increase output."

"I get that, but why you? Our land has the output it does because it's been organized and maintained the way the botanists told us to."

I don't think Gavin intended to insult me, but it kind of comes off that way. I smile.

"I doubt the warden knows that. I'll let him know. But to your direct question, I think the warden wants someone who doesn't really have a dog in the fight to look across the zones, find the best practices, and spread the word. Some people would say I'm biased toward Zone 3. I probably am. But I have no axe to grind with any of the supervisors, and I'm not part of your review process. That makes me the most neutral person in the camp to help us figure out how to get more from what we've got."

I can tell Gavin's not buying it, but still get an, 'I suppose.'

"I got several things out of today's tour. I'll have more perspective after I've toured the other zones, but this is what I have now and it's completely consistent with what you told me when I arrived.

"Your land is well used. The cane near the lake is virtually wild. It's not safe to go in and cultivate it, but it sustains your hives, so you have good fertilization rates. Except at the edge of the lake, your land is dry. You rely on irrigation. And your irrigation ditches are well maintained. You also draw from your compost production to fertilize your crop.

"The people thing I noticed is you have very experienced people who have specialized. For example, Brian has the lead on irrigation. Brenda knows more about composting and using compost for fertilization than anyone I've ever spoken with.

"Do you think I'm going to find that in Zone 5?"

Gavin makes an exasperated noise. "No, Rory, the super over there is a moron. His operation is chaos. It's amazing they get any cane at all."

"Does the warden know that?"

"Kind of."

"Does the warden know how to fix it?"

"No." There's several seconds of awkward silence. "I think I get it now. It's hard to find zone supervisors. The pay isn't great, the job is intrinsically hazardous, and you're basically working with slave labor.

"Rory and several of the others can't really be replaced, so he needs to figure out how to get them trained. There are no procedures or standards. And you've proven yourself to be pretty good at sorting that kind of stuff out."

I smile. "Thanks. I'll do what I can to put in a good word for you. And try to keep an open mind. Zone 3 seems to be working really well. I know that from my time here, which is why I wanted to start here. But there are undoubtedly ways we can do better. I may or may not find any. But at least consider possibilities that I might bring to you."

"Fair enough. By the way, the ladies have been asking about you. You should stop by. They're finally starting to let up on Vince a bit, but they really miss you."

We chat a bit more as we eat. Then I take off for Zone 5. It's too late to actually do anything there today, but at least I can talk with Rory a bit, get his take on the situation.

...

I pull up to Rory's office, but no one's there. Like Zone 3, the supervisor's office is close to the dining room, so I pop in to ask if they know where I can find him.

The dining room here is laid out a little differently, the opening between the kitchen and serving area is a lot bigger. The dining room itself is empty, but I hear noises in the kitchen.

I walk toward the kitchen, but I'm spotted before I get there.

"Hi, Jared."

The voice is familiar. Turning toward it, I see that it's Sophie Grant, morning assistant chef in Zone 3 when I started. She's the one that saved my bacon that first day.

"Sophie, what are you doing here?" I'm genuinely happy to see her.

"Substituting for the week. Emily, who normally has this shift is sick. It's not good, they moved her to the hospital."

I want to ask what she has but have been trained not to talk about inmate medical issues unless both parties have a need to know, which I do not.

"Any idea where Rory is?"

I see Sophie's expression darken.

"Down by the lake. There's been an incident. Someone was bit by a viper. I haven't heard anything yet, but he left about an hour ago. If he hasn't gotten them to the hospital yet..."

She lets the sentence trail off. We all know what it means if you aren't treated in the first hour.

"Thanks." I would prefer to stop and chat but know I shouldn't.

As I exit the building, I see Rory's cart speeding toward the dining room. Two people are in it. One looks like they're on death's doorstep.

Rory appears to be in a total panic. I know my cart is faster, so step out hoping he'll stop long enough to let me help.

He stops. The poor guy is falling apart. "Two were bit, I'm not going to get there in time. We heard Shelby scream and fall into the water. It took a long time to find her. Mike got bit fishing her out."

"You take Mike to the hospital. I'm going to take Shelby to see one of the old timers who's successfully treated a bite before. She'll be dead before either of us can get her to the hospital."

I pick up Shelby in a fireman's hold, then slap Rory's cart. "Go!"

He speeds away, kicking up dirt behind him. I run toward my cart with Shelby in my arms. It's obvious she's in a bad way. Her breathing is shallow. The wound on her ankle has turned black, as has most of the area below her knee.

We arrive at the ladies' cabin 10 minutes later. They are out on the porch as if they knew we were coming.

"Hurry up, sonny boy. We only have a few more minutes."

I grab Shelby and double time it up the steps. I'm directed toward the great room where I see that a sheet has been laid over the table. I lay her down as gently as I can. Ethel, who's tagging along behind me is already inspecting the wound.

"The idiots didn't even put a tourniquet on her." The words are spat out with anger.

Norah is there with a pan of some sort and a knife.

"Turn away if the blood is going to make you pass out."

Before I respond, the pan is under Shelby's lower calf. They slit her open and blood bursts out.

"We need to drain the venom and don't have the time to suck it out. If we get enough of it, the cream should counteract the venom."

Although I never really turned my head away, Ethel's body has blocked my view of most of the blood. Norah, on the other side of the table, is cranking down on a tourniquet.

"Is the blood going to make you pass out, Jared?"

The fact that Ethel called me by my name, not sonny boy, shows how worried she is.

"I don't know."

She makes a funny noise with her mouth.

"OK, come on over. We should start your education on how to treat this kind of wound."

I come over. The sight makes me swoon a bit, but I think I can hold it together.

She has a fork in her hand, holding it by the tines.

"See this?"

She uses the handle to stir some of the blood furthest from where its dripping from Shelby's leg.

"See how thick and gelatinous it is?"

I nod.

She stirs the blood accumulating directly under the wound.

"It's thinner," I say.

"It is." She confirms. "The venom from our snakes thickens the blood, binds it up like gelatin, shutting down circulation and eventually causing a heart attack.

"She's lucky. If the damn snake bit her closer to a vein, she'd be gone. But it didn't, so not that much venom got into the rest of her body. She also doesn't seem to be having an allergic reaction. If she was, she'd be dead already."

"What's next?" I'm already impressed by what I've seen.

"We're going to let a little more blood come out. Then we'll pack the wound with a special cream we've developed and wrap it up. She'll need stitches and possibly a transfusion. We'll leave that for the doctors to decide.

"How long is it going to take you to get her to the hospital?"

"Fifteen, maybe twenty minutes. It's not that far but the roads are terrible."

"They really need to fix the roads." Norah adds. "You haven't seen a harvest yet have you?"

"No." The question seems so out of context, it confuses me.

"You should see the mess that happens when they bring the trucks in to haul the cane. They must lose 10% bouncing out the sides. And lose another 10% of the juice from the excessive crushing action."

I need to file that thought for later. Seems like a simple fix that could have a significant impact on yield.

"Sonny boy. Go clear your cart. There are undoubtedly creatures on it at this point. We'll have her ready for transport in another minute or two. And the clock is ticking."

Ethel obviously thinks her patient is out of the woods if she's calling me sonny boy again.

I grab Ethel's impaling stick and step outside. Sure enough. Two snakes have dropped onto the roof of my cart. Another is on the ground waiting to pounce on anyone who steps down to get in.

A minute later, four vipers and one toad are dead.

The door opens. "Come get her. We'll keep the path clear."

I go in, grab Shelby and come hustling back out. They have the area clear and the back door open. I lay her in the back, close the door, then get in the front.

"Quick now. She's not out of the woods yet."

HOSPITAL

I pull up to the hospital 12 minutes later. It was a bumpy ride, but not as bumpy as it could have been. I found a couple smooth short cuts.

There are no hospital staff waiting for me. They probably know I'm coming. Probably think I'm bringing a cadaver.

I pull up to the emergency entrance and stick my head in.

"I have a snake bite victim. We got a lot of the venom out, but she's not out of the woods."

Several people stream out and do a quick triage.

"Ethel and Norah, right?"

"Yes," I answer in surprise.

"Good thinking on your part. They know what they're doing. Come on folks," she says to the nurses that have come out. "We need to get this tourniquet off or she's going to lose her leg."

There's a flurry of activity, then they're gone.

I park my cart, then go into the hospital through the front door. I see Rory in the waiting room. He's a total mess.

I go over to talk with him.

"I think we saved Shelby."

He brightens. "How? I was sure we'd lost her."

"I took her to two of the old timers in Zone 3. They've been here forever and know a lot about first aide for the snake bites. I got a bit of a lesson. I think we need to write up their techniques and add them to basic supervisor training.

"How's Mike?"

"Don't know. He was unconscious when we got here. They said they'd give me an update when they had one. So here I sit."

I slap him on the leg. "Let me check."

I stand and take a step toward the desk, then am hit with massive pain. It's as if someone stuck a knife in my brain. The room starts to spin. I know I'm about to go down, so drop to the floor as gracefully as I can. I really don't want to hit my head.

...

I wake to an incredible headache. The slightest movement results in piercing pain. I open my eyes, then immediately shut them. My head pounds. An alarm of some sort goes off and I think I'm going to die from the pain.

I hear the curtains open but am not going to open my eyes.

"Jared, are you awake?"

It's Dr. Avery's voice.

He takes my hand.

"Squeeze my hand if you're awake."

I squeeze.

"Would you like me to give you more pain killer? It will put you to sleep. Squeeze twice for yes, once for no."

I croak out, "What happened?"

"The activity yesterday caused a small blood vessel in your brain to rupture. I was hoping we were past this point. But scans show that you're still not fully healed from the beating you got in Heroldstown the day you arrived.

"It was touch and go there for a minute. We had to drill a hole in your skull to relieve the pressure."

I squeeze his hand.

"You're ready for more pain killers now? One squeeze for yes."

I squeeze. A minute later, the world fades away.

...

I start to come up from sleep. I know I'm in bed. It's comfortable and warm, so I just go with it. *I don't have anything on my schedule this morning, do I?*

I hear sounds, then realize I'm not at home.

I rouse myself and hear an alarm go off. It sounds like the ones in the hospital.

The thought, hospital, brings me fully awake, heart pounding. Another alarm goes off.

I hear a curtain open and footsteps heading my way. But I can't see anything. The footsteps stop next to me.

"Calm down, Jared. You're OK."

It's Doctor Avery again. His voice relaxes me. I know I'm safe.

"Why can't I see?"

"Do you feel the bandages over your eyes?"

I pause to think.

"Yes."

"How's the headache?"

"Muted."

"Good. We still have quite a bit of medicine in you. I'd rather not have to increase it." A pause. "Is it giving you pain to talk?"

"Not really. What happened?"

"Can I give you some good news first?"

"Sure."

"Shelby and Mike are on the path to a complete recovery. I don't think either of them would have made it if not for you.

"Running a hundred yards with Shelby over your shoulder came close to killing you. But it saved her. Saved both of them."

"My prognosis?"

"You started bleeding again yesterday. We had to go in to cauterize it. That's why you have bandages around your head. Evidence suggests that this damage happened some time ago. If I had to guess, I'd say it was the elevator incident. We now know what to look for and I think we got the last of it.

"So, another couple day's observation, then a light schedule with restricted physical activity for a month. Then a more complete schedule with no heavy physical activity for 2 more months."

"Does the boss know yet?"

"He's very worried about you, Jared. Also impressed that you saved Shelby."

"How soon before the bandages come off?"

"As soon as you're ready. They need to be changed. From there it will depend on how the wound is responding."

"I'm ready."

"OK, it will take a few minutes to get set up. In the meantime, there's someone here who'd like to see you if you're up for it."

"Who?"

"Someone you're going to want to see. I'll tell her she can come in."

Could Ethel or Norah possibly have come to see me?

I hear footsteps. They're quiet, shy.

"Hi, Jared."

It's Summer!

She takes my hand.

"Dad says you were very brave. Just about killed yourself saving two people. Two prisoners."

"I just made the best call I could. I didn't realize I was risking myself but hope I'd have made the same choice if I did."

She whispers something. For a moment, I thought she said... No, she wouldn't say that.

I hear some people and a cart rolling in. Summer lets go of my hand, then moves away from the bed. I think I hear her leaving.

APARTMENT

I ended up spending three days in the hospital. A surprising number of people came to see me. The warden stopped by. He seemed very relieved to see me on a path toward recovery. Summer came over at least once a day. We spent an hour talking each visit.

Gavin brought Ethel and Norah over to see me. I'm sure he was brow beaten into it. But he was very pleasant with both me and the ladies. He said he'd spent a little time with Rory. The ladies asked me to come by as soon as I was cleared to travel that far. They had something they needed to talk with me about privately.

Gavin came by a second time with Alex and Sophie.

Even my lawyer, Audrey Preston, stopped in. She was here on other business but stopped in to wish me well.

But the big surprise was Shelby and Mike. They were discharged a day before I was. When Rory came to pick them up, the three stopped by to wish me well. They were on medical work release for another week, but out of danger so released back to their cabins. Two people off for a total of 10 days was really going to hit Rory's numbers, which were already the worst. But my learning from all this was that Rory isn't that bad. He's clearly smart enough to do his job and cares for his people. I think the issue is solely the lack of training. My mission from now until harvest is going to be making him successful.

I'm mostly constrained to bed for the next week or two. My apartment is close enough to the hospital that Dr. Avery can stop by every other day to check on me. I'm allowed to get up to wash and use the bathroom. But that's it. Summer has taken on the role of bringing me food. I pay for two meals each evening. She picks them up then comes to eat with me. She's very pleasant company. I really like her. I've been splitting the rest of my time between working on another Jungle product and reading the news from the core worlds. There's nothing suspicious in the headlines. But I've taken a deep dive into the obituaries. I'm checking two or three cities on each of the top 10 worlds. Over the last couple years, reported deaths have doubled. And the percent attributed to 'a long-term illness' has more than doubled. It's suspicious, but not statistically significant.

...

It's been three weeks since the most recent brain trauma incident. I'm feeling good and Dr. Avery has approved me to go back to work starting tomorrow, but I'm restricted to light duty.

I want to go back out into the fields, which he thinks is a bad idea. After some back and forth we came to an agreement on the definition of light duty, which he's sending to the warden to make sure I won't cheat. The deal is that I can do light work in an office, use my cart, and talk to people. But I'm to avoid steps and cannot lift anything over 5 kilograms. To make sure I don't do something stupid, he's glued a blood pressure monitor on my arm. It will set off an alarm if my blood pressure goes over a certain number. It'll be interesting to see what happens if I get in an argument with someone and my alarm goes off. I chuckle at the idea.

As excited as I am about going back to work, I'm happy with what I accomplished while bedridden. I got the specs for a fourth Jungle product completed. This one's a little more complicated, so I've ordered a test copy. It'll take a month to get here, so the product is on hold for now, pending my approval. It's a fast-charge extended-power case for their most popular data pad. They sell hundreds of thousands of these things a month. I'll get 2 credits per case and if it gets their recommended label, we'll sell a lot of them.

News from the core worlds continues to be positive and cheery. But it's clearly a façade. The number of obituaries doubled over the last two weeks. None of them name the cause, just the vague 'long-term illness' language. And I can find no news articles pointing to some sort of health crisis. It's actually kind of creepy. So, I've finally started spending some money. I'm not sure where I'm going to put the equipment I've bought, but the first replicator will arrive in about a month. I'll be getting a shipment of bulk carbon along with the replicator. The instrumented test bench will be another month behind that. I hope to bring in a couple million credits over the next two years. It's my sense that it's about the amount of time we have left. Seems I need to visit Ethel and Norah again soon to see if we can glean more insight out of the news.

But enough of that! Summer is coming over for dinner tonight and we can actually eat at the table.

DINING ROOM

My apartment has a big open space that includes kitchen, dining area and sitting area. There's a large display on one wall that allows me to view the exo-net in 2-D. At home in Jaredstown we had a 3D holoprojector. They are specialty products, common on the core worlds, rare on protected worlds. I could probably get one and have it installed in my apartment, but really don't see the point in it.

I've set the table in the dining area. My alarm sounded twice while I was doing it. I really can't move as much as I thought I'd be able to. But after three weeks in bed, I'm easily fatigued.

There's a knock on the door and I get there in time to let Summer in. She has a key, but I want to meet her at the door.

"Jared, you're up."

"Dr. Avery cleared me for light duty today. I thought maybe we could eat at the table, then maybe sit on the couch and watch a show."

She seems to hesitate, then smiles. "Sitting at the table sounds nice. Why don't you sit? I'll heat things up. I'm worried about seeing you up on your feet."

I sit and watch her while she works. She's been doing this for the last couple weeks and at this point knows my kitchen better than I do. I'm mesmerized by her movements.

"Did you hear that Emily is back in the hospital?"

"No? What's the matter with her?"

"They don't know. It's stomach related. It seems to hit her every couple weeks. Each round a little bit worse. She's sick for a couple days, then gets better. They think it might be a parasite, something in the water in Zone 5. But they can't find anything. Weird, isn't it?"

At the edge of my consciousness, there's an inkling of déjà vu, but I'm too entranced with Summer to stop and think about it.

A minute later, a plate full of hot food is put in front of me.

"It's veal with a mushroom sauce, sauteed spinach and potatoes gratin. Lenna says it's one of her favorites, but the veal is hard to get so she can only put it out once every couple months."

Lenna is the evening chef at the staff café. Technically, she's an inmate. Prior to her being sentenced here, she was a chef at the finest restaurant in Ashcrag. She was eligible for parole, but couldn't find a

118

job, so wasn't eligible for release. Her cooking was so good, the warden hired her for the staff café. She has a staff apartment now and has free run of the property. But she's not allowed to leave the property. She seems OK with the way things ended up. But this is another one of those things that doesn't seem right to me.

...

Dinner and conversation were as pleasant as always. As Summer clears the plates, I ask, "Want to watch a show?"

She smiles and heads over to the sink to wash them.

"Jared, it's sweet of you to ask, but I need to be getting back home. My mom is worried that I'm spending too much time over here."

I try not to show my disappointment, but I'm crushed.

It only takes a minute for her to finish. When she's done, she comes back toward the table. "Do you think you can handle dinner on your own tomorrow? I can come back if you're not up to it yet, but I'm getting a lot of pressure at home to have dinner with them."

This is really hard. I try to put on a smile. "Thanks for all the help you've been giving me. But maybe you should eat with them tomorrow. I don't want to get into any trouble with your Mom."

She chuckles. Then says shyly, "I could probably go out to dinner with you Saturday, if you wanted to ask me out."

"I'd like that. Will you have dinner with me on Saturday?"

"Yes. I'd like that."

ZONE 5

It's the first day back on the job. As I walk over to my cart, I realize how nice it is to be back outside. The plan is to drive over to Zone 5, see if I can get some time with Rory. I haven't made an appointment, so the trip may be pointless. But I don't want to wait until tomorrow to get started. So, worse case, I just end up driving around a bit.

When I get to Zone 5, I find Rory in his office.

"Jared, you're back on your feet! Great to see you, buddy!"

There's a lot of warmth in his greeting. In truth we barely knew each other prior to the day of the snake bites. But the few minutes we spent together were truly a bonding experience.

"Good to be back, my friend. Good to be back."

He motions for me to take a seat.

"So, what can I do for you?"

119

"The warden has asked me to review operations and procedures. We need to increase production. There's a lot of demand for cane and normal sources of funding are starting to dry up.

"We're a prison camp. And as prison camps go, life here is better than the state is required to provide. So, we need to increase cane revenue if things are to continue at their current levels."

Rory gives me a concerned look.

"Our levels are down this year, way down." Rory says this as if it's a confession. "We're down staff and our crop just isn't growing. I've asked for help from one of the botanists but haven't received any. I don't know what to do."

"Well, that's what I'm here to help with. I'm doing a survey of all the zones to see what's working and what isn't. I'm going to compile a list of best practices and recommended procedures, then work with the zone supervisors to make the changes.

"It'll take a while, but I'm confident we'll be able to increase output in every zone if we can work smarter."

Rory eyeballs me for a couple seconds, then says, "I wouldn't ask anyone else this, but..." A pause. "Are you after my job?"

The question is so far from anything I ever would have expected that I'm shocked. Dumbfounded.

"No." Some stammering. "No. I'm better at designing things than doing things. And you've seen my health issues. It's going to be years before I can lift 10 kilos again, maybe never." As I blather, my blood pressure alarm goes off.

I sit back in my seat, put my head back and take a couple deep calming breaths. Fifteen seconds later the alarm stops.

"What was that?" Rory asks.

"Blood pressure monitor. If my blood pressure goes up into the zone that might trigger another aneurysm, it goes off. See what I mean about not being able to do your job."

I start laughing. The absurdity of the last couple minutes seems hilariously funny.

The alarm goes off again and I struggle to let the laugh go, so I can find my quiet place. The alarm stops and I'm flooded with a sense of good will.

"Sorry about that," Rory says with a lot of sincerity.

"It seems I'm not quite ready to be back on the job."

After another couple seconds, I look at Rory. "I need to sit still for a few minutes. Want to tell me about things here? What works? What doesn't. That sort of stuff."

"Sure."

...

An hour later, I'm back in my cart. I'm tired, but I learned a lot today. Zone 5 has more and different issues than I thought when I came here this morning. I told Rory I'd like to tour his zone with him, see some of the problems myself so I can understand them better.

He seems eager to start, but I told him I needed to get stronger before I could do it. He seems genuinely concerned for me.

APARTMENT

The trip to Zone 5 really knocked me for a loop. When I get back, I collapse into bed, even though it's only 4:00 PM. This morning, I'm still not right, so I go over to the hospital to see Dr. Avery.

I don't have an appointment, so am told that I'll need to wait a while. About an hour into my wait, I'm taken into the emergency clinic. There's a row of 10 beds curtained off from one another. One has its curtain open, so I assume that's where we're headed. About halfway there, a doctor emerges from the curtains two beds over. I get a glimpse of a woman, she's familiar but I can't place her. The doctor looks worried and my heart goes out to his patient. I've personally spent too many hours in these beds, so find it easy to sympathize.

I take a seat on my bed. The nurse tells me that Dr. Avery is running a few minutes behind and thanks me for my patience. Then she leaves and closes the curtain. Each curtained off area has quiet music playing that masks the sounds coming from behind other curtains. Nonetheless, I hear snippets of muted conversation that I can't make out. Then a surprisingly loud exclamation. "How can she have a keratin build up in her small intestine?"

There's some 'shushing,' but my attention is dragged back as my curtain opens. It's Dr. Avery.

"Hi Jared. I hear you're feeling worn down."

We talk for a bit. I mention that I spent several hours over in Zone 5 yesterday, which draws a stern look. Then he does a quick scan of my blood pressure monitor.

The look I get tells the entire story. I start to make an excuse, then let it drop. Any denial, any excuse will just be further incrimination. The evidence was all recorded.

"Jared, you're well liked here. A lot of people are worried about you. But it's all on you to regulate your behavior."

After thirty seconds of stern staring, he relaxes.

"I'm not going to report this to the warden, but next time I will."

...

The brow beating was enough to keep me home for the rest of the day. I read the obituaries, check my jungle account, then read more obituaries.

As I browse, I spot the Great Alien War documentary I saw some time ago. Several more episodes are available. The last one in the series catches my eye, *Last Stand, The Fall of Doffenplod*.

I remember the name Doffenplod. It's where the aliens made their last stand. I decide to watch it. Thankfully, they don't show any of the old video clips of the aliens. This episode is more of a tribute to the people who lived there.

It features interviews with survivors taken in the years following the war. It's really something to see people who died some 7,000 years ago talk about their experiences in the war. The first interviews are with soldiers that fought. The later ones are much darker. They are with some of the children that the aliens captured and did medical experiments on. Many of the children had scales growing on them

The final scene is the grimmest. It's the well-known historian, Melvin Harsoal. He's standing on some dusty remains on the planet. Everyone there had ultimately died from toxins the aliens left behind. The Confederation quarantined the planet just before the end. Now 7,000 years later, the quarantine has been lifted. The historian standing in the dust is part of the first scientific team to step foot on the planet since.

The idea of voluntarily going back to that planet totally creeps me out. He apparently died shortly after filming this segment.

...

The next day, I'm still unnaturally tired, so stay home again. But as the day comes to a close, I can't take it anymore. The number of obituaries continues increasing and all the long-term illness is depressing. So, I get up, get dressed, and head out to my cart. It's time to go see the ladies.

CABIN 007

I tell them my sad story and get nothing but silence in return. Finally, Norah breaks the silence.

"It's here."

I almost say, 'what's here?' But thankfully, I catch myself.

Catching yourself at this stage in our relationship brings nothing but laughter. Finally, Ethel speaks.

"Sonny boy, you'd be better off coming here for medical treatment between crises."

Her comment is followed by lots of cackling.

"But that doesn't change the fact that it's here."

After a moment, it snaps. "The core worlds' plague is here?"

This is impossibly bad news.

"Emily has it. So does Lenna."

It takes a second to place the names.

"Emily. Morning chef in Zone 5? Lenna, evening chef in the staff kitchen?" A pause. "I saw Emily at the hospital yesterday. She didn't look good. Her doctor looked worried."

There are icy stares and a bit of head shaking.

"It's been a while since you've had your mind expanded, hasn't it?"

I don't respond immediately, then see Ethel shaking her hand as if trying to erase the words.

"Sorry. Sorry. You're still too weak. What you did a couple weeks back was noble. I don't want to criticize. But we need you back sonny boy. We need you back. There isn't much time left.

"We know what it is. But we just can't grasp it. You're the only one we know who can. We need you back."

The message is delivered with passion and urgency.

"Give me another day or two, and I'll go back in, ready or not."

"We appreciate your sincerity, sonny boy. But we can't wait. Is anyone expecting you home tonight?"

The question seems preposterous to me, then I remember that Summer has been over every night in the last three weeks, except the last two nights.

"No. Not until Saturday."

I hear Ethel's cackle, then think I hear her say, 'this boy needs to get laid.' But I refuse to let the words enter my mind.

Now both are cackling, and a weathered hand reaches out.

"Take one of these. It will do miracles for you."

She hands me something that looks like a piece of candy.

"What is it?"

"A few extracts that we added to some sugar water, then let dry."

"And what are these extracts?"

"Chemicals we've extracted from the toad and viper venom."

"And why would this be good for me?"

"Remember Shelby's blood, how thick and gelatinous it was when it had the venom in it?"

I nod my head.

"Remember the cream we put on the wound?"

Again, I nod my head, wondering where these questions are going.

"The cream had a blood thinner in it. It's extracted from the toad venom. We put that cream on to counteract the viper poison still in the wound. It's what enabled her to survive until you got her to the hospital."

I nod my head, acknowledging her words, but still am not connecting the dots.

"A tiny amount of that blood thinner is in the sugar, none of the poison. It will lower your blood pressure. The other ingredient is a calming agent also extracted from the toad venom. It will knock the edge off so that every surprise doesn't trigger a blood pressure spike.

"Between them, your blood pressure will be lower and your physical reaction to emotional stimulus will be slower."

I pop the sugar candy into my mouth.

"Don't swallow, just let it dissolve on your tongue. Once it's completely dissolved it's OK to swallow."

The sugar quickly melts. Its sweetness masks, but doesn't eliminate, the foul taste of the other ingredients. By the time I swallow, I already feel more relaxed.

Ethel can see its effect on me. "It works fast. The active ingredients get into your system faster in your mouth. There's good absorption there. Stomach acids break it down, so little of what you swallow will get into your system.

I'm impressed with the ladies' knowledge.

"Back to the disease. It's in the stomach. It starts mild, hangs on a day or two, then disappears. A month or two later, the cycle repeats. A year or two of that and the patient starts bleeding in the stomach. The patients become anemic and start losing weight.

"No one here has died of it yet, but it's only a matter of time. We suspect that it's a parasite. But have no evidence."

"How did you learn this? Do you know what data led to this conclusion?"

"We used your trick. The obituaries on Caladon and New Brazil. We asked Supervisor Barnes to print them out for us each day. We told him that we had relatives that we'd heard were sick."

"Clever." Once again, I'm impressed by the ladies.

Ethel stands and steps toward me. "Let me test your blood pressure."

I look around for the equipment, but don't see any. I look up at Ethel, who's now standing next to me, hand out as if waiting for me to give her something.

The cackling and head shaking start. After a moment, she says, "Give me your wrist."

I extend my right hand. She grabs my wrist with her left hand, the grip surprisingly tight. Then she starts probing my wrist with the index and middle fingers of her right hand. A moment later she stops.

"Strong pulse." She looks me in the eyes and smiles, then bam. It's like a lightning bolt has shot into my hand. Massive tingly-ness floods my hand as if it's fallen asleep.

I pull my hand loose and start shaking it.

"What the hell was that?"

"I just compressed a nerve bundle."

"Why?"

"Because it doesn't work if someone's blood pressure is too high."

"What?"

Norah had slipped out at some point in the process. Now she's back carrying a little tray with three glasses of cloudy liquid. She sees me, then looks at Ethel.

"He passed the test, right?"

She nods yes. "His blood pressure is fine."

I'm really struggling to believe that any of this nonsense is true.

Norah holds the tray out for Ethel.

Ethel takes the least cloudy glass of liquid and hands it to me. Then takes one of the other two for herself.

Norah puts the tray on the table next to her chair, then sits, takes her glass, and holds it out as if to make a toast.

"We distill this ourselves. It has a bit of a bite, so you may want to shoot it."

She raises her glass higher then says, "Cheers!"

Ethel raises hers and says, "Saúde!"

I go with "Cheers!" but wonder if it's a good idea to be participating.

The ladies shoot theirs, then look to me. I gulp mine down and choke a bit. Then a moment later, I'm out of body, sailing through the night sky.

...

I struggle to determine where I am. The people are different, the language unintelligible, clothing and architecture unlike anything I've ever seen. Then it hits me. In terror, I turn to look where everyone is pointing. Aliens!

Row after row march toward us, their scales shimmering in the sunlight. I float up above it all. The ocean of them goes as far as the eye can see. In the distance, I see a spacecraft of some sort lifting off into the sky.

In an instant, I'm there, among the humans on the ground. Some are firing weapons at the departing ship. Others are weeping. Children have been kidnapped by the aliens!

The visions are compelling. They put you there; put you in the moment. But with some effort, my rational mind allows me to rise above it. What I'm seeing, living, is from that documentary. It did not have this scene. But this scene is a direct implication I'm drawing from the commentary and some of the stills.

In another instant, I'm aboard the ship. What I see causes the bubble of the vision to burst.

Now, I'm in a hospital on Doffenplod, the one in the documentary. The war has been raging a long time. The previous scene was hundreds of years ago. The patients in this ward were captured by the aliens, apparently left behind when the aliens fled. But these are tortured people. Images of the torture they were subjected to starts to form, then the bubble pops.

I land on New Brazil. The war has been over for ten years. My rational self, injects the question... I know little of New Brazil. Why am I here?

I'm in a recording studio, the person talking is recounting the story of a young woman that the aliens had captured on New Brazil. My rational mind reminds me that I saw this clip in the documentary. And Ethel told me a similar story. Many children were abused in similar ways, injected with substances that killed the majority, but not all.

Suddenly, I'm gripped with understanding. The vision drops me back into the ladies sitting room and I'm weeping.

"Sonny boy, you found the answer, didn't you?"

I nod my head, but I can't compose myself enough to respond. The grief, the fear... They're overwhelming.

"Here, drink this. It will help settle you. The visions can be overwhelming at times."

I drink. This one is sweet, as most of their medications are. And like most of their medications, the sweetness masks an underlying foulness. But it works. Moments later, at least it seems like moments later, I'm back. And I notice it's daytime outside.

"Jared, you went for quite a ride."

The compassion in Ethel's voice is comforting. The fact that I have my name back, implies that she's worried.

"I know the cause, but I have no idea how to fight it."

"If nothing else, that's a step forward." Norah, the quiet one, pitches in. "If we know the cause of the problem, then we can start a serious search for the solution."

My mine becomes laser focused for a second.

"Norah, we lost the great alien war. We just don't know it yet."

As the words leave my mouth, I slide into darkness, not really sure they'd even been spoken.

CHAPTER 11: SOLUTIONS

I wake to darkness, confused about where I am.

"Jared, close your eyes. I'll turn a light on."

The voice belongs to Norah, so I do as I'm told. Even with eyes closed, I can tell the light in the room has come up.

I open my eyes slowly, letting them adjust to the light.

Norah, who's been sitting opposite me in the darkness, gets up and approaches. "Here, take this. Amazingly, your blood pressure monitor hasn't gone off. This should keep it in check."

She holds out two of the sugar candies I had last night.

I take them, set one on the table, then place the other in my mouth. In a minute, it's dissolved. I feel the peace coming over me and start to relax.

"OK If I hold off on taking another?"

"Sweet boy, you're the best judge of that. I was worried you might need two."

"Thanks," I say with genuine sincerity. "I think I'm good for now."

There's silence for a minute, then I ask, "How did you do this? How did you develop the medications?"

She smiles. "On Calderon, where I grew up, there was a saying. 'Necessity is the matriarch of all innovation.' If you need something and there's no solution, you find your own. The camp has decent health care now. It didn't when we started here."

"I get the motivation, but how?"

She smiles. "You're the bright one. We knew that the first day we met you. Not because of the stupid prophecy. But because you are the bright one.

"But it's a convenient coincidence, isn't it? The person predicted to be the great one, is the great one. Not because it was predicted. But because that's who he is.

"You need to stop fighting the legend, Jared."

"Thank you. But that doesn't answer the question how."

She looks at me a bit exasperated. "Jared, how did you find out about the visions? We didn't tell you."

"A toad gassed off underneath the floor in my room."

"Was that part of the prophecy?"

I look at Norah like she's crazy, then I get it.

"One gassed off under this cabin. Given its location, I guess that happened a lot until you figured out why."

"You think?" she says sarcastically.

"Then one of you... No, probably a friend rather than one of you, got bit by a viper."

She nods her head.

"OK, you found out these venoms have properties... But how did you isolate them."

She rolls her eyes. "Maybe you aren't the one after all."

There's silence for a moment, then the answer comes.

"You made a still."

"More like we made a still long before we knew about the other things."

I almost say, 'stills are illegal in the camp.'

The cackling starts before the thought is fully dismissed.

"Sweet, innocent boy." She shakes her head. "The fate of our species lies in your hands. Don't let the rules bind your view of things. Few great people do."

We've apparently made enough noise to awaken Ethel.

"Has he explained himself yet?"

The question is directed to Norah, but the accusatory stare is directed toward me.

"No," Norah answers. "I didn't see the need to go there before you were up."

I note that these two have a relationship that's more like an old married couple then conscripted roommates. It's one of those thoughts that you know is true before its even completely formed.

"Hope it isn't a disappointment for you," Ethel says as if I'd screamed it out loud.

"Leave him alone. He's an innocent."

I'm not sure which surprises me more, that Ethel seems to be able to read my mind, or that Norah is defending me. Another realization hits with all the power of a vision. *I'm so out of my league.*

"Only in the sense that we play in different leagues."

Ethel's words and her stare paralyze me.

She shakes her head. "Jared, it affects us differently. I seem to be able to read people. Norah seems to be able to read events. You..." She sighs, seemingly struggling to find the right words.

129

"You have a scientifically trained mind. Our lives were different. You can see things we'll never be able to. We see things you probably never will. It's the complementary skills that may give us a chance at solving this."

There's a long silence. Ethel's words make a lot of sense to me. There's also an unaccustomed vulnerability.

I realize that two sets of eyes are on me. They hold pride and confidence, worry and fear, and a lot of vulnerability. I sigh, then explain what happened.

"During the Great Alien War, the aliens did a lot of experimentation on humans, mostly on children. At some point, they realized that they were going to lose. Lose that round anyway. So, they developed a virus as a vector for gene therapy. The gene therapy implants some of their DNA in us.

"It killed a lot of the children they tested it on. Others just started growing scales. None recovered to the point where they could live normal lives. Everyone on the planet Doffenplod during the war died in the years following. The Confederation put the planet under quarantine. The quarantine was lifted a year or so ago.

"You see, the aliens understood that the children would go back home and infect their parents, enabling the virus to spread. So over time, it would either change us into them or kill us, leaving our worlds open to their eventual return."

HEADQUARTERS

It's Friday. The warden sent me a message asking me to come by today around lunch time. No topic is given. I think he wants to know when I might be able to go back to work.

I enter the building and see Summer at the front desk. She gives me a warm smile. I'm certain that I'm sporting a goofy grin.

"Hi." I'm so bad at this.

"Hi, Jared. Thanks for coming over. Dad wants to talk with you. He's worried about you. He needs you back. But he doesn't want to ask unless he thinks you're OK."

"That's what I guessed."

"You can head up to his office."

I just hang there for another second, lost in her eyes.

"Save that for tomorrow," she whispers.

"I will. Guess I better head up."

...

I enter the boss's outer office. His secretary, Lillian, smiles at me.

"Good to see you, Jared. You gave us a bit of a scare."

"Trust me, I didn't do it on purpose." I chuckle.

The door into the boss's inner office is open. He hears us and comes out. "Well, look who's here? Really glad to see you, Jared."

"Glad to be here, sir."

"Come on in." We step in and he indicates the sitting area at one end of the office. I see a food service cart on the far side of the table that separates the chairs.

"I had some food brought up. You're welcome to help yourself if you're hungry."

I move toward the designated chair and hear the door close behind me. I take a plate with half a sandwich and some chips. Then one of the bottles of water.

The warden does the same.

"So how are you feeling?"

"It's been a mostly boring week. The trip over to Zone 5 on Monday, I think it was Monday, really wiped me out. I went to see the doctor the next day and got a talking to for having overdone it.

"I spent most of the rest of the week browsing the exo-net and sleeping. Then yesterday afternoon, I went over to see Ethel and Norah. I haven't seen them in a while, so thought that might be a good test."

The warden's expression darkens a bit.

"I heard you spent the night there."

"Yes. That wasn't the plan. I fell asleep in my chair and they let me sleep. I didn't wake up until a little before sunrise. Norah was already up, so we talked a bit, then I came back."

He's slow responding. "A male employee staying overnight in a female cabin is enough to get you in a lot of trouble. If it had been in anyone else's cabin, we'd be having a different conversation."

"Sorry. They gave me one of their herbal medications and it knocked me out."

"Let's put that aside. It's not why I wanted to see you."

He pauses. It's clear our conversation hasn't gone the way he wanted it to.

"Did you make any progress on your assignment before the incident?"

"Some. As you know, Gavin Barnes in Zone 3 has the best numbers. I learned enough about what he does to know why.

"In contrast, Rory Manning in Zone 5 has the worst, on a headcount basis, and it's clear why. He doesn't know enough about what he's doing. But what I've learned about him is that he's more than smart enough, he's just undertrained. If not for the incident, I would have expected him to already be doing better."

The warden is slow to respond to my comments.

"The harvest will start in a month or so. According to the botanists, Zone 3 will be ready by then with a harvest at or above target. Most of the others won't be. They will run late and yield well below target, which will put us in a real pickle.

"Did you come across anything that might help?"

"Yes, I did actually."

The warden smiles, "Tell me."

"Two related items. The roads are a mess. I'm told a lot of cane bounces out and stacks up along the road. There are several things we might be able to do to reduce the cane loss.

"The trucks are stacked high enough that the weight from the bouncing cane crushes the cane on the bottom, which lowers the juice we get paid for. Again, there are several ways to deal with that.

"I have no data to support this number, but I'm told we could increase revenue by 20% if we solved those two problems."

"What do you have in mind?"

"Idea 1: Get some work crews out on the roads filling in potholes. Less bouncing, less cane and juice loss.

"Idea 2: Build wooden, or plastic, inserts for the trucks that we load the cane into. We can do this to prevent cane from bouncing out and to reduce the weight crushing the cane on the bottom."

"Can you prepare me a plan for that with labor and material estimates?"

"Sure, no problem. When would you like it?"

"I'm headed out of town tomorrow for a week, so a week from Monday?"

"No problem," I say with a huge smile.

"Looks like you're anxious to get back to work."

It takes a second for his meaning to sink in, then I get it. He thinks I'm excited to make this plan. I'm actually excited that Summer's father is going to be away.

I nod my head enthusiastically. "Yes, sir. I'm very excited to get back to work."

...

I make my way back down to the lobby and see Summer is still there.

"Jared, something came for you from Jungle."

It's a small package, must be my new battery cover. She holds it out for me, and I take it.

"What were you thinking for tomorrow?"

The question makes me realize that I'm the one that's supposed to be sorting out dinner tomorrow.

"Is there any place we can go outside the camp?"

"No place better than the staff café until you're in Heroldstown."

"Would you consider the Zone 3 dining room?"

Her sour look answers the question.

"Then I guess it's the staff café. Want to eat there or pick up and go back to my place?"

"Would you consider letting me cook for you?"

"Are you sure you want to do that?"

"Yes." She smiles. "I'm a half-way decent chef and I already have the ingredients we need."

I'm confused by the statement.

"Mom and dad will be away. Come over to my place and I'll cook for you. It'll just be us."

This feels like incredibly dangerous territory, but it's not like I can resist her smile.

"Sure."

LAWYER

Last night's revelations and my conversation with the warden have a number of implications. The biggest is the fact the Jaredaan credit is going to crash. The metal trade is what gives our currency its value. The 'spread' between the Jaredaan credit and the Confederation credit is what finances our government. If mining revenue stays down, the spread will collapse. And with an epidemic spreading through the Confederation, demand will drop. I have a ton of Confederation credits that will get converted to Jaredaan credits when received at the bank. I need to stop those credits from coming in, so I call Audrey.

"Jared, good to hear from you."

"Hi Audrey. I'd like to set up a bank account on a member world, so I can hold Confederation credits off world. Most of the money coming in will be spent off world, so it seems safer to hold it there."

She's quiet for a moment as she thinks.

"There are tax implications associated with holding money off world. It's had enough of an impact on the protected worlds that they got the regulations changed so you can hold Confederation credits in special accounts locally. If I'm not mistaken, the Bank of Heroldstown has those types of accounts. If they do, I'm sure that's a better option for you."

"OK. Is that something you can help me with? I have a lot coming in soon, that I would prefer to hold as Confederation credits."

"OK, let me get the ball rolling with Miles Brown over at the bank. There are fees associated with these types of accounts. I'll get back to you with more info as soon as I can. I still have an active Power of Attorney agreement with you. OK if I use it?"

"Yes, and thanks, Audrey."

CAMP ENGINEERING

None of the equipment I've ordered has arrived yet, so I detour over to the camp's engineering department. It's not much. They mostly do repair and maintenance on the camp's carts. We have limited electricity and running water in the camp. The headquarters building and staff residences are better. But the rest of the camp is hit or miss.

But they do have Confederation standard electrical outlets and a voltage meter, and I know the staff there.

I walk in and see Leslie Wilkins, the manager.

"Hi Leslie. OK if I use one of the benches for a few minutes?"

"Hi Jared. Glad to see you up again. What do you need to do?"

"I just got a trial product from Jungle. I want to make sure it works right."

"Sure. Help yourself. You know that stuff better than any of us do."

Leslie's in her early thirties. Like too many people on Jaredaan, she lives apart from her husband most of the week. They have a home on the west side of Heroldstown, eighty-some kilometers away. He works in the space port. She rooms in staff housing with another one of the women here. A boarder takes a spare room in their house in Heroldstown to make up for her rent here. I feel bad for them.

I go over to the bench and quickly check the charge on the unit. It's supposed to come fully charged. I turn it on. It comes up, but there's only a 5% charge. Makes sense. It's been in transit for a month. 5% is within spec for 30 days, so no problem.

I plug the unit in. Specs say it should have a full charge in 2 minutes. I designed it to have a full charge in a minute thirty seconds. When the timer hits 1:30, I unplug it. A quick voltage check shows that it's taken a full charge.

Next, I put on a maximum load. It holds the voltage for 5 minutes, confirming that it has taken a significant charge and isn't overheating. Then I try the short circuit test. The unit cuts out perfectly. No sparking, no overheating. Perfect.

I leave the short circuit in place while I noodle around setting up the capacity test. It takes 5 minutes. The capacity test is a bit more tedious.

The short circuit test holds up, so I remove the short and plug the unit back in. It shows a full charge in seconds.

My original plan was to leave the unit here for the next couple days while the capacity test runs. But too many people seem to have taken an interest in what I'm doing, so I ask Leslie if it's OK to take the test set up back to my apartment for the weekend. Only one piece of equipment is hers, and I think I'm the only one that uses it.

"Sure, Jared. You can take it. No one else here even knows how to use it."

Her reply seems off to me. But I gather up the test set up and take off.

...

Back in my apartment, I start the test. The product specification requires the nanotube capacitor in the case to support 110% of the design load for 48 hours. I designed it to have even higher capacity that might last hours longer. The test setup will record how long the unit can hold voltage above 110%. From there it will continue recording until voltage drops to 95%. At that level, the tablet is supposed to shut itself down.

Now that the test is launched, I can cast my attention elsewhere.

What I need to do now is more research into the scales I saw on those children on Doffenplod. Did the people of that day confirm the cause? And did they make any progress at all toward a solution?

...

It's coming up on dinner time. I'm hungry and tired.

But with Summer's parents away the next seven nights, I'm hoping to spend a lot of time with her, so I pack up and head over to the ladies' cabin. I've learned enough that another round of stimulation may be useful.

ZONE 3 DINING ROOM

By the time I get to the Zone 3 dining room dinner is well underway. At this point, I'm known to almost everyone there. Finley Nevin, the dinner chef, even comes out to greet me.

"You're going down to Cabin 007, right?"

I smile. "I am. I assume their meals have already gone out."

"They have. Want me to put together a box for you? I have some of your favorites."

"Thanks."

"Come on back with me."

I head back into the kitchen with the Chef.

She points to one of the cabinets.

"Grab a tray and one of the bowls with a cover."

I know the drill and am smart enough to do exactly as the Chef says.

"There's a lot of talk about you spending the night with the ladies last night. Is this going to be a regular thing? I didn't think they were all that interested in men."

I groan. "There's nothing like that going on. They're friends. They have lots of stories. And I need to document their medicine. They're the ones that saved Shelby, not me."

"Yeah, right."

"Finley, you can't be serious."

"Jared, you're the top catch in the camp at the moment. Lots of women are getting jealous."

This line of discussion is starting to make me angry.

"Why do people say things like that? I'm being kind to the camp's two centenarians, and I get crap for it?"

She looks at me a bit embarrassed. "Sorry, but it is a bit odd."

The last part is said lewdly.

She finishes loading my tray, then hands it to me.

"Go get 'em, tiger."

I shake my head, then we both break out laughing.

"I put some of their favorites on your tray. Seems they should get some reward for keeping you out of trouble."

CABIN 007

It's almost dark by the time I get there. But the door opens immediately. I grab my tray and bound up the steps.

"We were hoping you'd be back tonight."

"Wouldn't miss it. Even brought some dinner. But I can't stay over tonight. I got a talking to by the warden this morning."

"Fair enough. But remember, he needs you more than you need him. And none of us are prisoners under sentence anymore. Besides, we wouldn't want your girlfriend to get the wrong idea."

In the kitchen we unpack my tray and I notice them eyeing my food.

"You ate right? They said your food had already been sent."

They're quiet and I can tell that something's wrong.

"What's the matter?"

"The garbage they sent us was inedible. Vince was actually apologetic. He said the budget's been tightened up, there's not enough to go around. So, the priority was to the field workers."

I'm hit with a kind of anger I haven't experienced before.

"Calm down, sonny boy. Some things are what they are. But if you're willing to share, we'll take some."

"Divide it three ways. Give me the smallest one."

They just stare at me.

I put out my hands, indicating everything on the table.

"We're either in this together, or we're not."

Norah, usually the quiet one, speaks up.

"You're too good to us, sweet boy."

...

Now that the immediate food crisis has been dealt with, we get down to the things I want to talk about tonight.

"I did some research. The Confederation did determine that the aliens were attempting to create a contagion that would rip through humanity, turning us into creatures more like them. They targeted a handful of human genes to replace with alien genes and developed a vector for each one..."

"What's a vector?"

"It's the mechanism that identifies the gene to be replaced. If you want to replace a gene, you need a.) a vector that can find the gene you want to remove, and b.) the new gene you want to install in its place."

"That can be done?" Norah seems flabbergasted that such a thing could be possible.

"Humans learned to do this back in the first age. The idea is tricky, and most of the early techniques for doing it came with a lot of risk. But yes, it can be done."

"And the aliens tried to do that to us?"

"They tried and had some success. Given more time, they might have done what they set out to do. Instead, they made a big mess that killed all the people on their test planet.

"But back to what they did. Human viruses are the easiest vectors to make for modifying the human genome. Why? The virus already knows how to get into your cells and hijack their metabolic processes.

"As I was saying earlier, they chose a virus that could also reproduce in the human system. So, they could release this thing, it would spread, then slowly it would start changing people. Where they may have overshot was trying to modify more than one gene.

"Anyway, when they released the viruses on Doffenplod, many people started developing scales on their bodies. Others started experiencing changes in their digestive system. Then the whole thing mutated, and people started developing scales in their small intestine. It's painful, very fatal, and spreads like wildfire.

"The Confederation isolated, then quarantined, Doffenplod. The quarantine held for 7,000 years. Then, a couple years ago, some historians got the Confederation to lift the quarantine, arguing that no human disease could last 7,000 years on a planet where there are no humans.

"Apparently, they were wrong and brought the disease back with them. And as you said, it's here. Emily is at the point where she has scales growing in her small intestine."

"How do you know that?"

"I accidently overheard one of the doctors puzzling about Keratin formations in her small intestine. Keratin is what fingernails are made from."

"Sounds terrible," Norah mutters.

There's silence for several seconds, then Ethel calls my name.

"Jared?"

I look at her.

"You've never asked about our gloves."

I have no idea where this is going, but what's new?

"No, I haven't."

She starts to take one off. "They're not a fashion statement."

I'm completely befuddled, waiting for the punch line.

The glove is off now, but she's covering the ungloved hand with the other. She seems hesitant to continue. Then smiles and holds out her hand.

"Our daily meds do this."

I stare in astonishment at her hand. She has no fingernails.

She smiles at me. "We may already have the cure."

"What exactly are you taking?"

She gives me a funny look.

"There's a supplement that we make from four of the components. Sometimes we'll add a fifth. We put a dollop of it in raw cane juice. This much supplement." She holds up the little finger on her right hand and uses her left hand to indicate the amount. "Most days Norah takes a little less."

"And what's in the supplement?"

The two ladies look at each other. Norah gives a nod.

Ethel stands. "Probably easier if we show you. You're sworn to secrecy, right?"

"I'm in this with you."

It wasn't exactly a direct answer. She looks at me a bit, then says come on. She leads the way to what looks like a linen closet, then opens the door. It is a linen closet. She grabs a stack of towels and hands them to me.

"Put them on the table." She indicates the table behind me.

The process repeats until two racks are clear, then she removes the thin wooden racks. Behind it, I see that the wall is cut. The seam in the wall had been perfectly hidden by the wooden racks and towels. She gently lifts the piece of wall out, revealing two small stills that had been hidden behind it.

The one on top has five vessels. The one on the bottom has six. The middle pots are labeled 1, 2, 3 on the top; 1, 2, 3, 4 on the bottom.

"Raw venom and water goes in the pot on the left. The components come out in the middle pots. Excess water from the distillation and any residuals from the venom go in the pot on the right.

"It's not in use at the moment, so let me cover it back up. Then I'll show you more."

We rebuild the closet and stack the towels just right, then we head for the kitchen. She opens a cabinet door. Right in front is a blue liquid medicine bottle with an eyedropper lid.

She pulls it out and sets it on the counter, then proceeds to take the shelf out, revealing another hidden compartment. In it are seven more blue bottles with eyedropper tops. Each bottle is labeled, as is its top. The labels are T1 to T3 and V1 to V4. She starts with the bottle on the left, T1.

"This one induces the visions, this one is calming, then blood thinning." She points to V1. "Then, clotting, stimulant, numbing, and feel good."

"Feel good?"

"Yeah, makes you feel good."

"And what's in the supplement?"

"One part each of calming, blood thinning, and stimulant, plus two parts feel good. And, if one of us is sick, one-part numbing."

"How many toads or vipers per batch?"

"One good milking of each."

"And how long does that last?"

"A month."

I ponder what I've just learned.

Ethel looks at me closely. "What are you thinking?"

I smile. She doesn't have enough context to know in this case.

"Cute," she chides, then starts putting her cabinet back together When she's done, we head back to the living room.

"If we're going to offer this to others, we're going to need a serious milking operation."

That apparently isn't something either of the ladies had thought about before.

"And a bigger still," Norah mutters.

I'd been thinking that finding a solution was going to be the problem. Now it appears that ramping up volume will be.

"How much venom is it viable to milk in a day?"

The ladies look at each other and hold the stare for a while. Ethel breaks first, and Norah says, "It doesn't take all that long. But every time we do it, it seems like it's going to be the last. These are dangerous creatures to be handling."

"Do you think you could recruit others? Any time I do anything interesting, my blood pressure alarm goes off."

We sit in silence for a moment, then I ask, "Emily is on her last legs. Do we make the attempt? Lenna is also in trouble. What about her? Then there's me and..." I decide not to go there.

"You're making a big ask of two retired women over 100 years old. We've already shared our secrets, surely there are others who can step up to be trained. It's not that hard. But it is the domain of younger people with faster reaction times."

I have so many questions. How are we going to get the venom? Where can we put the stills? How do we deal with the legal issues? Can we get real doctors to try this?

I'm worried. We think we have a cure. But at the moment I don't know how to get it to enough people to matter.

"Sweet boy?"

Norah's voice brings me back to the moment. I look up into her eyes.

"We have faith in you. Tell us what to do."

I look up and ponder the words for a moment.

"Write out your procedures. How do you milk a toad? How do you milk a viper? What are the still settings? What are the recipes for the various therapies you use?

"Tomorrow, I'll start the process of making this all legal. But I'll need the technical details if we're going to make it work."

Ethel smiles. "We'll do our best."

She starts to get up. "I was hoping you might go flying with us tonight, but..." She points to the clock. "We don't want you getting in trouble."

...

It's late, but not that late. As I ride back, I start making a list. But the only thing I'll do yet tonight is message Audrey, asking if it's possible for us to talk or meet tomorrow.

CHAPTER 12: CRISIS

I'm up early. Checking messages, I see that Audrey hasn't replied yet. It was a long shot, but I'm still hopeful. I take off for the staff café, pondering my To Do list. I want to make progress on something before dinner with Summer tonight.

I think the top three items are acquiring a still of appropriate size, finding space where we can operate it, and forming a company with the proper licenses.

Audrey can set up the company and sort out the licenses. She can probably help with facilities as well, but I'm the one who needs to figure out how big a still we need, and how much space we'll need to operate a still that large.

The still Ethel and Norah use makes enough medication for 2 people for a month. If I want to cover everyone at the camp, a little less than 1,000 people, then I'd need 500 times the capacity. We'd also need to milk 500 toads and 500 vipers, which seems daunting. If I wanted to cover everyone on Jaredaan, then I'd need 18 times that number. Two thoughts go through my mind as I open the door to enter the café. Even if I can save everyone on Jaredaan, we'll all still die because the Confederation will die. If I'm going to save the Confederation, then I'm going to need a synthetic solution. Our planet does not hold enough vipers and toads to treat a significant number of people.

"Hi, Jared." The voice pulls me out of my thoughts.

"Hi, Lenna." Lenna is the evening chef, but she's not here working, just having breakfast. She's looking at me intently enough that I realize I need to stop.

"Could I have a few minutes of your time?"

I didn't come here to socialize, just to get some food to go. But it would be rude not to talk with her.

"Let me grab some breakfast and I'll come sit with you."

"Thanks." I head over to the counter to place an order, worried about what she wants to talk about.

A few minutes later, the order has been placed and I'm seated across from Lenna. They'll bring my breakfast out when it's ready.

"So, how are you doing? I heard you were sick."

She smiles. "I heard you had a close call."

"I did. It turned out to be a previously undiagnosed complication from an old injury. It was close, but I'm on a good track now.

"Have you recovered from whatever was bothering you?" I want to steer this discussion back toward her. The ladies say she has it.

She looks at me a moment, hesitant to say anything.

"How much do you know about it?"

"Your illness?" I'm still worried about her reason for asking to talk with me.

"The doctors don't know anything about it, but rumors are circulating that you do. What do you know?"

"OK, if I ask you about your symptoms? I'm not a doctor, but I have been doing some research into a disease that's spreading through the broader Confederation."

"It started as mild stomach upset for a couple days, then went away for a month or so. Then it repeats, each time worse. The last couple times there was blood. I'm scared."

I nod my head. "It's happening throughout the Confederation."

"Does anyone know what it is?"

This is dangerous territory. I'm not a doctor. I'm not qualified to diagnose her. I have no real data to support our belief that we have a cure.

"I've not found anything on the exo-net, which is mysteriously quiet about it." I want to say more but am afraid to.

"I can tell you know more, Jared."

"I think I know more. But I'm not a doctor. It's one thing for me to research and speculate. It's a much different thing for me to advise a patient."

"The doctors are telling me it's terminal. They say I have keratin formations growing in my small intestine. That's causing the bleeding, which will continue getting worst until it overtakes me. They say I only have a few more months." There's a sob. "I don't even know what keratin is!"

Her outburst is heard by several people.

She looks at me and knows immediately that I do.

"You know what this is don't you!"

More people turn to look at us.

"I think I may have something that'll help."

"What is it?"

"A supplement extracted from natural ingredients. Think of it as an herbal drink. I take it, so I know it's safe. What I don't know is whether it will do anything for you."

"How does it help?"

"It breaks up keratin formations."

"I'll try it. I'm dead anyway, so might as well try."

"You've got to promise not to tell the doctors. I could get in a lot of trouble for suggesting that my supplement might help you. Technically, it's against the law."

"I won't. I promise."

"OK."

"How soon can I get some? The next cycle is going to start in another couple days."

"I don't have any at the moment. I'll bring some to you as soon as I can."

...

As I walk back to my apartment, I worry that I've really screwed up. I don't have any of the ladies' supplement. They've implied they'll share some, but I don't have a firm commitment on that. I'll run over at 11:00, maybe take them their lunch.

Turning my attention to the still problem, I start searching the exo-net for options. There's actually a used still available in Heroldstown. But its gigantic and doesn't have all the vessels we need, so I start looking off world. Within an hour, I find a company that can make exactly what we want and can get it here in 7 weeks if I expedite.

I fill out and save the ordering information. If I push this button, 112,000 credits will be sucked out of my bank account. I'm more than willing to commit that much. I can afford it. But I need a delivery address in order to complete the order.

I checked my bank account earlier. It has over 700,000 credits. I also checked my Jungle account. My unpaid balance there is over 200,000 credits. They are also anxious to get approval to start shipping the new product. Hopefully, I can give them that go ahead on Monday.

But for now, I'm going to hold off on ordering the still until I have a lead on the real estate.

The real estate search doesn't go as well. It must be because we're a small world. I can find commercial real estate on most of the core worlds, but on Jaredaan, nothing.

My communicator sounds. It's Audrey!

"Hi Audrey, thanks for calling me."

"Your message was cryptic enough to pique my curiosity. What can I help you with?"

"A long list of things. The first is that I want to start a company."

"Really?" She exclaims with some surprise.

It puzzles me that she's surprised. I'm about to become the planet's first Jungle millionaire.

"What's this company going to do?"

"It'll make natural supplements."

"What?"

"New hobby. I've done a lot of research and think I have something people will buy. I actually expect demand to far outstrip capacity. But, back to the immediate need. I'd like to get the relevant incorporation documents, whatever licensing I need to sell supplements, and a building for my manufacturing plant."

"You realize that this is going to cost several thousand credits, right? And the producer license will be on the order of 1,000 credits, plus a comparable amount for a distribution license fee for every planet you want to sell to."

"Really?" This surprises me. "I don't have anything like that for my Jungle products."

"They cover that under licenses they already have."

"How long do these things take to get?"

"I can have your incorporation documents in two weeks. I'll need to check on the licenses."

"Can you help me with the manufacturing plant?"

"I can handle the legal aspects, but you'll need to work with a broker. I'll send a reference.

"I'll also send my incorporation questionnaire and an estimate. As this work is technically for the corporation, the corporation will need to pay the legal fees. I can't take it out of your personal retainer."

"Understood. Thanks for talking with me on a Saturday, Audrey."

CABIN 007

I got to the kitchen early enough to grab the delivery for Cabin 007. When I saw what they were going to send, I complained. Alex heard me out and begrudgingly upped the offering a bit, but he complained that they weren't getting enough food to feed everyone as well as they had before. This is an issue I need to investigate. I suspect there's more to it than what he knows.

When I get to the cabin, I pop out of my cart quickly, trays in hand, and run up to their door. I think that this is the first time I've made it all the way to the door without someone coming out. I stand there a bit, but no one comes. So, I knock. Still, no answer. Now I'm worried. I'm thinking about going in uninvited, when I hear some stomping around in the side yard. A moment later, I see Ethel coming around toward the front carrying a viper. Norah is right behind. She's carrying a small wooden box with a cover over it.

"Hey, sonny boy. You're back earlier than I would have thought."

I'm shocked by the sight of these two coming out of the yard, and of Ethel carrying a snake, its head in some sort of clamp.

"It's Milking Day. Want to help?"

I want to say no way, but a "Sure," slips out instead.

Norah sets her box on the floor, then goes over to open the door. She says, "Toads," as she passes me. She goes in first, Ethel carrying the viper follows. It's obviously unhappy.

"Wait there, sunny boy."

I can see the cloth cover over the wooden box starting to dance around. The toads appear to be attempting an escape. I also hear noises in the cabin. A moment later, Norah is back. She picks up the box, then heads in.

"Come in, shut the door, and put the food on the table in the sitting room." The orders are issued tersely.

I do as I'm told and, once I get the food on the table, I enter the kitchen to the most bizarre sight. Ethel is holding her viper in her right hand, a glass cup in her left. The viper's fangs are in the cup and it's pumped out a couple tablespoons of venom. Norah is guiding its body down into some ice water, and its thrashing like crazy.

"Sonny boy! Help Norah. I'm about to lose my grip!"

I run over, grab the part of the viper that's thrashing, and help the two lower it into the ice water. Within moments the snake goes limp.

"It's cold blooded. Cool it off and it shuts down. Drop it in a hot box and it warms up."

"Safe now." Norah cuts in as tersely as usual.

Ethel puts the glass with the venom on the table.

"Help me, sonny boy. It's limp now. But we only have a minute or two to warm him up or we're going to lose him."

She coaches me where to grab the snake. She still has a firm grip on its head, but I've got most of the weight. We walk together over to the wall adjacent to the side yard where I saw them earlier. There's a

146

chute of some sort, covered by a piece of wood that's locked over top. There's a pitcher of water sitting on a table next to it.

"OK. This is the drill. You grab the pitcher of water."

I do as I'm told.

"I'm going to open the hatch on the count of three. You're going to pour the entire pitcher of water down the pipe, then we drop the snake in."

As she speaks, I feel the dreaded snake twitch.

"Ready?"

I nod.

"OK. Here we go. 3, 2, 1..." She opens the hatch and screams, "Pour!"

I pour, and hear stuff getting washed down as she guides the snake's tail into the pipe.

"OK, let go of the snake."

I let go and she drives the snake down, letting go and withdrawing her hand quickly as the snake disappears down the tube.

Ethel slams the hatch down, then buckles it up.

"That was close."

The statement puzzles me. "How so?"

She shakes her head.

"It had already started twitching. If its body is twitching, then its mouth is ready to bite."

"They can move that fast?"

She shakes her head. "Jared, dear boy, its body is always way slower than its head."

I'm feeling a bit chided, but at least I'm a 'dear boy' now, not just a 'sonny boy.'

"Come on." She indicates the kitchen. "The hard part is done, now comes the disgusting part."

We enter the kitchen and I see four small pitchers of water lined up next to a pot.

"There are four post-juvenile toads in the box. They're the perfect size for milking. Each will put off a half teaspoon of yellowish foam when its assaulted. The foam comes out right behind their eyes.

"One by one, I'm going to grab and smack them. When the foam is at the right level, I'll place the toad over the pot. When I put it over the pot, slowly pour the water over the toad's head, washing the foam into the pot. Ready?"

I grab the first pitcher, noticing that Norah's wearing rubber gloves, not her normal white cloth ones. "Ready."

She lifts the cloth over the box and grabs the first toad. Its body is 10, maybe 12, centimeters long, the legs equally long. Her technique is interesting. Her hand approaches from behind. I'm not sure if it can see her coming, but it doesn't twitch until she touches it. At that point the toad jumps, but it doesn't move all that fast. Norah grabs the toad as it starts to jump, thumb and index finger around its waist, the now-extended legs in her other hand. Her grip is strong, and she caught it in a very vulnerable position with its legs extended and unable to attempt another jump.

The toad hisses at her, the sound so unexpected that I jump.

In a very smooth motion, she rotates her hand backward, smacking the back of the toad's head on the table. The hissing stops as the toad starts swelling up and yellowish bubbly liquid starts coming out of glands behind its eyes.

Norah expertly positions the toad over the pot, head and belly down, feet and back up. "Pour slowly, but I want the pitcher empty in 10, 9, 8, 7, 6.... Faster... 3, 2, 1."

I feel like I've just water-boarded a toad.

With lightning speed, Norah puts the toad back in the box, and grabs another. She has the second toad over the pot before I have the second pitcher ready to pour.

"Speed it up a bit, Jared."

The way she says that reminds me of my Mom, who for the most part only called me Jared if I was in trouble.

With two toads milked and the third starting to foam, the smell finally hits me. I struggle not to retch.

"Told you this was the disgusting part." Ethel cackles behind me.

...

As Norah returns the toads to the side yard, I collapse into my normal chair. It feels like I've been struggling with wild animals for hours, but a quick glance at my chronometer suggests that it was more like 10 minutes.

Norah comes back in, sets the box by the door, then comes in to sit across from me.

"Good job."

"Did we get what we needed?"

148

She smiles. "Yes. We have about 2 liters of diluted viper venom and 2 liters of diluted toad venom. We'll let it sit for an hour to ripen a bit, then put it in the still."

"And you do this once a month?"

"Did. We're starting to ramp up. With the equipment we have, we're hoping to get up to 10 batches a month. That will give us enough to get you and several others on our daily regimen."

"What about people who already have it, like Emily and Lenna?"

"That's a more difficult discussion."

I'm deflated by her words.

"Why?"

"It took a long time for us to lose our nails. Longer than the duration of the illness implied by the obituaries we've read. If our supply is limited, then we should probably allocate it to the ones it might actually protect."

I see the logic in Norah's comment, but don't like it. I also think it misses an important point.

"At one level, I agree with you. But I think there's a problem with that reasoning. We don't really know if your supplement can cure or only protect against the disease. The only way we will know is if we can cure someone."

"You want to give this to Emily and Lenna, don't you?"

"Yes. I spoke with Lenna this morning. She's between cycles but expects the next cycle to start in a couple days. She's at the stage where she's bleeding. She says the doctors think she'll only last a few more cycles."

"Poor girl."

The sympathy and sadness in Norah's voice are unambiguous.

Ethel, apparently finished with her clean up, comes into the room.

"You two don't look very cheery."

"Lenna thinks she's near the end," Norah replies with no preamble.

Ethel looks at me.

"You want to try it on her?"

I'm always impressed by how much Ethel can read into a situation and the speed with which she does it.

"We think your supplement will prevent or cure this disease, but we don't know that for sure. If we can heal Lenna, or even slow the disease progression, then we will know."

Ethel stares at me for a bit.

"You're right of course. Until we've healed someone, all we have is speculation."

"And enough belief to try," I add on.

She nods her head in agreement.

"Have you looked into getting us a larger still?"

"Yes. I found a beauty that we can have in seven weeks if I can find a place to put it. I'm looking for real estate on the west side of town."

"How will you get the venom there?"

"Haven't thought about that yet."

"What do you think the warden will say about you taking truckloads of cans out of the camp?"

"Haven't thought about that either."

"It seems you have some thinking to do. But back to Lenna, will she take the supplement if we give it to her?"

"Yes, she's desperate for an option."

"And you? Will you take it?"

"Yes. Would I need your blood pressure treatment also?"

"No, I don't think so."

"Any chance you could give me some to take back today?"

She smiles. "Let me go get you some."

STAFF CAFÉ

Before I headed back, Ethel gave me a bottle of her supplement. She suggested that I take one teaspoon a day, mixed with sugar or cane juice, so I could hold it in my mouth for 30 seconds or more.

She suggested that I do the same for Lenna, slowly increasing to a tablespoon a day if she tolerated the supplement.

I actually had some cane juice in my apartment, so took my dose, then mixed one for Lenna. Her shift started two hours ago, so I'm back hoping to give her a dose.

I inquire at the counter and one of the workers takes me back into the kitchen, where I see Lenna sitting, not looking so well.

She looks up as we come in and she nods to the person that escorted me back. Once we're alone, she whispers, "It's starting again."

I pull out a little jar that has her dose.

"No guarantees this will work for you, but you're welcome to have it."

She takes the jar. "Thanks."

"This is one dose dissolved in cane juice. The supplement itself tastes terrible, which is why I added the cane juice. You could take it with sugar if that would work better for you.

"One important thing... You need to hold the supplement in your mouth about 30 seconds. The active ingredients absorb into your tongue and gums quickly. It breaks down in your stomach, so not much of what you swallow will help.

"I'm on one dose a day as a preventive. I could feel that first dose starting to take effect while it was still in my mouth. So, wait for it."

She nods her head in understanding.

"Want to try it now?"

She unscrews the cap and takes a sniff.

"Ugh. Smells nasty."

She stares at it for a moment, then pours it into her mouth.

I start the timer feature on my communicator and hold it up for her to see.

"You might get a little more kick out of it if you swish it around a bit."

She swishes and I can see the disgust on her face. After a few more seconds, the timer beeps, and she swallows.

"Oh my god, that stuff is awful."

She grabs her glass of water and takes a large gulp.

"Did you feel it at all?"

She smiles. "Yes. Yes, I did."

"I think you need more than one dose a day. Message me in the morning. If you've tolerated this OK, we can do another in the morning. And if, after a couple days, you're tolerating two doses a day, we can increase to three."

"Thank you, Jared. I know this may not work, but at least it gives me hope. I'll message you in the morning."

DATE

I show up at the warden's home a few minutes before 7:00 p.m. It's the first time I've been here and, in truth, it's a bit intimidating. I knock and a few seconds later, I hear someone coming.

The door opens and there's Summer, in tight jeans and a pale-yellow blouse that accentuates her figure. Wow.

"Hi Jared, come in. Dinner's almost ready."

As I step into the house, I'm overwhelmed by a delicious aroma that's vaguely familiar.

"Smells wonderful."

She leads me to the kitchen, which has already been cleaned up.

"I made you my Dad's favorite. Men all seem to like it."

I'm a bit worried about being compared to her father, but this smells like it might be my new favorite meal.

"What did you make?"

"Braised ribs with root vegetables and greens."

I think my mother may have made something like this once, but I've never smelled anything this good before.

"Sounds good. You're very tidy." I indicate the clean kitchen.

"That's one of the things I like about this dish. It's relatively quick to prep, then bakes for a couple hours, which gives time to clean up before dinner."

"Oh, I brought this for you."

It's a fancy flower, the name of which I can never remember. Ethel cut one for me and told me to give it to her.

"Hibiscus! They're so beautiful. Thank you."

She puts it behind her ear, then kisses me on the cheek.

The kiss shoots through me like an electric shock. I'm so in love with this girl.

We decide to eat in the sitting area of the kitchen, and I'm instructed how to set the table. As the youngest in a large family, I've set a lot of tables. But I'm actually enjoying setting this one.

We chit-chat as the table is set and the food is brought out. When we finally sit, she puts her hand over mine.

"Thanks for coming over."

"Thank you for inviting me."

I sound so sappy.

She dishes up my plate then instructs me on which items to taste first. I don't think I've ever been this doted over.

We eat in silence for a moment, then I ask, "Does your father go out of town often?"

"No, it's been years since he's left the camp. But there's a special meeting of the planet's elders this week. Apparently, there's a crisis of some sort. As one of the planet's senior government officials he was invited to join."

"Did he give you any clues about what's going on?"

"Not directly. I know there's a crisis going on up in Jaredstown. There's also some issue with incoming shipments. From what I understand, we've missed the last two supplemental food shipments, which is putting a squeeze on the camp and probably putting an even bigger squeeze on Jaredstown."

I fear that this is dire news. There's a lot we need to do before we become self-sufficient, if we ever can.

I'm sufficiently lost in thought that Summer prompts me.

"So, what are you up to these days? Are you fully recovered yet? Dad mentioned that he talked to you yesterday."

So much has happened in the last 24 hours that it's hard to believe it was only yesterday I spoke with the warden.

"I tried doing a full day on Monday. That proved to be too much. Dr. Avery gave me a real dressing down about it. So, I took the next couple days off as instructed, then did some light duty on Friday, including seeing your father."

She looks at me with big eyes. "Jared, please take care of yourself."

I don't think of myself as being that weak, but the evidence against me on that point is undeniable. I was always a book worm, never a body builder. My brothers exploited it, as did the thugs in jail the night I arrived in Heroldstown.

I meet her eyes sheepishly.

"I'm doing better and learning to self-monitor. I've also started taking a dietary supplement that's helping."

She smiles at me. And once again, I'm entranced by her eyes.

"So why are you spending so much time at Cabin 007? They're both really old."

For the first time I sense a coldness in Summer that I don't like. She can apparently read my concern.

"Sorry, that came out wrong. But I'm still curious. Most young men don't voluntarily spend this much time with old women."

I sense curiosity, not condemnation.

"Do you know how old they are?"

Seeing no response, I blurt out, "They're both over 100. They've seen things, they know things, and they're incredibly interesting people."

We're both 17, about to turn 18. But my comment about the old women being interesting seems to have landed wrong. So, I try a different tack.

"Did you get to know your grandparents?"

The question seems to take her off guard.

"I didn't. I was the sixth child. My paternal grandmother was still alive when I was born. My earliest memories are of her. But she passed before I was old enough to actually know her. Ethel and Norah are the closest thing I have to a grandmother.

I see my words have landed.

"No," she whispers. "They were gone before I was born. My parents were both the youngest children."

We sit in silence a moment, then Summer breaks it.

"Would you take me to go see them?"

I can feel a smile bloom and see Summer's response.

"Fair warning. They can be a bit cantankerous. Ethel calls me 'sonny boy.' Norah sometimes calls me 'sweet boy' if I've done something right. I'm only Jared when I screw up."

Summer snickers. "Sounds like fun."

The small talk continues for a while, then Summer gets up to clear the dishes. I carry my stuff in, then make a second trip back for the serving dishes while she washes. The scene is completely domestic. And I love it.

I dry as she washes and when the last of the dishes are done, she says, "Thanks for coming over. I really enjoyed the company."

I'm a bit crushed, I was hoping she'd ask me to stay. When we get to the door, I ask, "My place, tomorrow? I'll cook."

"Thanks, that would be nice."

I go to give her a hug and kiss on the cheek, but somewhere along the way, lips meet, and I'm totally electrified. It breaks quickly and she says, "Good night."

STAFF CAFÉ

I'm up early. I take my daily dose of supplement, then prepare one for Lenna and head over to the café.

I see Lenna in the same seat she was in yesterday morning. Maybe it's my optimism but she seems better somehow. I approach and take the seat opposite her.

"How did it go last night?"

"No negative side effects that I noticed. Last night, I was feeling more of the queasiness of onset than I am this morning."

"I have another dose, if you'd like to have it."

"Please."

I pull out the jar and push it across the table.

"Remember to hold it in your mouth for at least 30 seconds."

I set up my timer, as she takes the dose.

She's taking it a bit differently today. More vigorous swishing. Less scrunched up face. And she holds well past 30 seconds before swallowing. Then she takes a big gulp of whatever it is she's drinking.

"It didn't taste as bad today. Did you change it somehow?"

Her statement sets me thinking for a second. I didn't think it tasted as bad this morning either.

"I measured out exactly the same amount of supplement. I just eyeballed the cane juice. Maybe there was more of it."

I notice her seeming to relax.

"Are you OK?"

"Great. I can feel it working."

I continue watching her. She seems to relax more, and I'm worried I've drugged her somehow. But after a few seconds, she pops up.

"I'm actually getting hungry. You want something?"

"Sure." I get up to go with her. I plan to buy. In the presence of Lenna, a parolee on assistance, I'm increasingly self-conscious about the fact that I'm functionally a Jungle millionaire.

When we get back with our food, we sit and talk. Lenna has always been nice to me, but I've thought of her more as an acquaintance than friend. We're in such different stages of life that I wouldn't have thought we'd enjoy each other's company.

She seems to be on a roll this morning. She gives me an update on Emily. So much for restrictions on staff talking among themselves about prisoner medical issues. But maybe Lenna's telling me this because she thinks I have a need to know. It seems that Lenna's illness had progressed faster than Emily's. Lenna's symptoms started a month or two after Emily's did, but it seemed to be moving faster.

John, a kitchen worker in Zone 9, who I haven't met, was just diagnosed this week. It worries me that our camp now has three cases, all of which are among kitchen staff. If I'm right, this is communicable, and the kitchen is the perfect place for a communicable disease to be spread.

She also tells me about the food shortage. Inbound shipments from off world have ground to a halt. On paper, Jaredaan produces enough food to feed itself. But given waste and the way we're spread out, the backstop has always been imported dry bulk: pasta, rice, and the like. According to Lenna, we only have 30ish days of dry bulk left, at which point, real trouble will set in.

If nothing else, I was right about one thing... I'd be totally screwed if I'd let all my Jungle royalties be converted into local credits. At this point I may have more Confederation credits than any other entity on the planet.

JUNGLE

My first task once home is to check the new product test that I've been running. According to the monitors, the unit has been running for 40 hours now. The load is steady at 110% of nominal. Voltage is holding at 110%. Remaining power is 67%, a little higher than I would have expected. That could mean one of two things. The actual capacity of this unit is higher than the design spec, which would be good. Or, the battery level meter is not reading correctly, which would be bad. By this time tomorrow, I'll have a better idea about which it is.

Next, I log into my Jungle account. Sales of my current products are up. I respond to several messages from the New Products team. The first confirms my intent to complete testing in the next 48 hours. The second is to accept a promotion offer costing 25,000 credits. It will begin the day the product is released, tentatively Friday. Their demand forecast is up to 150,000 units a month. At 2 credits a unit, I will be looking at over a million credits over the next four months. Crazy.

Since I'm online, I start looking at various products I might need going forward. An item catches my eye, a bottling machine. It can support liquid bottling operations for a variety of bottle types and sizes. It even has an optional labeling station. I fill out the forms for a configuration that seems appropriate, it can form 150- and 450-ml plastic bottles from bulk pellets, fill and cap up to 1,000 bottles per shift, with a labeling system that can print and attach labels.

The price quoted is 125,000 credits for the machinery, plus a delivery charge of 25,000 credits, plus another 20,000 credits for the recommended initial load of bulk pellets. Looking at the site requirements, I can tell that this is going to be expensive and, of course, there are no authorized installers on Jaredaan.

Changing gears, I look for food supplies. It takes a while to find bulk dry goods that are actually bulk. I find a supplier that will ship to Jaredaan, so put together an order for 1,000 kg of pasta, 10,000 kg of rice, and 1,000 kg each of dried corn, beans, onions, and carrots. The items themselves come to 75,000 credits. Then the shock. No shipping available.

Wondering if this is a bulk issue or a shipping issue, I try creating and order for a 10 kg package of linguine. The product comes in at 47 credits, which isn't so bad. But expedited shipping is quoted at 100 credits with a minimum shipment time of three months.

Worried that something has gone terribly wrong with shipping in the Confederation, I check the shipping to New London and get the same answer. Then to Caladon. Same price, delivery in 14 days. Trying Jaredaan again, I get the same result as before, only this time I notice a link to shipping details. Tracking that down, I get my next shock. All shipments to Jaredaan are on hold until the quarantine is lifted.

After another hour of searching, I finally find a press release from the Confederation Health Ministry.

Today, Health Minister, Ingrid Bjorn, adds Jaredaan to the list of planets quarantined following confirmed cases of the Doffenplod Acquired Genetic-disorder Syndrome (DAGS). All shipments from, as well as all travel to or from, this system is banned until a cure or vaccine can be found for the disease.

Now that I have a name for the disease, I look it up.

Doffenplod Acquired Genetic-disorder Syndrome, known as DAGS, is a virus-born mutagenic pathogen that targets human Microfold cells (M-cell) found in the small intestine. In normal cells, the virus simply replicates, spreading through, then out of, the body. In M-cells, the virus cannot replicate. Instead, a portion of the virus' genetic material is inserted into the cell's main DNA sequence. The modified cells cease functioning as part of the human immune system, and instead become matrix cells for the production of keratin-based scales. The scales stop nutrient absorption in the small intestine, leading to weight loss and fatigue. Eventually, they grow large enough to cut surrounding tissue, resulting in blood volume loss, anemia, and ultimately death.

The disease is highly contagious and has a 100% mortality rate. There are no known survivors of this disease. It can be spread by ingestion or fluid exchange. No confirmed cases of air-borne transmission have been found. The disease is believed to be an engineered bioweapon created by the aliens at the end of the Great Alien War.

I stare at the page, lost in shock. We're too late. It's here. Our sanitary procedures were insufficient. It is being spread through our food.

An uncontrolled barrage of thoughts floods my mind. At the top of the list is the pending food shortage. I'm sure there must be a procedure for emergency supply delivery. That must be what the Elder's meeting is about. But even if there is, other things like medical supplies and medicine will go on allocation and I doubt the camp will be a priority recipient. Things are going to get bad here quickly. I need to start working a plan.

I'll start by researching emergency supply deliveries. There must be a way. Amazingly, I find the law concerning quarantines, and the section regarding quarantine boycotts. Deliveries are permissible, but the space craft making the delivery cannot enter the atmosphere. There's a link to a long list of planets and the standoff distances. Amazingly Jaredaan is listed. The stand-off is 1,000 km. Any space craft coming closer will be forbidden from returning. This exclusion is from the planet, as well as any space stations or ships.

There are two acceptable delivery methods. The first is to leave the package in space. It must be equipped with a transponder. And the receiver must accept delivery before the package is left.

The second method is much more expensive. An automated reentry vehicle can make delivery, but it must remain on the planet under quarantine.

There is even a table of allowable shipping rates. A quick scan shows that the minimum delivery fee is 100,000 credits for a 10,000 kg package, not to exceed 10 cubic meters. That means for food stuffs the order needs to be large and the shipping costs will be three or more times the cost of the goods. Prices from there increase at about 2,500 credits per 1,000 kg.

Maybe I can piggyback my shipment on whatever the planetary government is going to do. It would lower their costs. I wonder if the elders would be open to such a deal.

DINNER

I need to see the ladies and Summer wants to meet them. So, we change up tonight's dinner plans. Instead of me cooking, we're going to pick up four meals at the staff café and take them to Ethel and Norah's cabin. It also gives me the opportunity to bring another dose to Lenna.

We enter the café and are greeted by one of the people at the counter. I've spoken with her before, but don't actually know her name.

"Hi, Summer, are you and Jared going to be eating with us this afternoon?"

"Martha, good to see you." Summer snuggles up to me possessively as if I belong to her. In truth, I do, and apparently, she knows it. "We're just picking up some food for dinner."

Martha turns to me. "Hi, Jared, Lenna would like to see you for a minute if you have the time."

"Thanks, Martha. OK if we order? Then I'll go back."

Order placed, I mosey back into the kitchen. I'm sure I'm going to be cross examined on the ride over to the ladies' cabin.

Lenna is up and active, which is a good sign.

"You're looking better." I start.

She turns to me. "I am. It's still coming on, but nowhere near as bad as last time. Do you have more for me?"

I smile and pull the little jar out of my pocket.

She opens the jar, takes the liquid, and starts swishing. I don't even need to prompt her. After about a minute, she swallows and takes a drink of water. Then looks at me oddly. "Are you sure you're not changing the formula? It still tastes bad, but I barely notice it."

"I think you must be getting used to it."

"Maybe." She looks at the order that just came in. "This yours?"

I look at the order and think it is. "Yes, for four. We're going to share with some friends."

"Lucky friends. I'll slip something sweet in on the house."

...

Back in the cart, the questioning begins, and I realize that I need to make a decision. Anything I tell Summer that hides the DAGS problem will be a deception. I will eventually be caught, and she will be rightfully angry. I don't want this to come between us. I want her on my side.

Apparently, I'm too slow responding.

"Aren't you going to talk with me about this?" I can hear the disappointment in her voice.

"Sorry. I'm going to tell you all about it, was just trying to figure out where to start."

"Just start with what Lenna wanted to talk with you about."

"She's sick. She has a very scary disease." I pause. I want to ease Summer into the issue, but don't know how. "Did you know?"

"Yes, well no. I know she's been to the hospital a couple times but didn't know it was serious. But why would she want to talk with you about it?"

"My supplement. When I went to the hospital on Tuesday, I overheard one of the doctors talking about her condition. She intercepted me at breakfast yesterday and asked if I know anything about the disease. I tried to deny knowing anything, but I'm not a good enough liar. I think my supplement will help her so offered her some. Technically, it's a food, not a drug. But I'll still get in a lot of trouble if the doctors conclude that I'm trying to treat her."

There's silence for a few seconds, then Summer breaks it.

"I overheard my father talking about a new disease sweeping through the Confederation. Is this what she has?"

"Yes, I think it is. I'm actually certain that it is."

"How can you know that?"

We're getting into very dangerous territory. But I suppose that's the real reason I wanted Summer to come meet the ladies, so maybe it's time to dive in.

"The disease is call DAGS, short for Doffenplod Acquired Genetic-disorder Syndrome. It's a little present left behind by the aliens at the end of the Great Alien War. It killed everyone on the planet. The Confederation has kept Doffenplod under quarantine for over 7,000 years. They recently lifted the quarantine so scientists could go in and study the planet. They brought the disease back home with them. It's now spread to several planets, including Jaredaan. We were recently placed under quarantine. That's the reason for the elders meeting that your father is attending."

"How do you know this?"

"It's on the exo-net. If you look hard enough, you can find it. I've had a feeling that something was wrong, so went searching."

"And you think your supplement will cure it?"

"Not cure, just stop it."

"And why do you think that?"

"The disease is a bioweapon. It's carried by a virus that spreads slowly. Once you are full of the virus it finds its way into your small intestine. There, it triggers a mutation that causes scales to grow. The scales are like fingernails. In fact, I'm sure they are fingernails. My supplement causes your fingernails to fall out."

She looks at my hands. "But you still have fingernails."

"I do; it acts slowly. Ethel and Norah have been on it for years, and they have no fingernails."

We sit silently as we enter Zone 3.

"We're almost there."

160

"We're all going to die, aren't we?"

"That's what I'm trying to stop."

She looks at me angrily. "You're going to stop it?"

The sarcasm in her voice really hurts.

"I'm going to try. It's better than just waiting here for the end to come."

As we enter the swampy area, I see Summer getting nervous.

"Is it safe for us to be here?"

"I've learned how to come here safely. And you'll be safe if you follow my lead and do what I ask you to."

She shivers.

"I think you'll understand by the time we leave tonight. That's why I wanted to bring you here."

...

The ladies are waiting for us when we arrive. They expertly get Summer inside without incident. Norah and I take the food into the kitchen. Ethel takes Summer into the sitting room. The only words I hear as we turn the corner are, "Summer, dear. I've been so looking forward to meeting you."

I smile at the thought of what she's about to experience.

I stash the food while Norah warms the tea.

"I'll bring this in a moment. Why don't you go rescue your girlfriend?"

I come around the corner and can hear Ethel talking. I pause a moment hoping to discern where the conversation has gone.

"Jared is a very special boy. He's very much in love with you if you haven't figured that out yet, which makes you very lucky."

I almost snort at the words, take a second to calm myself then enter.

"I hope you two have had a chance to get acquainted. Norah will be in with some tea in a second."

"Summer tells me that you told her about Lenna. How is she doing?"

"Her next cycle is starting. She's had three doses now and says it's moving slower than before. She knows it might be placebo effect, but it's the most optimistic I've seen her since I met her."

"Summer loves you very much Jared and was worried about you seeing Lenna privately like that. You need to be more open with her."

We both blush. Then I burst out laughing.

"Thank you for the advice Ethel. I'll try to do better."

"Don't try. Do." She says sternly. The line seems vaguely familiar. Norah comes in with the tea.

"Tea anyone? I see we got the introductions out of the way."

Summer squeezes my hand. I think she understands why I like it here, which is good because the night is young.

Over dinner, I share everything I've learned with the ladies. I sense that all doubt has left Summer at this point.

"So, you're thinking we might be able to piggyback the equipment we need on the emergency shipment," Ethel asks.

"I'm sure it could be done and that the elders would be better off for it. What I don't know is whether they will allow it."

"But you know all the elders, don't you?"

"To date, every elder that has served on the board has had a direct blood connection to the founder. At some point in my life, I'd met all the elders on last year's board, and I'm sure they know me. My father was scheduled to rotate on this term, but he died, and I don't know who replaced him."

"Aaron." Summer says.

"Did you have a good relationship with Aaron?" Ethel asks.

"Aaron and my father were the two family members hurt the most by my conviction and sentence. Neither thought I was guilty. But I wouldn't be surprised to find out Aaron holds a grudge because I chose not to return when I was released."

I'm sure Ethel figured out the implications of my answer before I even got it out.

"There might be a different solution." Norah ventures.

All heads turn toward her.

"There's a fellow named Brock Newton in Heroldstown. He's a copper smith. Did some work in Zone 2 last year. He might be able to build a still for you."

"You want to make a still?" Summer seems taken back by the idea.

"That's how we separate the good stuff out of the venom."

"What venom?" She seems shocked.

"Ah, he hasn't told you that part yet."

I get the evil eye from Ethel.

"The viper and toad venom are both complex mixtures of compounds optimized for killing prey or fending off predators. Several of these compounds if taken by themselves in the right quantity have very beneficial effects. For example, toad venom kills by causing hemorrhaging. It does that using a blood thinning compound, another compound that makes you sleepy, another that puts your mind into overdrive and another that is a neurotoxin. We can separate the components out using a still. The neurotoxin has no beneficial use, but the other three do.

"These two developed what I'm calling a natural supplement. It has incredibly beneficial effects but caused their fingernails to fall out."

I can tell Summer isn't buying it.

"Summer, dear," Ethel starts. "How old do you think I am? Guess high."

"Early 70's?"

"You're closer than he was. I am 127 years old, third generation. Norah's a youngster, she's only 114.

"We stopped aging when we discovered the secrets in the toad venom. We started getting younger when we discovered the secrets in the viper venom.

"We haven't been able to optimize the recipe to fight the disease. But we are certain that our basic daily formula will slow or stop disease progression."

She looks down and says quietly, "We've made enough for you to take it too."

"Me?"

Ethel glances at me, and Summer seems to get it.

"Thank you."

In a seeming change of subject, Norah turns to me. "You've learned enough that you need a dose of cognitive enhancer, don't you, sweet boy?"

"Yes."

"I think we could all use a little taste."

As Norah goes to get it, Ethel reaches out to take Summer's hand. "You don't need to do this if you don't want to, dear. But I think you should. It will help you understand. We'll only give you a tiny dose, one that will clear your mind and help bring understanding."

I can tell Summer wants nothing to do with this, and I'm not going to twist her arm. But I hope she gives it a try.

Norah returns with four glasses of liquid. She's poured a full ounce for me, smaller portions for themselves, and a tiny amount that barely covers the bottom of the glass for Summer. There's also a pitcher of water.

"Jared, you first."

I take mine into my mouth and hold it there a second. The alcohol in the mix burns. As I feel it taking effect I swallow. If burns all the way down. I refill my cup with water and guzzle it, then fly out of body into space.

From a distance, I hear Norah say, "Don't worry dear. He'll come back to us soon with all the answers. He's the smartest person on our world without the neuroenhancer. With it, he's the smartest human being alive. Now, take yours so you can understand. It won't hurt you, but I will dilute it for you first."

I return to the room in my enhanced state.

"The first emergency shipment of supplies has arrived. It's in orbit. They're having an issue at the spaceports that makes deorbiting the supplies dangerous. Another round of supplies is on the way. Costs so far have just about depleted the elders' off-world reserves. They may not have enough left to get the parts they need to fix the problem."

Then the ah-ha. "But I do."

I notice Summer, entranced and smiling. She apparently decided to try it. I go zooming off again.

...

I return and see that Summer has also. The ladies still have not taken theirs. Ethel sees that I notice their cups still full.

"We thought it best if we waited for the two of you to return. You found out what you needed to know?"

"Yes." I look at Summer. "How did it go for you?"

She smiles. "I learned what I needed to know."

Her words are uncharacteristically cryptic, but I can tell that I'm not going to get any more.

Ethel stands. "Since you have what you came to get, maybe its best if you go now. We're good on our own."

I stand. "Ethel, Norah, thanks for your hospitality."

Summer echoes my remarks. "Thank you. And thank you for letting me visit."

"Thanks for the meal, sonny boy. There's enough left over for tomorrow, so we won't have to endure whatever slop it is that Vince brings us."

As we exit, the usual menagerie has gathered on and around my cart. We have it cleared in a few seconds, then Summer runs down and jumps in. I follow, waving at my hosts and saying good night.

Once we're on our way Summer asks, "Mind altering drugs, right? You're good with that?"

164

The question surprises me. I hadn't thought about it that way before.

"When you put it like that, I don't like the sound of it at all."

"And there was alcohol in it to. Is there alcohol in your daily dose?"

"No, I don't think so."

"But they obviously have a still."

I don't answer. This conversation seems to be headed someplace I don't want to go.

"You're a camp employee. You're required to report things like this." She says with a bit of exasperation.

"If they were producing alcohol for the purpose of getting drunk, I might. But they are using it for the purpose of saving the camp. The rules need to accommodate that."

"I understand. I'm not accusing you. But my father will eventually find out. I won't be the one that tells him, but he will find out. A lot of people are curious about the amount of time you spend with them.

"And when he does find out, he will throw you out and he will throw them out as well. Before the quarantine, you had the money to get away with anything. But now, your money is useless on this planet. So when he throws you out, you'll starve."

"Is that what you saw?"

She's quiet.

"Is it?" I demand.

"No," she whispers quietly. "I saw something very different."

We drive back the rest of the way in silence. I pull up to her home and she gets out, then sticks her head back in.

"Promise you will take me with you."

Now I know what she saw. "I promise."

...

I'm in bed but can't sleep. There's so much that needs to get done. The camp has become my home. I need to help them become more self-sufficient. Cane juice and camp grown food are the only things I can see helping. I already have authority to start making changes that will increase cane volume and quality. While the warden is gone, I can assume the authority to mandate vegetable gardens in each zone, but I'll need to get that project too far along to cancel before the warden gets back.

On the disease front, I need a still. So I need to connect with Brock Newton. I also need a place to put it, so I need to contact the commercial real estate broker, Audrey recommended. This is going to be a busy week. I hope my daily dose is sufficient to keep me alive until the end of it.

As I start to drift away, I snap wide awake. Summer is right. I will be thrown out of the camp in a week or two. Maybe I can go exploring for a place in the wilderness this weekend. As daunting as that thought is, I finally drift asleep.

CHAPTER 13: QUARANTINE

I wake with focus and urgency. I take my daily dose and prepare one for Lenna, then head off for the staff Café. She isn't there when I arrive, so I order breakfast and set up shop at one of the tables.

The first thing on my docket today is a work process update regarding composting. The directive is simple. Starting immediately, all zones are to prioritize fertilizing their fields and vegetable gardens, over expanding their fields to the south. Specific instructions on appropriate fertilization procedures are included. They're basically the ones Zone 3 has used for years.

This directive was mostly done last week. I had planned to hand deliver it to each of the zones, but instead send it to the supervisors, promising to stop by and see them within three days.

Moments after the directive goes out, my breakfast arrives. Then a minute or two later, Lenna comes in. She doesn't look as good as I was hoping she would. She sits and I put her jar on the table.

She smiles at me. "Thanks."

A moment later she's swishing. I can see her starting to relax before she swallows. She's quiet for a moment. I can see the calm passing over her. "That felt really good." She pauses, exhales, and lets the calm spread some more.

"I was hit with a round of intense queasiness this morning." The statement was made as if it was a confession.

"I'm four days into this cycle now. Last time I went into the hospital on day 3 and was drugged into oblivion for three days. Even if this cycle lingers, it's still moving slower. Giving me more time."

I put my hand over hers. "We'll just take it one day at a time."

I'm encouraged by her words. I think I'm as desperate for it to work as she is. If we end up losing her, it doesn't bode well for the rest of us.

"I'm going to grab some breakfast. You going to hang around? Or do you need to run."

"Sadly, I need to run once I'm finished. I have a lot to do today."

"Good luck. I hope you have a productive day."

OFFICE

Although I haven't used it much, I actually have an office in the main headquarters building. I arrive shortly after reception opens, so stop to flirt with Summer for a minute before heading upstairs.

My next task is a clarification of policy statement regarding gardens. Apparently, the zone supervisors seem to think it's against camp rules for a zone to maintain an herb and vegetable garden. A quick search of the camp rules shows that there is no such rule, but there is a policy on garden operations.

A quick read through the garden operations policy, and the problem is immediately obvious: equipment requirements. *Zones must separate equipment and equipment closets for garden use. Equipment used in the garden cannot be used in the fields.*

A little more research and I find the rationale for this policy. Some years ago, a blight in one of the vegetable gardens spread into a nearby field. Cane production in that field dropped 30% that year. Shared equipment was blamed for the transmission.

I'm a bit skeptical, but realize I have no real expertise in this area, so don't want to challenge the policy. Instead, I start a search for equipment. The first couple calls turn up nothing. Then I hit pay dirt. The nursery at the far end of the lake has the equipment I need. When I ask for 20 sets, the call gets passed 'upstairs' and I end up talking with the owner. After a little back and forth, he asks how long it will be before the Request for Proposal is released. I tell him I have the discretionary funds and would prefer to bypass the usual government processes, if he can do that. After a little more back and forth, he agrees to meet me for lunch at their facility.

I'll pass through Heroldstown on the way to the nursery, so I call the number on file for Brock Newton, the coppersmith Norah mentioned last night. He agrees to meet me at his workshop at 3:00.

According to the guidance system on my communicator, the nursery is 95 km away by road. It puts the travel time at 100 minutes but cautions about possible traffic delays through Heroldstown.

I run down to check the charge on my hovercraft, which at this point I'm thinking of as my truck. It's about half full, which should be enough. But in an abundance of caution, I hook up my charging unit. Satisfied it will have a full charge by the time I need to leave, I head back up to my office to tie up a few loose ends.

WEST LAKE NURSERY

There was virtually no traffic on the trip over, even while passing through Heroldstown. My sense is that the economy here is dying, which may be to my advantage.

I arrive about a half hour early to an empty customer parking lot. But I see other vehicles over in an employee parking area, which is assuring. I go into the retail store and am immediately greeted by a salesperson.

"Good morning, sir. What can I help you with today?"

"Hi. I'm Jared Daan. I'm here for a meeting with Jayce Carlson at noon. I'm a bit early, so thought I'd poke around and see what kind of stuff you have."

"Ah... So you're Jared Daan. Dad's expecting you. He prefers to go by Jay, by the way. I'm Brooke. Pleased to meet you."

She sticks out her hand to shake.

"I'm sure he's ready for you if you want to go up, but I'd be happy to show you around."

"That would be nice."

I can tell she's happy to see me. I'm guessing they need the business. I also sense a bit of a flirt in her tone. I'm guessing she's 20 or 21.

She takes me on a short tour through the plants in the retail section of the store. There are fruit trees, and a small display of herbs. But it's mostly landscaping plants.

The retail shop is in the foothills. The land here slopes down from the retail shop toward the lake. She stops to point out the extensive green house and growing fields at the far end of the property. They're 20, maybe 30, meters lower than the shop. The view from here is quite extraordinary.

As we head back to the shop, she asks. "What are you looking for exactly?"

"I want to establish herb and vegetable gardens near each of the kitchens in the camp. Ten gardens in total. Camp rules require us to have separate equipment and equipment storage for each garden, so I need a lot of equipment."

She nods her head sadly. "I remember the incident seven years ago, the one where they lost most of a cane field. I used to help out in our growing fields back then and was amazed to hear how sloppy procedures had been at the camp."

I chuckle at her brazen honesty.

169

"Sorry, no offense intended."

"None taken." I reply. "I wasn't there then. But I'm glad to hear you understand the problem."

"So, you're really going to restart the gardening operations?"

"I'm going to do my best to."

We reenter the store to see an older man coming down the steps from upstairs.

"Dad!" Brooke calls out. "Mr. Daan is here to see you."

He gives a big smile and approaches to shake my hand. "Jared, a pleasure to meet you in person."

"Likewise, sir." I shake his hand. "I got here a bit early and Brooke agreed to give me a little tour."

"Glad to hear that. And please call me Jay. Shall we head upstairs?"

A minute later, we're upstairs and seated in his office.

"Brooke will be up in a bit with some sandwiches and drinks." He looks at me as if sizing me up. "So, you want to restart the gardens?"

"Yes. I do. Over the years, the camp has done a good job fulfilling its mission as a prison facility. And it's done so in a way that contributes to our economy at minimal expense to the government. But with budgets tightening, we will better serve our mission if we're more self-sufficient. Adding gardens that reduce our external food purchases is one way to start."

He looks at me critically, still sizing me up.

"Most food production operations have long payback cycles. I'm surprised the camp, or the elders for that matter, would want to invest money in something with such a long payback cycle."

I can see that Jay is a clever guy who already knows there's something odd about what I'm trying to do. The question is how to play him. But even as that thought passes through my mind, I know I need to play this straight up.

"You're aware of the pending food shortages, right?"

"I've noticed that inventories in the stores are down but haven't heard anything about a food shortage."

"Maybe there will be. Maybe there won't. It's hard to say. But I personally believe there will be, so am looking for ways to protect the people at the camp. And I'm willing to put up personal funds to make it happen. I live there, so if nothing else, I'm acting in my own self-interest."

"And you have enough money to do this?"

"I have a lot of credits. I want it done. And I want it done fast."

170

"How large do you envision each of the gardens to be?"

"How large would they need to be to make a difference?"

He shakes his head. "Define a difference."

"Say 10% of the food required to feed 1,000 people."

He snorts. "That would be food for 100."

He snorts again. "One hectare, if managed properly, can feed 2.5 people. That means you'll need 40 hectares. Broken into 10 plots, that would be 4 hectares per garden. Do you have that much space?"

I think for a minute. The gardens would have to be 100 meters by 400 meters. The answer is obvious. "No." I sigh, worried that this great idea is going to be a bust. "We have a lot more land than that, but I can't reallocate that much land at this time."

"I didn't think so. Want a suggestion?"

"Please."

"Herbs require little maintenance, but they make marginal food more palatable. Fruit trees are similar. Minimal maintenance, flavor that enhances, and decent calories. Potatoes. Again, minimum maintenance, lots of calories. My point is that there are things we can put in that will take minimal maintenance, so are viable for kitchen staff to maintain. Some will help with palatability. Others will help make up the calorie deficiency that comes with a food shortage. That's where you should concentrate your effort."

There's a pause. I realize I'm in over my head. Jay knows it too.

Jay sighs. "We put in camp gardens ten or so years ago. The warden wanted... Let me say this differently. They didn't want to go with the strategy I just described. They wanted a mix of more gourmet items that were intrinsically high maintenance. They couldn't do the maintenance, so ended up losing the gardens.

"I know the land you have. I have a plan that will give you the best value for that land. If this were a government contract process, I'd bid 55,000 credits for the job. If you have that much personal funds and you want to pay cash, I can do it for 45,000."

I put my hand out to shake.

"You have 45,000 credits?" Jay seems flabbergasted.

"Yes. Write up the invoice. I'll take it over to the bank and you'll be funded this afternoon. Half upfront, the rest on completion."

Jay looks at me with a frown.

"25,000 up front, 2,000 on completion of each zone."

I put my hand out again. "Deal. If I get you the money today, can you start tomorrow? I want as much of this done by Friday as possible."

"Tomorrow, maybe. Friday, unlikely. But we'll work through the weekend to get it done ASAP."

"Deal." My hand is still out there. This time he shakes it.

He's still staring at me when Brooke comes in with the sandwiches.

"You've made a deal already?" She is genuinely surprised.

"Seems we have and there's a lot of work to do. Can you ask Brian to come over?"

"Sure." The word is directed toward her father, but her smile is directed toward me.

COPPERSMITH

I arrive at Brock Newton's workshop a minute early and take in the look of the place. It looks like it's been idle for a long time. I step up to the main door, which is ajar, and knock.

"Come in. I'll be there in a moment."

I push the door open, step in, and know I'm in the right place. There's copper everywhere. Sheet, wire, tubing, things half built. The place is full of copper stuff. There's also a lot of dust. I might be right about it having been idle for a while.

I hear noise at the back of the shop and seconds later see a wiry man of 40-something years come in from another room along the back.

"You Jared Daan?"

"Yes I am."

He looks at me with a bit of disdain. "I was expecting someone a little older."

"I'm of age," I state with confidence. "And I need something I'm told you can make."

"On the phone, you said you wanted a still. But you really don't look like someone that wants to make their own moonshine."

I'm admittedly a bit amused at how poor a salesman Brock is.

"I want two stills actually. One with five precipitation chambers, the other with four."

"What the hell type of alcohol do you make with that?"

"I'm not making alcohol. I'm doing chemical separation of a complex botanical solution."

"You mean like perfume?"

"Natural remedies, not perfume."

"Well, I'll be damned. I've studied such systems, but never thought I'd see one built on Jaredaan. How big?"

"I have specs if you'd like to see them."

...

We talk through the specs. He has suggestions for improved heating of the source material; suggestions for more consistent condensation of each of the components. And I'm generally feeling like this is going to work. Then he stops midsentence and looks at me.

"This is going to be expensive. You got the money for this?"

"I think I do."

"I'll need to do some work to make a proper estimate on which I'll put a 20% contingency. But there's no way this can be done for less than 50,000 credits. Do you have that kind of money?"

"Yes."

He scowls and fidgets a bit.

"I'm going to need some proof."

"Do you know Miles Brown, general manager down at the bank?"

"I know of him."

"Would a phone call with him be sufficient?"

He thinks for a second.

"I don't know him that well."

"Want to go down to the bank with me?"

He fidgets some more, then sighs. "I suppose that's the best option."

We pack into my vehicle and take the 3-minute drive to the bank. I call ahead, hoping that Miles will be available.

We arrive and are whisked immediately into his office.

"Jared, a pleasure as always."

It seems that Miles has figured out I'm here because I want to spend some money.

"Mr. Newton, a pleasure to make your acquaintance. How can I help you today?"

I start.

"I'm attempting to engage Mr. Newton's service for a relatively large project that will cost 50, maybe 75,000 credits. He wants assurance that I have the ability to pay before he'll sign the contract."

"Mr. Newton. My client, Jared Daan, is one of the wealthiest men on this planet. He has more than enough to honor a 75,000-credit project."

My banker turns to me. "Is this related to the new company I hear you're forming?"

"Yes. Yes, it is."

"Would you like me to work with Ms. Preston to get accounts set up for the company? There are regulations regarding such things. I know you're busy Jared, so maybe Audrey and I could get everything set up for your signature ahead of time."

"Yes, please. Brock and I need to get back to his studio now. Would it be OK if I dropped by at 4:00 on another matter?"

"I'm always here for you, sir."

...

Back in the studio, a very contrite Brock Newton presents me with a 1,000-credit retainer agreement.

"This will let me get started. I think I have all the material you'll need in inventory. It'll take me a few days to work through all that, but this will get the ball rolling. I understand your urgency. This will move things along faster."

A retainer of this type is new to me. But it's only 1,000 credits, credits that will bind Mr. Newton to me and my project. Money well spent.

APARTMENT

The second stop at the bank went much like the first. My banker is worried about the rate at which I'm spending money. But the 25,000-credit transfer to West Lake Nursery is made with minimal whining.

I'm back in my apartment. It's 6:30. I messaged Summer on the way back saying I would be late. We agree to meet at the staff café at 7:00. I have a half hour, so connect back into the exo-net, where I have a flashing message from Jungle.

I'd totally lost track of my validation of the extended-charge tablet-cover project. I quickly check on the prototype. The timer says 63 hours. The voltage has dropped to 95%, which is still an operable level. This is more than 25% higher than the product spec. The charge remaining gauge says 3%. I find this to be very encouraging. I don't need to do the math to know that this design is sound.

I message my acceptance of the design to Jungle and within minutes get a notice that my design has gone live.

I quickly package up Lenna's next dose and head over to the staff café.

STAFF CAFÉ

I'm a few minutes early, but Summer is already there. She asks if it's OK for her to come into the kitchen with me.

As I enter, Lenna is finishing up 5 plates that are about to go out.

"Be with you in a minute, Jared."

"Would it be OK if Summer comes in, too?"

She pauses mid-motion, then restarts in a rush. "Sure," she says after turning back to her work. I can tell that she doesn't want Summer to come back and am now unhappy with myself for having asked.

The plates are put out in the window for the servers to take, then she turns to me with a big smile and says, "That's better."

Not seeing Summer, she calls out, "Summer, come on back."

Summer comes in, and the two embrace.

Summer whispers, "Sorry, I didn't know, then didn't know what to do when I found out."

This is the last thing I expected. I surely wish I had Ethel's skill.

There's the odd tear, then they separate.

No explanation is given, so I start in on my doctor's routine.

"How are the symptoms?"

"I still have mild queasiness, but it's a lot better than this morning."

I pull out her little jar. She has real technique now as she empties the jar and holds the liquid in her mouth. I see her close her eyes and relax, then swallow when she knows most of the medication is in her system.

She gives me the jar back with a meek, "Thank you."

Then a second later, she's back in motion. "I'll get yours out next."

SUMMER'S HOME

Back at Summer's place, the food is dished up and we sit to eat.

"Oh, I almost forgot. Did you get my dad's message?"

"Ah, no." I pick up my communicator and see that its set for silent running. I turn it back to normal and multiple messages pop up.

"Let me guess. You turned inbound service off and forgot to turn it back on?"

"Yep." I'm tempted to read and listen to the messages but am not going to do that to Summer. I put my communicator down. "Do you know what he wanted?"

"No. He called your office and it rolled over to me. I told him you were away from the office and he should try your mobile. He said he had and needed to speak with you ASAP."

"I'll call him after dinner."

She smiles at me. "Did you have a successful day?"

"Very. I contracted to have gardens installed and to have a pair of stills built."

Summer looks at me with concern. "You're spending your own money on this, right?"

"I am."

More concern. "Jared, this isn't normal. No one spends their own money on prison improvements. And you're making a big change without Dad's approval."

There's silence for a moment.

"You're right of course. What do you think your father will do when he gets back and there are full gardens in each zone?"

"It didn't go so well last time and ultimately cost a lot in lost revenue. So, I suspect that he'll want to rip it all out."

"That would be a shame. They chose poorly last time, putting in finicky, high-maintenance plants not suited to the land. Everything I've ordered is low maintenance, calorie rich food to help us ride through the famine that's coming. I've even bought new equipment and sheds to store the equipment."

"How much did you spend?"

I hear an edge of hysteria in her voice.

"45 thousand credits."

She looks at me in shock. I think she's going to cry.

"You know people will starve if we don't do something. We should just sit and watch it happen?"

After a long silence, she whispers, "No. Dad hired you because he thought you might be able to save us. But he's still going to be mad that you did this without telling him."

"I'm sure you're right."

After a little more silence, I change the subject.

"What was that between you and Lenna?"

"We've been close friends for a while now, since she started working here actually. We had a stupid argument just before she got sick. She seemed to be avoiding me, so I just let it be.

"When I took that stuff Norah gave me, one of the things I saw was Lenna, suffering from the illness and wishing she had a friend. I had to make up with her."

"You going to tell me anymore about what you saw?"

"Probably, but not yet. I need to process it some more."

APARTMENT

Back in my apartment, I screw up my courage and call the warden.

"Jared, what took you so long to get back to me?"

"Sorry, sir. I turned off inbound calls for a meeting this morning and forgot to turn it back on. It wasn't until Summer told me you called that I realized the problem."

"Done the same myself," he says ruefully. He's quiet for a moment, then starts in. "There's a lot we need to talk about. Now that I have you on the line, I'm not sure where to begin."

"I assume this is about the DAGS, the quarantine and food shortage."

"How did you find out about that?"

He sounds shocked.

"It's on the exo-net. The disease, its origins, the quarantines... It's all out there."

"Seems you're ahead of me, as usual. Have you given any thought to what we should do about it?"

"Yes, but I may have gotten a bit ahead of myself."

"Go on."

"Food in the camp, for the prisoners, is already a problem. So, I looked into what it would take to restart the gardens."

"Not the gardens..."

He says the word garden as if it's some sort of nightmare.

"I went over to West Lake Nursery this morning to talk with Jay Carlson. We came up with a low maintenance plan that will add calories and flavor—things like herbs, fruit trees, and potatoes, things that take some effort to plant but little effort to maintain."

He sighs. "Jared, I appreciate your initiative. It's one of the things I love about you. But we'll never get the budget to do that."

I smile. I'm about to find out how much trouble I'm in.

"Not a problem. An anonymous donor came forward to fund the installation. They're going to start tomorrow."

There's silence on the line.

"You bought new gardens and authorized their installation without asking me!"

There's silence on the line for a moment. Although the line is quiet, I can 'hear' his blood boiling.

"Damnation, not gardens again." This is said in resignation.

"It will work. I promise," I whisper quietly.

I hear laughing on the other end of the line.

"I met your brother Aaron yesterday and was in meetings with him most of the day today. He's a big fan of yours. He actually said at one point today that you probably have the problem solved already. I just wasn't expecting it to be gardens.

"What else have you done that I don't know about yet?"

"I put out a new work directive this morning regarding composting. All zones are directed to prioritize crop fertilization over field expansion. We're basically switching everyone over to Zone 3's work process. That could bump yield up by as much as 10% this year."

"Anything else?"

"Finished, no. But there's one thing I've started that I don't think I've told you about yet. In the recent viper incidents, we almost lost two people. It should never have been as close as it ended up being. I've been working with Ethel and Norah to document their field procedures. There are simple things we can train any of the zone supervisors to do that will add an hour to the critical time between bite and death."

"So that's what you've been doing down there."

"That and more. They have a wealth of knowledge we need to get into more people's hands."

"Understood. Keep up the good work, but no more sleepovers down there."

I chuckle. "Understood."

"That brings me to another issue, several actually. It seems that I may not be able to return on time. An issue of some sort has come up with our shuttle operations. So, I'm going to appoint you deputy warden in my absence. I don't know how long I'm going to be detained, but you're the one I think I can trust the camp to if I'm detained for an extended period. But please, let me know before you do something like the gardens again."

"Understood, sir."

"Next, and this is more sensitive..."

The fact that he's hesitating puts me on guard.

"The power situation in Jaredstown is becoming critical. If the shuttles were still working, the elders would probably summon you by the end of the week. A retiree named Levi Grayson has been called back to service, but he can't do very much. They only have one surface certified engineer left, a fellow named Rylan Graham, but he recently suffered an injury. They've been able to redirect some power from Ashcrag, but Jaredstown is in trouble. You seem to be their only hope."

I don't say anything. But the temptation to get in my truck and drive out into the wilderness is almost irresistible at the moment.

"Anyway, your brother Aaron sends his regards."

"Please send mine to Aaron as well."

...

Once again, I find myself in bed unable to sleep. The thought of being compelled to return to Jaredstown haunts me. The thought of being separated from Summer is soul crushing.

If they come for me, I'll run. And if Summer will come with me, I'll take her.

THURSDAY

Tuesday and Wednesday fly by. Lenna continues to improve. The current cycle seems to be finishing.

I've visited all 10 zones multiple times. The supervisors are surprised and grateful that we're adding the gardens. It'll be a while before there's a harvest, but food supplies have become tight enough that the gardens give them hope. I've not mentioned that I've personally funded this, but they all seem to know.

The composting directive has also been well received. More than one zone supervisor has said they're waiting for an irrigation directive. It's been on my mind. I have a draft. But as Logan Reid, the Zone 10 supervisor, pointed out this morning, it's hard to prioritize good practice until directed to. There are a lot of other directives on the books. I'm sure all of them were relevant when issued. But the essence of most are deeply engrained at this point. So, the older directives can mostly be deleted, not because they're irrelevant, but because they've been superseded. The old ones create more confusion than clarity.

My evenings have been spent with Summer, dinner at her place, then more work once home. I've tried to keep the warden in the loop. Tonight, I message today's progress and advise him of the irrigation directive I plan to issue. I also mention that I plan to review the active directives in the hope of eliminating contradictions and redundancies.

I get a message back as I head off to bed, thanking me for my work and agreeing that a directive review is overdue. I get the sense from his response that things up north are not well. In some sense, they brought it on themselves. If they'd been smart enough not to railroad me, Dad and I would have kept their electrical system running. But I need to check my emotions on that topic. If I were still there, Dad and I might both be dead already from the disease.

Tomorrow will be more of the same with one exception, Summer and I will be going out to look at real estate. It'll be the first time we've been offsite together. It will be a test of sorts for our relationship. I hope I pass the test. I also hope I find property.

REAL ESTATE

The day starts well. Lenna claims to be symptom free, the cycle is done. I desperately hope that's true. Morning rounds go quickly. I start in Zone 10 and work my way back in the hope of seeing more garden development in Zones 1 to 5.

The gardens are coming along well. Zones 1 and 2 are completed. Their supervisors have organized watering and fertilizing duties. I worry, as the warden does, that this will slack off over time. But as of today, everything is good.

I pick up lunch for Summer and me at the staff café. For the first time I hear the lunch chef complaining about food availability. The shortage is finally reaching the staff. I'll need to start being careful about my consumption.

After a quick bite in my office, we head out to meet my realtor. Her name is Macy Frazer. Audrey, my lawyer, recommended her. I spoke briefly on the phone with her to set up the appointment but haven't met her yet. I didn't tell her Summer would be with me but doubt that will be a problem.

We arrive in Heroldstown about 20 minutes early. Its eerie how little traffic there is. I don't have all that much experience, but the roads are emptier today than I've seen them before. Macy's office is two doors down from the outfitting shop, so I decide to stop there.

"Why are we stopping here?"

Summer seems puzzled.

"I need to head out into the wilderness before too much longer. My visions always point in that direction. I was thinking about maybe going out this weekend. Possibly spending a night. I have all the equipment, but no food. I'm hoping they still have some dehydrated food available. Want to come in with me?"

"Sure."

We enter and a salesperson greets us immediately. It's the same guy that sold me my shelter and other gear. I'm blanking on his name, but thankfully he's wearing a name tag.

"Cody, good to see you again. I'm Jared Daan. I was in a couple weeks back to get a tent and other supplies."

"Jared, I'm glad to see you back again."

I notice him eyeballing Summer.

"This is my friend Summer."

He smiles and shakes her hand.

"So, what can I help you with?"

"Last time I was in you suggested that I get some dehydrated food. I'm hoping you still have some."

He looks at me oddly.

"Stock's a bit low, the shipment we've been waiting for still hasn't come in yet. But I've got more than enough to feed two for a week. Want to see?"

The question is apparently rhetorical because he takes off for the food section before I reply. We follow, then start browsing through his inventory. Summer and I each pick several items, but I can see she's hesitant because of the prices.

The alarm on my phone goes off, interrupting our shopping. I confirm that it's the alarm I set for our meeting. We only have 5 minutes.

"Cody, we have a meeting in 5 minutes. Could you pick out a week's worth of food for us? Seven days, 3 meals, two people, and maybe some snacks? We can come back to pick it up at 4:30."

"Sure, Jared. Good luck with your meeting. I'll see you at 4:30."

As soon as the truck's doors close, I hear the question I was expecting.

"Are you really going to buy that stuff? It's incredibly expensive and I struggle to believe it will be any good."

"Yes. That stuff will last forever. I'm tempted to buy his entire inventory, but that would be too suspicious."

There's no immediate reply, she's obviously chewing on the implications of my comment.

181

Macy's building is just down the block, so it only takes a minute to get there. As I pull into her parking lot, Summer finally responds.

"You're already making contingency plans for us if everything falls apart. Aren't you?"

"Yes, but more than that. You nailed it the other day. Once everyone knows we're under quarantine, my money will be worthless. So, I want to spend it now, while it still has value, on things that might save us if everything does spiral out of control."

"But if things don't spiral out of control, won't that leave you broke?"

This conversation is not going someplace I particularly want to go, so I answer simply. "No, not really." Then open my door to get out.

I get a slightly cross look. I think it's mostly a warning that this topic isn't finished yet. Thankfully, she's smiling again as we open the door to Macy's office.

...

There's no one in the reception area. But the bell attached to the door rings as we enter and moments later an older woman comes out.

"You must be Jared Doon." She marches out hand extended. "I'm Macy Frazer. And who might your lovely companion be?"

She shakes my hand, although her attention is now squarely on Summer.

"I'm Summer Glenn, Ms. Frazer. It's a pleasure to meet you."

As she shakes Summer's hand, Macy seems to have an epiphany. "You're the warden's daughter, aren't you? Goodness, I remember when you were born. Look at you now!"

She holds Summer by the shoulders at arm's length the way older people do sometimes when inspecting a youngster.

"Are you two a couple?"

I can't help but chuckle at her gregarious behavior.

"My specialty is commercial real estate, but I'm sure I could find you the perfect home to settle into and start a family."

I'm laughing now.

"Well someday maybe..." Her voice trails off, then she looks at me with lightning focus.

"Jared, you really should have come to see me before you started your buying spree. Rumors of rampant spending have been ripping through town. Asking prices are up 10% despite the recession."

"I've got a lot to do and little time to do it in," I explain, hoping this doesn't launch us down another line of interrogation.

"Entrepreneurs. Got to love 'em. They're certainly good for business." She invites us into her office and indicates seats.

"The market has a lot of inventory as you might expect. The recession has brought all the owners to their knees. So, it's a buyers' market. The buildings best suited to the description you sent me are all to the north. But there are buildings available in the east, if that's what you want."

"It needs to be in the east, we need proximity to the camp."

"Then that's where we'll concentrate our search."

She looks at me curiously as if trying to figure out where to go next.

"You know..." Her voice trails off as she turns to grab a thick notebook on the shelf behind her. She plops it on the desk, then starts flipping through the pages. She comes to a page, looks at me again, flips a few more pages, then goes back and forth between a couple before finally settling on one.

"This is it." She declares, skewering the page with her finger. "It's not what you asked for, but I'll bet it's the one."

She turns the book around. I see an old industrial building that appears to be in good condition, but also appears to be in the middle of nowhere. There's a road leading up to it that's in less than good condition. And a tall chain link fence running around the building. There's enough dead bramble and other trash caught in the fence that it's hard to tell what condition it might be in.

Other than that, there's nothing. No other sign of human existence. Not even powerlines.

"I think that's the eastern most building ever build on Jaredaan. It's downstream of the ethanol facility, difficult to spot from the main road. It's maybe 5 km from the camp. It was set up for specialty alcohol production. It even has its own furnaces for steam-based heating. Technically, it's owned by the government. The idiots built it, then realized the charter doesn't allow the government to produce alcoholic beverages. It didn't have the capacity required to produce ethanol-based fuel, so they tried to sell it. There were no takers, so there it sits. It was listed for sale for years, but the listing was eventually withdrawn. Last asking price was 100,000 credits as is. Bet I could get it for 50,000. But it would be a purchase, not a lease. The government can't own, or lease, alcoholic beverage production facilities."

"We're not planning to make alcohol. We're doing chemical separation of naturally occurring organic products."

She pins me with a stare. "Doesn't matter what you call it. The facility was built for vodka and whisky production. That's the way it's zoned. That's the way they'll classify the purchase. Doesn't really matter what you do with it."

"Can I put an apartment in it?"

"Technically, no. But don't let that stop you. Most housing in Heroldstown isn't technically legal. There's only one legal dwelling in the camp. The one Summer grew up in."

From the body language, I can tell Summer doesn't like this idea at all. She hasn't said anything, but I know she thinks it's crazy to buy. I kind of like the idea of buying it.

"Can we look at it?"

"I'll need to call and make arrangements."

"You can read people, can't you? You knew what I wanted by just looking at me."

"I wouldn't put it that way, but I've been in this business a long time and almost always call it right in the first half hour."

"Is it worth looking at anything else on your list?"

"You actually thinking about buying it?"

"If the price is right, yes."

"Give me a half hour. Let me talk to the seller."

"Great!" I stand. "We have a short errand we need to run. We'll be back in a half hour."

I reach out to shake her hand and she smiles.

"See you in a half hour."

As we walk out, I hear her whisper, "Love doing business with entrepreneurs."

...

As soon as the truck's doors close, Summer starts in. "Jared, what are you doing?" She's clearly distraught.

"I really like this idea. With our own space, especially in that location, the opportunities are endless."

"But 50,000 credits..."

As her voice trails off, I realize we need to have the money talk. I've been wanting to keep this private. But Ethel's words haunt me. If I don't come completely clean with Summer, it will eventually come between us.

"We need to talk about money." I say, not looking at her. "I have a lot. I haven't wanted to talk about this, because I don't want you to think about money when you think about me. I don't want that to be an issue in our relationship.

"But it's becoming one. So, I'll tell you if you ask."

"Do you have a million credits? That's what people are saying."

"Close, but that's about to change."

"Because you're spending so much?"

"No. My target income this month is about 300,000 credits. It will plateau a little higher than that next month."

"You're making over 3 million credits a year?" Again, her voice is tinged with hysteria.

"I haven't made that much yet. May never. But that's the current forecast. I currently have over half a million on planet. Another 200 thousand off planet."

"So, this really is nothing to you."

"I don't like it when you put it that way. This project is everything to me. I take that back. You're everything to me. But I need this project to keep you alive. The money is just a tool. I didn't set out to make it. But since I have it, I'm going to use it."

We enter the outfitting store's parking lot and I turn into the parking spot we vacated a half hour ago. I've kept my eyes straight ahead since we got in the truck in the hope of keeping my emotions under control. Now I turn to look at Summer.

"Are we still friends?"

"Yes, and I understand now. Let's go in and get a lot of food, then go buy your building."

The words are offered quietly. I can tell she's struggling with something. But one thing I know. She will tell me when she's ready and any prying on my part will just delay the eventual reveal.

ALCOHOL FACILITY

It took a little longer than expected, but Macy succeeded in arranging a tour of the facility at 5:30. She conscripts a younger colleague to drive her down. We follow along behind. I'm really excited to see the place.

Summer has been quieter than normal. I can tell she's brooding over something. So, I finally ask.

"Penny for your thoughts?" It's something my mother used to say, though she would usually tack a sweetie on the end.

She smiles. "There have been a lot of revelations this week. Lenna, the disease, the quarantine and embargo, my folks away with no return date in sight. You," she adds with emphasis, "and the visions, Ethel and Norah... I had no idea about any of these things. It's like... I really don't have the right words, but it's like a veil has been lifted. And sadly, the world it reveals isn't the one I thought I lived in. It's hard to take it in. I used to think I had some idea of what my life would look like, but now I know that I don't."

"For what it's worth, I know the feeling. I thought I knew what my life would look like and worked really hard to make it happen. Then my brothers framed me for a crime they committed, and I got sent here, all my dreams wiped away.

"None of that was any fun, but it has put me in a much better place, given me a much greater purpose."

I look over and see her smiling at me.

"I'm glad you ended up here," she says.

...

We finally turn off the highway onto the road headed toward the ethanol fuel facility. The facility is a lot bigger than it looks from the highway. This portion of the road is smooth and well maintained. To me, this road always appeared to be the long driveway leading to the ethanol facility. But to my surprise, I see other buildings along the road that are hidden from view of the highway.

As we pass the ethanol facility, my building comes into view. From this distance it looks as good as it did in the pictures. The fence looks as covered in bramble as in the picture, but the road looks a lot worse. It was obviously paved at one point. Now the road is little more than gravel.

As a hover car, the road quality doesn't really affect us very much. But Macy's car bounces so much that we proceed at a snail's pace. Looking ahead, I see the gate to my building is open and a truck sitting in the parking lot.

Ten minutes later, the bumpy kilometer is behind us. As I pull into the parking lot, I have the strange, but visceral experience of being home. It must be a side effect of the visions. This feels too real, too mine, to explain rationally. When we get out, I notice Summer looks the way I feel. She must have seen this place, or something like it, in her vision.

A rugged looking guy in a coverall with the ethanol company's logo comes over to greet us. He exchanges cards with Macy, who introduces Summer and me.

"So, you're Jared Daan. I was expecting someone a little older. You're interested in buying the place?" He indicates the building.

"Very interested," I reply.

"Well, let's do the tour." He says good-naturedly. "Let's start in the boiler room." He points the way. "There are several entrances, but let's go in through the loading bay. The electricity's off at the moment, so I opened the loading bay doors to let some light in."

The building is L-shaped. The loading bay is the foot of the L. It's small compared to the main building, but there's room here for two large trucks.

Charlie points out several loading features, and the storage area above the parking spots in the main garage, then heads to the back door. He takes us out back where there's a large fuel tank.

"If you buy the place, the first thing you'll want to do is fill up the ethanol tank. We'll clean it out and put a little ethanol in before title transfer, but this tank feeds the main boilers which produce the electricity and steam to power the plant. They put in a really nice unit that's never really been used. The only time it's been fired up was to do the 12-hour burn-in test."

I notice that he says this ruefully.

"Were you part of the team that built this plant?"

He smiles. "That obvious?" Then he chuckles. "Yah, we went top shelf on everything. You really have to for food grade products. A lot of credits were flushed down the tube on this place. I'm glad someone might actually use it."

We linger for a moment. Charlie's obviously reminiscing.

We're about a half kilometer south of the river, facing due north. I notice that we're on a bit of a plateau, at least 20 meters higher than the river. This too rings a bell, but I can't place it.

Coming out of his reverie, Charlie says, "Come on. Let's go checkout the boiler room."

We reenter the loading area and Charlie closes and locks the door. Then he hands us each a small high-intensity flashlight.

"It'll be dark inside, you'll need these."

As we enter the boiler room everyone turns their flashlight on. The room itself is relatively small, maybe 10 by 20 meters. There's a classical boiler tank feeding a pair of steam lines. The one steam line feeds a small steam turbine that sits a meter or two away from the tank, enough room to work on either unit, but no wasted space.

The other steam line goes through the wall into the main still room.

In the still room there are three large column stills wrapped with steam jackets. Each has continuous feed lines, condensation unit and collection barrel. It's not what I need, but it's beautiful.

"Any chance Brock Newton built these units?"

Charlie looks at me curiously. "In fact, he did. You know him?

"I do. I've hired him to build the new stills we need."

"You're not going to use these?"

"They don't do what I need. I'm not making alcohol. I'm doing chemical separation of natural solutions. My solutions have four or five components that need to be separated, isolated, and purified. Each has a different evaporation point, so we have multiple condensation and collection steps for the first pass."

"I had no idea that anyone on Jaredaan was doing anything that sophisticated."

"Our prototype system is tiny. We can produce 250 ml in 3 days. It's time to scale up."

"I'm sure Brock can modify this equipment. He's quite capable. And the bones on this place...," he indicates the building, "...are perfect for food quality separation."

He pulls out a business card and hands it to me. "If you decide you need a facilities manager, give me a call."

Charlie walks us through the rest of the building. There are separate spaces for raw material and finished product storage, a packaging line, men's and women's changing rooms, several offices, even a reception area.

When the main tour is done, Charlie asks if I want to walk the building perimeter. I do, so we exit out from the reception area, which faces the parking lot where our vehicles are parked. Summer joins me, but Macy and her colleague stay in the reception area.

We turn left and walk the length of the building. Charlie points out several features, stopping periodically to knock on the metal wall, showing how sound it is. We turn left again to walk along the south face of the building, following the same routine.

"How much did it cost to build this place?"

"Probably less than you think. The building is a basic steel shell. The important walls around the boiler and main still rooms are reinforced concrete. The rest is mostly just cosmetic. The dual-purpose boiler and steam turbine cost less than 50,000 credits. Each of the stills cost about 20,000. I think the whole building as you see it was well less than 200,000.

"My boss told me you were looking to pay 40,000 credits. If they give it to you for that, it's a steal."

We've only walked a quarter of the way around the building, but are now facing due east, out into the wilderness. Charlie notices that I'm looking that way.

"It goes on forever. The access road goes maybe 50 km. Beyond that it's just the wild unknown."

"You ever ventured out there?" I ask.

"A couple times to the end of the road. I'm not sure why they built it. But there are a number of test wells, or at least relics of test wells, along the way. Rumor has it that Herold thought there might be something interesting out that way, but I have no idea what."

We finish the tour and say goodbye to Charlie, then head back toward the main highway. As agreed, Macy pulls over at a rest area, so we can debrief. There's a small pavilion with a couple picnic tables. It seems so incongruous to find a facility like this here. But it's here, so we use it.

I'm no sooner out of the car than Macy says, "Called it right, didn't I?"

"You sure did."

"When I called their office, they hesitated to talk price. I told them I needed an asking price, or I couldn't show the property. They said 60,000. I'm sure they'll go lower."

"While we were walking the perimeter, Charlie mentioned 40,000."

Summer nods her head confirming my number.

"It would be risky bidding that low, if you really want it. Too low an initial bid can backfire. How much do you want it?"

"I want it."

She smiles. "That's why I like working with entrepreneurs. You know what you want. So many clients don't." She pauses. "We can go in at 45, maybe 47.5. I'm sure they'll give it to you for 50."

"How about this? We go in at 52.5, but want the ethanol tank full, and the steam and electrical systems tested and certified to be in working order."

"You really do want this." Macy smiles. "My commission is 3 percent. Tradition is that the seller pays. If they balk, can I say you'll split it with them?"

"If you have to."

I put out my hand to shake. She shakes it and smiles.

APARTMENT

The last several nights we've headed over to Summer's place to eat. Tonight, she wants to come over to my place. It's a little further away from the staff café, but not much.

Summer has really changed this week. I can't read her very well, but the change in her demeanor is worrisome.

We get to my place. I set the table as Summer gives the food a quick warm up. We're like an old married couple. She seems to own my kitchen in a way that I don't.

"So, what's on your schedule tomorrow? You've been all over the place this week."

"In the morning, I'm back out into the fields. It's only been a week, but we're already seeing changes in the health of the fields. My presence seems to motivate. So, I want to spend 15 minutes or so checking specific items in each zone. I also want to see how the new gardens are taking."

"I'm still struggling to believe that Dad's letting you get away with this."

"I thought he was going to blow a gasket at first. But he agrees with the rationale and I sense things have gone poorly up north this week. Desperation can go a long way toward changing one's mind."

I let the statement hang there for a minute, then ask, "Do you know any more about when they might get back."

"No." She looks at me very seriously. "Jared, you're doing what this place has needed for a long time. My father can't do that. I'm afraid that he's going to mess it up when he gets back. And I'm afraid the two of you are going to come to blows over it."

"I don't want to fight with your father."

She chuckles.

"Well, I hope you're willing to fight for me."

I have no idea what she means by that. She gets up and starts clearing the table. I bring the rest of the dishes.

"What did you see in your vision?"

"Several things, it was like a series of forks in the road. Reconciling with Lenna, living in the warden's mansion with you. Living in the wilderness with you. You living in the wilderness on your own, our world dead other than you and a few survivors that you lead in the wilderness.

She turns and wraps her arms around me. "I don't want to lose you Jared. You're the one who will save our world. And you're the one

190

who will survive if it can't be saved. I want to be there with you, wherever you are. But my father will oppose it."

STAFF CAFÉ

I'm up and out early. Summer stayed over last night. She's up and out early with me. I've been meeting Lenna at 7:00 to give her the morning dose. We're early and she's not here yet. Summer sees me fidgeting and puts her hand over mine.

"I can handle this, if you need to go."

I've been becoming more and more protective of Lenna. There is so much hope in what's happening with her that I don't want to take any risks. But it occurs to me that it's not only protectiveness. I also have trust issues. Every time I trusted my brothers with something, anything, it came back to get me. If I'm going to have the life with Summer that I want, then I need to trust her.

Unexpectedly, that conjures thoughts of Nana and the ultimate betrayal of trust that came with that relationship. But I guess that's the point. I had no relationship with Nana. I just thought I did, based on a couple dinners and a roll or two in the sack.

It's not that way with Summer. We are bonding. We had a very tender, but platonic night last night. Lots of caring, no rolling. I'm hoping to change that, but I'm more interested in her and her wellbeing, than I am in rolling around. Well, for now anyway.

I look up and smile. "Thanks. I've got a lot to do today." I give Summer the little jar, then stand. I take one step toward the door, but it opens and Lenna comes in with real spring in her step.

"Jared, sorry I'm late." I get a quick hug, then she's saying hi and hugging Summer. I can't help but notice her hug with Lenna is different than with me.

"I've got your medication," Summer says to Lenna.

Lenna turns to me and says, "Thanks."

In that moment, I realize two things. The first is that I've been dismissed. The second, and by far most important, is that I'll have partners on my side when everything goes sideways. Something I expect to happen soon.

FIELDS

I'm working the fields in reverse order today, starting in Zone 10 and working my way back. At this point, Zone 10 is my biggest problem. Their land is underdeveloped, and they are understaffed.

Proportionally speaking, you need more staff during development than you do during maintenance. As just one example, it takes more effort to dig a new irrigation ditch than it does to maintain an existing one.

Rory's irrigation ditches, in Zone 5, were a mess. But it didn't take all that long to clean them up. Zone 10 has irrigation to less than half its land. The cane growing in the other half is useless. It's as bad as the wild cane along the road into camp. Most of it will not yield enough juice to pay for the harvest and transport.

The good news is that the quarter of the land they've been focusing on is yielding well. Their garden also looks great. I congratulate supervisor, Logan Reid, on the work he has done and tweak his priorities a bit, then head off to the next zone.

...

I just finished the review of operations in Zone 4. I'm impressed with all the zones I've seen so far today. It's taken months of stop and go work to get this project moving. This week, with my health fully restored and the additional liberty the warden's absence has given me, it's finally happening. But I'm running late, so stop in Zone 3 long enough to talk with my old boss Gavin Barnes. His zone has been, and still is, the standard of reference. This stop is more about thanks than it is review. He reminds me that I need to get the new irrigation directive out soon. I thank him for the reminder and promise to put it out this afternoon.

Curiously, the garden in Zone 2 is the first one completed. Turns out the land there needed the least preparation. This garden is beautiful, and larger than I was expecting. It's oriented such that the north west corner of the garden lines up with the south west corner of the dining building, the side the kitchen is on. The stairs down from the kitchen land a meter or two from the herb corner of the garden. A variety of herbs are in a raised bed, high enough that the toads won't get in. Rosemary is planted in the ground perpendicular to the raised bed forming one corner of the garden. A tight mesh fence surrounds the entire garden, keeping the toads out. On the far side are fruit trees. The trees are surprisingly mature, each has newly budded fruit that will be ready for harvest in a couple months. I see apple, orange, lemon, lime, and banana trees. Then recognize a fig tree in the far corner. I've seen pictures of fruit trees on the exo-net. I got a glimpse of the dwarf apple tree in the garden in Jaredstown once. But the sight of this many trees in one place is mesmerizing.

In the main gardening area, I recognize tomato plants, but am clueless about the rest. One of the installers from West Lake sees me and points out the remainder of the plants for me. Corn, potato, several types of squash, pepper, and others. Target annual yield for this garden is about 1 metric ton, or 10 kg per resident. One month's food spread across the year. At one level it's not that much, on another, it may be the difference between malnutrition and full nutrition. I'm thinking it's money well spent.

OFFICE

I get back to the office and find the real estate offer sitting on my desk awaiting signature. Summer printed it out and brought it up. There's a message from Macy complaining that it hasn't been returned yet. I do a quick read, then sign. It's 3:00. There's still time for Macy to submit it today. Summer comes to get it. She'll have a scanned copy in Macy's hand momentarily.

Next on my list is the irrigation directive. I finished it yesterday and am disappointed with myself for not getting it sent until now.

I'm just about finished for the day when a call comes in from Warden Glenn.

"I hear you've had a busy week."

"I have." I give him a quick update on all the camp business.

"I also hear that you're buying the old alcohol distillery that never got put into service." I can tell from his tone of voice that he disapproves.

"Attempting to, yes. But it isn't my intention to make alcohol."

I hear something of an exasperated noise on the other end of the line.

"It doesn't matter what you call it. Stills are used to make alcohol."

I can't believe I'm having this conversation.

"Or ethanol; or perfume; or flavoring ingredients. Or in my case a natural dietary supplement that I think people will want."

"A dietary supplement? Why are you making dietary supplements?"

I let the question sit there for a second, then ask one of my own.

"How many days' supply does Jaredaan have of basic pain killers, blood thinners, all the other drugs we take for granted? There are numerous herbal remedies that are easy to make and don't require governmental approval.

193

"I'm using my resources to do what no one else on this planet seems to be doing. Finding a path to survival on a quarantined world."

It's me who's exasperated now.

"One of our meetings today was on that topic. If we can get people to pool their supplies, we might have three months. We're hoping this will all blow over by then." His voice is a bit more contrite.

The stupidity of this statement almost sends me over the edge. I calm myself.

"You mean someone's found a cure?"

"No. But it has to end at some point."

"You realize that they quarantined Doffenplod for 7,000 years, then lifted it so scientists could go do some research. I would bet that the quarantine of Jaredaan will be closer to 7,000 years than 3 months."

There's silence on the other end of the line. It lasts an uncomfortably long time.

"Do you know when you might be able to return?"

More silence.

"Hello? Are you still there, sir?"

There's a sigh. "No. The fusion system that powers the shuttle is almost out of fuel. The fuel we need is stuck in the shipment floating in orbit. The Jaredstown lightning capture system is down to one-third capacity. Without the means to evacuate Jaredstown, they need to divert the power remaining in the fusion system to Jaredstown. So, we're stuck. I should never have agreed to come up here. But I didn't know what was going on until I got here, so had no reason to suspect that we'd get stuck." The voice coming over the line sounds defeated.

"And there are a lot of sick people in Jaredstown. I hear conditions there are dire. We're staying in Ashcrag, as is your brother. The elders have placed Jaredstown under quarantine."

"I'm sorry to hear that sir. Does Summer know that you're stuck up there?"

"She knows we won't be back tomorrow."

There's silence, then he asks a question that I would never have expected to hear.

"Jared, promise me you'll take care of her if we don't make it back."

"I promise." It's possibly the most solemn commitment I've ever made.

...

194

After the call with the warden, I go downstairs to talk with Summer. I want to go out into the wilderness this weekend. Maybe leave this afternoon. I'm hoping she'll come with me.

CHAPTER 14: VISION

I'm finally headed out into the wilderness. Summer agreed to come with me but asked me to wait until morning. She stayed over again last night. I made up four doses for Lenna, enough to cover her for the weekend. Summer and I both have her number. If we should be detained, I'll tell her where she can find a key to my apartment to get more.

Just before the close of business yesterday, I talked with Jack Johnson, head of camp security. He'd been the default assistant warden until I was given that job recently. I told him that I would be away on Saturday and Sunday so was leaving him in charge in my absence. I also brought him up to speed on the gardens and new directives, asking him to call me before taking any action that would impact these changes.

Jack's a straight arrow, a standup guy. I'm confident that he'll do a good job in my absence.

Summer and I are up early again. We pack our gear onto the flatbed portion of my truck, then head over to the staff kitchen. Lenna is waiting and looking positively radiant. Summer gives Lenna the bottle with four doses and tells her we're going to be away for the weekend. I caution her to take her medication on time, not to double up.

As we pull out, Summer says she's never seen Lenna looking this good. We're both full of optimism.

As we leave the camp, a certain weight seems to lift off my shoulders.

"So, what's the plan?"

I smile. "It's simple. We're going to follow the road south of the river until it ends. Then see how far East we can get over the open land. I suspect that'll be slow going. We'll stop an hour before sunset and set up camp. Have a pleasant evening, then come back tomorrow. It's uncharted territory, so who knows how far we'll get. But we're on our own, so I don't plan to take any risks."

In a seeming change of subject, Summer says, "I talked to my parents just before leaving work yesterday."

"I'm surprised you didn't tell me that last night." I say light heartedly.

"Dad told me that he talked to you yesterday."

I'm wondering where this is going. Last night I told Summer I'd spoken with her father shortly after we sent the real estate offer out.

"And..."

"He's very proud of you, you know."

"I'm glad to hear that. I have a great deal of respect for him."

"He told me that he asked you about buying the alcohol plant. Said that he was a bit rude to you and you replied a bit sharply, which he thought he deserved."

Now I'm really worried about where this is going.

"I guess the upshot of the conversation was that he thinks you're our world's best hope, so he asked you to promise to take care of me."

"Which I will."

She smiles wryly, apparently the punchline hasn't come yet.

"I told him I want to move in with you and asked for his blessing."

My blood pressure spikes. I wasn't expecting that.

"And what did he say?"

"He rambled a bit, saying he thought we were too young, blah, blah, blah. But given the situation, the uncertainty about the future, whether there would even be a future..." Her voice trails off for a moment. "He thinks we should take whatever happiness the world offers while we still can. And that if you are able to save us, he hopes to be your father-in-law someday."

I'm momentarily frozen, not sure what to say. Then the answer comes with incredible clarity.

"Summer, I love you. Will you move in with me?"

"Yes."

I pull off onto the side of the road. Then turn to kiss her.

After a while we come back to reality and I realize we haven't even passed our manufacturing plant yet.

"Want to walk around our new property?"

...

As we pull up to the plant, I see that the gate's open, and Charlie's truck is in the parking lot. I pull in next to him, then get out. He apparently hears us and comes out of the loading area.

"Well, look who's here." He comes over to shake my hand then Summer's.

"The boss was impressed by your offer. He was expecting a lot worse. I'm not allowed to tell you this, but I think he plans to accept. He asked me to make sure all our stuff was out, then to schedule a test for the steam and electrical system."

"Good news," I reply.

"How soon do you think you'll start up operations?"

"As soon as possible, of course, but I don't have a good idea about that yet. A lot will have to do with Brock Newton and the still changes."

"Understood. I'd love to come work for you, if you're looking to hire."

"I'll keep you in mind."

Charlie points to my truck. "You headed out into the wilderness?"

"Yep. Been wanting to do it for a while. This weekend seems like it might be our last chance, so we're taking it."

"Well, I hope you have a good time."

We shake, then Summer and I get back in the truck.

"Hope to see you soon," Charlie calls out as we pull away.

ROAD TO NOWHERE

We pull out of the parking lot and turn east. The road here is not so good, but within 20 meters it gets worse. The road would be impassable in a regular ethanol-powered, two-wheel drive car. It's not too bad in the hover craft, but I adjust the controls to lift us up a half meter off the ground. At this height it does a good job of steadying our ride. But I still can't go very fast.

Ten minutes later, we spot the first test well. I stop, lower the truck, then get out. There's not that much to see: a cement pad with a capped pipe coming up out of it. Embedded in the cement are rusted bolts that are almost completely gone. The pump, or whatever device had been mounted there, had been removed long ago. There's a plaque mounted on the corner of the pad. It had markings at some point. Nothing is readable now, but I snap a picture anyway. Maybe with some postprocessing we can glean something from the picture.

I do a quick 360 to take in the whole scene. Our new manufacturing facility is still visible to the west, but just barely. Beyond that are the mountains and space port. Those landmarks will make navigation easy. There's a ridgeline just south of us that runs parallel to the river. We're about halfway up, so have a great view of the river and of the land downstream.

I notice Summer looking intently at something down river.

"What do you see?"

She looks at me, then points. "There's a palm tree and a bunch of sugarcane plants down by the river. There must be something there that causes them to bunch up like that."

Looking east, I can see plants of various types continuing on as far as the eye can see, although they appear to thin out. It makes sense, there are lots of plants grown outdoors in Heroldstown. Strong winds sometimes blow this way, no doubt carrying seeds that will grow if they fall close enough to the river.

"Well, let's see what else we can find," I say brightly.

...

We get to the end of the road around lunch time. There was another well every 5 km or so. 10 in total. Each was about the same. One had a completely rusted out piece of equipment on the platform. Each had a plaque. A few had a character or symbol that could be read.

There is still vegetation here and there on the ground, but less than there was near our new manufacturing facility. Vegetation near the river has remained fairly constant. The water either carries the seeds more consistently, or there is less rain as we move east from the lake.

We are now far enough downstream that the mountains in the west aren't the pronounced geographic feature they were before. We'll need to rely mostly on the river for navigation from here out.

Being this far from home makes me a little more aware of our limited food supply. We brought the dehydrated food we bought earlier this week and nearly 100 liters of potable water, so it's not like we're at risk of running out this weekend. But I'm very aware that once we go past the end of the road, it will be difficult for rescuers to find us if something happens.

"You're quiet," Summer prods.

We're sitting on the hood of my truck, sharing a liter of water and one of the sandwiches we bought at the café this morning. It's a good place to survey the land ahead. The land slopes down here. There's a gully blocking our way. That's probably why the road ends here. Several more gullies are visible ahead. We'll probably need to go down closer to the river to find a place to cross them.

"Just taking in the scenery and trying to figure out where to go next."

"So, we're not stopping here."

I point downriver. "See how the valley narrows, then turns north?"
She nods.

"If possible, I'd like to get down there. There's something like that
in my visions. We'll probably have to go further than that to find what
we're looking for, but I think that's all the further we can go today, if
we can even go that far."

"We might be able to see more from the top of the ridge." She
points up to a spot along the ridge about 5 km east of here.

"Good point. Think you can scout a path to get there? The gully in
front of us is a problem. I don't want to try crossing it. It's too deep."

I point up the hill to our right. "I lose track of the gully up there.
Maybe there's a crossable spot."

I point down toward the river. "I think we can cross down there.
See how it flattens out. I think I can crank up the levitation to at least a
meter, maybe two. Beyond that we risk crashing."

"Then let's head downhill toward the river."

She smiles and pops off the hood. "Let's go."

This is the most carefree I've seen Summer in over a week.

CROSSING

It takes us a full hour to get down to the river. There's actually a
sandy shoreline that's relatively smooth and runs a long way. Every so
often there's a copse of trees or a growth of sugar cane we need to
navigate around, but in the next hour we move 10 more kilometers
downstream. There we hit our next obstacle.

The sandy shoreline ends. Looking downstream, we can see the
riverbank getting higher and higher, at one spot at least 10 meters. As
we move up hill, we find another gully. This one runs all the way down
to the river, cleaving the riverbank at one of its high spots. We spend
the next hour climbing higher and higher up the slope toward the
ridge line.

We only need to travel another kilometer or two east to see
around the bend in the river. But we haven't been able to find a place
where the gully flattens out enough to cross. As we climb, we come to
what appears to be a grassy meadow, which seems extremely unlikely.
I stop, not wanting to venture out onto the meadow. Something
seems very wrong.

"What's the matter?" Summer asks.

"It looks like a meadow, but I don't think it is."

Summer rolls down her window and sticks her head out, then screams and pulls back in, rolling the window up as fast as possible.

"It's a swamp with some sort of swamp grass. And it's infested with vipers. We're already several meters in."

I slowly ease back in reverse, glad that I had the good sense to stop when I did. I can't help but wonder how this got here. Why is this much water up so high? How did it get here? And the vipers? I seriously doubt they swam upstream. And what do they eat? I don't see any toads. This doesn't add up.

My reverie is broken as things suddenly darken.

"What happened?"

Summer points at the ridgeline. "The sun dropped below."

I almost chuckle. Everyone calls our star the sun. It's as if that word means the local star. As the owner of a protected world, implicitly part of a protected system, my ancestor got to name all the celestial bodies. We're supposed to call our star, J-Sol. Embarrassing, but true.

"What's so funny?"

I look up and see Summer's questioning eyes.

I almost say, "Nothing." But that's not true and she knows it.

"Can I answer that tomorrow?" I plead. "The bigger problem is what to do. It's getting dark and we need to set up camp, but we clearly can't do it here."

"Then go around." She points to a trail that goes around the swamp and ends on the other side of the gully.

"Not sure how I missed that! Sounds like a plan." I smile.

RIVERSIDE

The crossing Summer pointed out worked. It's as if this problem had been solved long ago and trail markers set for idiots like me. As we start our descent on the other side of the gully, there's a blinding flash of light. Well, maybe not blinding, but certainly bright enough to get both our attentions.

Puzzling through it, I come to understand this illusion. We passed through the last rays of the setting sun. And in that moment, I get a glimpse of the great sea into which the river empties. It's too late to get there tonight. But there's no way we can journey there tomorrow and still get home tomorrow night. But that's a problem for tomorrow.

Casting my attention back to the moment, I see a beautiful little lake down by the river, an eddy in the bend. There's a steep bank on the uphill side, and a flat rocky surface above perfect for my shelter.

I point. "I think that's where we should set up our shelter."

"Looks interesting," Summer replies skeptically.

"Let's at least check it out."

"Agreed." She smiles at me.

I love the smile. I'm not sure if she believes that's the place. But I love the idea that we're working this out together.

CAMPSITE

It's starting to get really dark by the time we arrive. I use the truck's headlights, then a high-power flashlight to check the site before committing to it. Summer agrees, so we unload the shelter. It comes with a high-power bolt driver, so in a matter of minutes, the shelter's anchored and the auto-setup sequence initiated.

I set up the stove, as Summer selects pots and meals, then adds the water. We're having beef stew and grill bread, whatever that is. Twenty minutes later, we're sitting in our portable easy chairs and the last of the sunlight is fading. I hear toads starting to croak, so get up to put security measures in place.

The security is a perimeter shield. It's a dual electrostatic defense grid that's a meter tall, 2 centimeters thick and wraps around the shelter, fireplace, and truck. It plugs into the truck's electrical outlet and will electrocute anything that touches the inner and outer grid. Toads, vipers, adult centipedes... All will be toasted if they try to pass through. In the event of a full-scale creature assault, the system will set off a siren that can be heard for kilometers, hopefully giving us time to escape. The truck's charge is low at this point, so I plug it into my antimatter recharger. I feel remarkably safe, no doubt a harbinger of bad things to come.

Stars begin to light the sky to the east as the last tinges of red fades from the sky in the west. I settle back into my portable easy chair and take in the view. Summer comes over, one hand behind her back.

"Dinner will be ready in a half hour. Want to celebrate?"

I look at her questioningly.

The hidden hand comes out. It's holding a small bottle and two champagne flutes.

"Now that we have my parent's blessing, maybe it's time to celebrate."

"That sounds nice."

She pops open the bottle, then fills each flute about half full.

"To a successful adventure." She extends her flute toward mine and we clink.

"To a successful adventure," I echo.

The drink is interesting. It's a sparkling fruit juice of some sort, surprisingly sour, not sweet.

The last of the sunlight is gone and it's now dark. Our only light is the light coming off the fire.

...

Dinner is surprisingly good. I think the rich flavor is driven by the herbs. I suspect that observation is driven by my conversation with Jay earlier this week. The surprise is the texture. I was worried it'd be like cardboard. But this stew is almost as good as Lenna's.

"You're quiet." Summer prods.

"Just marveling at how good this meal is."

"I suspect it's the skill of the chef," she teases.

"Probably," I tease back.

There's silence for a moment.

"Do you think we could get to where you want to go if we left early tomorrow morning? We could probably go an hour or two and still get back home by dark."

Her question surprises me. I desperately want to go further but assumed she didn't, so wasn't going to push it.

Then it occurs to me. She knows I won't ask, so she's giving me permission to ask her to do something she probably doesn't want to do.

"We only need to go another kilometer or two. If we can spot a path, we could do that in an hour, which would give us plenty of time to get back tomorrow."

She smiles and stands. "Would you mind cleaning up? I'd like a couple minutes to myself."

"Sure."

"Thanks." She heads off toward the shelter, enters, then closes the door.

I hope she's OK. It's unlike her to skulk off like this.

I head over to the truck and grab a liter of water. I'll use it to wash the dishes. As I do so, I realize the water is going to be a problem on future trips. We drank two liters today, used two more making dinner, now another for the dishes. On a longer trip where we're making all our meals, washing more dishes, and washing ourselves we'll need at least 10 liters a day. That's a lot of space and weight for water.

As I set the dishes out to dry, there's a bright flash of light and a loud snap. Pointing my flashlight in the direction it came from, I see smoke rising from the charred remains of a large centipede. Seems the security barrier works.

With a last scan of the camp site, I head over to the shelter and knock lightly on one of the door supports. "OK, if I come in?"

"Been waiting for you."

I dial down my flashlight and open the door. It's dark inside. Summer's light is off. I back in and secure the door, then turn and see Summer on the bed. As I pass my light over her, I see that she's wearing nothing but a sheer nightgown that's more or less completely transparent. I'm transfixed by the sight of her and filled with desire.

"Well? Are you going to come and join me?"

...

I'm aroused by another snap outside. It wakes me enough to notice the predawn light penetrating the shelter and dimly illuminating Summer's naked form lying next to me. The sound apparently woke her too and within seconds we are once again wrapped around each other.

After a while, she pushes back a bit. "If we don't get up soon, we won't have time to explore further downstream."

I groan. I want more, but I also want to go explore.

I pull her in close, hold her for a second, then sigh and let her go. "Let's get up and head out."

Once moving, we dress and pack up everything that doesn't get folded up into the shelter. I open the door and push the packs out, then turn to tie down the last item that needs to be secured before I initiate the shelter's auto-shutdown mechanism.

Summer steps out and a moment later screams, "Jared!"

VISITORS

I come flying out of the shelter, my eyes drawn to where she's pointing. There, I see something I could never have imagined.

Two men are sitting in portable chairs outside the security perimeter, opposite our chairs from last night.

"So, you are Jared Daan?"

I'm shocked that he knows who I am.

"Who are you and what are you doing here?"

The man indicates our chairs. "Please come and be seated. We wish to speak with you."

I stand my ground and repeat. "Who are you?"

He indicates our chairs again, then replies.

"My name is Julian Daan. I'm the leader of the people of the East, the one you've come out here to find. And I believe that we are relatives. Please." He waves his hand at our chairs.

I slowly move toward them. Summer creeps along behind me.

"Why are you here?"

"Jared, we have common interests to discuss. Please."

Again, he indicates our chairs.

As I get closer, I notice his eyes. They're like Ethel's. His pupils are clear and coal black. But his irises are almost completely white. At one point, they were apparently blue. Now, they're white with thin streaks of blue.

As I take my seat, he turns toward Summer.

"The two of you are bonded?"

I'm a bit shocked by the question. Summer less so. She replies, "Yes, we're together."

"Good." The old man nods approvingly.

"So, what is this common interest?" I prod.

He looks at me oddly.

"You bear the name of my grandfather. I am second generation, the grandson of Jared Daan and Mirella Padilla."

I shake my head. "My ancestral grandfather was married to a woman named Emma."

The old man gets a laugh out of that.

"Yes. The one in Jaredstown. But he was a man of much greater appetite than poor Emma could satisfy. While still living on the space station, he had taken up with one of the settlers moving here from New Brazil, a young woman named Mirella Padilla. When they were found out, the old man sent her, and others in her group, to a settlement he'd built in secret along the shore of the great sea. He named the town Jaramor, and the sea, the Sea of Passion." Another chuckle. "He had quite the way with words and apparently no shame.

"Early in her study of the great *mystery*, she learned of you. She's the one that coined the saying... *The sixth son of the sixth generation will unite us all.*"

Not the sixth son thing again! I am so sick of that nonsense.

He looks at me oddly. It's as if he can read my mind.

As the thought passes through my consciousness, he nods.

"I trust you've found the solution." Julian speaks the words as if it's a statement, but it's clearly a question.

"You mean the disease?" I reply.

He looks at me in shock, then turns to his silent and unintroduced partner. The two lock eyes for several seconds, then lift their hands to the sky and Julian chants what sounds like a prayer. Not only do they anoint me with a new version of the old saying, but they carry on like mystics.

After a moment, his gaze falls back on me.

"You have not learned of all nine components yet?"

"Nine?"

Julian turns back to his companion, who again nods.

Turning back toward me, Julian stands. Somewhere along the way, he'd reached inside his robe. I know this because I see his hand coming back out of the robe as he stands. He extends his fist toward me, then starts to open it palm up. As the fingers come into view, I lean back in shock. His fingers have no nails. The shock is so complete that I miss the small candy made of compressed brown sugar sitting on his palm

"This is a gift of immense value. Few ever taste it. But it is given to you freely. We call it *profecia aumentar*. Place it on your tongue and hold it there while it melts."

I'm frozen in my seat, paralyzed by the implications of what I'm seeing, and the words spoken. Profecia aumentar, I've heard Ethel say this. It's Portuguese for increased prophecy.

"If the two of you are indeed bonded, then best if the partner takes some also."

I continue sitting and staring, but surprisingly Summer stands, takes the candy, breaks off a piece, and turns to me.

"You going to join me?" she asks, then pops her piece in her mouth.

I take it, place it on my tongue and feel it immediately. Then the world expands. I sense dozens of people hidden around me, all of whom think I'm their leader. Then Julian's thoughts pass through my mind as if he's speaking out loud.

So, it is as the prophecy foretold. The woman will go first.

I stand and focus my mind on what's happening to me. This isn't like the visions induced by the ladies' concoctions. It's different. It's changing me. I can feel it.

Summer's voice sounds in my mind. *Jared, are you OK?*

I close my eyes and cast my mind in her direction. Curiously, I can feel her. Feel her breathing, the air coming in and going out. I can feel her heart pounding, afraid of what's happening.

It's OK, my love. I need a moment to myself, then we'll go exploring.

I feel her heart pounding harder. I see Julian through her eyes. She's asking him what's happening to me. I see him answering, but don't hear the words. It's a bit overwhelming experiencing the world through Summer's senses.

Then I snap back into myself fully awake, fully aware. I take Summer's hand, then we're off. First stop, Ashcrag.

I see the warden. Love and worry for his daughter radiate out of him. Next, I see Aaron. Pain of loss radiates from him. He seems lost without Dad and desperately wishes I had been chosen to be an Elder, not him. He's out of his depth and knows it. The Elders are deeply divided about the path forward. Unfortunately, they're totally clueless about what's actually going on. If they act on any of the things they're considering, our presence on this world will soon come to an end.

The next stop is New London. I pass through city after city where only a few souls still live. This was the first stop Melvin Harsoal's research team made on their return from Doffenplod. This world is now dead.

Next, I'm off to the Confederation's capital world, New Beijing. Senior government officials are terrified by the reports coming in from the protected worlds along the rim. Another alien armada is inbound. They are currently in the void separating our spiral arm from the next one out. They will be here in a few years and no one knows what to do about it.

Next, I'm in the void approaching the incoming armada. Now I'm on the bridge, where the King commanding the flagship takes notice of me. He reaches out to grab me, but when the first, fleshy, pale digit touches me, he shrieks and pulls away. His hand seems to burn, and he falls to the floor. And in that moment, a blinding truth fills my consciousness. Their bioweapon is far less dangerous to us than our cure is to them.

A moment later, I'm in the office of the Commander of the Confederation's Joint Military Forces. The eyes of Admiral Arthur Tang lock onto mine.

Admiral Tang, can you hear me?

Who are you, and why are you here?

I'm Jared Daan, from the planet Jaredaan. I have a cure for the disease and a powerful weapon that could destroy the inbound alien forces.

As he starts to reply, I'm distracted by Summer's voice sounding in my mind. *Jared, come back to me.*

...

I feel someone shaking me.

"Jared! Jared, are you OK?"

It's Summer. I slowly open my eyes but am not sure what I'm seeing. I'm sitting in my chair. Julian and his companion are still in theirs. I thought the sun was fully up by the time we had spoken with Julian, but now it's not.

Julian is the first to realize I'm back.

"You were gone for nearly 12 hours Jared. I hope you found what you needed to find."

I turn to Summer. "Is that true? Was I really gone 12 hours?"

She holds out her communicator. It reads 7:29 PM.

"I just got back, a minute or two before you did. But yes. I think that's the right time "

"Where did you go?"

She chuckles and shakes her head.

"I followed you, sucked along in your wake so to speak."

"You were with me?"

Julian answers. "Bonded ones on a small dose usually do. They have little ability to influence where you go but are likely to remember details that you won't."

I look at Summer. "You were in Ashcrag?"

"Yes. It was hard seeing Dad like that. Aaron asked you to stay."

"I remember looking at them. But I don't remember either looking at me or trying to communicate."

"As I said," Julian asserts himself. "A bonded partner is more likely to remember details. Particularly ones not material to your purpose."

"And on the alien flagship?"

I see Summer shudder.

"Yes, you killed him."

Julian interrupts again. "So, it's true. The aliens are returning."

I can still hear Julian's thoughts. They're muted, but more than clear enough to make out. He wants us to return to Jaramor with them. *We can do a more thorough debriefing there. If we leave now.*

"We will go with you. Please show us the way."

208

"Let some of our people help you pack."

The words are no sooner out of Julian's mouth, then dozens of men on horseback appear from hidden spots in the area around us.

We are packed in minutes, then follow the caravan along trails we would never have found on our own.

Within an hour we are around the turn in the river and a great sea stretches out in front of us. The sunset lights the sea ablaze. It's a sight I could never have imagined.

We spend another hour descending the last of the foothills onto the plain, then we enter Jaramor. It's larger and in better condition than Heroldstown. I can't wait to learn its secrets.

JARAMOR

We are led to a building that looks like a pub. When we enter, Julian and his still unnamed companion lead us to a private room in the back. We enter and see four more people already seated there.

"Jared, Summer. The six of us are the town elders."

He indicates the woman sitting next to him. "This is my wife, Elder Sofia Paschal Daan."

He indicates the unnamed man and the woman sitting next to them. "You've met Edson Jardim. Next to him is his wife Elder Clarissa Fontes Jardim. Edson lost his voice years ago. He communicates telepathically now as you and I did for a while. We have both spent enough time exploring the *mystery* that we have formed a telepathic link."

This is the second time he's used the word *'mystery'* in this way. It must be the way they refer to the visions.

Julian points to the last two people. "This is Ryan Lake and his wife Elder Aurora Simpson Lake."

He then addresses the others.

"Friends, this is Jared Daan, the one foretold by my grandmother, and our first elder, Mirella Padilla Daan. With him is his bonded partner Summer Glenn Daan."

I smile when I hear Julian introduce Summer as a Daan. I sense that she's less comfortable with the idea but going with it for now.

"They have learned many of the properties of the venoms, but not the one that allows them to probe the future. I gave Jared his first dose earlier today. Summer accompanied him. He was able to confirm that which we suspected. The aliens are returning.

"He also learned something new."

Whispers rip through the room at those words.

"Yes, more proof that he is indeed the one foretold."

Julian pauses for effect.

"Our medications hold off the disease and are toxic to the aliens. Jared made telepathic connection with one of their kings, and it killed him."

After noisy whispering among the Elders, Edson stands.

All eyes turn toward him.

Julian speaks for him. "My friend proposes that we call on the proprietor to bring us a platter of beef and a pitcher of his best ale."

"Agreed," Ryan replies enthusiastically.

...

As we waited for dinner, I gave the elders a summary of my vision. Summer elaborated a number of things that I completely missed. She seems to have seen a lot more than I did. Something that seemed to put the elders more at ease with our story.

But as the conversation went back and forth, one thing became increasingly odd.

"You make this sound as though the work here at Jaramor is the real reason our founder acquired this world. As if Jaredstown and Ashcrag are just covers to divert the Confederation's attention."

Julian looks at me oddly. "It may not have been at the outset. But something happened before the expedition actually got underway." A pause. "Have you ever wondered why so many of the settlers came from New Brazil? Our ancestor and his brothers were all born on Caladon. Your namesake made a huge fortune there, then at some point sold it all and withdrew from society."

Julian's question gives me pause to think. "I always assumed he withdrew because he was planning to leave."

"No," Julian replies. "He attempted to run for political office. He sensed something going wrong in the Confederation and wanted to help correct it. His attempt failed. He was shamed in the process, ostracized. So, he started looking for another path to his end goal. Jaredaan, with its wealth of gold, platinum, copper, and nickel seemed like it might be enough to help him rise within the Confederation's social hierarchy.

"At some point before the colonization mission's departure, he took a trip to New Brazil. He ended up staying there a month. His plans changed at that point."

"Do you know how they changed?"

Julian looks at me again as if puzzled that the answer to my question could possibly be unknown.

"Have you ever wondered why our world was terraformed using sugar cane? Why not corn? We certainly have the land and atmosphere? Why not algae? How could that not have been faster?"

I think I know the answer, but don't have the courage to venture a guess.

Julian shakes his head. "Given the circumstances, one would think the answer is obvious!"

Getting no reply, he continues, "The cane ecosystem. Vipers, toads, centipedes... For thousands of years, the people of New Brazil have known that these creatures secrete the substances needed to see the future. Periodically, someone with the gift of foresight, would start to rise then quickly get swept away by the Confederation.

"Our grandfather's dream was to create a place like New Brazil, but far from prying eyes. A place where someone with the gift could rise and gain power."

Julian pauses and shakes his head, then chuckles.

"His mother came from that region of New Brazil. He thought he might be the one with the gift. That turned out not to be true.

"His wife, Mirella, did have it, but was nowhere near powerful enough to plot his rise. As the truth settled on him that he would never lead the Confederation, the old man began to decline.

"Mirella, hoping to give him comfort, began probing the *mystery* in earnest. The sixth son prophecy was eventually revealed to her. It gave the old man enough hope to press on, spread the word, and eventually die in peace."

CHAPTER 15: RETURN

I'm startled awake by the sound of an alarm clock going off. It's been a long-time since I've used an alarm clock. I always wake early, so stopped using one. Summer must have set it.

I look at the time on my communicator and am shocked to see it's 8:00. I never sleep that late. Yesterday's journey must have taken a bigger toll on me than I would have expected. The long evening with the elders and the second ale might've had something to do with it as well.

Our discussions last night covered a lot of ground. Possibly the biggest disagreement was about our plan to return home. They want us to stay. In truth, Summer and I would both like to stay longer. But if we don't return home, the warden will send a search party looking for us. And if that happened, Jaramor's long held secret would ultimately be revealed.

Possibly the best news of the evening was that they have significant milking capacity and are willing to give us as much venom as we want, in exchange for getting half of the end product back. They also gave us the 'recipes' for several useful medications.

Summer is slower waking than I am, so I hop in the shower first. Fifteen minutes later, I'm out, dressed, ready for the day. Summer's ready a half hour after that, which allows us time to get to a breakfast meeting with the Elders at 9:00.

PUB PRIVATE ROOM

We arrive back in the pub's private room a few minutes early. Everyone else is already there and has helped themselves to the buffet.

Julian is the first to greet us. "Jared, Summer. I trust you slept well."

"Yes. Thank you for the accommodations last night," I reply.

"Think nothing of it. It's your room whenever you're here."

Among the things we learned last night is that Julian and his wife Sophia owned the pub and the inn that it's part of.

We grab some food, then join the others at the table.

Julian takes that as his cue to start.

"In the interest of honoring our agreement to be finished by 10:00 AM, I'd like to start. I've arranged for two of our rangers to accompany you on the first part of your journey. They know the fastest trails and can get you to your half-way point fast enough to get back home themselves."

Having just stuffed some food in my mouth, Summer answers for me.

"Thank you, Julian. If we can reduce the transit time, we can spend more time with you next time we visit."

Julian nods his agreement. "The next thing I'd like to discuss is the possibility of sending one of our pharmacists back with you. Would you be able to shelter him, keep his presence secret?"

"At the moment, no. In a couple weeks, probably. I hope to close the deal on our manufacturing plant this week. We plan to add one or more apartments suitable for overnight stays. Once that's done, he can stay there. We can get him in and out without being seen.

"I assume your intent is to help us bring up the plant quicker."

Julian nods his head. "Just like you, we need to get your disease preventive in the hands of our people. We'll do everything in our power to see that happen as quickly as possible. Which brings me to the next topic..."

He trails off. I suspect he's worried I won't be as willing to accommodate as he is.

"We need to get you out there exploring the *mystery*. Our prospects here on Jaredaan are not very good if we can't save the rest of humanity from the aliens. The only person who has a chance of finding that path is you, Jared."

Although I've come to believe that Julian's words are true, I don't like the idea of destiny or predetermination. I am who I am because I strived for it. But even as the thought passes through my mind, I know it's not wholly true. I worked hard for my educational accomplishments, but my apparent visionary power has more to do with innate attributes inherited from my parents and the work of people like Julian, Ethel, Norah, and their ancestors, who discovered the properties of the venoms.

I notice all eyes on me and realize I've been off in my own head somewhere. I look at Julian with intensity.

"I sincerely hope that I'm not humanity's last defense. But I acknowledge the gift I've inherited. Is there a way I can take shorter trips? Twelve-hour trips like the one yesterday will be hard to hide from others, especially if Summer comes with me."

Julian nods, then smiles. He pulls a small tin from his case and slides it across the table to me.

"Open it."

I do.

"See the different sizes? The largest ones are like the one I gave you yesterday that took you away for 12 hours. The smallest might be more like 3 hours for you. If Summer is to accompany you, she should take about a quarter of what you do. Much more than that and she will take her own journey."

"Understood and thank you. I have a lot to do when we get back. This will allow me to get that done, then probe the *mystery* in the evenings at home in private."

Surprisingly, Ryan's wife, Elder Aurora Simpson Lake, the least spoken of the Elders, says with compassion, "Do what you need to do, dear boy. But remember, you are the one with the gift. Using it to chart our course is the most valuable use of your time. Everything else is of lesser importance, so should be left to others. Others called to those purposes."

Her words are surprisingly tender. And as much as I hate the implications, I know they're true.

TRAIL HOME

As we leave the pub, I see four men on horseback near my truck. I also see that the truck has been fully packed already and there are a couple extra boxes that weren't there before.

I turn to say something to Julian, but see he's staring at one of the horsemen in the way he does when speaking with them telepathically.

He snaps out of it, then turns to me.

"The rangers have decided to provide a larger escort than the one I requested. These four will travel with you directly. Four more have already been sent ahead to scout the trail. Apparently, there was rain last night. I'm surprised that we hadn't seen it.

"Our observation teams near the prison camp have noticed the food shortage that's developing. So, we're giving you about a month's supply of dehydrated food from our stores. Probing the *mystery* can be very draining. It is important that you remain well fed."

He pauses, seemingly hesitant to continue.

214

"Jared, I know it's in your nature to want to share this food with people in the camp. Please do not. We don't have enough food in our stores to make up for the camp's food shortage. If we are to survive, this food must go to its designated purpose, fueling your search."

"Understood. And thank you again for your generosity. Is there a way I can contact to arrange our next visit?"

Julian chuckles.

"In time it will just be a matter of directing the thought to me. You can contact me at any time during your journeys, just by visiting. If you need to contact me without journeying, take a quarter or less of the smallest candy. Wait until you can feel its effect. Then extend your mind toward me. Don't worry. It will come naturally."

JOURNEY HOME

The team escorting us is remarkably quiet. I eventually deduce that they are slightly dosed, enough to communicate telepathically among each other and with the scouting team. Periodically the team leader, a fellow named Jason Tanner, comes back to check in with us. The rain has caused the swamp level to raise a little. It turns out that the swamp was made, and is maintained, by the sourcing team in Jaramor.

It was created over 100 years ago. Every viper in the swamp is tagged, its DNA mapped, and its venom characterized. Vipers with poor quality venom, meaning ones with higher levels of toxins and lower levels of the useful compounds, are killed, eliminating them from the gene pool. Over the years, this evolutionary force has vastly improved venom quality.

Anyway, the sourcing team is in the process of lowering the swamp level, so it should be passable by the time we get there.

...

We arrive at the swamp to quite a spectacle. The water level has been adjusted down, so we pass with ease. But lined up along the edge of the swamp are a dozen milking stations. Each station milks one viper every five minutes or so. In the half hour it takes us to circumvent the swamp over 200 ml of high-quality venom has been harvested.

With a known path, we've made good time. We left Jaramor around 10:15 and now, at 12:45, we're saying goodbye to our escorts. We say our farewells along the riverside at the gully where the road from Heroldstown ends. Ten minutes later, we find the road. Another hour and a half later we are at our manufacturing building. It's all buttoned up, the gate closed. There's also a sign hanging on the gate saying sale pending. The sign lifts my spirits. Soon this building will be ours. A few weeks later, the updated stills will come on-line. A few weeks after that we'll have our first production quantity of my nature-based remedy for DAGS.

HOME
True to her word, Summer unpacks her stuff in my apartment. She's moving in with me. A quick inventory of my kitchen shows that Lenna took a little more of the medication than she was asked to take.

It's only 3:30, so we head over to headquarters to check-in. Larry, Summer's co-worker seems relieved to have Summer back.

I head up to my office. There are about 20 messages waiting for me, but I skip past them and call Jack Johnson, head of camp security, to let him know I'm back.

He reports that the camp has been calm, no real issues came up while I was away. The mood is as upbeat as he's seen it in a while. He thinks it's the gardens, which are being well received. He's skeptical about how much impact they'll have on the food supply but likes the upbeat vibe. He reminds me that a happy camp is a safe camp.

There are messages from my lawyer Audrey, realtor Macy and coppersmith Brock. I dash off quick replies and promise to speak with them tomorrow. The only message of concern is from Dr. Avery who needs to speak with me urgently. He wants me to come over to the clinic at my first opportunity. He'll make time to see me when I arrive.

HOSPITAL
I arrive at the hospital and am immediately taken to a conference room in the administrative area. A few minutes later, Dr. Avery comes in scanner in hand.

"Jared, I have something urgent I need to talk with you about, but would you mind if I scanned your blood pressure monitor first."

"Sure." I take my shirt off, he places the scanner on the blood pressure monitor, still glued to a spot near my right armpit.

"No incidents," he mutters. He paces for a moment, then stabs me with a stare. "Are the rumors true? Did you start taking a dietary supplement after the last incident?"

"Yes, I did."

"Is it perhaps the same one Lenna has started taking?"

I've been found out. I want to say no, but I can't.

216

"It is," I whisper.

He exhales with great exasperation. "Jared, you can't go around treating people with some unknown supplement. It's even worse to do it without the consent of their doctor."

"This is just a natural supplement. It's a food, not a drug. It makes me feel better. She wanted to try some. I gave her some of mine. I'm neither treating her, nor bypassing her doctor."

There's silence as he stares at me, then he seems to wither. "It's working. Her last cycle was minimally symptomatic. She was in today for an appointment booked a while ago. I shouldn't tell you this, but I did some scans. Her keratin buildup is shrinking. At the current rate of shrinkage, it'll be gone altogether in a couple weeks. There's not been a single documented case of DAGS remission. This is the first."

There's silence again for a few seconds.

"You knew this would happen, didn't you Jared?"

"I hoped it would."

"How? Why?"

"I recently learned of it. It's a traditional remedy that's been used on New Brazil for a long time. People there use it to lower their blood pressure. It has the side effect of making your fingernails fall out. I tried it on myself and my blood pressure issues just went away. I haven't been on it long enough to lose my nails..."

I can tell that Dr. Avery's figured it out when he says, "But Ethel and Norah have. Ethel's from New Brazil. This is something she knew about and made here."

I nod my head. "Something like that."

"So that's why you're buying the old whisky distillery. You want to make this stuff in quantity."

"I do. Ethel and Norah have been taking this stuff for years, so it's proven safe. And as you say, it is the only thing that's ever reversed a case of DAGS."

"How did you even find out about DAGS?"

"Exo-net. It's pretty well hidden, but there for public view if you look for it."

"How much of this do you have? We have two active cases in the keratin accretion phase, and several more suspected cases."

"We have enough for Ethel, Norah, Lenna, Summer and me. I think I can get enough for the other two."

"And how long before you have quantity?"

"I'm targeting six to eight weeks."

"Would you agree to let me start an official clinical trial on this?"

"Would that require us to divulge the formula?"

"Yes. Results must be tied to a specific substance or method."

"Sorry, I can't do that at this time."

Dr. Avery looks at me in shock. "Why?"

"We know how to make it, but we don't know what it actually is."

He stares at me for several seconds.

"Then that means you get a lot of batch-to-batch variance."

I nod my head. "The plan is to go to a continuous flow process to produce the precursors. Then a purification step or steps, then blending. Until the new facility comes up, we'll only have small quantities with more batch-to-batch variance than we'd like to admit."

"Now I understand the food supplement approach."

He mulls on it for a bit, then looks up at me.

"Word will get out, you know. And when it does, we'll come under Confederation pressure to convert this to a drug, one that's been put through the appropriate approval process."

"Maybe, but you understand that this isn't a cure, right? It just counteracts the effects of the genetic modifications the virus makes. Until the virus is killed off, we'll continue getting new cases. And once the genetic modification has been done, you have it for life. Our supplement will prevent you from becoming symptomatic, but it doesn't fix the underlying problem."

Another light seems to click on for Dr. Avery.

"And who ever controls the formula, controls the human race."

JUNGLE

Back in my apartment, I check on my Jungle account. I've not checked it since I released my new product for sale, almost exactly one week ago.

My message box has a surprising number of messages in it. There's a notice that the new product is up for sale; a notice about an adjustment they made unilaterally to the promotion package I'd signed on for; another product suggestion; multiple promotion offers; and a complaint about my slow response to another offer I don't even remember receiving. Then one that stops me in my tracks. It's a list of planets where delivery is no longer available. There are about 70 of them in two lists. One list is of planets where deliveries are temporarily suspended. They hope to restore operations from local delivery centers that should come online in the next 30 days. The other is a listing of planets from which orders will no longer be accepted. Jaredaan is on the list.

It makes sense. But it's still shocking to see it so plainly written out in black and white.

Checking on my sales levels, I see that sales of my older products have dropped about 20%. This is no doubt related to the delivery restrictions. But my new product more than makes up the difference. The last forecast was for 150,000 a month, 5,000 per day. Today is its seventh day on the market and total sales stand at 37,000. Between the two, my deferred payments increased 50,000 credits last week, unbelievable.

STAFF CAFÉ

Summer called to tell me she'd be staying at work an extra hour. Apparently, Larry got little done in her absence, so she wanted to get more caught up to lighten tomorrow's load. She's a bit grumpy about it, so I volunteer to pick up dinner. We can start using the supplies Julian gave us tomorrow.

I place our order, then go around to the kitchen to check on Lenna. She sees me and comes over to give me a big hug.

"Jared, I got some good news this morning."

"Tell me."

"They did a scan and my keratin levels have dropped in half. The doctor thinks I'm getting better. Your supplement is working."

"That is good news. How's your supply? You took a little more than I was expecting."

"Sorry," she looks really guilty. "I got confused as I poured and didn't want to risk contamination pouring it back. I'm good. I have enough for tonight and tomorrow."

I smile at her. "Good. It's going to be several more weeks before we have ample supply, so we need to watch it closely. And I can't tell you how happy I am that it's working for you."

JOURNEY

Summer looks really tired when she gets home but perks up as we eat. "You plan to probe the *mystery* tonight?" she asks in a saucy voice.

I laugh and nod my head. "You coming with me?"

"Sure. Where are we going?"

"I spoke with Dr. Avery today."

"We're going to see Dr. Avery?" She teases.

"No. Lenna's getting better. The keratin buildup in her small intestine has dropped in half and he figured out that our supplement is the reason why. He wants to do a clinical trial on it, but that will require us to disclose the chemical formulas used."

"You're not going to disclose them, are you?"

"We don't even know what they are."

"So, you want to go searching for the formulas?"

"Kind of. I want to find out how. Is there equipment on planet that can do the analysis? Can we buy or rent time on it?"

"You want to do this so you can run a clinical trial?"

"No. I want to figure out how we can mass produce this stuff. With Julian's help, I think we can treat everyone in Heroldstown and Jaramor. And I think that's something we need to do. But that isn't sufficient. We need enough to treat the Confederation. That's trillions of people. If we don't know what this stuff is, we'll never be able to mass produce it. There just aren't enough toads and vipers."

"Sounds like fun."

Dinner is done, everything's cleaned up. I open the tin and pull out a three-hour piece of *profecia aumentar* for myself. Summer takes another, cuts it into four pieces, and puts three of them back. We settle into our easy chairs and on the count of three, place our piece on our tongue.

In moments, I'm flying. I look for Summer and find her next to me, then cast my attention toward Heroldstown. Within moments I find multiple analytical chemistry setups capable of doing what we need. There are two at the main hospital, two at the ethanol plant, one at one of the food-packing plants, and one in each of three different government testing facilities. I thought it would be hard finding equipment like this, but it wasn't. The question now is how to get access to it.

Scene after scene passes through my mind and the answers become clear. The hospital won't help. They don't allow their equipment to be used for non-diagnostic purposes. The ethanol plant's equipment is too specialized and part of their continuous flow production process. They never contract it out. But the government facilities and the food-packaging company provide contract services.

I probe several approaches. It's a curious experience. When I look at a building, I can tell what it is. When I enter a building, I can see what's inside. When I look at a person, I can read them, learn something about them. But I can't tell how they'll react until I think about what I'll say to them. Then I can see their response.

I finally figure out that I can't see past my next decision, unless I specifically test that decision. Probing this way takes a long time. At some point I hope I can do it faster. But by the time the effect of the *profecia aumentar* starts to fade, I know exactly what I need to do, which component should go to which lab, who to talk to, and what to ask them.

At this point I'm absolutely confident that I can learn the exact composition of my supplement.

ZONES

It's been three days since I've been in the zones and I'm feeling incredibly guilty about it. The gardens are mostly planted and looking beautiful. The work supervisor from West Lake assures me that they will be done by the end of the week.

My 'problem' zones are doing surprisingly well. Both Rory, in Zone 5, and Logan, in Zone 10, have really embraced the new directives.

Rory appointed a fellow named Blake King to be his irrigation lead. Blake spent the day yesterday with Brian, the irrigation lead in Zone 3. Today, during my tour of Zone 5, Rory and I stopped to check in with Blake's work team. We arrived to see Blake instructing the team on the best way to cut the soil, the easiest way to gauge ditch depth, and common-sense defenses they can put in place to protect themselves from vipers that periodically venture into the irrigation ditches.

When I check in with Logan, he tells me that he, too, has assigned an irrigation lead, a woman named Kali Marrow. As we take our tour of the fields, I see that Logan has arranged for Brian to be in Zone 10 today. He's apparently giving Kali the same training he gave Blake yesterday.

I stop in Zone 3 at lunch time. I catch friend and former boss Gavin Barnes as he's heading over to the dining room.

"Gavin, thanks for loaning Brian to the other zones. It's already making a difference."

"Glad to hear it." He's quiet for a moment. "There's something I need to get off my chest."

I look at him curiously.

"You were right. I get it now. I had the benefit of some training and assistance when I started. The newer guys didn't. They had no idea what they were doing, and the warden was too detached to get it. You've made an incredible change. Not because you knew how to run a zone, but because you got involved, spotted problems, and rallied people to solve them. And it's done more than just improve productivity and output. It's improved morale."

"Thanks," I reply sincerely.

"OK, if we just grab a sandwich and head back to my office? I have a sensitive matter I'd like to discuss with you."

...

We're back in Gavin's office with today's sandwich and some sparkling water.

"So, what's on your mind?"

"Emily. She's back in the hospital today. Rumor has it that you have a cure. Are you going to offer it to her?"

"I've agreed to let Dr. Avery give it to her, but I'm short supply at the moment."

"There's another rumor going around, several actually. Is it true that you bought the old whisky distillery to make your cure in volume?"

"I'm trying to, yes."

"And you hired and paid for the gardens to be installed before you got the warden's permission."

"I was deputy warden at the time. I'd just found out that we are facing a food shortage, which made securing additional food the camp's top priority. It was within my authority, and I could afford it."

"But you didn't tell the old man until after it was done."

"I told him before the first plot was tilled, and he could have stopped it. But he didn't."

"And he didn't fire you?"

"Gavin, the warden is one of the good guys. He gave me a lot of latitude before I was released, then gave me a job once I was. And he did that knowing that I don't need a job, so the relationship would only work if it was collaborative.

"Yeah, I pushed the boundaries a little. But the real problem with the garden was budget, not rules or policy. Gardens are clearly allowed. I could provide the budget, which solved the real problem. I thought he would ultimately approve and the problem, to the extent there was one, would be that I personally funded it."

"But why? Why use your own money?"

"I do live here. If I can feed the camp, I can feed myself."

"It's that bad?"

"Unknown, but yes. There's a chance it will be that bad. And it's a problem that can be solved if we get ahead of it. This was the best I could do to get ahead of it."

Our discussion is interrupted by a call from headquarters on my camp radio.

"Jared here."

"Jared, we need you back at headquarters immediately. The Heroldstown police chief is here to see you."

"Understood, on my way."

I look at Gavin. "Sorry, but I need to run."

"Any idea why the police chief is here? Seems odd unless there was supposed to be a prisoner drop today."

"No idea."

HEADQUARTERS

As I come in the front door, Summer points upstairs. "He's in the conference room."

"Know why he's here?"

"No, just said it was urgent and he needed to talk with you."

"Wish me luck."

I double-time it up the steps, then knock on the conference room door and enter.

"Hi, I'm Jared Daan."

The police chief looks at me sternly, then offers his hand as he introduces himself.

"I'm Nicolas Santana, Heroldstown police chief."

We shake and he indicates a seat. Odd given it's my conference room.

"Chief, what brings you out to the camp today? Is there a problem I can help you with?"

"Confederation military command reached out to the elders council inquiring about a Jared Daan. The elders, including your brother Aaron, referred the complaint to me. They told me you are deputy warden here. Is that correct?"

"Yes. I'm the deputy warden here."

"The commander of the Confederation's joint military forces, a fellow named Admiral Arthur Tang claims you contacted him. Is that true?"

"I attempted to contact the admiral on Saturday."

223

"Did you attempt to contact him, or did you actually contact him."

"I contacted him but lost the connection after a few words."

"And where did that contact take place?"

"I was camping out in the wilderness, 50, maybe 60 kilometers east of the main road into camp."

"And what were you doing in the wilderness?"

"Camping. May I ask what the issue is?"

"The admiral says you appeared in his conference room, then left moments later. He wants to know how that was done. His conference room is heavily guarded with transport blockers in place."

"I never left Jaredaan. I contacted him telepathically."

The chief rolls his eyes.

"You contacted him telepathically, did you?"

The sarcasm in his voice angers me a bit.

"Do you know any other means of contacting someone 100 light-years away, while off-grid in the wilderness?"

"Cute."

"I'm serious. I know of no other way. So, if I contacted him that must be the way I did it."

The sheriff stews a bit, obviously not buying it.

"Why did you contact the Admiral?"

"I think I know how to defeat the aliens."

The chief snorts. "You're about 7,000 years late for that aren't you, son?"

"Chief, they've obviously not briefed you. The disease going around was left by the aliens to weaken or kill us. When it began spreading, they apparently found out. A large armada of alien ships is crossing the void as we speak. The admiral knows this and is looking for a solution.

"I've been experimenting with telepathy and thought maybe I could contact him so we could open a dialogue. I didn't know it would work."

"I don't know what your game is son, but I'm not buying it. The elder council asked me to come interview you, see if there was anything to this request from the Confederation. Seeing that you admit to having contacted the Admiral, I'm supposed to bring you into town for questioning. You going to come peaceably, or do I need to come back with a warrant?"

"You have no jurisdiction here, chief. This is a central government facility, not a city facility. I report directly to the elders. If they want to question me, they know how to reach me."

There's a knock on the door. It opens and camp security director Jack Johnson comes in.

"Good afternoon, Chief."

"Afternoon, Jack."

"Everything OK, boss?"

I take the question as a declaration that camp security is on my side.

"I think so. The chief had some questions. I answered them."

Turning toward the chief, I ask. "Is there anything else I can help you with Chief?"

"No. I think I got what I came for, but this isn't over yet, Daan. You can't go off doing stuff like this and not expect it to come home to roost."

The chief gets up and heads for the door. "I think I can find my way out."

He shakes hands with Jack, then opens the door. "Jack, you may want to think carefully about whose side you're on."

Then he leaves. As his footsteps recede down the stairs, Jack shuts the door. "What the hell was that about?"

I exhale and deflate a bit.

Jack pulls out a chair and takes a seat.

"Jared, he's not someone to mess with."

"No one on this planet has any idea what's going on."

"Want to tell me?"

"You know that Lenna and Emily have been sick, right?"

"Yah. I've heard that John in Zone 9 has it too. Is this about the disease?"

"The disease was left behind by the aliens on a planet called Doffenplod, which has been quarantined since before the end of the war. The quarantine was lifted a couple years back and the disease has spread like the plague. It's here. We've been placed under quarantine. Only no-contact deliveries are allowed, that's why we're running out of food."

"So, that's why you put in the gardens!"

"Yeah. I also found a treatment for the disease. It's not a cure, but it does put the disease in remission. Lenna's on the road to recovery. I'm trying to create the means to make more."

225

"That's why you're buying the old whisky distillery, isn't it?"

"Yep."

"So why was the chief here? You're not giving him the medicine?"

"When I have the supply, I'll give it to whoever needs it. But no, that's not why the chief was here. He doesn't even know about the disease. Probably doesn't know about the food shortage. The elders are holding that close to their chest."

"How do you know?"

"The exo-net. It's all there if you're persistent enough to find it."

"So why was the chief here?"

"Word of the release of the quarantine somehow got back to the aliens. Another armada is headed our way."

"You've got to be kidding me!"

I shake my head no.

"How do you know this?"

"I just do. The Confederation knows it too."

"So, the Chief was here because you know something you're not supposed to know?"

"Close. I think I know how to stop the aliens. I tried to contact Confederation military to tell them. They sent an inquiry to the elders wanting to know how I found out and was able to contact them. The elders sent the chief.

"Neither the elders, nor the chief, know about the aliens. When I told the chief, he didn't take it so well."

Jack starts chuckling.

I look at him questioningly.

"This seems to be your pattern, Jared. You're so far ahead of everyone else, you get in trouble for it." He chuckles some more. "I'll ask Summer to call me first if the Chief returns. With our help, he may have trouble finding you."

OFFICE

I'm back in my office, catching up on paperwork when my communicator sounds. It's Macy!

"Jared. I just got word. The ethanol facility has accepted your offer for the distillery. If you fund tomorrow, we can close on Friday."

I confirm my intention to fund immediately, then contact Miles Brown, my banker. He is also the banker for the sellers and the escrow company, so will have everything available for my signature tomorrow. It's frustrating that I need to go to Heroldstown to complete the financial transaction. But as I've come to learn over the last month, some things are done the way they're done and complaining about it just slows it down more.

With that out of the way, I decide that I need to do something I really don't want to do. Talk with Aaron.

I place the call, and surprisingly it connects.

"Jared, is that you!" Aaron seems overjoyed at the fact I've contacted him.

"It's me. Sorry, I didn't reach out sooner. The way I left... Dad's death... It's been easier to just put it off. That was wrong of me, but..."

"Me, too."

There's silence for a while. Both of us are emotionally involved enough that it's hard to talk.

"I'm calling about a visit I got from the Heroldstown Police this afternoon."

"Stupid idea. I told Walter we should do this ourselves, not involve Nicolas, but he wouldn't listen."

It takes a second for me to place the people. My uncle, Walter Daan, is the prime elder this year. So, he is the ultimate planetary decision maker. I've met him before, but don't really know him. He lives in Ashcrag. Nicolas is the chief, whom I spoke with earlier.

"Aaron. Did you see me on Saturday? Like in a vision or a dream?"

"Yes. How did you know?"

"I've acquired something like telepathy. I'm still learning to control it. I thought about you and was suddenly there with you, then it slipped away."

"So that was real?"

"I think it was. I thought I spoke with you, but don't remember what was said."

"I asked you to stay. But you were with that beautiful girl. Is she the warden's daughter?"

"Yes."

Aaron starts laughing. "I wouldn't have that much courage. I like Archer, but he's a bit strict. He sure seems to like you though."

"I have a great deal of respect for the warden and love his daughter."

"So, she's part of your telepathy thing."

"It works better when we do it together."

"Oh, don't start my mind down that path."

I chuckle and shake my head. Aaron's turned out to be a much nicer guy than I would have believed when I was little. But he can be a bit simple.

"One of my next stops on that telepathic journey was with Admiral Arthur Tang."

"You've got to be kidding me!"

"No."

"What for? Do you know this guy?"

"Aaron, the aliens are coming again. A full armada is on their way. The Admiral knows that, most of the Central Council does as well. They're trying to keep it secret, which I understand and respect. But I think I've figured out a way to stop them, so needed to tell someone that could do something with it."

"So, you went to the top admiral to offer him a solution to a problem no one is allowed to know about? Jared, have you lost your mind?"

"Now that you know the story, can you tell me what the government asked you to do?"

"Nothing really. They just asked if you were a real person and attempted to contact the admiral."

"OK, you have the answer. Can you get Walter to call off the sheriff?"

"I'll see what I can do. So, are you going to marry this girl?"

I just shake my head. "I'd like to."

"Then I hope it works out for you. You deserve someone good."

"Thanks. OK, if I ask about something else?"

"What."

"I know about what's going on. The disease, the boycott and embargo, the no contact delivery rules, the delivery you haven't been able to land..."

"How? That's supposed to be secret too."

"It's on the exo-net. All you have to do is look for it."

There's silence for a moment.

"And the point of telling me this?"

"Maybe we can cooperate? I have a lot of money off world. I don't have the standing to place an emergency order, but there are things I'd like to get. Maybe if we worked together, the elders could get another delivery and I could get the equipment I need."

"What kind of equipment do you need?"

"Scientific instrumentation, chemical synthesis equipment, bottling machines, that sort of thing."

"What the hell, Jared."

"I have a treatment for the disease that puts it in remission. I need stuff like that to put it in mass production."

More silence, then... "You've got the money for that? How?"

"Best-selling products on Jungle."

More silence. "You're in a whole different league than we are, aren't you?"

I let the question sit there.

"I'm sure Walter will be willing to deal. The situation is bad, really bad. But play your cards closer to your chest when dealing with him. If he knew what you've told me, he'd be coming to seize your assets. He's a gangster at heart with no compunction against theft, especially if he can wrap it up in '*the good of the people*' nonsense."

"Thanks for the warning."

"You've got a good heart little brother. They'll take advantage of it if you let them."

After a little more chit-chat, the line drops. I miss the brother I never really got to know until I was ripped away from him.

JOURNEY

Tonight's destination is the void. I need a better sense of how much time we have left. Summer's not happy about this choice but is going anyway. The bond between us has grown amazingly strong in almost no time. I never sensed anything like this between my parents. They were more like business partners than a bonded pair. I can't imagine doing anything of consequence if Summer isn't part of it.

We settle into our easy chairs and moments later are in the void between the galactic arms. With just a thought, I hover near the flagship. Hundreds of others stretch out behind it as far as the eye can see. Further, no doubt.

I don't want to enter the ship but do want to get a feeling for how many are aboard. The answer comes almost immediately. There had been two dozen pairs of kings and queens. The senior king died recently. His queen is in her death throws, unable to function without his pheromones. Their dedicated crew of nearly 1,000 drones have ceased to function. The 23 remaining pairs of rulers can't figure out what happened. Their unease has spread to the 23,000 drones remaining. The newly elevated senior king is struggling to consolidate his power, but it's been slow going. Some of the younger kings are concerned he's not up to the task.

A moment later, I'm outside the next ship. It too has 24 pairs.

I move down the line of ships. All have similar configuration. The large ships have 24 pairs and their drones. The smaller ships have half that number. Probing a little differently, I see that their plan is to assign 20 ships per planet. The initial target is the 100 core planets, so they've brought 2,000 ships.

In an instant, I'm back in Admiral Tang's office.

Admiral, I am Jared Daan from the protected world Jaredaan. This is a telepathic connection. I have important data for you. The alien armada consists of 2,000 ships. Their target is 100 of the core worlds. I have developed a poison that kills them on contact. I will lose this connection shortly. Please contact me by conventional means tomorrow.

The admiral looks at me sternly and nods an acknowledgement.

I will contact you tomorrow.

...

Moments later, I wake in my easy chair. Summer is still out. I look at my communicator, we were gone for six hours. How?

I hear Summer stir. I get up and take her hand. The contact allows me to hear her thoughts. She seems lost. Apparently, I retreated too fast for her to follow.

"I'm here. Come back to me."

A moment later, her eyes open.

"How long were we gone? It felt like days."

"Only six hours."

She looks at her communicator. "Six hours on a tiny dose. Would we ever come back if we took another one of the larger ones?"

I put out my hand to help her out of her seat.

"What did you see that I didn't?"

She smiles at me. "Probably most of what happened."

She laughs in a way that turns to tears. "They're really coming, aren't they?

"They're really coming, but at least this time they're afraid."

She looks at me a bit confounded. "A few of them are. Most are just thinking it's their chance for leadership. They've been waiting a long time to get a second chance at us. No one in this armada has been in human space before. Most are just hungry to prove they can do what their forefathers couldn't. Apparently, we are one of the few species they've ever encountered that they couldn't just roll over."

"How did you learn that?"

She smiles at me. "I hear their thoughts. While you're busy probing, I just observe and listen. I think that's what Julian was trying to tell us. Not that we would do it this way, but that when we do it together, we will take complementary roles. I can't probe the way you do, but I can watch and listen, and learn things that you won't because you are pursuing something different."

"What's your take on the admiral's intentions?"

"He's desperate. He has no idea how to combat them that will lead to a better outcome than before. But he doesn't believe you. He's not convinced you're real, not convinced you have a solution if you are real."

"Any ideas on how we might change his mind?"

"Maybe." She takes my hand. "It's late. Tomorrow's another day. Let's sleep on it."

...

Once in bed, Summer falls asleep immediately. I don't. Something's nagging at the edge of my consciousness, but I can't put my finger on it. I let my mind drift, but I can't let go of the feeling that I'm at the edge of a discovery.

After a couple minutes, it comes to me. Summer said it. *Six hours on a tiny dose.*

I purposefully cast my attention toward the space station and in a moment am there. That's when the realization dawns. The *profecia aumentar* has changed me. Could it possibly have changed me enough that I can probe the future without it?

I look at the space station a little more closely, but quickly lose interest in it. Maybe it's just the residual effect of the last dose. I'll need to try this again after a longer period off it.

With that thought, I return to myself, then slide into a deep sleep.

CHAPTER 16: BREAKTHROUGH

It's Wednesday. I'm up early as usual. Summer gets up with me, which is not so usual. She seems to be in good spirits this morning. I was worried our encounter with the aliens last night would still be dragging on her. But not so. Maybe it's because she'll be doing the daily medicine delivery to Lenna, then over to the hospital for Emily.

My principal objective today is to get the distillery purchase funded. I'm irritated that I have to go into Heroldstown to get it done. But I resolutely head out early enough to be at the bank by the time it opens.

As I come into town, Chief Santana spots me. I wave and continue on my way. The reception at the bank is the same as always. I'm obsequiously greeted as Mr. Daan, then advised as Jared that I'm spending a lot of money. It's comical.

As I leave, I see the Chief coming in.

"Morning Chief. Hope things are well with you today."

He growls, "Daan," while giving me the evil eye, then continues over toward the tellers where he gets in line. Apparently, Aaron, or one of the other elders, told him to leave me alone, which I'm happy about for now. But I need to work the relationship with the chief. He's someone I need on my side. Yesterday's encounter was a step in the wrong direction. Our interests are aligned, he just doesn't know it yet.

The next stop is at Macy's office. The escrow agent is there with all the remaining documents. The only odd one regards the fuel tank, which has been inspected and recertified, but not filled. Instead, I get a purchase order confirmation marked pre-paid. My agent explains that it's traditional for purchases that include fuel to be fulfilled after the property itself changes hands. The ethanol company offers delivery Friday afternoon, if I can be there to receive it.

Once all the papers are signed, I head over to see Brock Newton. I'd contacted him on Monday to let him know we'd put the offer in on the distillery. He was ecstatic about the opportunity to work in that facility again.

Today goes a little differently. He gives me a long litany of issues that need resolution now that we're putting the new stills in the old distillery. I assume this is a lead up to a higher price tag. But it's not.

Apparently, it's his engineering way of telling me we'd be coming in on budget and possibly early.

I love the drawings he's put together of the new layout. Most of the other stuff is over my head, but my big take away from the encounter is that he's become a believer. No more 'I was expecting someone a little older' or 'I need proof you can pay.' Now, we're best friends, and he can't wait to move the project forward. I actually like the guy and am happy to have him on my team.

I make one last unscheduled stop over at West Lake Nursery. I'm greeted by the owner's daughter, Brooke Carlson.

"Jared, what an unexpected pleasure. What can I do for you?"

I smile. "Was in the neighborhood, so just wanted to stop by to say thanks. Is Jay here?"

She nods and points up, "Dad and Brian are upstairs doing the final check list on your project. Go on up, I'm sure they'll be happy to see you."

I trot up the steps and see Jay and Brian immediately.

Jay jumps up to shake my hand. "Jared, what a pleasant surprise. Come on in." He points to a chair.

Brian offers his hand as well. "Jared, good to see you. What can we do for you?"

"I'm in town on another project and finished early. As I started back, it seemed wrong to leave without stopping by to say thanks. I haven't had the chance to tour all 10 gardens yet. In fact, Zone 2 is the only one I've really looked at. It's beautiful. And the morale in all the zones is up, so thanks."

"Thank you," Jay replies, then points to Brian. "Want to give Jared a status report and the recommendations you've compiled?"

He smiles. "Sure."

My sense is that this is the first big project on which Brian has had the lead. I'm also sensing that his father is pushing him to start working the relationship side of the deal.

"Zones 1 through 8 are finished. We expect to finish Zone 9 today, Zone 10 tomorrow. Both have been started, the ground prepared. What remains is mostly the final planting of the smaller plants.

"One thing has come to my attention that I think you might be interested in. The drier parts of Zones 4, 5, and 6 are perfect for citrus. We've put citrus trees in the gardens, but you could put small orchards in those three zones that could help your population nutritionally and with supplementary calories. You also have a lot of under used land in Zone 10. The problem there, as you know, is irrigation. We have machinery that could put in irrigation. And we have corn seeds that would do well there. For about 10,000 credits, we could irrigate, plow and plant corn on 20 hectares, about 0.2 square kilometers, less than 2% of the land. That will yield about 350,000 ears of corn, or one per person every day of the year. There's only one harvest per year, so you would need to manage consumption and storage, but that's a lot of corn."

"What about the orchards?"

"I think we can go as low as 3,000 per zone, so 9,000 for the three target zones. Each zone will produce 40,000 kg per harvest, starting in year 3. Years 1 & 2 will be lower. If you did all three zones, that would be the equivalent of one orange a day for your entire population.

"To put that into context, one orange and one ear of corn per day is 5% to 10% of the daily calorie requirement."

I like Brian's pitch. It's well matched to my concerns.

"How soon could this be done?"

"Optimal planting for the corn will be in about two months. The project can be done in a week

"The citrus is harder. I think we can put in the first orchard now. It will take less than a week. I need to check on some things before committing to that. We could put in the rest of the trees in two to three months. About a week per zone."

"I'd like to do both these projects, but it'll take at least a week before I can commit either way."

Jay asks, "Will you be covering this personally again?"

I smile. "Yes. The camp has no budget. But I ruffled a few feathers putting the gardens in, despite the fact it was completely within my authority. This will not be, so I need to get approval from the powers that be before I can contribute the trees or the corn."

"Understood. Thank you, Jared."

JOURNEY

Tonight, Summer and I are headed back to the alien armada. Last night, I'd succeeded in determining their strength, but not when they would arrive. Summer and I agree that our principal objective tonight should be to make that determination. The plan is to attempt to determine their location and speed. I really don't know how to do that, so the backup is for me to further probe the ships to see what I can learn from their navigation systems or navigators. Summer thinks she'll be able to read their thoughts if I can probe them in a way that makes them think about their timeline.

We settle into our easy chairs, then moments later are there. It's amazing to me that I can travel all the way out to the void just by thinking about it. I doubt that I'm actually in the void, at least not in any real sense. What I'm seeing must be a mental construct of some sort. But how is it informed?

This line of thought has left us sitting here doing nothing and I can sense Summer's frustration. So, I cast my attention back to the aliens. I once again enter the ship, then the bridge. This time I focus on the navigator, who is a young queen. She notices me, hisses, and leaps from her chair. As she does so all eyes turn toward me, and I'm slammed with a wall of hate. I'm neither controlled by, nor hurt by, their psychic assault. But it is loud, which makes it difficult to concentrate on my objective.

I step toward them and they all back off. They seem to know that I'm the grim reaper. Instead of pressing the assault, I go to the navigator's station. Neither the controls, nor the displays make any sense to me. So, I push an arbitrary button to see what will happen.

Turns out I can't push the button. I'm a psychic entity, not a corporeal one. But I do learn what the button does. It's the same phenomenon I noticed the other night. I can't see past an unmade decision. The act of attempting to push the button, allows me to see the future past that point of the button push.

I rapidly cycle through all the buttons, then start trying some combinations. This activity infuriates the aliens. The female whose station I'm messing with comes at me screaming. The alien kings and queens are giant blubberous creatures that wear no clothing. The angry queen's ponderous breasts sway as she comes at me. Something about the motion makes me dizzy and the next thing I know, I'm falling, overcome with vertigo.

I wake in my easy chair screaming. It takes a while for me to calm myself enough to move. I turn to Summer, who is not moving, but I can hear her thoughts. Once again, I've left so quickly, she can't find her way back. But the aliens have spotted her and are coming for her.

I take her hand and coax her back. She also wakes screaming. But unlike last night the scream turns to laughter.

"Oh, that was too funny."

"What?"

"The look on your face. She'd been screaming at you for about an hour, becoming increasingly hysterical. Then she jumps at you. Each of her boobs was larger than your head. With all four of them going in every which way and your head spinning to track them..." She starts laughing again. "It's no wonder you got dizzy and fell over."

Then, in a sterner voice. "Jared, you've got to learn to keep your eyes on a girl's face!"

We both laugh.

"Did you learn anything on this trip? I certainly didn't."

She laughs more. "Yes. They're two plus years out. Twenty-eight months to be exact. They want to do simultaneous attacks on all 100 target planets. They realize now that lingering on the first planet as long as they did last time cost them the war.

"They have a stealth mode they can travel in that will keep their approach secret. But using stealth slows them enough that they can't engage it until they're close, so any attack we make must be done while they're still far away.

"By the way, that queen jumped on you once you were down. The contact killed her. Her king immediately fell. So, your toxicity is again confirmed, but I don't get it. We obviously aren't actually there. Your button pushing spree clearly proved that.

"Direct psychic contact is sudden death for them, but apparently not for us."

"Anything else?" I ask.

"I wonder how many you would need to kill, before they turned back. Suppose instead of trying to learn anything, you just went and killed all the kings on a ship. If you took down a ship a day, you'd kill a third of the ships before they got here. Suppose you could take Julian and Edson, then we'd get them all before they got here."

"I doubt I could do that. But I like the idea. If we could raise an army of psychic warriors, we could stop them before they got here."

"Do you think Ethel and Norah could do it?"

"Good question."

ZONE 1

Today's plan is to tour the zones, starting in Zone 1. It's the oldest of the zones. Its numbers are good. Its population is older. Its supervisor, Hunter Park, is the oldest of the supervisors. He'll be eligible for retirement in ten years.

I've spent less time in this zone than any of the others, so want to spend an hour here this morning to get a read on Hunter's perspective on the changes I've been making.

I catch up with him as he's leaving the dining room and ask if he'd mind taking me on a tour of his garden. Like a lot of the older people here in the camp, Hunter is mellow, easy to be around.

"I'm surprised you got away with this." Hunter motions to the garden. "The last time it was tried, it turned out to be a disaster."

"So I've heard. But things are different now. We need to shore up our food supplies or people are going to start going hungry. This garden, your garden, gives your chefs more options when the external supplies we provide aren't enough."

"Why the shortage?"

"Multiple reasons. Power issues up in Jaredstown have reduced their garden output. Dry bulk imported from other worlds has ground to a halt because of the transportation issues. It could be quite a while before all that is fixed. Given the budget cuts imposed on the camp, I wanted us to become more self-sufficient."

"Well, it's been well received. Your approval rating in the zone is sky high."

"I'm glad to hear that."

"So why are you here today, Jared? Our numbers are about the best, arguably the best when adjusted for our retiree population."

"Your numbers are a good reason for me to be here. There are undoubtedly things you're doing that the other zones are not. But I haven't spent enough time here to know what they are."

"I think the answer to that question is easy. Our people are older. Most are happy to be here. I don't think I have anyone who was sentenced here from Jaredstown or Ashcrag that wants to go back when their time is up. I have no young troublemakers, no real slackers. Yeah, some of us don't move that fast anymore. But as a whole, we're more like a commune than a prison camp. That's not a process you can replicate in another zone."

"Fair enough." I'm about to ask his opinion on expanding the gardens when my camp radio goes off.

"Excuse me for a second, Hunter.

"Jared here."

"I have Admiral Tang on the line. He wants to speak with you. I can run it through the radio, but the quality of the line will be terrible."

"It will take me 10 plus minutes to get back. Ask if he wants to talk, wait or reschedule."

"Will do, please hold."

"Looks like I'm off the hook," Hunters says good-naturedly.

"That it does. But give some thought to my question. What are you doing that you don't think the others are? I buy that your population has a lot to do with your numbers. But I bet it's not the only reason."

Summer's voice comes back on the radio.

"He'll call back in 10 minutes. You better hustle!" I can hear the humor in her voice.

"OK, I'll be back in a few minutes. Thanks."

I return my attention to Hunter and shake his hand.

"You're doing a good job here my friend."

"Thanks." He nods toward the radio. "And good luck with your other problem."

"Should be interesting."

As I head out, I reflect on our interaction. Hunter is a great supervisor, one I hold in high esteem. But he likes the status quo, and I can tell he's happy to be rid of me.

CENTRAL COMMAND

I'm back in my office and have the warden's 3D holoprojection system connected to the Admiral's line. I'm on hold. Images of spaceships drift across the room in front of me as dramatic military music plays softly in the background.

The image suddenly morphs into a conference room with the admiral sitting across the table from me with other officers in the seats on either side.

"I'm Admiral Arthur Tang. You are Jared Daan?"

The power of the admiral's presence pushes me back in my seat. He's a stern man whom the officers next to him follow without question.

"Yes, I'm Jared Daan. Thank you for contacting me, sir."

"You claim to know about the aliens. How did you learn this?"

"As you've experienced, I've telepathic powers that allow me to perceive things few others can. Shortly after learning of DAGS, I attempted to perceive the aliens, and to my surprise found an armada of 2,000 ships making their way across the void.

"Since then, I've spent hours probing their ships, attempting to discern their intentions and plans. I have much yet to learn, but now know their strength, timeline, and the basic outline of their plan."

"Go on."

I can tell the admiral doesn't believe me but is just stringing me along for reasons I'm probably not going to like.

"There are 2,000 set to arrive at the rim in about 28 months. The majority of ships have 24 king-queen pairs, each of which has 1,000 drones. There are also some smaller ships with only 12 pairs and their associated drones.

"They plan a simultaneous attack against 100 of the core worlds, 20 ships per world. Their ships can operate in a stealth mode. They cannot move as fast in that mode, so have not gone into stealth yet. But they plan to engage stealth as they approach their targets."

"And you say you have a weapon?"

"I have found a treatment for DAGS. It will be entering clinical trials soon. It turns out to be highly toxic to the aliens. A small amount on their skin causes them to wither. It happens fast enough you can see it happen."

"And why should I believe any of this?"

I let the question hang there for a second, because I really do not have an answer. But I suppose that is the answer.

"I've seen it and know it's real. And I'm searching for solutions. But I cannot fight the aliens on my own. And even if I could, I wouldn't succeed without your backing. But it would be irresponsible for me to hide or withhold the information that I've found. Therefore, I attempted to contact you.

"It's really up to you to decide whether or not to act on it. If you already had this under control, then you'd have no need for me. But I don't think you do, so am offering my help."

His eyes remain locked on me. After several seconds, he says, "Please hold." And the screen goes blank. I don't have a mute button, or if I do, I don't know how to use it. So, I sit stoically and wait.

My intercom is muted, but I see a blinking light that indicates Summer is trying to reach me. A few seconds later, I see a message come in saying the elders want to speak with me. I message back that I am on hold with Central Command. As I send the message, the admiral and his conference room appear before me.

"Mr. Daan. I would like to dispatch a ship to get you but see that your planet is under quarantine.

"I still don't believe you but would like to keep this channel of communication open. Someone from my office will be in contact with you to establish a secure messaging channel. Use it if you learn more. But be advised, it is a treasonous offense to interfere in any war the Confederation is prosecuting. If it should be determined that you are interfering or collaborating with the enemy, then you will be found and destroyed, quarantine or no quarantine."

With those words, the connection is cut and the 3D holoprojection shuts down. Summer apparently sees that the connection dropped. She buzzes me.

"The elder board is on the line. OK if I connect them?"

"Sure."

ELDERS

The elders appear. They're seated in their conference room. But it's different than the connection with the Admiral. It reminds me of being in Jaredstown. They're obviously underground up north. I smile because I'm glad I'm not.

Great Uncle Walter starts off the meeting by welcoming me.

"Jared, good to see you. It's been a long time."

"Indeed it has, sir."

"We have a number of things we'd like to discuss with you. You seem to be in the middle of many of the issues we're struggling with."

"I look forward to helping you with them, sir."

"I'd like to start with this inquiry that came in from Confederation Central Command. Is it true that you contacted, or at least attempted to contact, this Admiral Tang fellow?"

"Yes, sir. I have spoken with him twice now and just finished a conference call with him and his command staff."

"What the hell for, son?"

"The disease that has placed us under quarantine is a prelude to another alien invasion. I've been able to confirm the aliens will arrive in about 28 months and they have vulnerabilities we previously did not know about."

"How do you know this?"

"Information about the disease, its cause, and the quarantine is on the exo-net and easy enough to find. Its role in the pending invasion I found by accident, but it is true."

"What? You figured out how to turn on Herold's crazy alien detector?" He laughs at the notion.

240

"Alien detector, sir?"

"Yes, a series of detectors in wells stretching east from the lake. What a hair-brained idea that was. He spent a load of money, then died before it was done. No one ever understood it, so a hundred thousand credits went down the hole with nothing to show for it."

So, that's what all the wells were for!

"I did find those wells, sir. But had no idea what they were for."

"Then how can you know anything about the aliens?"

"Since coming south I've discovered that I'm telepathic. I've cast my mind out to find them and did. There are 2,000 ships inbound. The Admiral knows this. Other protected worlds out here that were able to bring up the detection systems have reported it. I've been able to use that knowledge to refine what we know."

"You shitting me, son? I don't believe in any of that hocus pocus."

"I'm sorry you don't, sir. It's a powerful tool that could be the difference between life and extinction in the coming war."

He stares at me shaking his head in disgust.

"Aaron tells me you have money off-planet. Money you want to use to buy scientific and other equipment. Money you'd be willing to use to pay for an emergency delivery.

"Is that true? Or, just more of your voodoo?"

"It's true, sir."

"How much money do you have? Emergency deliveries are incredibly expensive."

"I don't know the exact number, but I have more than enough to cover an emergency delivery."

"Where could you have come up with that much money?"

"I have three bestselling products on Jungle."

The mention of Jungle earns me several dark looks. I don't understand why people hate Jungle so much. Before the quarantine, it was the best way to get things not made on Jaredaan.

"I'm going to want to see that money upfront if we're going to go down this route."

"I don't think that will work, sir. I'll create a purchase order for the things I need. You can add whatever you want to it. Then request the emergency delivery. I'll pay the invoice."

"I'm not sure that's good enough."

"That's the deal I'm offering. You're more than welcome to pursue a better one."

Uncle Walter looks like he's about to blow a gasket. I notice Aaron nodding at me approvingly. A couple of the other elders do the same. I sense that the elders as a whole do not like Uncle Walter's leadership.

...

After a little more back and forth, we come to an agreement on the emergency delivery. This is going to cost me nearly half a million credits.

As an almost sincere gesture of good will, Uncle Walter says he hopes that I will visit if I ever venture north again, then adds, "... and Warden Glenn wants to speak with you when you have a chance."

WARDEN

I call the warden. It'll be the first time I've spoken with him since Summer moved in with me. I sincerely hope that's not the reason he wants to talk with me.

"Jared, thank you for contacting me. Seems you don't spend that much time in your office. I haven't been able to reach you there."

Although he says this in a friendly manner, I detect an implication that I'm shirking my duties to the camp.

"Sorry sir. This has been an unusual week. When I'm on site, I spend quite a bit of time out in the zones. But this week, I spent about a day and a half off-site on important camp-related business."

"What kind of business?"

"One day was spent working to secure enough raw materials to treat everyone in the camp for DAGS. The half day was spent tracking down additional food sources, which is one of the things I'd like to discuss with you."

"Go on. What did you find?"

"The garden installations have gone extremely well. Camp morale has really improved. West Lake Nursery wanted to pitch me two more projects. These involve using a tiny amount of the space designated for cane, 23 of our 15,000 hectares to be exact. The hectares in question are currently unused. I'd be happy to finance the additions if you'll work with me to get space reclassified."

"What will we get for this?"

"The working proposal is to put in 3 hectares of citrus trees in undeveloped areas well suited to citrus. By year three, they will yield the equivalent of an orange a day for everyone in camp. The other proposal is to install irrigation to 20 hectares in Zone 10 that are not currently irrigated, then plant it with sweet corn. That will yield the equivalent of one ear of corn per day for everyone in camp. If we want to convert this field to cane next season we could, because it would already be irrigated. If the food crisis persists, we could plant another season of corn."

He looks at me with new respect. "That'll be an impressive accomplishment. You are performing the economic miracle the camp has needed for years. Can we do more?"

I would never have guessed that reaction.

"Yes, sir. It will take longer. West Lake does not have that many citrus trees at hand. They plan to ramp up nursery operations to get that many seedlings. I don't know what their limit is, but I'd be surprised if we couldn't double that number. I don't know about the corn. They said they had the seed for 20 hectares. I don't know if they have more. But I'd be happy to ask."

"Please do. If we don't get import of bulk dry goods restarted soon, we're in for big trouble. The situation the elders are grappling with is quite grim. Maybe if we got seed added to the next emergency shipment, we could reposition the camp to be supplying food in addition to the feedstock for ethanol."

"That would certainly be good for the camp."

"Thank you, Jared. I'm so glad we have you looking out for us."

When the call is done, I reflect back on what was said. I find it ironic that I'm busting my butt to save the camp, the planet, and all mankind for that matter. Yet if I'm not in my office, the assumption is that I'm slacking off.

CABIN 007

I got word to Ethel and Norah that Summer and I planned to come over for dinner and would bring food, if they were up for it. Vince asked the question when he made his morning delivery and let me know they looked forward to seeing us.

I thought we could bring some of our dehydrated food and actually cook. Summer suggested that we buy food at the staff café. We arrive around five o'clock, early enough to go on a journey with them and still get home at a reasonable hour.

The front door of the cabin opens as my cart comes to a stop. Ethel pops out and hustles Summer inside. I follow with the food. I enter to see Ethel and Summer settling in the sitting room and Norah preparing tea. The first thing I hear is Ethel saying, "Thank God you finally did it!" I just shake my head.

I set the food on the table, then ask Norah how I can help. She smiles. "Not to worry dear. Why don't you go join the others? I'll be in with tea in a minute. We can bring the food out a little later."

I come into the sitting room and hear a question about our intimate relations, one I never thought I'd ever hear spoken out loud.

"Ethel? Really?"

"Just want to make sure you know what you're doing. This girl deserves satisfaction."

I bury my face in my hands.

"Spoil sport." Seeing that I'm not taking the bait, Ethel changes subjects. "So, you finally headed East. I can tell you've found something exciting but can't discern what."

Norah comes in with the tea. "What did I miss?"

"Nothing. Jared is apparently an adequate lover, and they've discovered something in the wilderness that they haven't told me about yet."

The thought goes through my mind that Ethel has no discretion.

"Oh, but I do, sonny boy. I'm saving the juiciest parts until after you've left so as not to embarrass you."

I put my face back in my hands.

"So, what's the most interesting thing you learned?"

Summer indicates that I should answer.

I smile. "There are nine components, not seven. And the new ones allow you to see the future, but not in the way I was expecting."

"And how did you learn that?" Ethel demands.

"Why don't we discuss it over a meal." Norah suggests.

...

As we eat, I tell the ladies about meeting with Julian and Edson in the wilderness, taking the profecia aumentar, and the ability it gives to see the future. Then tell her about our trip to Jaramor, meeting with the elders, and the basic deal we made. Then I finish with the return trip, seeing their viper breeding operation, and the high points of their supply practices.

"So, our founder took a second wife and built a secret settlement for her. There, she refined skills she learned from my people on New Brazil. And she's the one that made the prophecy." Ethel cackles. "Truth can be so much stranger than fiction."

Her musing suddenly becomes more serious as she stabs me with a stare.

"You've brought this new formulation and want us to try it. Why?"

Summer looks at me. "You need to tell them about what's actually going on."

Ethel's look takes on a darker tone.

"What are you holding back, sonny boy?"

"Word got back to the aliens that the disease finally escaped Doffenplod. They've launched another invasion. Two thousand ships are in route. They're about 28 months out."

"You know this how?"

"I've gone to visit them, probe their ship. I've even killed two of the king/queen pairs."

"In your telepathic state?" Norah asks incredulously.

"Yes."

"But how can you be sure?" Ethel counters.

I nod to Summer.

"This type of probing, or voyaging, is best done in pairs. In our case, Jared leads. He prosecutes the agenda he wants to explore. I kind of come along for the ride. The formula makes him laser focused, as if he's blind to other things going on around him. I'm the one who actually sees what's happening. He's likely to find what he's looking for. I'm likely to discover many of the things his discovery implies.

"The Elders use this technique. Both roles are valuable. They tend to put more weight on what the observer sees than what the leader does. They say this only works for bonded pairs. We think it might work for the two of you."

I add, "I don't know if we can collaborate, do this as a foursome somehow. If I can take you to see the aliens, one of you could probe, the other observe. Doubling up like that might help us find a way to defeat them faster. If you can kill them the way I can, then you might be able to be a warrior in this fight."

The two look at each other for a moment, then Ethel says, "We're in."

...

We all make ourselves comfortable. I give Norah and Summer a quarter of one of the three-hour pieces of profecia aumentar. Ethel and I get the remainder. On the count of three, we each place our respective pieces on our tongues. Moments later I'm up, hovering above our bodies, then the three ladies appear next to me.

Let's go, I send, then head out. I start slowly. Ethel follows without issue, so I increase speed. Moments later, all four of us appear near the flagship.

245

I hear Ethel think, *Mãe dos Deuses*. It takes me a moment to recognize the Portuguese, *mother of the gods*.

Without my prompting, I see her plunge into the ship with Norah trailing behind. I decide to do the same, this time in engineering. Similar to last night, I approach a panel. My goal is to understand how propulsion on this ship works.

I start pushing buttons. Each time I learn its function. An engineer, a king, sees me and, in a panic, attempts to intervene. He charges, and when he hits me, I just pass through him. It's an odd sensation for me, catastrophic for him. I see him shriek and shrivel. Smoke comes off him, then he stops moving, clearly dead.

Another engineer starts to charge me, but when I turn toward him, he stops and retreats. In a sudden flash of insight, he goes for a blaster of some sort. I flash over, hitting him. He collapses. I check out another panel. This one seems to have a speed indicator, so I start probing the controls and find one indicated as *port thrust trim*. I touch the control again and gain the same insight. Then think, "Increase."

The ship immediately starts to turn. That answers the question about whether we can do anything here. As the ship continues turning, alarms start going off. Again, I think, "Increase."

A queen comes running into the room with a rifle of some sort. Thankfully, she's a bad shot. A laser beam of some type sears a panel near me. I flash over to where she is. She screams and collapses, her finger still on the trigger. I flash out of the beam's path as it wreaks destruction to more instrumentation and kills two more kings.

I've learned a lot and am ready to get out of the hot zone. As I flash away, a beam catches my foot, nicking my big toe. Pain flows through me and I feel myself falling. In an instant, Summer is on me, then we're gone.

I wake back in Cabin 007. My foot throbs with pain. Summer has my shoe off, looking at my foot.

"How bad is it?" I grunt out. "It hurts like hell."

"No markings on shoe or foot. That's not what I saw out there. It looked like you lost a chunk of both."

I look and confirm that the throbbing toe is intact. I reach down to touch it and immediately the pain stops. I'm absolutely baffled.

I suddenly realize that Ethel and Norah are not back, they're still out there. I get up and walk over to Ethel's chair. When I'm close enough to touch, it's like I'm there on the ship with her. She's systematically destroying the ship, trashing every system she can get her hands on, killing every king and queen that gets in her way. The aliens are in a panic.

Then I see something that worries me. All the aliens have turned and run. There's a flashing red countdown timer. They must have activated the self-destruct.

I touch Ethel's hand and send, *Ethel, get out of there. Find Norah and run. Now!*

A moment later, Ethel and Norah stir, then wake.

I ask, "You OK?"

Ethel turns to look at me, a big smile starting to form. "Now, that's what I call an alien ass kicking!"

I look at Norah. "They started an autodestruct sequence, didn't they?"

"Maybe them, maybe her. It's hard to know. I tried to get her attention but couldn't."

"It's very difficult to reach them when they're in deep like that," Summer says. "Ethel, Jared tried to call you back. Did it work?"

She smiles at me. "Yes, I heard him say self-destruct, say the countdown timer, then heard him say Norah. I jumped over to where Norah was, then came back."

I'm surprised by her answer. I was worried the aliens had started a self-destruct sequence, but don't recall mentioning it.

I ask, "So, do you think it's real?"

"Well, I agree with what you said earlier. It sure feels real. But how are we able to hurt them?"

"We can also activate their controls. I was able to turn the ship by adjusting the port thruster. But I have no idea why?"

"Maybe what we're seeing is what would happen if we were there."

My first thought is that Ethel is right, but... "How could we move that fast?"

Norah suggests, "Maybe it's like a break between scenes. You know, we do something and see what the reaction would be. Then we pop somewhere else and see what the reaction would be."

I'm a bit deflated. I thought maybe we'd killed an alien ship. Now I'm thinking we're just playing what-if games and wondering whether or not touching the aliens will really kill them.

Ethel, who seems even more attuned to me than before, answers the unasked question. "This formulation isn't going to be of much value, if the things it lets us see don't actually happen."

It occurs to me that this will be easy to test.

"I think I know how to test this. I'm going to go back in. This will only take a minute."

I put my head back, then shut my eyes and moments later am flying.

I pop over to my apartment. I'd been expecting it to be dark, but there's a light on in the kitchen. Summer must have left it on.

I select a light in the living room and attempt to turn it on. I can see and feel the switch, and in the same strange way as on the alien ship can sense what it does. But can't physically move it. I think 'on' and the light comes on.

I go into the kitchen and do the same thing with the water spigot. Water starts coming out and, to my surprise, a cockroach scurries up out of the drain and disappears behind a cabinet. The cockroach startles me, and I want to smash it. But that's a problem for another day. With the water flowing slowly, I turn the light in the kitchen off, then return.

"I thought you said it would be quick." Summer says with some heat. "You were gone nearly an hour."

"It only felt like 5 minutes."

Ethel intervenes. "So, what did you learn?"

"Nothing yet. I just did an experiment. I popped over to our apartment. I turned off a light that was on, turned on one that was off, and turned the water on in the kitchen sink. When we get home, we'll know if this is real, or if it's a what-if."

"Good thinking. If it's real, you'll know that for sure. But if it's not, that doesn't mean it's a what-if."

"Point taken."

I look at Summer. "Ready to go find out?"

We say our goodbyes. Norah packages up two one-month-for-two people-bottles of supplement for us. And we head home.

APARTMENT

We enter to see the kitchen light on, living room light off, and no water flowing in the kitchen. In truth, this is what I expected, but it's still really disappointing.

"So, it's not real after all," Summer whispers, hope slipping away.

I turn on the living room light, then go into the kitchen to turn off the light in there. I pause, looking at the sink. Then walk over to it and turn on the faucet. Water trickles out, then a cockroach erupts from the drain and scurries off behind the counter.

I'm so startled that I jump, and a quiet scream escapes my lips. Summer comes rushing in.

"What's the matter?"

I look at her and start laughing. In the preposterousness of the moment, I laugh so hard, tears start to flow.

"What?" She demands, starting to smile.

"It is future vision. In my vision I turned on the living room light, then came into the kitchen and turned on the water. When I did a cockroach came running out of the drain and ran behind the cabinet."

I point to the cabinet.

"Just now I did the same thing. I turned on the light in the living room, then came in here and turned on the water. And a cockroach shot up out of the drain startling me."

"So, we ARE seeing possible futures," she says in awe.

THURSDAY

My plan for today is split. I want to tour the zones. Things happen when I show up on a regular basis. I think this is Warden Glenn's biggest failure. But I also need to do some research into chemical synthesis systems. For most things, I think a natural solution is best. But when the natural solution involves toad and viper venom, I can't help but believe that a synthetic one would be better. But even that thought is meaningless. I might be able to treat everyone on Jaredaan with the products of the toad and viper venom. But we'll need a synthetic solution to treat the preponderance of humanity. And without that, what difference does it make? For all its aspiration and bluster, Jaredaan is not self-sufficient. Add to that the aliens... Well, there's really no point to all the other work if we can't save a big slice of humanity.

Summer and I do what now feels like the morning split. She handles supplement delivery to Lenna and to Dr. Avery for the other patients. I do the rounds in the fields, then shift to our strategic initiatives in the afternoon. Yes, this is only day four of this normal split, but in less than a week Summer and I have gone from friends with latent romantic interests, to inseparable partners with a separation of responsibilities. At least that's how it feels this week.

I'm starting in Zone 4 today. It's another well-performing zone that has received too little of my attention. I'm almost there when the call comes in from headquarters.

"Jared, you just got a message from the Elders marked urgent. I think you need to deal with this ASAP."

It's Summer. If the message had come from anyone else, I might ignore it. But I trust her instincts on this implicitly. I turn around about a half kilometer from the Zone 4 supervisor's office and head back.

I come into the headquarters building and get a wry smile from Summer.

"It's in your queue." She points upstairs.

My eyes linger on her as I head up. Oh, to spend the day with her, instead of dealing with whatever nonsense is coming down from above.

I saddle up to my desk and open the urgent message. Amazingly, it's a planetary purchase order to be fulfilled via emergency relief protocol for quarantined worlds. The message that accompanies lays out the bounds of the modifications I can make. They're very one sided, which is a bit cheeky given that I'm paying for the entire package. I have the primal instinct to trash it. But thankfully my rational mind kicks in. Walter is saying the same thing I said to him. There's an offer on the table. I'm more than welcome to try to find a better one.

I have to smile. It's time to do the math. If I can get what I need in the weight and volume this order provides, I'll do it. If not, I'll modify and return it to him for approval. We're both desperate. His desperation is more short-term, so undoubtedly more poignant to him. If I need a change, I'll also need a reason that either appeals to his duty or satisfies his greed.

...

My heart's a bit heavy at this point. This purchase order will wipe out enough of my reserves that I might not be able to sponsor another one. The equipment I need exceeds the weight allowance and the volume allowance I've been given. The synthesis equipment puts me over the top. If I knew for sure this was the right synthesis equipment, I'd fight for it. The problem is I don't. The analysis and control equipment are necessary to get the supplement to everyone on planet. I can't compromise on that. But I can't bring myself to accept what's in front of me. So, I set off to do something I know I shouldn't do... Probe the *mystery* for insight, in the middle of the day with no companion.

I come down the stairs quietly, hoping to avoid Summer. That doesn't work. She sees me and immediately knows what I intend to do.

"No! Not on your own." She says loudly.

I go over to the front counter where she's seated, not really knowing how to explain myself.

"I know," she whispers. "Let me get Larry to cover."

Then more sternly. "Two hours max!"

APARTMENT

Back in our easy chairs, I explain what I intend to do. I'm going to attempt an analysis of the components. Assuming I get somewhere, I'm then going to attempt to synthesize them.

Summer shares my skepticism about our likelihood of success, but she is a willing participant in the inquiry. A moment later, I'm in the government analysis lab with the person doing the analysis of the first component. I watch as she injects a drop of the component into a liquid chromatography system. She explains that chromatography systems separate the elements in a solution. Lighter ones come out early. Heavier ones come out later. She points to the screen. It just shows a flat line.

"As a chemical passes the sensor at the end of the tube. The line will lift up ultimately forming a peak. The peak will look something like the classic bell curve you may have seen in a math or statistics class. The taller and narrower the curve, the purer your sample is. Run time is expected to be an hour."

I jump forward an hour and see an exceptionally clean peak emerging on the screen. The purification we did before submitting the sample was remarkably successful. The lab person diverts the effluent to a mass spectrometer and tells me we will know the chemical composition in another hour.

Again, I jump forward to see the next result. The computer analysis is done. The sample we sent was 96% pure, excluding the water in the sample. The primary ingredient is one of several possibilities. The computer puts the highest probability on a protein known to exist in the venom of several common viper families. I'm worried that there's no way I'll remember the name of this protein. She opens a book that I know we have at headquarters and points to the listing and commentary. It's on page 256, the third item listed. That I can remember.

I repeat the process, this time on component 2 at a different lab. I time the jumps better and in minutes am looking at another page in the same book. This one is a relatively simple organic compound used in many medications.

I repeat the process a third, fourth, then fifth time and am convinced I now know the five compounds I need. I realize that I've been running on adrenaline. I'm beat and barely able to stay awake. I try for a graceful return. I need to write down the answers when we get back.

I wake in my easy chair. Summer got back before I did. She has a pen and paper ready for me. I write the items down, then fall into a deep sleep.

...

I wake, still in my easy chair. Weak light penetrating from outside makes it feel like dawn. Summer's asleep in the chair next to me. Her breathing is soft and gentle.

I don't want to wake her so am tempted to just close my eyes and relax. But I'm hungry and have a ton of work to do. The notes sitting on the table next to me are a reminder that I need to look up the component identifications.

I get up slowly, grab my notes, get my tablet, then head toward the kitchen. I almost make it when my foot lands on a squeaky board. I hear Summer startle awake and feel immensely guilty.

"You're up."

I turn to look at her as she's rubbing the sleep from her eyes.

"Sorry, I tried to be quiet."

"You had quite the ride yesterday. I dropped out during hour 11. I couldn't hold it any longer. Impressive technique by the way. Did you get them all?"

"The five in the daily supplement, yes."

"What's next?"

"I need to look up the five items, then determine what's involved in synthesizing them. If we can synthesize them, then we could do our clinical trial. We could also sell it off world."

She comes over as I'm talking, then wraps herself around me. After a minute she releases me.

"How about I make breakfast while you look up the things you need to look up?

252

"Deal."

...

It doesn't take long to find the references and sanity check them. There are two proteins, two common organic compounds and one exotic one. All of these are known to be associated with naturally occurring venoms. The two simpler organic compounds are used in existing medicines.

I launch an automated search sequence as Summer serves breakfast. I'm trying to find machines capable of synthesizing the proteins.

About halfway through breakfast, my tablet dings, indicating one of the searches is done. A minute later, there's another ding. Apparently, my gaze lingers on the tablet a little too long. I know this because Summer laughs and says, "It's OK if you look at it to see what you got."

I know how much she hates it when I take my attention off her during a meal, and I attempt to resist the impulse to look. But now that I have permission, I truly cannot help myself.

She laughs again, clearly sensing the tug of war I just lost.

I quickly look at the results. There's a relatively long list of machines for each protein. A couple of them show up in both lists. This is incredibly good news. Good enough that I can put the tablet back down and resume conversation with Summer. She's so sweet.

OFFICE

As much as I want to spend the day in the zones, it's impossible. I need to get the purchase order sorted out. So, instead, I go into the office. Once there, I check messages. I was offline most of the day yesterday and am rewarded with a long list of urgent messages. At the top of the list is one from the elders, specifically from Walter. He was expecting to have received the purchase order back for processing yesterday and wants to know what the problem is.

I write out a quick reply saying they gave me less space and weight than I was expecting, which is problematic. There's a certain minimum I need to go through with this transaction. I'm looking for another way to get what I need while keeping the colony's requirements intact. I hope to have an answer tomorrow. If not, then we'll need to reconnect to see if there's a different deal that can be done.

The next message is from my realtor, Macy. She reminds me that the distillery purchase will close this morning and asks if we can meet at the distillery this afternoon to take possession. She also notes that

253

the ethanol company would like to make delivery this afternoon at 2:00. I write back accepting the meeting.

The next message is from Brock Newton. He would like to meet, so we can review his work. He'd heard from Macy that we would be taking possession of the distillery this afternoon and wanted to know if he could come by at 3:30 to meet and take a tour. I send him an acknowledgement accepting the meeting.

There's a message from Jay Carlton at West Lake Nursery, confirming their intention to complete the garden project today. He wants to come by to do a final inspection with me to close out the project. I send him a message saying I'm booked today but would be happy to do that over the weekend or on Monday.

...

Finally finished with yesterday's messages, I turn my attention back to the purchase order situation. Yesterday's visions have given me enough certainty about the venom components that I'm thinking I can drop the analytic equipment and replace it with synthesis equipment.

This morning's automated searches turned up several pieces of equipment that could synthesize the components. That's where I decide to start.

...

It took a while, but I've narrowed the search to two units and watched the demonstration videos for each. I think that's all the information I need to go back tonight and probe the suitability of these units.

DISTILLERY

Summer and I arrive at the distillery five minutes early. For the second day in a row Larry is covering for her and he's not happy about it. Everyone else is already here, as is the tanker that will be filling our tank.

We exchange greetings, then Charlie Tanner, the ethanol company's representative presents me with the keys. We do a quick tour to confirm that everything is as expected, then we go into one of the conference rooms to review the results of the tests Charlie ran earlier. I sign the test acceptance, then sign for the delivery.

Ten minutes later, the tanker is connected and filling our tank. When it's done, Charlie walks me through the startup process and ten minutes later, the electrical system is up, and the lights are on.

For now, we'll run the generator round the clock in low power mode so we can keep lighting and security on around the clock. Eventually, I'll build a storage unit that charges during the day on waste energy, then powers lighting and security at night.

Brock Newton arrives just as the tanker is finishing up. Even though his official duties are complete, Charlie asks if it's OK for him to sit in on the meeting with Brock. At this point, I know I want to hire Charlie, so I say yes.

Brock spreads his drawings out on the main table in the conference room. The drawings are beautiful. Every major component has a supporting document with the calculations supporting its mass and energy balance. I don't know this branch of engineering all that well. It's different than electrical power generation. But I'm as impressed as can be by the quantity and quality of engineering that's gone into it.

Charlie, who is intimately familiar with this branch of engineering, drives most of the questioning. Any doubt I previously had about hiring him is gone. I have to update my financial models before I'll be able to issue a job offer. That'll be a priority for the weekend.

I note that a critical element of the system is missing, the chromatography column we use for batch protein separation. Brock apologizes, saying he doesn't have the specs on that yet. Then points to the placeholder box on the drawings.

Once the drawing review is done, we go into the main still room. Brock uses a handheld laser measurement instrument to find the spots where the various vessels will go, painting small spots on the floor so we can better visualize the new layout.

...

When we finish, I give Brock the approval to start building the vessels. It will take about four weeks for that to get done. I ask him to send me two copies of the plans.

Once Brock leaves, I ask Charlie if he still wants to come work for me. I get a resounding yes, so ask him what terms he needs. He's expensive but not as bad as it could have been. I reaffirm my interest in having him on my team and promise to get back to him next week one way or the other.

APARTMENT

"You want to go back in tonight, don't you?"

By the way the question is asked, I can tell Summer would rather have a night off.

"I do. Can you guess why?"

"You want to see if the machines you were so hot on this morning will actually make the supplement."

I nod in renewed respect for her ability to read me. "Exactly, and I need to do it tonight so I can get the purchase order back to Walter tomorrow."

"That's what I thought."

I can hear the conflict in Summer's voice.

"Are you sure you're up to it?"

"I'm tired. But I don't want you doing this on your own, so I'll come too."

"Thank you."

After a quick meal, we settle ourselves in our easy chairs. Then moments later are flying.

I chose the test lab for the machine I like the most. The set-up is that I want them to do a proof of concept run on a formula I want to make. They charge me a ridiculous sum but accept the sample request.

The person running the test sample walks me through the process and an hour later I have a sample kit with 5 tiny 50 ml dropper bottles.

I mix up a dose, then take it to a test lab. They are not very efficient, so I have to skip ahead frequently. The report I'm given at the end confirms the contents of the dose.

Then I spend 5 days dosing a volunteer with late-stage DAGS. I spend two minutes talking and dosing then skip ahead to the next dose.

After a ton of skipping ahead, I'm finally in the doctor's office reviewing the test results. The patient is still seriously ill and at risk. But keratin buildup is substantially reduced. It works!

I come back to myself and wake to a pitch-black room. I hear Summer asleep next to me. She apparently came back before I did. I check the time on my communicator. 2:30 AM. Once again, I was in for eight hours. Despite the excitement that a solution is at hand, I'm exhausted. I close my eyes for a minute, trying to collect the energy to get up and go to bed. But in seconds, I'm fast asleep.

CHAPTER 17: PRODUCTION

A month has passed, and a lot has changed.

The cane harvest has come in, and we've done surprisingly well. Net delivered yield was up 18%. The harvest itself was good, the plants healthy and full of juice. We weren't able to get the roads repaired, but the new transport structures we added to the trucks materially reduced the transportation losses.

I've spent so much time probing the *mystery* that Summer and I had to go back to Jaramor for a night to pick up more of the profecia aumentar. Things are far less than well there. Their probing has produced nothing. And they've logged their first case of DAGS. I can only leave a one-month maintenance supply for two. We are still short. The distillery isn't up yet. Brock is still building the vessels. We're just about at the point they're due and I have to credit him for what he's been able to accomplish. But we're resource constrained and the food shortage is now plainly manifest.

Even though they're young, the gardens have matured enough that they're yielding some food. The corn went in and has sprouted. Some of the plants are as tall as my hand is wide. I'm told they'll be up to my knee in another month. So ironically, things aren't quite as bad in the camp as they are in Jaredstown.

Things off-world have really gone down the tubes. Our emergency supplies are delayed, which has everyone here in a panic. The great irony of course is that my products on Jungle are selling better than ever. The forecast for the last four weeks was 300,000 credits. Actual royalties came in just short of 400,000. My local funds are down to less than 200,000. There was a day when I could not imagine such a sum. Now it's scary low. Of the many options I have to help Jaredaan, none are within my financial means until the distillery comes up and I get delivery of my chemical synthesis equipment.

DISTILLERY

Today is the day. Brock Newton is delivering the first of the vessels he's built. He's also bringing the final specs for the entire system. I'm worried about his design for the packed columns used in the first two steps to separate out the two protein-based components. Brock and

Charlie think these are perfect and to spec. But none of the three of us understand the spec all that well. So, I'll be taking the designs to Jaramor for review.

I arrive at the distillery at 9:00. Summer stayed at headquarters. Larry has been complaining loudly about the hours she's missing and filed a complaint with me and her father. I need her more than the camp does, so I've been pushing to get her transferred to work as my assistant. Of course, the state won't allow that. Summer doesn't want to quit her job. But the whole situation is coming to a head. I think the solution will be for her to resign from the camp and join my company. When the warden finally returns, I suspect I'll need to do the same thing.

I see the doors to the loading bay are open, then see Charlie's truck in the parking lot. The ethanol company agreed to allow Charlie a slow exit. He's a quarter time with me now, the rest with them. But that will change soon. If Brock's columns check out and he can bring the rest of the system up this week, then production will start next week.

I go in through the office entrance and see that Charlie has a pot of coffee brewing. Traditional coffee beans are grown on Jaredaan but are hard to get. Most 'coffees' on Jaredaan are some sort of herbal substitute. Charlie refuses to disclose what his is made of or how it's processed. But I think he makes it from the pulp mash that comes out of the ethanol plant. I kind of like it, so take the cup that's offered.

We go outside to sit at one of the café-style tables at the edge of the parking lot to wait for Brock.

"So, you think we'll start production next week?" Charlie asks.

At this point he knows what we're trying to do. I'm not sure the degree to which he actually believes we have a treatment that will reverse the effects of the disease. But he's fully onboard with the plan to bring the distillery back to life. He also knows about the synthesis equipment we're waiting on.

"I hope so. We've *cured* two patients at this point and have a third on treatment. But that just about taps out our home brew capacity. We now know of 24 people on Jaredaan who have it, and I suspect we will all get it at some point. Those 24 will succumb to it within a year if we cannot get the supplement to them."

"And how long do people stay on it?"

I snort. "Forever. No one knows how to cure this disease. All we do is shut it down and keep it from starting back up while you're on therapy. Go off of it and it will return. We don't have good data on

258

how quickly it will come back. But my gut tells me that it will come back quickly."

"You're going to make a fortune on this aren't you?"

"On Jaredaan, no. I'll eventually need to charge for it, enough to keep the operation here open. Off-world, yes, I'll make a fortune."

"You going to gouge people?"

I shake my head in disappointment at the question. "No. But along that line of reasoning, how much do you think we should charge for it?"

"I don't know... a credit a day?"

I chuckle. "Think about that for a second."

"What do you mean?"

"How many people are there that will want this therapy?"

"I don't know. I guess all of them."

"There are over 1 trillion humans. If I got a credit a day from all of them the government would eventually come after me. Even at a credit a month, I'd be a target."

"And I'm your first employee."

We both laugh.

A loud bump gets our attention. It's Brock. He just started down the 100-meter-long, bumpy access road. At some point I'm going to need to do something about that.

...

We're in the conference room doing a quick review of the final drawings. Brock's brought two copies. One for the company to hold here at the distillery, the other for my personal use.

"Brock, I'm still concerned about the two packed columns at the start of the process."

He smiles. "So am I. I've not built a process like this before. I've studied up on it and the math works out, but..." He just lets the sentence hang there.

"Understood. I think I know someone off-world who has experience with this. OK, if I send him the drawings and get his opinion?"

"The drawings belong to you Jared. But what does that mean for the timing and installation?"

"Let's continue with the plans as they are. I think I'll have an answer in three days. So, to the extent that you can, work everything else first."

He smiles at me. "Will do."

A bell rings, indicating that someone has come in through the front door. I look out and see that it's one of Brock's men.

"We've off-loaded the first five vessels and are ready to install when you are."

I turn to Brock. "Ready?"

ROAD TO NOWHERE

Summer and I take off just before first light. I messaged Julian last night, letting him know that we were coming and the purpose of our trip. We will be met at the far end of the beach that starts just after the end of the road.

By the time we get to the distillery, the sun is up, and I can kill the truck's lights. Shift change at the ethanol plant is less than an hour away. I'd rather not have people seeing headlights on the road to nowhere. There's a lot of speculation about what we're doing. I don't want to fuel the rumor mill with obvious sightings of my truck heading out into the wilderness.

Summer sleeps all the way to the end of the road. The job, followed by six hours of probing most evenings, is wearing her out. Both energize me. But our roles are different. I drive the queries. She observes. And as I get better at it, I'm constantly skipping through scenes, spending the least amount of time in any one as possible. I'm thinking that I should be spending more time probing the *mystery* on my own. I'm worried for Summer.

We come down the slope toward the river, then continue east. It's obvious that there's been an unusual amount of rain down this way. The river is swollen. It's carrying more debris and there's an unusual quantity of debris on the shore. Up higher on the ridge, I see signs of a mudslide. I'm glad we're going to have an escort who's already scouted the way.

Because of the higher water level, the far end of the beach is very narrow. At the risk of increased bumpiness, I head up the hill a bit, stopping at a level spot just above and in clear sight of the rendezvous point. We've made good time and are early, so Summer breaks out a snack for us to munch on.

She hands me a tart and a hot cup of Charlie's coffee poured from a thermos. "Do you really think we'll get the distillery to work?"

"Yes, I'm sure. When... That's a different matter."

"It's the packed columns, isn't it?"

"Yes."

"Haven't you probed that question?"

I smile. She has so much faith in me.

"I have but can't read the result. I must be approaching the query wrong. But I can't think of another way."

"Any chance Julian can help?"

"Don't know, but I'll ask."

There's a pause in the flow of conversation. I sense that Summer wants to tell me something that she doesn't think I'll want to hear.

"Out with it," I prod.

"I need a break from the probing. The drugs are messing with my head and I'm not accomplishing anything. You skip scene to scene so fast I can't follow."

"I know. It's OK. I'm getting good at posing the questions and sequences in a way that's revealing. Each trip reveals more and more of the future."

"And my parents will be coming home soon."

This is probably the first thing she's ever said that throws me into a panic.

"What about your parents coming home?"

"I barely see you anymore. You're off probing every night. Working all day. There's a cursory breakfast and dinner, then you're gone. You haven't even attempted to make love with me in a week."

Earlier I'd been thinking that Summer needed to quit her job so we could spend more time together. Now, I'm thinking I should.

"Please don't move out. I need you. I'll quit my job when your father gets back, so I can do what I need to do during the day and spend the evenings with you."

"Don't quit your job," she whispers. "The camp needs you. We'll work things out."

With her words still ringing in my ears, I'm taken by a vision. In it, she's in her room in her parent's home. I'm installing a new and larger still in Jaramor. *Oh, dear God. Please don't let that be my future.*

JARAMOR

We arrive in Jaramor in the early afternoon. We're shown to our room and given a few minutes to freshen up, while Julian fetches the settlement's chemistry team.

A half hour later, we're in the pub's private dining room meeting Julian's two experts, Matthew Lee, who prefers to go by Matt, and Darcy Santos. Darcy's specialty is the first part of the process, analytical chemistry. Matt's specialty is the last part, distillation. I've heard the expression analytical chemistry, but don't really know what that means.

The drawings are laid out on the table and the discussion begins. Overall, the feedback is positive. They think Brock has done an outstanding job on the distillation end. They concur with his thermal analysis and the column packing specification for components 4 & 5. This comes as a shock to me.

"I thought that the first two columns were the only ones packed!"

They look at me oddly, then laugh. Darcy takes it on herself to explain.

"Jared, all the columns have an interior structure. The first two are packed with the powder-like medium needed for High Pressure Liquid Chromatography (HPLC) separation. The third one has evaporation plates. The last two have evaporation plates and glass beads. This is how you narrow the precipitation window. The boiling points for the last components are only a few degrees different. This is the mechanism that allows us to separate them."

Now I'm totally confused.

"The first two columns are packed with more of a powder-like material that separates the two proteins based on their molecular weight, not their boiling point. This part is better described as an analytical chemistry process than as distillation.

"Your designer has done a wonderful job on both halves, but the two analytical chemistry columns are not connected in the right sequence. And we need diverters at the last two drop points."

She points to the connection between columns 1 and 2, and at the one between column 2 and the distillation boiler.

As she does that it clicks. Ethel has little stop cock valves there.

Darcy continues, "Initially all material passing through column 1 just passes through to column 2. At the right time, it is diverted to column 1's collection bin. Once all of component 1 has come through, the flow is diverted back so everything continues to column 2.

"Column 2 is handled the same way, initially everything passes through to the boiler, then at the right time is diverted to collection bin 2, then back to the boiler. You could have done this almost as well with just one column. But the two-column approach you've chosen works well."

I kind of follow, but one question isn't clear to me.

"How do we know when it's coming through?"

"It's easy to calculate. But the short answer is that we need instrumentation at both points to detect it.

"What's missing from these drawings is the estimated timing, the two sensors, and the two valves they control."

Darcy's explanation triggers a momentary vision that answers why I couldn't see this before. I'd queried whether the columns were right. The answer is that they were. I didn't query whether they had been connected correctly. They weren't. That's why the trial runs I'd sampled were hit or miss.

"Jared?"

Julian's voice brings me back to the moment. I turn to look at him.

"We seem to have lost you there for a moment. Did you learn something?"

I smile at him. "Yes. I now understand why I couldn't find what was bothering me while probing the *mystery*. I was posing the questions wrong."

He looks at me oddly, which triggers another thought. *They don't probe the same way I do.*

I hear Julian's telepathic response. *No. We apparently do not. You'll need to instruct us. And while I have you privately, you need to resolve whatever issue it is that's separating you and Summer.*

Then I hear Edson chuckle. Apparently, our exchange was not as private as Julian thought.

I turn to Matt and Darcy, who are watching me patiently. They are apparently used to the elders going telepathic on them. Funny that I'm included in that group.

"Thank you. I knew something was wrong with this design, but I wasn't sure what. Can you propose a change for us with drawings of the new components, cutouts showing where they go, and any supporting documentation my engineering team will need?"

"Yes. That won't take long. Tomorrow morning maybe?"

"Thank you."

...

After a short break, the three elder pairs reconvene with Summer and me.

"So, Jared. Can you give us an overview of your probing method?"

"I'd be happy to. I discovered this technique while pondering the actual chemical composition of the components we draw from the venom. In order to register for a clinical trial, we need to disclose the formula. Unless we get clinical approval, we will not be able to get our treatment out to the rest of the Confederation.

"The components have chemical formulas, which will eventually be determined. So, I tried probing for them but got nowhere. After several attempts, I gave up and started looking for labs on Jaredaan that can make those determinations. Turns out there are several. I contracted with several of them so no one contractor knew too much. And that's when the thought occurred. If those tests are going to be run, can I move forward in time to observe them. And that's what I did.

"You see, the problem is that you cannot see past your next decision. In this case, I was going to be the one that was going to cause the chemical formulas to be known. If I didn't do it, no one would. We'd all be dead. So, by committing to that course of action, I could probe past the point of that decision."

There's silence for a moment. I can tell they're talking privately among themselves and do so discreetly enough that it's not leaking to me. I'm sure I could break in but respect their privacy.

Julian's attention snaps back to me. It's obvious he's been selected as the spokesman.

"We understand the principle and agree with your conclusion. But are not sure how to apply it, what it looks like in action."

I'm about to start down a path that's going to take way too long, when Summer puts her hand on mine.

I hear the message, *Let me*.

I smile.

She reaches into her purse and grabs a pad of paper that she carries with her.

She scribbles a short message on each of three sheets, then puts them face down on the table.

"I want you to figure out what's written on these sheets. Julian, you have the first one. Edson you have the second. Ryan, you have the third."

Ryan raises his hand and points at his wife Aurora. "She leads. I'm the observer."

"Oh, sorry about that."

Summer's clearly embarrassed but continues on.

"Does anyone know their answer yet?"

They all shake their heads, no.

"How might you go about finding out?"

264

There's silence and puzzlement for a moment, then the light goes on for Edson, who turns to look at Julian.

The door to the private room opens and their server comes in with a pitcher of house ale.

Julian indicates that he should put it on the serving table and not serve it yet. As the waiter does that, Julian's eyes settle on me.

"Jared, I'd like you to read those pages to us at 7:00. Will you do that for us?"

I look to Summer for permission.

She nods, then says, "Agreed."

Julian pulls out his little box and plops some tiny sugar candies on a plate, then starts issuing orders.

"Aurora, Ryan. You take the first one. Write down the answer when you come back but keep it secret until we're all back.

"Edson, Clarissa. You take the second one. Sofia and I will take the third."

They all take an appropriately sized piece for this incredibly short mission, then each goes into a trance.

I take the opportunity to help myself to some ale.

"Want some?"

Summer nods. "Just a little."

About ten minutes later, Aurora and Ryan are back. They both quickly write down their answer, then compare and nod smiling. Then Ryan asks, "Ready for some ale?"

A moment later Clarissa and Edson return and jot down their answers. When Edson shows his to Clarissa, she smacks him. "Behave yourself!" They laugh, then Edson gets up to fetch some ale.

Curiously, Julian and Sofia are gone for a half hour.

When they finally return, they too jot down their answers, snicker a bit, then get some ale. When they take their seats, Julian asks.

"We all know what was on our page and I'll bet we all know what was on all three. Which leads me to a question... Does Jared really need to read those sheets now? We've all seen him do it. Will the answers change if he doesn't? Or if he never does?"

All eyes turn to me. But as I ponder the question, Aurora asks another.

"Similar question, what happens if Summer changes what's on the pages."

"Good questions. What you saw was one possible future. There are undoubtedly many possible futures. But the fact you saw something implies that if you stay the course, the future will be as you saw it. If you make different decisions, then you should expect a different answer."

The door to the room opens, and a beef buffet is brought in.

Julian thanks the waiters, then says to the group. "Let's let this experiment run to its conclusion. I think it has served the purpose it was constructed for. Thank you, Summer."

We all help ourselves to the meal, which works its magic. Earlier tensions melt away and the room takes on a party feel. An alarm goes off. Apparently, Julian set an alarm for 7:00. It takes a few minutes to regain control of the room and to find the slips of paper I'm supposed to read.

"OK. I'm about to read the first sheet. Aurora, you'll show us your answer once I've read the first sheet, right?"

She nods and a huge smile starts to spread.

"OK, here goes." I flip over the first sheet and read, "Jared!", then turn to Summer, "you put an exclamation point after my name?"

Aurora points to the clock on the wall, then turns over her piece of paper. It says, 'Jared!' including the exclamation mark. She's also noted the time, 7:04 PM.

I'm stunned. I've been going on faith, based on the episode with the cockroach, that the visions were true. But this clear a presentation, played out with sentient beings, is stunning. My hand trembles, heart pounds as I turn over the next sheet and read, 'would you please.'

Edson slaps the table as Sofia reads, 'would you please.' Then they both start laughing.

With heart pounding even harder, I grab the next slip of paper. The power of this demonstration is hitting home in a way I could never have imagined. I turn the last sheet over and read, 'make love to me tonight.'

The words are out before their meaning sinks in. I stare at them, eyes wide open, as the guffawing reaches a crescendo.

Julian pipes up. "Sounds like you have more work to do tonight, young man." He puts his piece of paper out showing the same words.

After a few more minutes of laughter, Edson stands, then Clarissa says, "Edson suggests that we let these two get on with their evening. Shall we meet in the morning at 9:00?"

266

MORNING

I wake to Summer's alarm. That usually means that I get up and ready, then wait a half hour on her. Not today. Yesterday was exhausting. I just cannot wake up. That changes when she says the only way we'll make it on time is if I jump in the shower with her. God, I'm so easy!

We make it to the private room in the pub a minute before our meetings are to start. Everyone else has empty plates, but there's still food on the buffet. Before I even get to the buffet, Edson envelopes me in a huge hug. Julian comes in close behind.

"We're both relieved the situation has been resolved."

What, a moment ago, felt like brotherly affirmation is now embarrassment.

"Oh, don't take it that way, dear boy."

It's Sophia. Why do older women always call me 'boy' with some adjective stuck in front?

"Because we see our husbands and our sons in you."

Sometimes, it's really hard working with telepathic people.

"I know, I know, Jared." Sofia kisses me on the cheek. "But that's part of living with the *mystery*."

Darcy Santos and Matt Lee, the analytical chemistry and distillation specialists, come in just as Summer and I are taking our seats. Greetings are exchanged. I shovel in food as they roll out drawings at the other end of the table. As I watch them, I wonder where their technology comes from.

Edson, who's sitting next to me, pats my hand. I look over and see him smiling at me. Julian speaks for him. "I didn't hear your thought, but Edson says you probably already know the answer to your question."

"Where your technology comes from?" I'm perplexed that he thinks I would know the answer to that question, but even as I think the thought, I know. "You have collaborators, presumably in Heroldstown."

"Indeed, we do. Some in Jaredstown as well. But it's hard to work that channel these days."

"Have you been getting supplementary food?"

"On occasion, but rarely. And none these days, of course. For most things, including food, we are self-sufficient unless there is some sort of disaster. That happens now and again. And when it does, our sympathizers help to the extent they can."

It seems that I learn more about my world every day. What's shocking is how much of it is hidden from the general population.

Darcy signals that they're ready, and Julian gives them the floor.

Essentially all the changes are in her domain, and it's clear to me that she's a master. Her descriptions are clear and cogent. Her drawings are beautiful, at least to a layman. And her documentation is comprehensive. I have no doubt that Brock and Charlie will be able to build it out.

When they're finished, they package up the documents in a protective carrying case, then take their leave.

Once the door is shut, Julian takes on the last item on his list.

"Jared, what are our priorities for the next month? What are you going to be doing? And how would you like us to help?"

"My priorities are clear. The top priority is to get the still up and working, so we can start distributing our supplement here and in the camp. Then to expand distribution to the rest of the planet and the space station.

"Next will be to get the synthesis line up and use it for clinical trials. To save the Confederation, we need to distribute off planet. To distribute off planet, we need the clinical trials.

"Next, we need to find a way to defeat the incoming alien horde. I've already made a little progress on this. But it's not something we'll be able to do without Confederation involvement."

"And how can we help?

This question is harder.

"Have you attempted to find the aliens?"

"Attempt, yes. Find, no."

"I could probably guide you if I had the time. But I need to get these..." I pat the drawing case, "...back tonight."

"Is there a way you can think of to help?"

Julian pauses to think.

"We need to learn your probing techniques. We got a glimpse of it last night. Maybe we can make some progress applying what we've learned."

Summer, who's been writing on her pad this morning, pulls a few pages off, then looks up smiling.

"I'm not really involved in the distillery engineering process, so started writing down some of my observations about Jared's probing technique while you were reviewing the drawings." She slides the pages to me to look at. "Maybe they'll help you, Julian."

There's silence for a moment as I read through them.

"Wow. These are really good. Thank you."

I hand them to Julian. He bows his head in thanks to Summer.

"Thank you. This is a real gift."

RETURN

As we leave the pub, I see that the truck has already been packed for us and four rangers on horseback are waiting to guide us back. These sessions are way too short. Six-to-eight hours of meals and meetings sandwiched between two six-to-eight-hour tiresome trips through the wilderness. Hopefully, we will get to spend a full day here at some point in the future.

We say our goodbyes, then get in the truck to leave. Jason Tanner is the lead ranger again today. He guides us out of town via a different path, then starts into the canyon leading home at a different place than before. At a level spot about a kilometer in, Jason stops, then gets down. I lower the window as he approaches.

"Some unusually heavy rain hit last night. There's been a wash out. Want to see?"

Summer and I get out and follow him to a place nearby with an excellent view of the entire valley. He points to a spot 10 kilometers upstream.

"See the lower area, where the river's blocked a bit. To get past it, we're going to need to travel higher on the ridge essentially the entire way." He points to a trail visible high on the ridge.

It looks really narrow to me.

"It's narrower than the lower trails were. But we can ride two abreast the entire way, so I think your truck shouldn't have a problem."

"Are there other ways?"

"This is the only one we've found so far."

For the first time, I'm worried. On our first trip down, we could turn back if we got stuck. But we really can't do that now. We need to get home.

"Then, let's do it."

Jason nods, remounts, then leads the way.

For the next hour we climb, nearly to the ridge top. There we stop to water the horses, who are really struggling.

I get out to check on them.

"Everything's fine. We're dependent on the horses, so stop to water them after any long climb." He points back behind us.

"This is one of the best view spots in the area."

I turn to look and am amazed at what I see. We have a clear view of the north shore of the great sea. It stretches to the horizon. In the distance, I notice what appears to be smoke. Looking closer, I see what appear to be buildings.

"Is there another settlement further east along the north shore?"

"We think of it as being part of Jaramor. But yes, there's great agricultural land up there. It's where most of our food is grown. The smoke is from our drying facility. It's wood and trash powered." He points to a green area a little closer. "We've cultivated a forest in the valleys over there. It's mostly a local strain of eucalyptus bred for that environment. Wood from the forest is used for construction purposes and as fuel. There are also several groves of fruit trees. We have some incredibly sour apples that make great cider."

Again, I'm impressed by the people of Jaramor and they're resourcefulness.

Once the horses are watered, we resume the trip back. It's slow going. The trail is very narrow in places with steep drop-offs on the right. But after six hours, the trail widens and starts down. Jason stops again at a shallow stream to water the horses.

I get out to chat.

Jason points northwest. "From here the trail goes down the hill to the road. We checked it earlier today and it's good. If you're OK with it, we'll leave you here. You shouldn't have any trouble getting home. It'll take us four to five hours to return. I'd like to get past the narrow cliff area before we lose the sunlight."

"I'm good with that. Thanks for the help and have a safe trip back, Jason."

I get back into the truck and restart the crawl west. We wave as we pass the horses.

"I like Jaramor," Summer says quietly. "I look forward to the day we can stay there longer."

"Me too."

TEST RUN

It's been a little over a week since we got back from Jaramor. Brock and Charlie have been working around the clock to finish the first production line. This line is for the viper venom. It has five collection points, plus waste collection. A preliminary test of the distillation section passes with flying colors. The test is done using plain water. The purpose is to confirm heating functionality, evaporation rates, precipitation temperature stability and other process attributes that I don't fully understand.

Brock runs a second test, adding a test substance that should precipitate in the first collection bin. 99.9% lands in the first bin, the measurement limit for this test.

He runs another test, adding a test substance that should bypass all the collection bins and land in the waste. Again, 99.9% gets through, the measurement limit for this test.

The final test is on the HPLC protein separation system. I had totally misunderstood this step until the last trip to Jaramor. Although it's not connected into the rest of the system yet, Brock runs a test on it. 95% of the test material is separated out, the rest goes to waste. This step is a lot less efficient than the previous ones, but within spec. So, I approve it.

Knowing that all the parts of the viper line are functioning, I authorize Brock to finish connecting it up. As the toad line will be basically the same, I authorize Brock to build it out also.

He says both lines will be ready to start operation in 10 days.

I've brought Charlie on full time at this point, so give him the responsibility to drive this phase of the project to a close. My job now will be to secure the raw materials and sort out an appropriate packaging scheme.

CAMP

Things at the camp have become routine. Production in all zones is up, but the food supply has become a real issue. Summer and I have stopped eating camp food. Lenna and her team always have good stuff for us, but I feel guilty taking it. Instead, Summer has been cooking using our dehydrated food supplies. It's not as good as Lenna's food, but it's good enough, tasty actually. But the average daily calories going out to the labor force are dropping. And we're getting a lot of complaints from people whose cabins or work assignments are the farthest from the dining rooms, about the food quantity and quality when they finally get there. The gardens have only been in for 6 weeks, so aren't yielding enough yet to make a difference.

We are up to eight confirmed cases of DAGS. The actual number of cases is undoubtedly higher because symptoms lag infection by months. We've dropped Lenna and Emily to one dose a day. They are symptom free at this point. We've put them on maintenance, so Dr. Avery can have more doses for symptomatic patients. We need to get the production lines up soon. Ethel and Norah are doing what they can, but their absolute maximum capacity is maintenance doses for 20 people.

It's now broadly known that I'm working on a treatment for the disease. Many people have figured out that Ethel and Norah are involved somehow. The ladies don't want, or need, the attention, so I deflect as much attention away from them as possible.

But now that people are starting to realize we have a serious problem that I'm trying to solve, others are stepping forward to cover as many of my camp duties as they can.

Warden Glenn has become quite distant. I think he's become bound up in the palace intrigue up north. Shuttle system operation should resume a week or so after the emergency delivery. He should be returning on one of the first flights back. That's when things will get really interesting. The camp operates much differently now than it did the day they left. Summer is convinced I'm going to come to blows with her father. I hope that doesn't happen. But my priorities are clear, and I will not waiver from them: save the camp, save the planet, save mankind, then defeat the aliens.

RAW MATERIALS

I got word from Charlie today. System construction will be completed tomorrow. Test and calibration runs will take the next four days. Then they'll be ready for the first production run. The supply tanks have been installed and cleaned. We can take delivery of the raw materials as early as tomorrow.

I take a tiny dose of the *profecia aumentar*, enough to enable me to connect with Julian.

Jared, is it time?

Even at distance, Julian seems to be able to read my mind once we connect.

Yes, it is. We should be ready for the first run in four days. Do you have the raw materials?

Yes. Can you come to collect them?

I can if I must, but it'd be better if you could bring them most of the way. My plate is still too full.

272

OK. Three days from today. Meet Jason where you parted company with him on your last return. They will have a wagon with four half-barrels for you. They will be there by noon.

PICKUP

Quite a few people know that Summer and I go camping in the wilderness. Most think it's strange. But no one suspects that we're meeting people out there.

That makes this pick-up tricky. I will be picking up supplies at noon and coming back to civilization with them during the daylight hours. I don't want to take those supplies home with me and don't want to risk getting caught up in a surprise inspection. Instead, I take a different kind of risk by staging an elaborate deception.

At first light I'm off to Heroldstown. I stop at the outfitting shop to buy a tarp and anything else that looks interesting.

I enter and see the same sales guy. This time I remember his name.

"Cody, good to see you again."

"Jared, good to see you too."

I immediately sense that something's wrong.

"Ah..." Cody starts. "I hope you're not here looking for more food. We're out."

"Sorry to hear that. The food we got last time was really quite good, I'd love to get some more. But that's not why I'm here."

He brightens. "Then what can I help you find?"

"A tarp. We got a little rain on the last trip out into the wilderness. Thankfully, nothing got wet. But I want a tarp to tie over the back of my truck."

Minutes later, I have exactly what I want and Cody's pressing me for anything else I might need. He shows me some of his more unique items and before long I have two of the most ridiculous things I've ever bought, a pair of inflatable easy chairs.

Cody helps me load the tarp and deflated easy chairs into the passenger compartment, then I'm off to the hardware store. At least that's what I tell Cody.

...

There is a hardware store in the industrial area. There's also another rarely used picnic area in one of the few wooded parks in Heroldstown. I stop at the picnic area and make sure no one is in sight. Then I put the easy chairs on the truck's flat bed and inflate them. Once inflated, I put them on their side, tie them down under the tarp, then step back to inspect my work. It's less than perfect, but from a distance this will pass as four half barrels of raw material. The next part of the deception is going to be a bit harder to pull off.

...

I pull into the distillery parking lot and see that both Brock and Charlie are already in. Their trucks are in the parking lot. I park in a spot clearly visible from the conference room, then head inside. If I've timed this right, they'll be having a cup of Charlie's coffee and reviewing the work plan for the day.

I enter the building and am immediately greeted. They're having coffee. Charlie can see the truck and is really excited. "You've got the raw materials?"

I smile. "I do."

"Want us to help unload?"

"Yes, but later. Something's come up."

Brock, who has real trust issues, frowns. "What happened?"

I can tell he thinks the project's been cancelled. I pull a copy of a news article from my pocket. It's a bit salacious but will serve my needs. I place it on the table, and the two men are stunned by the headline. "Alien Sensor Array Malfunction"

They look at me incredulously.

"Apparently there was a blip on the alien sensor array on Taramoot, a protected world another 20 light-years out along the rim. I got a priority request from the elders to check our array."

I plop down a message from Uncle Walter asking if I knew anything about this and had any means to check on Herold's array.

"We have an alien sensor array?"

"Herold tried to build one, but apparently screwed it up. I need to go check out the one at the end of the road. It should be making a sound if it has made a detection."

Walter had made this request about a week ago. We both know the array is nonfunctional, so his request was to check it out if I was ever in the area. I deleted that part of the message as well as the date before printing this out.

Both men seem to be in shock.

"Look, it's nothing to worry about. But I need to run out that way. The materials are safe on the truck. Just wanted to let you know I'd be back by later this afternoon to off load."

Charlie starts to protest, but I cut him off.

"Don't worry. I've got this."

I turn and exit. As I'm starting to leave, Charlie runs out.

"Are you sure you don't want me to come with you?"

I smile. "No. You have work to do. The elders want me to check this out personally. No sense both of us losing half the day."

He waves. It's obvious he doesn't completely believe me. But hopefully any residual curiosity about this journey has been deflected away from the raw materials which will be on the truck when I return.

...

I reach the end of the road, then start up the hill toward the area where Jason should be waiting for me. It's surprisingly windy. I can periodically hear the wind moan as it cuts through the peaks.

I arrive at the pickup spot, but don't see Jason, which is worrisome. I go a little further toward Jaramor, then see one of the rangers stepping out from behind some brush. He waves me over.

"Thought it best if we waited off the trail. What do you have in the truck?"

I laugh and tell him about the deception.

I get a simple, "Good idea," then he and his team start loading the barrels as I deflate the chairs.

Fifteen minutes later, the deflated chairs are back in the passenger compartment, exactly where Cody put them, and the barrels are secured under the tarp.

Jason, who has behaved oddly the entire time, comes back to say they are done then asks, "What does this detector do when it senses something?"

I look at him curiously then admit that I don't know.

He points at the nearest well. It's about 2 kilometers away, but clearly visible down below us.

"That thing has been making moaning sounds all day long. We couldn't figure out what it was. One of the men went down on foot to confirm it was coming from that well."

"What?" I'm completely shocked. "Isn't the sound coming from the wind?"

"No. It was doing that when we got here a little after dawn. The wind didn't start up until an hour ago."

In 60 seconds, I've gone from thinking that I've been working a sketchy deception to thinking that we have a serious problem.

"If you're supposed to be reporting this, you better get moving." Jason prods.

"You, too." We shake, then head our separate ways.

I stop at the well at the end of the road. Heading in for the pickup, I hadn't come this close. Where I am now, 5 meters from the well head, I can feel the truck vibrating. When I step out of the truck it's so loud, it's uncomfortable to approach any closer.

I speed on to the next well. It too is moaning, but not as loud. The same is true for the next two wells. After that, I can hear the moaning if I step up onto the cement pad and approach the small opening in the well cap, but really cannot hear it from the truck.

The idea that our alien detectors are going off scares me to the core.

FIRST RUN

I arrive back at the distillery. Technically, I was never out of comms range, but I couldn't bring myself to call this in from the truck. So as Brock and Charlie unload the truck, I call the elders council emergency line. I tell the dispatch officer what I've found and am greeted with skepticism. But the officer is professional. I'm an elder's brother, and my instruction letter is on file, so I'm routed directly to Walter. He's far less professional than the dispatch officer and truly in a quandary about what to do next. I suggest that he use his Confederation connections to find out more about the detectors and how they sound the alarm. Apparently, this is not one of Herold's hairbrained schemes, but a Confederation program tied directly to our standing as a protected world. Who would have ever thought?

...

Back in the distillery, Brock and Charlie have loaded the diluted viper venom into the HPLC separation system and are ready to start the run. In a little less than an hour, component 1 will be separated out into the protein bin. Overnight, the rest of the volume plus a little added water will be in the raw bin for its distillation run.

While it is running, we load the toad venom into its HPLC separation system and start that run. From here, everything is automated. The first distillation runs will start in the morning.

JOURNEY

Over dinner, I tell Summer about the day's developments. She's as shocked as I was, astounded that the alien detection system appears to be working. Thankfully, she suggests that we probe the issue. I've backed off a bit on probing the *mystery* since our last trip to Jaramor.

Once dinner is cleaned up, we relax into our easy chairs and start our inquiry.

The first stop is Taramoot. This world is much different than ours. Our world is cold and dry. The only place you can go outside is along the equator. Taramoot is hot and wet. Eighty percent of the planet's surface is water. There are no ice caps. All human life is concentrated north of the 60th parallel. The land that far north is richly cultivated. There's a 100 km circle at the north pole where there's not enough light to grow crops. For the most part, only trees grow there. It's also where their alien detectors are. And they are going off. Their detectors make a similar moaning sound, but it's loud enough to be killing the nearby trees. This seems to confirm the theory that our alien detectors work.

The next stop is much more confusing. We are at scientific headquarters on New Brazil. I'm at the back of a long lecture hall where the speaker is talking about the theory behind the detectors. They apparently work by sensing a vibration in the pressure between layers of space-time. This has something to do with how the alien propulsion systems work. The sensors basically convert that pressure fluctuation to physical movement of a membrane positioned at the end of a long horn shaped tube. Everything else I hear makes no sense to me.

The next stop is with the alien armada. Again, this is difficult to probe. The aliens seem to be able to sense me, so it's harder to eavesdrop. But what I hear is terrifying. An advance force has been hiding closer to the rim. They have been cloaked in stealth mode, sitting idle waiting for reinforcements to get closer. They've been given orders to decloak and begin their mission. That's what set the alien detector off.

There's a world the advance force has been instructed to find. One of the alien kings on the bridge where I'm hiding turns and looks in my direction. He makes no attempt to approach or hide his interest in me. He just smiles. His advance force has been sent to look for me!

...

Reality comes slamming back. Usually, I come out of the *mystery* slowly as if I'm waking up. Not this time. It's more like I've been dropped into my seat from the second floor. My heart is racing. I notice Summer startle awake as suddenly as I did.

"What the hell!" she screams.

I have never heard Summer use foul language before. But seeing my sweet, innocent partner startle awake that way seems incredibly funny and I can't hold back the laughter. In a moment, we're both laughing so hard we're crying.

After a minute we settle.

Thinking through what I just saw, I'm confused. So, I ask Summer, "The detectors are sounding now, so the advance force must have already de-cloaked and started moving. They think they've found us, but that's at some point in the future. Did you get any sort of read on when that might be?"

"That's not the way I read it. They started moving. That's why the sensors have gone off. But they're still cloaked and moving slowly. They're looking for something, but it may not be us. When they find what they're looking for, they will decloak and attack. My sense is that it isn't us. He was gawking at you because you're human, not because you're you. He seemed to be lusting for something else."

"How long were we on that ship?"

"Maybe an hour. You spent a lot of time transfixed. About what, I couldn't tell. I spent a lot of time reading the minds of the bridge crew. They are definitely looking for something. When you're up for it, we should go back. I think it's important."

TEST

It took three days to process the venoms. Each day we put the proteins through another HPLC pass and each of the distillation components through another distillation pass. On each pass, we lose a little. But at this point, I'm confident in the purity of the results.

In some sense we didn't gain any speed on Ethel and Norah. Their process takes three days. But ours is much purer. And we have about 1,000 times as much. I'll be delivering half of that to Julian as promised. But I'll also be delivering a dose to the local analytical lab first.

I've already used the *profecia aumentar* to confirm the results the lab will produce, but don't want to tempt fate. So tomorrow, a sample of each component will be delivered to the appropriate lab and I'll watch as they run their tests.

But I'm not going to wait for the lab results. Today, I'm taking my first daily dose to confirm safety. Assuming I survive the next 24 hours without consequence, we'll start distributing. I've already probed the future on this matter, but one more day for one more safety test seems a reasonable precaution.

NORTH SPACE PORT

Word reached me today that our emergency order arrived 10 days ago, and the required shuttle repairs were made. I'm a bit pissed that I paid for this and am only now finding out. But that seems to be the way Walter operates. I tend not to hold grudges, but I'll do my part to make sure Walter will become *persona non grata* once his term is done.

Over the next several days the supplies will be delivered. Supplies headed to Jaredstown and Ashcrag will get priority. I don't like it but understand it. The shuttle will be running in a circle for the next several weeks. Supplies will come down to the north space port. People and goods will travel from north to south. Then people headed north or to the space station will travel to the space station, where the cycle will repeat. Once the north deliveries are complete, the cycle will switch to the other direction—station, south, north—until all deliveries are made and we switch back to the ping pong strategy of the past—station, north, south, station, south, north, station.

I've sent a request to the elders for priority treatment of my synthesis equipment. I've advised the elders that my treatment for DAGS will not head north until a week after the synthesis equipment is delivered, best case.

WARDEN RETURNS

The first north-south shuttle that's operated in months will have Summer's parents aboard. It arrives a little before sunset, so Summer and I drop everything at 3:00 to go collect them. My truck will not hold four people, so we take one of the ancient ground vehicles owned by the camp. For the life of me, I cannot figure out how these things operate. So, Jack Johnson, head of camp security, drives.

Jack drops us at the front entrance and goes to park the camp's van. Although I've been here before, nothing is familiar. It takes a while, but finally the penny drops... I've only been in the secure prisoner transport areas, not the public spaces. The realization puts me in a serious funk.

Summer senses that immediately and tries to perk me up. When her normal charms have no effect, I get a telepathic blast.

Wake up or plan on sleeping by yourself for a while.

279

I hear the reprimand. But it's delivered with a degree of compulsion and humor I cannot resist. I turn and kiss her before the effect wears off. It seems I'm not the only one for whom the effect of the *profecia aumentar* lingers. Jack returns from parking the van moments before the warden and Ms. Glenn come through the arrivals exit.

The greetings are a bit awkward. Summer's mother seems to be completely briefed on and OK with my relationship with her daughter. She gives me a big hug. The warden... Not so much. He treats me more like a camp laborer or subordinate, than like a son-in-law. He's more distant now than before he left. I can tell it's going to take a while to work through this, but I'm resolved to make it happen.

We collect their bags, pack the van, and head back to the camp, then the interrogation begins.

DISTRIBUTION

One of the things I wanted, but could not get, in the last delivery was a bottling line. It would have allowed us to distribute a bottle containing a month's supply of the supplement to about half the people in the camp.

Without the bottling line, we need to go with larger containers for distribution. We ultimately decide on a system where each zone gets a large bottle that has 30 daily doses for 25 people. The supervisors are responsible for distributing it. No one is required to take it and so far, most don't want to. But those who have DAGS, know someone who has had DAGS, or are starting to have symptoms are clamoring for it. The hospital also has a large bottle with enough for two doses for every DAGS patient in the hospital and any of the staff that want to start taking it.

At the moment, supply exceeds demand, but that will change.

I also made a predawn trip out to the exchange point to return the barrels, one of which had been filled with a month's supply of daily doses for 500. Once again, Jason headed the team of rangers sent for the pickup. He told me that the next round of raw materials would be ready in about a week. Julian would contact me when they were ready.

The alien detector is still sounding the alarm. Its creepy moaning, ever so slightly louder than before, makes my skin crawl. The only good news is that Walter has asked me to check the detectors every week or so. It gives me the cover I need to go collect materials without drawing unwanted suspicion.

SYNTHESIS EQUIPMENT

A week has passed since the space shuttle repairs were made and my synthesis equipment has finally been scheduled for delivery. I've been given a 3:00 pickup time this afternoon. Summer and I leave headquarters at noon. Although he says nothing, I get the evil eye from the warden. Larry, on the other hand, is very vocal about the fact he is being stuck with the extra load again.

As we reach the north shore of the lake, where the road finally turns west, I hear the sonic boom of the space shuttle entering the atmosphere. Several minutes later, I see it coming toward the space complex on final approach. Today, I'm the lucky guy getting something from another world that I've been waiting for a long time.

JUNGLE

It feels like it's been weeks since I checked my account on Jungle. There are numerous messages waiting, but I skip by that to check on sales.

Since the last time I checked, two months have finished. The first of those had royalties of just less than 400,000 credits at that time. That month closed at 412,000. Last month closed a little lower at 389,000. I check my sales by planet report and immediately see why. Several of the smaller planets are under quarantine. Sales on those worlds have functionally dropped to zero. Sales on worlds still operating have held steady or increased. One week into the new month, royalties are just short of 100,000.

A quick check of my bank account is encouraging. I still have over 100,000 Jaredaan credits and another 100,000 Confederation credits. My next payment from Jungle will put me up over half a million, enough to get a bottling machine, if Uncle Walter will let me have that much space. But he will, because I won't do the deal otherwise.

CHAPTER 18: SYNTHESIS

When I arrive at headquarters this morning, there's a message asking me to check in with the warden when I arrive. I stash my stuff, then head down the hall.

His secretary greets me with a big smile as she always does.

"Morning, Jared. Go on in." She indicates the boss's open door.

"Thanks, Lillian." I return her smile, then enter the inner office.

"Hi, Jared. Thanks for coming by. Would you mind closing the door?"

I close the door and take a seat. I'm sure I'm in some kind of trouble, but not really picking up on what that might be.

"First, I'd like to say thank you for the work you've done here. I can't recall the camp running this well before and, despite all the problems associated with the plague, camp morale is as good as I've ever seen it."

The warden's words are gracious, but I hear a 'but' coming.

"But here's the problem. You're not really doing much at the camp these days. You're spending a lot of time out in the wilderness and even more time over at your production facility. When's the last time you've spent a day out in the zones? Or, a day in your own office for that matter?"

The warden's claims are accurate, and I understand his concern. But this is one of those things that makes me angry. Nonetheless, I rein in the emotion. Letting any of it slip out will work to everyone's disadvantage.

"I do my best to work the biggest issues facing the camp. At the moment, those issues aren't in the zones or in my office. They're mostly out there. Getting enough medication to contain the disease. Finding and securing the supplies we need to continue operating. Responding to the elders' request to monitor the alien sensors.

"Is there anyone else here at the camp that can do those things? And where would we be if I hadn't taken the initiative?"

"But people talk."

I find the response so comical that I almost snort.

"I presume you mean the people in this building. I'm hearing nothing but praise from the people at the hospital and most of the people in the camp that I meet outside this building."

The warden seems uncomfortable with the direction this conversation has gone.

"Can we start this conversation over?" I ask. "There's obviously something bothering you, and I expect there's something you want from me that you're not getting. We both have the camp's interest as top priority. So, we should be able to work this out."

The warden exhales.

"Jared, camp rules do not allow employees to run outside businesses. It's been easy to overlook your products on Jungle. But the fact that you're being paid by the camp yet spending a lot of time at the facilities of a company you own and operate, sits poorly with the board. This is a problem. The board hasn't forced my hand yet. But they want you in or out, not straddling the fence."

It's been a long time since I've looked at my paycheck. I don't really know how much I'm paid. But it's something trivial—20, maybe 25 thousand credits a year. I've spent more than twice that amount on the camp and give them their drugs for free! It's hard to contain the emotion.

"Well, maybe we should change that up. I can quit and move to Heroldstown. You can contract out and pay for the next corn planting on your own. Same with the remainder of the citrus plantings. And I'd be happy to sell you the medications I'm currently supplying for free. Going rate is a credit a dose."

I'm embarrassed by the amount of anger that slipped out, but it doesn't seem to affect the warden. He actually smiles.

"I think we both understand the problem now. Want to help me solve it?"

His words break the tension and I chuckle. "Of course, I do. What options do we have?"

"I really want you here. I don't want you to move away. But you can only have staff housing if you're on staff."

At first, I'm puzzled that we're starting with housing. Then it sinks in. If I move, Summer will move, and he'll move heaven and earth to keep her here if he can.

"So, how can I stay on staff and still do the things we both need done."

"Leave of absence?"

"I'm assuming that would be an unpaid leave and I would still need to pay for my apartment."

He nods his head.

"Maybe we can strike a volume deal for the medications." I shoot back.

His visage darkens at that suggestion.

"Or maybe go a different direction altogether. Summer is eligible to have my apartment, isn't she?"

"She doesn't make enough money."

"But there are rules for life partners to live with employees on site aren't there?" I cite two couples I know about that have partners living with them on site.

He's quiet for a moment.

"I'm going to push back against the board. You're already spending enough money on us and giving us a lot of free product. The status quo is tremendously beneficial to the camp. And I know you'll be back out in the fields when you need to be.

"Regulations are regulations. But they're not always in the camp's interest. I'll file for an exception. We can take this up again later if I don't get it."

...

As I leave the warden's office, I realize several things. He knows what's going to happen if he can't keep me. In short, the camp will be in real trouble. I give the camp more money than he pays me. He'll never get the budget to replace the money and product I'm putting in. And if I leave, Summer will probably go with me.

And possibly more importantly, he knows that I will work with him to make things happen because I care for the camp as much as he does.

FIRST RUN

Today is a scary day on multiple fronts. The synthesis line is up. The programming appears to be right. It's mostly based on the results of the analytical chemistry runs I did at the labs. But it's also based on the pseudo-clinical trial results gleaned from the *mystery*. At this point, I'm betting everything that the *mystery* has revealed truth to me. But who can really know?

True. I've probed it to the best of my ability. And equally true, every test, the few there were, showed the *mystery* to be reliable. But this bet is on a whole new level. I'm willing to, and will actually, bet my life on it. But objective scientific proof that this will work... Well, there is none, at least none of the type I've been trained to accept. And that's the conundrum. I believe. Not because I'm following the conventional wisdom I've been taught. But because I'm following the truth that's been revealed to me.

I smile and laugh at myself. As best I can determine from the history written down for us, truth is one of those things that's evaded humanity since the dawn of time. Good, evil.... Right, wrong... I strongly believe in those principles. But is that really what's been revealed to me?

...

It seems the time for such philosophical nonsense has expired. The line has been set up and checks out. It'll work, or it won't work. I've spent huge effort and most of my fortune to get to this point. It's time to find out which it is.

But I'm going to be the first to take it. If it's going to kill someone, then it needs to start with me.

ALIENS

I got a telepathic message from Julian on Thursday. They think that they may have discovered something. He asks us to come on Saturday if at all possible. He says the upper road is clear, so we should be able to make it most of the way on our own. Jason and his team will be dispatched for arrival at the pickup location around 1:00 PM. But he asks us to continue down the road until we meet them, so we can have more time in Jaramor.

I tell the warden that Summer and I will be leaving early on Saturday morning to go take more test measurements on the alien detectors. I also tell him that we're planning to camp out so we can explore another site further downstream. He knows we've done this before, but still worries. I hope he doesn't send a security team to keep an eye on us.

Summer and I take off just before dawn. I suspect our time in Jaramor will be busy.

...

At this point, I've made four trips to the end of the road to pick up raw materials for the manufacturing plant. Each time the volume from the alien detectors is slightly louder. I know because I now carry a DB meter to measure the volume. I've taken three measurements so far. At well ten, they were 89, 90 and 92 dB respectively. This is less volume than they're getting on Taramoot, where levels are alleged to be well over 100 db. But I take little comfort in that. There is no official test procedure. I've marked a spot about 5 meters from each of our wells where I take my measurement at that well. This gives me some comparability from test to test. But this is not done precisely enough to make a strong comparison between the wells.

I don't know how Taramoot takes their measurements. And there is no calibration between their sensors and ours. So, as I said, the fact that my volume readings are lower than theirs means nothing. But I'm increasingly worried that the aliens' advance fleet is getting closer.

...

We are at well 10. The first two still do not make a perceivable sound. But the remaining eight do. Today well 10 checks in at 95 db. Taking the measurement is hard on the ears, and it reveals the largest increase to date.

The ten tests probably cost us an hour. But we arrive at the rendezvous point before Jason and his rangers. I stop to survey the road behind us. There is evidence of our passing, but not much, and I see no sign that we're being followed. So, I start down the trail toward Jaramor.

We're making great time and come to the narrow spot along the cliff around noon. I can see that Jason and his team have widened the trail by cutting into the mountain side a half meter or so. In an abundance of caution, I stop to get out of the truck, then check the stability of the narrow pass and the clearances. As I walk across the pass, I see the rangers on the steep part of the trail maybe 5 km ahead.

The narrow pass seems stable as does the rock on the mountainside above. So, I get back in the truck and start inching my way across. As I go, I realize now how harrowing it is to cross without someone guiding. Even with the extra space I feel like my truck is about to scrape the wall or fall over the edge. After five minutes of inching my way across, we're clear. I stop, put my head back and take a calming breath. I let go of the steering wheel to wipe my brow and realize that my hands are trembling.

Summer laughs. "You had plenty of room on this side all the way across."

I'm surprised by her comment, then moments later caught up in the humor of it. After a good laugh, I race down the wide trail hoping to catch the rangers before they reach the top of the long slope. There's no sense wearing their horses out.

When we get to the steep descent, I see that Jason and the rangers are watering their horses at the rest stop about halfway up. They must have realized we could make it there on our own. When we meet up, they lead the way into town.

JARAMOR

We arrive in Jaramor early. The rangers and inn staff help us unload. Among the things brought over this trip are the four barrels that have been supplying the raw materials. One of them has a month's supply of our supplement. The others are empty and ready for refill. We also brought our shelter. There was no intention to use it. We brought it as a prop to support our cover story if we bumped into someone.

We take a moment to freshen up, then head downstairs. The pub is surprisingly busy given the hour. We look for seats, but Julian sees us and whisks us into the private room. The others haven't arrived yet, but Julian wants to speak with us privately. A waiter comes in with a pitcher and a tray of snacks. He sets them on the table, then leaves.

Once the door is shut, Julian starts by pouring us each a taste from the pitcher.

"This is fresh mulled cider. It's a treat for us here in Jaramor. We have an apple orchard planted with a local variant that we can harvest twice a year. The harvest started last week. This cider comes from the first pressing. It's been mulled with spices."

He chuckles. "Our cider is an acquired taste, but most of us love it.

"The first hard ciders from this harvest will be available in another week. This one is non-alcoholic. But if you like it, we use it to make a buttered hot toddy in the evenings that is alcoholic."

We both take a sip. I cringe at the sourness. This will take getting used too. Summer on the other hand loves it.

Julian fills both our mugs, then asks, "Mind if I switch to business?"

I nod as I take another sip.

"We've had something of a breakthrough. It took a couple days to learn your techniques, but we've mastered them enough to start probing the alien advance force in some depth.

"Their mission is not what I was expecting. The main armada is powered by zero-point energy devices. We are not aware of any ship in the Confederation that can travel as far or fast as the alien ships do.

So, it makes sense that their ships are powered by a source that we do not have.

"Although their ships don't burn fuel per se, the catalyst at the heart of their zero-point energy systems does erode away. So, their first stop after crossing the void will be for catalyst replenishment.

"They've found two planets along the rim that have the material they need. One is an ice giant, the other is Taramoot. They want to minimize their exposure to humans until they're ready to strike, so have tried mining the ice giant. Unfortunately, the ice giant's deposits have been difficult to access. And the small amount of material they've been able to extract is of poor quality. The advance force is on its way to Taramoot now. They will get there in another month or so. Their plan is to exterminate the human population there, then spend the next two years mining and refining the material."

"Could you determine what this material is?"

"Yes. It took a lot of work, but we found it. It's one of the so-called rare-earth elements, thulium. Specifically, they use the isotope ^{169}Tm.

"Taramoot is a mostly agricultural world. But the founders of the settlement there knew of the thulium and have been mining it for export to other worlds. They are apparently more isolated than we are. No DAGS cases have been reported there. I suspect they have little trade, mostly periodic thulium exports in exchange for equipment and other things they can't make themselves.

"There's a lot more news to share with you, but I'll let the others share the rest when they get here." Julian smiles at us. "They're the ones that made those discoveries. They'll be along soon."

...

Time passes. Jason and some of the other rangers we've met come by to see us. They celebrate the cider enough that I suspect that's the reason they decided to come.

But I'm totally good with that. I get it. Julian has asked a lot of his people to support our welcome in their community. Summer and I appreciate the reception we've received, as I'm sure the Jaramor elders do.

Nonetheless, my broader sense of the community is less welcoming. We come from what they perceive to be the more privileged side of our world. I understand the perspective. On paper 'we' have more. But that's the irony. I'm possibly the wealthiest person on the planet. But how did that come to be? Familial persecution? Betrayal? A sentence to a prison camp?

I'm doubting many people here have been through the same heartbreak. I'm sure our side of the world has more stuff in total. But it's totally corrupt. I'm the victim of that corruption, not the beneficiary. I have yet to see any corruption of similar magnitude on this side. It may exist; I don't know. But few people have had to walk through the persecution and torment that I have. We've all grown up with the sixth son nonsense. But where they see it as some sort of blessing, I see it for the curse that it has been.

...

For all the rant, I've really enjoyed our time with the rangers this afternoon. I wish I were more like them. They're enthralled with Summer and, in truth, she seems a little more enthralled with them than I'm comfortable with. But they clear out quickly as the elders arrive. Julian orders up a huge platter of smoked pork and several pitchers of ale.

Elder Aurora Simpson Lake, Ryan's wife, offers up a blessing for the meal and our time together. My family had a tradition like this that my parents practiced for the big holidays. But this is different. She probes the *mystery* for hours every day. Enough that the *profecia aumentar* is never absent from her system. Her blessing has a spirituality that I've never experienced before. It's as if she's speaking from inside me.

Food is served. Ale and toddies poured. But despite the food and drink, the mood in the room is more somber as the ever-so-serious briefings and discussions begin.

Julian explains that Clarissa and Edson took the lead on assessing the aliens' capabilities. Aurora and Ryan took the lead on the Confederation's planned response. He indicates Clarissa, who begins.

"We set out to make assessments on four fronts: propulsion, cloaking, weapons, and defenses. Their propulsion systems are similar to our own, although they have pushed the technology a lot further than we have, no doubt aided by their zero-point energy systems. Their basic propulsion is via ion-drive. Their maximum thrust is generated when all 16 ion emitters are ejecting 1 kg of ions per second at 0.95 the speed of light (C). Their maximum sustained sub-light speed is 0.1 C, not because they can't sustain the thrust, but because of policy related to time dilation. The main long-distance propulsion system is a multiverse system."

Clarissa turns to Aurora.

"Would you or Jack like to compare that to the Confederation's sub-light propulsion?"

Aurora points to Jack.

"The Confederation's most powerful sub-light propulsion systems have a fraction of that power. They are powered by antimatter reactions, which limits both the quantity and speed of the ions emitted. It was hard to find this, but our most powerful system has four emitters that can emit up to 100 grams per second at 0.90 C. The ships that use those systems can get to a speed of 0.1 C, but it takes a lot longer. We do not have a policy restriction on max speed, but the highest recorded speed I could find was 0.18 C."

He nods back to Clarissa.

"Possibly the biggest difference in propulsion is the way they use the multiverse. They have found multiple layers with different properties. The one they use to cross the void gives them an effective speed of 1,500 C.

"The ships approaching Taramoot are coming in at a relative speed of only 25 C. It could be that they are actually traveling in the same layer of space time as the others, just moving at a much slower speed. But I think they're traveling in a different layer.

"Which brings me to cloaking. I think that, too, is done in a separate layer of space time. If I'm right, that makes them invisible, and it puts them out of reach of our weapons.

"Regarding their weapons, they have all sorts, including railguns, energy projectors, and one that disrupts the fabric of space time. The later always results in the total destruction and annihilation of anything in the target zone. But they don't like using this one. Their real purpose isn't to destroy us. It's to eat us. Their optimum outcome in this encounter would be to turn the Confederation into a giant farm, where humans are raised for food."

I feel Summer shudder next to me.

Julian asks Aurora to present their findings. Again, she points to Jack.

"We found out a couple things about our defenses that are relevant to discuss before Aurora starts. The first is that we may have an ace up our sleeve as regards propulsion. The Confederation has an experimental jump drive that it's trying to get ready in time. It works by creating an artificial worm hole that a ship or ships can transit through. In principle, we could travel through the worm hole to mine the alien armada's path.

"The Confederation is also working on something they're calling a transporter. It can move things from here to a distant place in an instant. Their prototype has had some success. Simple objects, like rocks or metal slugs, pass through more or less intact. Most machines sent through do not function properly on the other end. And to date, nothing living has survived transport."

Ryan's words trigger a thought.

"In my probing of the aliens, any contact seems to kill them. I think it's either the supplement or the *profecia aumentar* that does it. If we could transport that aboard their ships, we might be able to kill them without destroying their ships."

"Good thought," Aurora replies. "Most of my work with Ryan has been focused on the Confederation's preparations and planned response. What we've found is a bit discouraging. Our military strength today is less than it was at the end of the Great Alien War. Our propulsion has advanced a little in that time frame. Our weaponry has not. The idea of using the transporter as a weapon is interesting. But we have nothing like their space-time disruption weapon.

"We won the last war mostly on the ground. The government is thinking we can do that again. They don't see the viability of a space-based war. My big concern with that is the aliens. Last time they apparently realized they could not establish a food generation operation here and got tired of the ongoing losses among their workers. Their last-ditch effort to contain us was a bioweapon, which we contained until a few years ago.

"My fear is that they will start destroying planets in the hopes of breaking our will. This time around is different than the last. I don't think they will retreat like they did last time. I think they'll set a loss limit, then destroy what's left.

"But I haven't found a way to get the central government to even consider the possibility of taking the fight to the rim to stop them there."

...

As the evening wears on the conversation becomes less productive. I have several big takeaways that I need to ponder in the days ahead.

The first is that the aliens' technical advantage is something we can't reverse in the time we have.

Next is that the aliens want to enslave us, not destroy us. As we have no way to destroy them, they will continue to toy with us for a long time unless we find a way to really hurt them.

But something else has been tugging on my mind that I can't quite put my finger on.

"Jared?"

Hearing my name called startles me out of my reverie. It's Julian.

"You seem lost in thought. Care to share what you're thinking about."

I want to say, I don't know. Because I can't figure out what's bugging me. Then it snaps.

"Sorry if this sounds like a change of topic. But something's been bugging me that I'm struggling to put my finger on."

I pause to assemble my thoughts more fully.

Julian prompts, "Go on."

"The synthetic production line for our supplement has just come up. I'm going to start testing it when we get back. The reason I did this was to arrest the impacts of the aliens' bioweapon. We can't produce enough of it from venom to save the entire Confederation, so we needed a different solution.

"If the synthetic formula works, we plan to take it to clinical trials. If we get approval, then we can set up production on other worlds, bypassing the quarantine and boycott."

"And the relevance?"

"If it's true that the supplement is toxic to the aliens, and every human is taking it, then it won't take the aliens long to figure out that we are useless to them as a food species. Then what will they do? Leave? Or exterminate us?

"If we can convince them that we're no longer edible before they get here, will they turn around and go home?"

Aurora pipes up. "I don't know the answer to those questions, but I do know one thing. We need to get the people of Taramoot on your supplement. If we can't find a way to save them, they will be harvested. If all the aliens feasting on them die, it will send a cautionary message."

Julian adds, "It'll also be an opportunity for the Taramootans to use the supplement as a weapon, spraying it on the aliens as they approach. We need to do everything in our power to stop the aliens before they get to Taramoot. But if we can't, then we need to make the aliens pay dearly for having gone there."

FIRST TEST

The trip back from Jaramor is uneventful. As we get to our manufacturing facility, I see the gates are open and Charlie's truck in the parking area. His plan had been to babysit the synthesis line all

292

weekend. But I'm surprised to see him here at 4:00 on a Sunday afternoon.

We park and go in. Charlie hears the bell on the door and comes out to greet us.

"You two have a nice weekend in the wilderness?"

"I suppose you could say that. Our official mission was to take measurements at the wells. But we found references to other sites further downstream and went to look for them."

"Did you find anything?"

"Not really. No additional wells. Just lots of wilderness that thins out the further you go.

"How are things here?"

"Good. No incidents on the line. Production rate is slow, but we can clearly make more this way than via distillation. We're making about four liters an hour. We have a seemingly endless supply of raw material. We'll need someone here to reload it every couple hours, but if we can sustain this rate and it proves out safe, we'll have enough for everyone on Jaredaan."

"Are we set up to start blending?"

"Yep, want to see?"

Summer and I follow Charlie back into one of the rooms originally set up to be a quality assurance lab. There are five glass containers on a long test bench against the wall. Each has a cooling jacket on it. There are a couple dozen glass mixing vials on a drying rack.

Charlie explains it all, then asks if I want to make the first test batch. I grab one of the mixing vials, then go to the first station. I put the vial under the spout and press the button. The exact quantity required is emitted, filling the vial to the line marker for Component 1. I repeat for the remaining four components, each one bringing the level in the vial up to the next line. When that's done, I grab a stopper to seal the vial, then put it in a mixing machine. A minute later, I withdraw the vial, then pour the contents into a dispensing bottle

"OK, I just got my first month's supply," I announce.

Summer asks, "Can I make one for myself as well?"

I didn't expect this. I wanted to make sure it was safe before giving it to Summer.

She knows my concern, but says, "Better if it kills us both, than just you."

The thought of anything happening to her cuts into me. But I feel the same way, so hand her the mixing vial.

A minute later we have two bottles of the synthetic supplement.

Summer holds out the mixing vial for Charlie, who puts his hands up.

"I'll wait until I see how well it works for you. I'm responsible for the machine." He points at me. "He's responsible for the formula."

We all laugh.

I take the vial, rinse it, and place it in the drying rack. Then we head for home.

REPORT

With everything under control at the manufacturing facility, I decide to spend my first day back in my office at headquarters. The warden seems incredibly pleased to see me spending the day in the office. I'm going to spend as much of the week here or in the zones as possible.

The first item on my list today is to send Uncle Walter and the elders an update on my alien sensor readings. I also send along my analysis that the aliens are targeting Taramoot, in all likelihood because of their thulium deposits. I reiterate my belief that my supplement is likely to be toxic to the aliens and ask him to pass the information along. If the Confederation can find a way to get the supplement to Taramoot, despite the fact it originates on Jaredaan, then the people on Taramoot will have a better chance of surviving.

Everything sent is couched as being based on my analysis of the alien detector readings. I doubt he'll forward my suggestions to the Confederation, but send it anyway.

CENTRAL COMMAND

Although I haven't used it yet, Admiral Tang did have someone from his office contact me and get me set up with a secure messaging system.

I open the system, establish a link, then send a message. The message is terse. I tell him Taramoot is the aliens' initial target and the thulium is the reason. It's a critical material used in their zero-point energy devices. I also tell him about their new weapon.

I reiterate my belief that my supplement is toxic to the aliens and suggest that he arm the people of Taramoot with it.

Lastly, I tell him about the aliens' intent for revisiting human space.

I send the message wondering if it will be read, and I'm skeptical that I'll get a reply.

PATENT

I've been on the new synthetic supplement a week now and feel better than ever. It's not a clinical trial, not proof perfect that the supplement is safe or effective. But I'm confident enough at this point to move on to the next steps.

With a synthetic version of the supplement at hand, it's finally time to start a formal clinical trial. But I need to file patents on my formula first. I engage Audrey, who recommends that we work with a specialist with experience in pharmaceuticals. She estimates her fees to be around 20,000 credits, then warns me that the specialist she wants to use in the capital will be more. I'm worried about the rate at which I'm spending my Confederation credits, but this is what needs to be done, so I agree.

...

Audrey gets back to me with draft documents for five patents and one copyright. Since three of the components in our supplement are already in the public domain, she recommends that I file 'use patents' for each of the two proteins that we're synthesizing, and another for the overall formula. These proteins are known to science but have never been patented for a given use. So, use patents are likely to be granted. This combination of ingredients has also never been patented. She thinks a use patent on the combination is also likely to be granted.

We haven't discussed product form or packaging, but she's created blank patent documents for each. She needs more information from me to complete these documents. But the shell she's created is ready to go other than the content.

Last on her list is a blank copyright document for the labeling. Her argument is that the more claims we make, the more difficult it will be for someone else to make a knock off product. The price tag is up to 75,000 credits, which includes her specialist in the capital. That's a lot, but I still go for it.

CLINICAL TRIAL

With patents pending, I give Dr. Avery the go ahead to start clinical trials. The first step is filing for a license. There is a shorter process for regional food supplements that have been in use for a long time. Dr. Avery thinks this shortened process is most appropriate. The basic claim is that the toxicity and side effects of this therapy are reasonably well understood. So, the purpose of the trial is to prove efficacy and better clarify the side effects.

The data provided to support the use of this process is twofold. The first set of data is Ethel and Norah's medical records for the last 50 years. Birth certificates are also provided as proof of their age. The second set of data is the short-term medical records of the 500 people currently taking the supplement in the camp.

No toxic effects have been observed in either set of patients. The principal side effects observed are fingernail loss and improved life expectancy.

The preliminary evidence of efficacy is twofold: none of the people on the supplement have developed DAGS, and eight people with DAGS, two in an advanced stage, have all gone into remission.

The last element of the application is the test plan. It will be double blind with the exception that any patient that develops DAGS while part of the test will be put on the supplement once keratin formations are manifest.

Given the severity of the disease and the long record of use of the supplement, Dr. Avery thinks approval to conduct the clinical trial will be granted immediately.

CHAPTER 19: JUNGLE

With the clinical trial documents filed and an emergency trial approved, I need to find a way to produce off world. In previous browsing, I've noticed a number of supplements listed on Jungle that have Jungle listed as the producer.

As a best-selling Jungle partner, I have access to a special live chat support app. So, I decide to use it for the first time. As soon as I open the channel, I'm greeted by 'Heather' who will help route my query. Heather's interactions seem a bit mechanical, so I suspect she's a low-end AI, but that's OK. She certainly seems to know her stuff and before long we are working through the list of requirements for food grade products they can produce. All three of the organic compounds are on the list. Neither of the proteins are.

I assume that's the end of the road, but it's not. Over the last hour Heather seems to have morphed into a protein scientist. She's clearly an AI and I'm sure our session has been moved to a much more capable host system. I give her the chemical composition of two proteins and point her to an on-line resource that lists the details of the proteins, then I'm placed on hold.

About a half hour later, Heather comes back confirming that Jungle can produce my dietary supplement and they have distribution available for supplements with this composition on 58 planets.

Next topic is product form and packaging. After some back and forth, Heather tells me that they only have one option for products like this, fast dissolve gelatin capsules delivered in 30, 60, or 90 capsule bottles. Manufacturing costs will be 12.50 credits for the 30-capsule bottle, 24.75 for the 60-capsule bottle, and 37 for the 90-capsule bottle. She asks if I would like her to create three new products with these specifications in my partner account, where I can work the marketing, advertising, and pricing options.

I say yes and she advises me that the products will appear in my account within the next six hours. It took nearly two hours to work through the process. But the problem I had no idea how to solve two hours ago is now solved.

With a sigh, I turn my attention back to some camp work I can't put off any longer.

My concentration is broken by the sound of my communicator buzzing. I look at the caller ID. It's from off world. I've never received a call from off world on my communicator before and am a bit intimidated by it.

"Hello, this is Jared Daan."

"Mr. Daan. My name is Margot Fong. I am Sr. Vice President of New Products at Jungle. Three dietary supplement products registered in your name came to my attention today."

"Yes, ma'am. I have a dietary supplement that my team has developed. There's a lot of demand for it on our world and we would like to take it to market off world."

"This came to my attention because the ingredients listed are the same as those in a drug recently given emergency approval for clinical trial in Heroldstown, Jaredaan. The clinical trial is for the treatment of DAGS."

"Yes, ma'am. We've been using it here as a food supplement. About 1,000 people here take it. Eight of them had DAGS when they started taking it. All eight have gone into remission."

"According to the clinical trial application, a patent has been filed listing the drug's owner as Jaredaan Supplements."

"Yes, ma'am. I am president and sole owner of Jaredaan Supplements."

There's silence on the line for a moment.

"OK. There are a number of problems we need to sort out in order to list this product on Jungle. We would, of course, like to carry this product. In fact, we would like to have exclusive rights to it. But there are several issues we'll need to resolve before we can even post this product to a partner account.

"The first regards the titling. Jaredaan Supplements will need to establish an account with us. Your other products are patented in your name. This one is not. I will send the appropriate application documents to the message box in your personal account. Heather can help you fill them in if you would like. She has been assigned to you and will be the one to reply whenever you open the chat box.

"Next regards licensing. It is legal to sell food supplements that are in clinical trial. But you'll need a supplement license in each jurisdiction. Given the exposure this supplement will get, you will need your own, you can't use ours. Our legal team will work with you to get that done if you like, but it will be expensive.

"Lastly, the claims you make for the product are restricted. The new products team can work with you to get that done.

"Would you like me to send you a proposal where we supply these services?"

"How much is this going to cost me?"

"I don't know yet, but it will be more than 100,000 credits."

I ponder Ms. Fong's words for a few moments. "I think I would like you to do this, but the cost must come from my pending payments. Jaredaan is under quarantine and I need the money I have to pay for emergency shipments to feed our people."

"Understood. I think I can do that. Can I call you at this time tomorrow?"

"Yes, that would be good."

"Mr. Daan, I think you're on the path to becoming the wealthiest person in the Confederation."

ZONE 1

The whole Jungle thing has my head spinning. It's remarkable what they're able to do. But at the same time, it gives them a lot of power, which they use to tip the scales in favor of one vendor over another. So far, I've been the beneficiary of that influence. But I'm sure that will change.

I close my eyes and take a deep breath, allowing my mind to relax. As calm settles, I realize that I need to get out of the office. I need to work on something more tangible, more real. So, I take off for the zones. That's where reality lives.

...

I arrive in Zone 1 wanting to continue a conversation that was rudely cut off a few days ago. I look for supervisor Hunter Park at his office, but he's not there. I have momentary sympathy for the warden when he can't find me. I'm rarely in my office and for the first time understand his frustration. I need to work on that issue.

But that doesn't address the problem of Zone 1's missing supervisor. I chuckle at my own frustration. I truly hope that he's not like poor Rory, trying to save two of his people who have gone sideways with the local fauna.

The most hopeful place to find a supervisor who's not in his office is the dining room. I know from both the prisoner's perspective, and from camp management's, the best place to look for a supervisor, if he's not in his office, is in the dining room.

Not seeing him, I go to ask at the front counter and am met by a woman whose name tag reads Alana Bellucci. I recognize the name from the employee files. I'm trying hard to memorize them all. She recognizes me even though I don't remember ever meeting her.

"Assistant Warden Daan. How can I help you?"

The question takes me by surprise. When it comes to taking official action, I've started to think of myself as assistant warden, but It's certainly not my self-image.

I put out my hand to shake. "Alana. So good to meet you."

I love meeting everyone. I did the same as an inmate. But for the first time, the words sound hollow in my ears. Not because they're insincere, but because they're now said from a position of authority.

I smile. "I'm looking for Supervisor Park. Any idea where he is?"

I see her wilt.

"Supervisor Park was taken to the hospital last night." There's a snuffle. "He has it, whatever it is. They say you have a cure. Are you going to save him?"

For a while now, I've worn the self-imposed mantel of camp protector. It's now being projected back on me and the weight of responsibility is heavy.

"I'm sorry. Word hadn't reached me yet." I'm almost overcome by emotion that another one of my people is infected. "But I'll do everything in my power to make sure he gets through this."

I start to skulk off, then hear words that terrify me.

"Thank you, sir. If anyone can get us through this, it's you, the sixth son."

I know the words are offered with sincerity and good will, but they still cause my blood to boil. I hustle out of the dining room without reply, knowing I'll feel guilty about it later.

ZONE 2

My next stop is Zone 2. It's run by supervisor Vera Lopes. Her family emigrated from New Brazil just before she was born. She reminds me of Ethel, well the 50-year-old version anyway. She's a natural leader in firm control of everything around her. And she swears in Portuguese, just like Ethel does. Her numbers are second only to Gavin's, and like Hunter in Zone 1, they're better when adjusted for the retiree population. This is another zone where I've not spent enough time. As a result, Vera is a little less roped in, less

300

connected to the other supervisors as people like Gavin, Rory, or Logan.

As I pull in, I see her entering the dining room, so catch up with her there.

"Jared, welcome to Zone 2. We don't see you here all that often."

"Sorry. I haven't been ignoring you. You just weren't one of the problem zones."

"Does that mean we're a problem now?"

Her words are spoken with humor and I take them with the humor intended.

"Touché."

We grab some lunch and sit. I go through my normal pitch about codifying best practices to lift all the zones up so we can keep all the zones as whole as possible through the current hard times.

As I get to the end of my pitch, Vera stabs me with a stare.

"So, how bad is it? For over a hundred years, the camp ran the way it ran. There was always the need to produce and the older zones learned to do what was required. But there was always ample food.

"Now, there's directive after directive, and explicit pressure to do better. And we have done better. Even Zone 2, which has consistently been one of the top three zones. It may not show in the numbers you see yet. But anyone who knows our fields can see it. We have more, taller, healthier cane than ever before. I wouldn't be surprised if our yield is up another 20% this year.

"But we are losing people to the *maldito* stomach disease, and the food... There's not enough! And what we get is *merda*!"

I've heard Ethel use those words before and am guessing Vera is saying the damn stomach disease and the food is shit.

"Jared, the supervisors have been responsive to what you've done, and we respect you for that. The workers worship you. We all have more pride in our work than we did before. But that's changing and will eventually go the other way if the food issue isn't fixed.

"So, I repeat. How bad is it?"

Vera's voice is loud enough that half of the room is looking at us now. Some people scurry out. I'm guessing they don't want to see what they fear will happen next.

I put my head down and stir my fork through the tiny portion of rice I was given. Then after a few moments, I look up.

"It's bad. Food from off world has been cut off for something like two months. Jaredstown has lost most of its power. The disease is ripping through its population and they've lost most of their food production capability. Within a week of finding out about it, I got the gardens added. I've also secured medication that will put the disease in remission. But a series of catastrophes have hit the Confederation, and Jaredaan is mostly on its own until those are resolved."

"Are we all going to die?"

"Not if I can help it. But I'll need the help of the zone supervisors."

"How?"

"Zone 10 is less than half built out. I'm working a plan to build out the remainder with food crops. I'm working the issues of plant mix and availability, land use, everything related to what needs to be done.

"But the 10 of you, the 10 zone supervisors will have to figure out how we organize the labor force to get it done, all while managing the cane harvest."

"Well," Vera smiles. "That's something we can do. Want my first piece of advice?"

"Please."

"Reorganize the cane operation into 9 zones, make the food crops the tenth zone. Then put me in charge of it."

"I like that idea. Let me see if I can sell it. The warden's mostly onboard already, even though he hasn't heard this part."

Vera chuckles, then indicates the door. "Seems you have a lot of work to do. I'd advise you to get on with it."

OFFICE

The conversation with Vera helped crystalize many of the things I've been brooding over. Although I'd planned to spend the day in the zones, I've come back to the office. I need a viable proposal to cultivate Zone 10 with food and bring it to harvest before the camp starves. I need an ally in this, so I call Jay Carlson at West Lake.

"Jared, good to hear from you. What can I help you with?"

"Can we talk off the record? I don't want this conversation to go any further than the two of us."

"Understood. Does this have something to do with the food shortage?"

"Yes."

I hear Jay exhale in a defeated way. "On the news this morning, the elders announced that the food shortage is over. Dry bulk imports have resumed. They say we'll see relief in the stores within a week. That's not true?"

I was unaware the elders were going to make this announcement. The fools.

"As I understand it, three months' worth of supplies have been received. That will materially reduce the current crisis, especially in Jaredstown. But the planet is still under quarantine and exports are still prohibited. The elders think that will change in the next three months. I don't. So, I'm working a process to get up to 1,000 hectares of our land re-zoned for agriculture, instead of cane."

"Do you think they'll allow that?"

"If I have a compelling plan, maybe."

The line is quiet for a moment, then the penny drops.

"And you want me to help you come up with that plan."

I nod my head at the empty room. "Yes, I do."

"In Zone 10?"

"Yes."

"We can help you with things like prepping the fields and installing the irrigation. It's the seeds and seedlings that will be the problem. The commercial agriculture operation on the south-west side of the lake is struggling with the same thing. Imported seed is higher quality than the seed they grow, so they usually don't hold any back.

"Word that imports have been cut off only reached them a couple weeks ago. Way too late for them to have preserved the seed needed to replant. They barely have enough seed at this point to feed themselves next year. And they're not happy that I gave you the last of my corn seed."

Jay's words send a shiver down my spine. In all my planning models, I assumed that the commercial agriculture operation would continue undisturbed. But they won't. They don't have the seed. I need to get this word to Aaron. The next emergency delivery needs to prioritize seed.

"Jared, are you still there?"

Jay's voice snaps me out of shock.

"Sorry. It never occurred to me that the agriculture operation would be impacted by the supply disruptions."

"They also get their fertilizer off planet."

"Unbelievable," I mutter then fall into silence for a few seconds. "OK, this issue has really blindsided me. Let's divide and conquer. Maybe we can loop the agriculture operation in on this also. Can you work out what I should plant in order to feed my people? I have up to 1,000 hectares. I'll work out sourcing and fertilizer options."

"Have you met Evelyn Fontes? Her full name is Evelyn Fontes Daan. She married one of Herold's grandsons. Her family is one of the ones that came in from New Brazil when the colony was founded.

"She runs the agricultural operation now. She's a real steam engine. You remind me of her a bit. But, setting that aside, I have a good working relationship with her. I think the three of us might be able to pull this off if you can find a way to get the imports we need."

"I look forward to meeting her. Let me see what progress I can make."

...

When the line drops, I slide down in my seat. Our leaders have no idea what we're up against. I put my head back and close my eyes. I need a path forward.

My reverie is interrupted by a knock on the door.

"Come in," I call out, righting myself in my chair.

The door opens and Summer comes in, then shuts the door. She whispers, "What's wrong? I can feel you when things happen. What is it?"

"Have you seen the announcement from the elders?"

She brightens. "Yes. The food shortage is over!"

Her optimism slips away as she sees my look.

"Maybe, but the famine that follows is about to begin."

She plops into the chair across from me. "Why?"

"The agricultural operation, where most of our food comes from, imports its seed. The imported seed is more productive than the seed they produce, so they normally don't hold back any seed stock.

"This year was no exception. Most of the last harvest was sold. Although they did hold back some over the last couple weeks, it was nowhere near enough. So, unless we can get an emergency shipment of seed, Jaredaan's food production is going to grind to a halt."

Summer wilts the same way I have, but after a moment looks up.

"You need to call Aaron. If the Elders don't deal with this then we're all dead."

She gives me a wry smile. "On the brighter side, you and I can run to Jaramor."

"True, but that might not be a very bright side. The still and synthesis lines are on this side. They run on ethanol. We might not starve. But without ethanol, we'll suffer a much more painful death.

304

She stands, puts on a smile, and turns to leave. When she gets to the door she stops and points at me. "No one else here can learn of this, but you need to call Aaron. Now!" Then she's gone.

...

After some deliberation, I call Aaron on my communicator, not the camp phone. He picks up immediately.

"Jared, did you hear the good news!"

I can tell that Aaron really believes we're out of the woods.

"I heard that the dry goods are about to be made available."

"Great, right?" His child-like enthusiasm is infectious, so I enjoy the moment. Especially since I know it's about to come crashing down.

"Agreed. I look forward to having some pasta again."

"So am I." He drags the words out in emphasis. "So, what's up?"

"Do the elders know that the agricultural operation down here relies on imported seed?"

There's silence, then finally a tentative, "No. At least this is the first I've heard of it."

"Well, I learned of it today. We have small scale food operations here at the camp, always have, although I've expanded them recently. I reached out to the nursery we work with for more seed and learned that they are out. The agricultural operation just took the last seed they had. But what they got is just short of what they need to feed their staff."

Aaron groans, "Oh, shit."

"That means the next emergency shipment will have to be mostly seed, plus the remaining equipment I need. There will be little if any room for additional dry goods."

Aaron groans, issuing a string of increasingly more virulent expletives. "Walter will never agree to that."

"Then we're all dead. No seed, no food. No equipment, no medicine. It's as simple as that. Without food and medicine, every single person on this planet will die. Just like they did on Doffenplod."

I hear a lot of anguish on the other end of the line.

"What do we need to do to bring Walter around?"

Aaron's slow to reply. "I don't know. He's becoming increasingly irrational."

"If I testify, and the president of the agricultural operation testifies, will the elder board listen?"

Again, Aaron's slow to reply. "They'll listen. The problem will be getting Walter to let you address them."

"Then start working that process. The window we have before disaster strikes is closing quickly. The most critical crops need to be planted in 4 to 6 weeks."

There are more expletives on the other end of the line, then, "I'll start working it tonight."

...

When the line drops, I realize that I need to brief the boss. So, I get up and wander down the hall to his office. Lillian greets me when I come in. The boss's door is open, so she says it's OK if I go in.

He looks up as I enter and puts down his pen. "Jared, what can I do for you?"

"Mind if I close the door?"

He nods, and as soon as the door's shut, he asks, "What's wrong?"

I brief him on Hunter, my discussion with Vera, then the revelation regarding the seed crisis. His head droops.

"The one thing the elders took as given through all the discussions was steady output from the agricultural operation. If that's not there, then it's game over."

"I think we still have a chance. But we'd need to get another emergency order issued immediately. I called Aaron to test the waters with him. But he's not convinced Walter will go along."

"Did he say why?"

"He thinks Walter is deeply vested in the idea the crisis is over, and the quarantine will be lifted in three months."

"That may be true, but Walter's not stupid. He's scheduled to be at the camp board meeting this week. Now that I've been briefed and understand the magnitude of the issue, the rules require me to bring it to the board, so he'll get briefed. He may want to confirm the facts of the issue for himself, but he can't walk away from it."

I wish I had the warden's confidence.

PROPULSION

Over dinner, Summer and I decide we need to restart our efforts to probe the aliens. Everything else we're facing is too depressing. She suggests that we probe their propulsion technology. Her rationale is simple. If we can find a way to disrupt it, we can slow them down and possibly stop them from getting here.

When dinner is cleaned up, we settle into our easy chairs and moments later are flying. The probing method will be similar to last time. We'll go in with as much stealth as possible. I'll do things that will draw their attention to the propulsion systems. Summer will read their thoughts.

I choose a ship further back in the line of 2,000 ships in the void. Then enter an engineering space that appears to be unoccupied. Summer hides in an auxiliary space in the main engine room, close enough to 'hear' the chief engineer's thoughts, but out of sight.

I spend a few minutes scanning the panels. I've spent enough time at these stations on previous visits to recognize some of the controls, but still run my finger over them to confirm their function.

My plan is to make a change to some auxiliary system that will draw energy away from the propulsion system, slowing the ship in a non-obvious way that will cause the aliens to search for the problem.

I ponder the controls for a while, Summer will say hours I'm sure, before settling on a plan. Main propulsion is powered by over 100 zero-point energy devices that are ganged together. Each of these also powers other ship systems, all of which are currently turned off. My idea is to turn one of those systems on, draining some energy away from propulsion, hopefully enough to cause the ship's engineers to start investigating. I have a harder time figuring out what these systems are, so choose one at random and turn it on.

At first, nothing happens, then all hell breaks loose as alarm after alarm starts sounding. The once quiet control board in front of me, now has dozens of blinking lights. A massive vibration rips through the ship and I see power source after power source drop offline.

I feel Summer pulling on my arm, them BAM, I'm back in my easy chair. Summer is standing next to me. She must have come back first.

I'm still coming back to myself, but manage to blurt out, "What happened?"

When Summer sees I'm back, she starts laughing. "Do you have any idea what you did?"

"I tried to divert some power away from propulsion, hoping it would cause the engineers to start searching for the problem. Did you learn anything?"

She chuckles some more.

"Lots. Nothing particularly useful. But lots."

"You going to tell me?"

She laughs some more.

"Well, I found this perfect place to hide. Relatively close to the chief engineer and his assistant. They didn't perceive me at all, but I could hear every thought.

"Flying in the void between the spiral arms is apparently boring. The two sit there scanning their systems, but mostly gossiping about everyone else's sex life. The aliens do it a lot differently than we do.

"Anyway, this goes on for hours and I'm wondering if you're still on board, then suddenly everyone's in a panic. The landing gear is deploying, and no one can figure out why. It's locked out when traveling faster than light, because it will disrupt the space-time bubble the ship is travelling in.

"Then vibration starts, and they try to drop back into normal space but can't figure out how. Those controls are locked out while the landing gear is deployed.

"What happened next was hard to follow. These guys can carry on multiple telepathic communications at the same time. Between them they were yelling at like 50 people. The gist of it was that the ship would be ripped apart in a few minutes if the landing gear was not retracted.

"I assume you're the one that deployed the landing gear?"

"I didn't know it was the landing gear, but I'm sure it was me. The vibration hit moments after I turned on the system I picked at random."

"Well, I'm sure the ship was destroyed. The vibration was so strong when I bailed that it felt like the ship was starting to come apart.

"But I'm not sure how that helps us. It confirms they travel in space-time bubbles, which is what we thought before. It confirms what we were taught in school, a ship traveling in a space-time bubble will be ripped apart if the bubble loses integrity.

"But I'm not sure how knowing that landing gear deployment will destabilize a space-time bubble helps us."

"Good point. Want to go back out, try again?"

She holds up her communicator, showing me the time.

"Too late. It's already after midnight. Time for bed."

As we shut down and head into the bedroom, I ask, "So how do the aliens do it?"

OFFICE

I'm back in my office this morning. It's my intention to spend most of the day here. Normally, that wouldn't make sense, as there's just not that much that can be done in the office. But a lot came in last night and earlier this morning.

Margo Fong, Jungle's New Products VP, sent a meeting request for 2:00. She claims to have several offers to present.

Jay Carlton sent a meeting request for 11:00 this morning. Evelyn Fontes, from the agricultural operation is also included.

To my surprise, Vera Lopes, Zone 2 supervisor, organized a meeting with the supervisors in Zones 3, 4, & 5. They are all on board with the idea of rejiggering the zones and letting Vera take the new Zone 11. They want to meet tomorrow to discuss the changes. Vera plans to meet with the other zone supervisors today. She also suggests that I look into the possibility of composting waste fiber from the ethanol plant.

I'm a bit blown away by the quick response from the people I spoke with yesterday. I guess the prospect of starving to death is enough to get people in gear. Anyway, I now know what my first task is this morning.

...

"Jared, good to hear from you."

"Charlie, how's it going at the plant."

"On the distillation front, we've run all the raw materials and finished purifying all the components. I just about finished the expansion to the mixing system that will allow rapid blending and easy large container bottling. Brock has given me a proposal for 8,000 credits to automate that process if you're interested.

"On the synthesis front, everything is running smoothly. The entire process is automated and runs round the clock. Our biggest problem at the moment is quantity. We're making so much I don't have room to store it all. I'll need to throttle back tomorrow if we can't start moving the product."

I suppose having too much is the better problem, but it's not. Until I get a proper bottling system, distribution north isn't possible. Demand up there is right at the limit of our capacity.

"Understood. Contact Brock and work with him to expand our storage. We need every drop of our capacity."

"Will do."

"Changing subject, the camp needs more compost. Do you know if the ethanol plant has excess compost, or excess fiber?"

"It does. It's one of the plant's bigger operational problems. We've been dumping the post-fermentation fiber across our property for decades. We don't actively compost it, so it decays slowly.

Periodically, we need to do a controlled burn to get rid of it. You've probably seen the black smoke it gives off."

"Do you know who I could contact to see about getting some of that fiber?"

"Your best bet would be to just call Martin."

"Martin?"

"Ah, Martin Vargas, the president of Jaredaan Ethanol Corp. Technically, he's the one that sold you this place. I'm sure he'd take your call."

"Thanks."

...

"Jared, how can I help you?"

"Martin, thanks for taking my call. The prison camp needs more fiber for composting. I'm told you have an excess."

I hear a chuckle on the other end of the line.

"Seems like you're out to take all my problems off my hands. We have tons of excess fiber, literally tons. We'll even pay to ship it to you if you want it."

"We're at the very beginning of making changes to our composting operations. It may take a couple weeks to sort this out. I'll get back to you when I know more."

AGRICULTURE

As much as I would have liked to head over to the agriculture operation today, I have to call in on the 3D holoprojector. Jay went down in person, so when the line connects, I see the two of them in Evelyn's conference room.

After quick introductions, we get right to business. Evelyn confirms that they only have enough seed to plant 750 of her 10,000 hectares, enough to feed her 1,250 workers and half her livestock.

She sends me a copy of her seed requirements and her recommendation for our property. She tells me that her seed is available and reserved, but unless shipment is organized within the next week, her supplier will sell the seed elsewhere.

"If I can get the shipment organized, do you think your supplier will be able to take my order as well?"

She smiles. "Yes. I talked with him this morning. They understand our situation and want to work with us to get this done. But fair warning, this will max out normal shipments to Jaredaan. We would have to ship in a different way to get anything else in this shipment."

I look at Jay. "What about equipment? You know what I have and our current operations. Do we need additional equipment? And do you have it?"

"It'll be a stretch."

Evelyn interrupts. "That's not going to be a problem. We have everything we need for the coming season. If you can get us the seed and Jay can help with the planting, we can supply all the other equipment.

"The problem will be fertilizer. We have the manure, but that's not sufficient."

"We have compost. It's mostly from cane. I'm also trying to line up post-fermentation fiber from the ethanol plant."

Evelyn's eyes light up. "We can blend our own then. Maybe in the small strip of land between our properties?"

"Works for me." I reply.

...

The conversation drags on a while, but the only real hurdle yet to be overcome is Walter. He's the only one empowered to request an emergency shipment. And at this point, I'm the only entity on the planet who can finance it.

OFFER

Margot calls exactly on time. She has several people in the room with her whom she introduces, but the introductions go by faster than I can write the names down.

To my surprise, Heather is also on the line. Her voice is smooth and natural. Her demeanor friendly, but professional. I've got to hand it to Jungle, Heather is an amazing piece of technology.

"Jared, we've worked round the clock to come up with options for you. I'm going to start at the top. We would like to buy your patent."

It's an audio call, so I'm safe rolling my eyes, which I do.

"I am authorized to offer you 100 million credits, 5 million today, the remainder on successful completion of clinical trials."

"Sorry, not interested." I say as soon as she completes the sentence.

She chuckles. "I didn't think you would be, but that's where our executive committee wanted me to start. Let me flip to the other extreme. As a supplier of your standing, there are a number of things we can do for you at no cost. The first and simplest is to set up a new account for Jaredaan Natural Supplements. Heather has already looked up your company's registration and other public data, so with your permission she can set up the new account and register it as a new products team select account.

"Would you like her to do that for you?"

"Yes."

"Done." Heather answers.

"Next, we can set up the three products based on the specifications you already provided. We have given some thought to product naming and descriptions that we'd like you to consider. Would it be OK for Heather to set up these products for you? And if so, may she preload our suggestions?"

"Yes."

"Done." Heather answers again.

"Next, we've prepared the license applications in your company's name for each of the jurisdictions we can sell to. We cannot file these for you. But we can load them into your account for you. You can launch them from there. These mirror our licenses, so we know they will be approved. But you should have your legal team review and approve them. Jungle's interests are not the same as Jaredaan Natural Supplements', so terms that work for us may not work for you. We offer no warranty that these are appropriate and accept no liability if they do not satisfy your needs.

"Would you like Heather to upload these to your account for your review?"

"Yes."

"Done." Heather replies.

"Next is pricing. We've done an analysis of pricing based on preferences you have expressed in previous transactions. These price suggestions are not binding, just our best guess at what you want.

"Would you like us to preload these prices for you?"

"Can you give the short description of what they are?"

"They maximize your profit based on our analysis of price elasticity and the underlying costs in each market. For the small bottles you would get 6.5 credits on average."

"Yes, please preload those."

"Done." Heather replies.

"I have two paid services to offer you, which have been approved for financing from your personal pending payment account. The first is legal assistance. Once your lawyer approves the license applications we've uploaded to your account, we can provide expedited processing. Each planet in question has an expedite process that is difficult to access from off world. We have lawyers and local currency funds in each locale and can get the approvals in 3 days, not the 30 to 45 days you would otherwise be looking at.

"We cannot and do not influence the approval process. That is in the planetary government's hands. But we have the local representation in each jurisdiction that gets the approval or rejection fast. This will cost 108,000 credits for all 58 jurisdictions. It includes the application costs and expedite fees. Would you like us to do that for you?"

"Probably, what's the other offer?"

"It's an advertising and merchandising offer, which is contingent on the expedited application offer being accepted. We will make you our number 1 product recommendation for 30 days. You will appear at the top of every list on more or less every search."

I've seen their top product recommendations and always hoped I could get one of those. Who would have thought it would be for a supplement? But this is going to be crazy expensive.

"How much?"

"I've talked our executive committee into giving this to you at a discount price of 242,000 credits."

The number takes my breath away. My first thought is not to do it, then the strange price settles in.

"Why that price?"

"You said you needed funds for emergency supplies. We did some research into costs for Jaredaan and found an open order for seed pending emergency shipment. We don't know if that's the shipment you are concerned about. But we used it to inform an analysis of how much you still have available to pay. We came up with 350,000 credits. The normal price for expedited legal and top product promotion would be quite a bit higher. We can't do the promotion without the legal, so we discounted the promotion because we want this product."

"Why do you want it so much?"

"Yours is not the only supplement out there that claims a DAGS benefit and has been approved for clinical trial. But the data filed to support your clinical trial is by far the strongest. Because of recent regulatory changes, we can provide a link to your clinical trial application in our promotion. The forecast for our promotion is 1 million bottles in the first month."

"I would like to do this but need to confirm the funds availability."

"May I make a suggestion?" Heather asks.

Hearing no reply from Margot, I say, "Please."

"There is a three-day cancel right for promotions of this size."

From the sounds I hear in the background, I'm guessing Margot did not know this.

"That means you can accept the package and the expediting will begin. It takes three days, which gives you three days to confirm what you need to confirm before the promotion is binding."

There's silence on the line and I'm assuming Heather would be in trouble if she were human.

So, I ask, "Is that true, Margot? I want to accept this offer and will do so now if you acknowledge this cancelation policy applies. But I have to double check the funds availability issue before I irrevocably commit to the promotion. If accepting, then cancelling will sour our relationship then I'd rather wait."

There's more silence, then... "Accept the legal now. I'll leave the promotion open for up to three days. But leaving an offer like this open comes at a price, so please accept or reject as soon as possible."

"Then I accept the legal expedite offer and promise to get back to you ASAP."

"Heather, please process acceptance of offer 1."

"Done."

...

When the line drops, I put in a call to Audrey. Thankfully, she answers.

I quickly brief her on what's happened and the applications, then give her access to the company's new Jungle account, so she can review the applications. She promises to get back to me with some initial feedback by the end of the day.

At this point, I'm so buzzed on adrenaline that my hands are shaking. There's a discreet knock on the door then Summer slips in.

"What happened?"

"I just got off the line with Jungle. They're accepting our supplement as a product. And they're psyched about it enough that they're giving us some free promotion and licensing assistance. Well, they're charging me for some of the licensing assistance, but they're never this generous. They really want the product."

"Are you going to make a lot of money on this?"

"Yes, but..." I realize I don't want to have this conversation right now, there are still too many unknowns.

Summer looks at me questioningly.

"I expect to make a lot. They threw out a ridiculous number that I really don't want to say out loud, because I don't believe it yet. Let me work it a little more, then we can talk about it tonight."

"OK." She slips back out.

I access the company's Jungle account and start looking at the products that Heather's set up for me. As I look through the first product, I'm shocked by what I see. The product labeling and packaging is beautiful. The description and use instructions are masterfully constructed. It conveys all the hope of remission and life extension without actually saying these are provided.

The use instructions and recommended dosing mirrors what's in the clinical trial without mentioning DAGS. And the link to the clinical trial application goes straight to the government site and opens to the executive summary section. I could not have created this in a thousand years.

My communicator sounds. I pick it up and see that it's Audrey.

"That was quick," I say without preamble.

"The first application I looked at was for New Beijing. They have the strictest rules. The application is perfectly filled out, the discretionary parts are done the exact same way I would have done it. It's as if they read this right off my computer and fixed my typos. I'll scan the rest of them. They're all different, but close enough that it won't take that long."

"I can't believe that Jungle did this for free."

"Not completely free. They're going to make a lot of money on this. More than I will. So, I think they wanted to minimize the likelihood I'd get this screwed up somehow."

"Seems reasonable. I'll finish these before quitting for the evening. I'll message you when I'm done, but you'll be able to release them in the morning if you want."

"Thanks, Audrey."

AARON

The only thing in our way at this point is the emergency shipment authorization. Given the narrow window we have, I need to push this along. So, I call Aaron again. It's only been 24 hours since the last call, but we need the authorization now!

The line connects and it's immediately apparent that he knows why I'm calling.

"Walter says no. You can have up to a third for seed and equipment, the rest will go to food and some toys he wants."

"Has he said how he'll pay for it?"

"He says you'll cave."

I almost shoot off a hot-headed denial, but rein it in.

"In school, I remember them telling us that there was a recall process for elder board members. Do you know what it is?"

The question seems to take Aaron by surprise. He's quiet for a moment.

"Interesting idea. Let me look it up."

The silence drags on for a while.

"Any sitting elder can request a vote of no confidence. If all other board members concur, then the elder is recalled and a new one can be selected.

"I doubt we can get six votes to recall him. Let's see what other criteria there are.

"If there isn't unanimous consent among the other board members than a super majority can vote to replace a board member. For a board with seven members, it takes five members to form a super majority. The vote must name a replacement for the member being recalled. The replacement has to have the same or higher paternity rank.

"Walter's a three. I'm the only rank one in the colony at this point. Jonah's rank is two. I think there's another two, but I'd have to look him up. Walter is the only three I know. But I know there are other threes. I'd have to look them up as well.

"But this feels hopeless. No one will vote for me to replace Walter. I doubt they'd vote for Jonah because he's my brother. Brothers are technically allowed to serve together, but it goes against tradition."

Ironically, I think Julian is a two. But no one knows he exists.

"OK." I acknowledge. "There must be another way. You keep working the rules. There must be a way we can compel him or replace him. I'll work on our pitch to see if we can change his mind. I'll also start looking for off-world options."

WARDEN

I've had the door to my office closed most of the day. Now that my calls are done, I open it. I've learned the warden prefers for me to have my door open when I'm in and not on a call.

But there are two things I still want to progress this afternoon. The first regards the emergency shipment rules. It would seem that commercial enterprises with Confederation credits should be able to place such orders. The other item regards my pitch. The basic claim is that without seed, we will all starve. I need to strengthen the argument that there really isn't another option.

Task one goes surprisingly quickly. Now that I know how to find the quarantine order and associated emergency procedures, I go straight to them and start reading. The legalese is difficult to wade through, but the answer is clear. Non-governmental entities can request shipments. But the shipments must be paid in advance with Confederation credits and the applicant must provide a certificate from the relevant authority verifying that they have the ability to land the shipment.

A quick check of Jaredaan commercial arrangements with the space station shows that a company can request such certification, but it is subject to governmental approval.

So, I don't need Walter to request the shipment, I can do that myself. But I do need the government to allow the space station to land the shipment. That Walter can block. But would he?

As I ponder this, there's a knock on my door frame. It's the warden.

"Jared, you look lost in thought."

"Guilty as charged. What can I do for you?"

He points to one of my chairs, "May I?"

I nod, it's not like I'd say no, but I still appreciate the courtesy.

He closes the door, then takes a seat.

"The board meeting is tomorrow. I need to explain the food shortage issue to the board. Do you have any material I can use?"

"I have lots of raw information. I could have something cogent for you in an hour."

"What's the general outline?"

"We buy just over 90% of our food. The largest single supplier is the agricultural operation, which makes up about 75% of the total. Next is the bulk dry goods supplies, which is about 10%. The remaining 15% is miscellaneous local and specialty supplies, like the Heroldstown Cheese Company.

"I've spoken with Evelyn Fontes, the president and general manager of the agricultural operation—Jaredaan Agricultural. She confirms that their output will drop to essentially zero for the coming year if her current seed order is not shipped within a week. I have a copy of her order.

"My proposal has been to supplement, using enough of our own land to offset the difference. But we are stuck in the same place unless we can get a seed order. I have the proposed order and confirmation that it can be added to the shipment, if the emergency delivery is scheduled within the next week.

"There are other issues like, equipment and fertilizer. But I have local solutions for us and for Evelyn in cooperation with West Lake and the ethanol company."

The warden nods his head.

"Well done. I like it. And what do we need to arrange for the emergency delivery?"

"The elder board can coordinate the process. We could also do it on our own, but we'd need a certificate from the space station confirming their commitment to land the delivery."

"Good work, Jared. Can you get a draft document to me by the end of the day?"

"Will do, sir."

JULIAN

It occurs to me that we may have another option for seed. Jaramor. When I get home, I ask Summer if she's OK with me taking enough of the *profecia aumentar* on my own to connect with him. She's become increasingly protective and I've promised not to venture out on my own unless she agrees. When I show her how little I plan to take, she agrees.

A minute later, I'm away. I cast my attention toward Julian and in short order I'm sitting with Julian and Edson in the pub's private room. I tell them about the problem with the seed and before I know it, they've dragged updates on all my initiatives out of me.

Walter sounds a lot like Herold. Julian sends.

This surprises me. *You knew Herold?*

Yes. I worked on his well project. He didn't know who I was. He assumed I was a rogue of some sort. But he really didn't care. Anyone able bodied and willing to work was his friend.

Edson, who seems less interested in our family history interrupts. It's the first time I've heard him speak, even if it is telepathic.

Your best bet will be to fight for your off-world shipment. There are better seed producers on the major planets than there are here. But

318

our dried food serves a second purpose. It's dried using a process that preserves the seed. Essentially all the fruit, tomatoes, peppers, squash, and cucumbers will grow if you plant them. We intentionally do not clear the seeds before drying. And although it's not particularly palatable, most of the roots, leaves, and stems that you grow from those seeds are edible.

Julian gives Edson a stern look. *We don't have enough dried food to feed Heroldstown, barely enough seed to grow enough food for Jaramor over the next six months. This would be an option of last resort.*

You must confront Walter to get the off-world seed. And if he doesn't budge, then you need to remove him—one way or another.

There's a darkness to the way Julian sends the word 'another.'

After a moment of silence, Edson sends an even darker thought. *We don't like to talk about this, but your telepathy can be used against others—mildly, or in the extreme, if necessary.*

After several seconds of silence, Julian changes subjects. *Summer contacted us regarding your probing of the aliens' propulsion. Clever idea. I know you didn't accomplish what you wanted, but it got us thinking about the same problem from a different perspective.*

As you found out, the aliens get their speed by traveling in space-time bubbles. If the bubble destabilizes, then they will drop back into our space time. If it's a controlled exit, they come back at a sub-light speed. If it's an uncontrolled exit, then their ship gets ripped apart.

The alien detectors that Herold built sense that resonance. If we could run the detectors backward, inducing a different space-time resonance, we could destabilize their bubbles. In the best case, it would destroy their ships. In the worst case, it would leave them stranded in the void traveling at sub-light.

Julian's conclusion seems reasonable to me. *Any idea how to do that?*

Edson replies this time. *No. We don't know how the alien detectors work. But the Confederation probably does. It wasn't Herold that designed the detectors we put in.*

CHAPTER 20: CRISIS

To my surprise, Warden Glenn invites me to the camp's board meeting. He wants me to brief the board on the food shortage as we see it, our proposal to solve it, and the problems we've run into.

The meeting is held in the warden's office on the holoprojection system. Once we establish the meeting, the various board members start joining. It occurs to me that I don't know who the board is, or their interest in the camp.

To my surprise the first to enter is my cousin Kinsley Daan Gosling. She's the eldest daughter of my father's younger brother, Tobias Daan, who was mayor at the time of my conviction. She's a year older than Aaron, 15 years older than me, but she was always friendly toward me when I was a kid.

"Jared, what an unexpected pleasure to see you."

"Kinsley, what a pleasant surprise. How did you get on the camp's board?"

I can see from the body language that the warden wasn't expecting this. He answers in Kinsley's place. "Kinsley is the new mayor of Jaredstown, her father died of DAGS a couple months back. She won the special election to fill the rest of his term."

The news of Uncle Tobias' death hits pretty hard. He was stern and of little help during my arrest and prosecution, but he was a decent human being and a close friend of my father's.

"Kinsley, I'm so sorry to hear about your father."

"Yours too, Jared."

An awkward silence settles, then the next person enters, Evelyn Fontes of the agricultural operation.

"Hi Jared, I'm glad to see that you're joining us today."

The warden whispers, "She's the mayor of Heroldstown."

The next person to enter is someone I don't know. Greetings are exchanged around the room, then the warden introduces me.

"Everett, this is Jared Daan, the assistant warden here.

"Jared, this is Everett Dawson, the civilian mayor of the space station."

The last two board members enter more-or-less at the same time, which confuses the holoprojector for a few seconds. When it clears, I see Uncle Walter and Marten Vargas, the president of the ethanol company.

I learn that Uncle Walter is the chairman of the board for the camp, by virtue of his position as the head of the elder board. The other members represent the jurisdictions that sentence people to the camp and the camp's primary customer.

Uncle Walter calls the meeting to order and goes through the opening formalities, then turns it over to Warden Glenn to give the quarterly update. The update is surprisingly comprehensive. He has charts for a long list of metrics that show the camp's current and historical condition. What surprises me is the kink in each of the curves that starts in the month I joined the camp staff. All the good things are up. All the bad things are down, with one exception: the retiree population, which has continued up at the same steady rate.

As the warden concludes his report, I see Walter giving me the evil eye. When the warden opens the floor to questions, Walter throws the first zinger.

"All the trends took an impressively positive turn about the time Jared joined the staff. How can that be when he's busy running his own company and getting rich on the side?"

The Heroldstown board members do not look kindly on Walter's question. I really haven't had that much interaction with them, but they know what I've done and why I've done it. The other board members seem curious to hear the answer to this question.

The warden clears his throat. "I'll let Jared answer directly if you'd like, but before we do that I must weigh in on this issue. Jared's top priority is the camp. Everything he does is to the camp's benefit. He's made numerous changes that no one before him could have imagined. On the side, he's made a lot of money on Jungle. But look at what he's done with it! He's installed gardens, planted crops, found a cure for DAGS, and formed a company to produce that cure, which he supplies to the camp at no cost.

"Things would be much different here without him."

Walter shoots back, saying, "Well if he's doing all that, why do we even need a warden?"

I raise my hand. "If I may?"

All eyes turn to me, including Walter's evil eye. But he doesn't stop me from speaking.

"I'm an engineer by nature. I focus on the problems that need to be solved and find solutions for those problems.

"But I'm not an administrator. I can substitute for the warden for short periods, but I would not be good at his job. We make a great team and I'm happy that I've been given a chance to serve here. But he holds the camp together. I just fix the problems."

The warden seems surprised by my comments. And I can see that I've won Cousin Kinsley over to my side. I also seem to have taken the steam out of Walter, who moves the meeting on to the next topic: current issues at the camp.

The warden points to me and I walk people through the pending food shortage, my plan to fix it, and the broader issue of seed supply. Walter sputters and argues that the food shortage is over, but Evelyn will have none of it.

"Walter, get a grip! Without the seed, we will starve. Period! Imported food has never covered more than 20% of the food supply on this planet. Even if the quarantine goes away, which it won't, the mines have never made enough money to feed us all. That's why the family gave Uncle Herold the money to establish the ice transport system.

"We have one week to get that seed. If we don't, then its starvation, guaranteed! Do you want that blood on your hands?"

Struggling for some sort of win, Walter asks, "But why divert field labor away from cane to grow food?"

I can tell that Evelyn has more she wants to say, but she signals me to go first.

"The big investment of labor is at the front end, creating the irrigation system and preparing the fields for the first time. I plan to contract that out, so that it has no impact on camp operations. I also plan to pay for it myself, so it will have no impact on camp finances.

"During the growing cycle, things are slower, so we can handle the increased load with no real impact.

"Harvest is the only time that we're capacity constrained. But for the crops in question, with the exception of corn, the harvests are at different times, so there is no trade-off. We get more output from the same labor because the busy times for each crop happen during slow times for the others."

I can see Evelyn nodding her head and smiling at me. All she says is, "Agreed. Good summary."

Walter appears convinced that the board is on my side, so he turns to me.

"How much space can we spare for dry bulk and the equipment I want?"

Evelyn answers for me. "None. The seed maxes out the emergency delivery."

He doesn't argue, but asks me, "And how long until you can afford another shipment?"

"Approximately three months."

"Well, how's that going to work?" Walter snorts. "I thought you needed that equipment to package your medicine so it could be transported up north."

"I'm looking at options."

"What options?"

"Wine barrels, maybe copper lined vats. I haven't had enough time to sort that out. But it's a lesser problem than getting the food. I'm sure I'll find a way."

I can see Walter winding up for another swipe, but Warden Glenn beats him to the punch.

"I think we have a recommendation for the elder board. Are we agreed?" He raises his hand indicating that he does. I raise my hand also and within a second every hand is up except Walter's.

OFFICE

To my surprise, the emergency supply documents arrive on my desk a few hours later. It only takes a moment for me to append the funding authorization the bank will need. A huge weight comes off my shoulders as I send the emergency request back for submission to the Confederation.

That frees me to log into my Jungle account. Audrey has approved all the license applications, so I release them for Jungle to process. A couple minutes later, I accept the 242,000-credit promotion offer.

When Margot extended the offer yesterday, my initial reaction was to reject it out of hand. Today, I enthusiastically accept it, even though it will leave me with almost no Confederation credits for the better part of three months.

I take a moment to savor the prospect of making six-plus million credits a month. That's enough that life in Jaredaan can return to normal even if the quarantine is never lifted.

After savoring a moment of peace, I move on to the next problem that needs solving, bulk transportation of the supplement to the north. It occurs to me that Brock Newton may know something about this, so I give him a call.

"Shipping liquids on the shuttle is tricky, but there are several options I've created for others. Do you know how much you need to ship?"

"Yes. About 2,600 liters every four weeks."

Brock groans. "That's a lot of liquid for the shuttle system. But I think the solution is simple. All normal shipping is done using containers. For the passenger shuttles, there are eight of the standard 180 kg containers. For the cargo shuttles there are several configurations using a mix of 180 kg and 400 kg containers. Your best bet for liquid shipment will be to use the 180 kg containers. There's a standard configuration that holds 12 15-kg plastic bottles.

"Henry, up at the plastics factory, usually has these in inventory."

JAREDSTOWN

I hadn't seen Kinsley in over 5 years. Now I'm talking with her for the second time in the same day.

"Jared, I didn't expect to hear from you so soon. What can I do for you?"

"We're ready at this end to start shipping our supplement to you. I wanted to discuss arrangements."

There's a pause on the line, then she says, "Let me tie in Walter."

After a minute Walter joins us.

"You found a solution for your bottling problem already?" Walter asks in a way that suggests I've been sand bagging on my end.

"Yes and no. It turns out that there's a standard bulk liquid shipping solution for the shuttle, using 15-liter plastic bottles. So, I can get the supplement to you in bulk via the shuttle, but you'll need to figure out the financing for that. I'm out of money.

"Once you get it, you will need to figure out the local distribution. In the camp, we do bulk delivery to the hospital, who administers it to the patients. Then we have bulk delivery to each zone, where the zone supervisor gives it dose-by-dose to people in the zone that want it."

There's silence on the line, which Walter breaks with a sigh. "I think I finally understand the bottling problem."

There's silence for a moment. This time Kinsley breaks it.

"When you think about it, we already have a solution for this problem. Both the garden and the restaurants have To Go packaging for liquids via reusable glass bottles. They require a deposit for the bottle, then refund it when you return the bottle. If you come in for a refill, then there's no additional deposit required.

"We probably have the discretionary funds to acquire the reusable bottles. We could have refilling operations in the garden, or at restaurants or the food stores."

Walter gives a harrumph, then says, "Good idea. That will work and it puts the work out in the hands of existing commercial operations. Can you take the lead on that?"

"Sure, if your office will take the shuttle issue." Kinsley smiles.

Walter grumbles a bit, then says, "Sounds fair. Approving government shuttle operations falls to me."

Then he points to me. "How soon before you can have the first shipment ready?"

"If the local supplier has the bulk containers in stock, then 2 days. Let me check that, then get back to you."

"Deal." To my surprise, Walter smiles as he says deal.

OFFICE

Now that I have a deal of sorts with Walter for bulk shipment, I need the bulk containers. Quickly searching through the local directory, I find the number for Henry Barros, President of Heroldstown Plastics.

"Jared, what a pleasure to hear from you. You've been the talk around town the last couple months. What can I do for you?"

I quickly explain the situation regarding bulk delivery of my supplement to the north.

"I'm glad to hear that someone has a cure for this thing. I know a couple people who have it. It's a scary thing. Regarding the containers, they're durable and will have no problem surviving the flight. We've had really good experience with them. The only downside to these containers is that they're relatively expensive. The 15-kg plastic bottles are 30 credits each. Twelve of them to fill the standard shipping pallet will cost you 360 credits. But I'm guessing that you're going to need more than 12 of them."

"Yes, I need to make 10 shipments per month to cover everyone, so that will be 120 bottles per month."

There's silence on the line.

I break it by asking, "Is that going to be a problem?"

"Ah, yes. I make these bottles from plastic pellets that I source off-world. I'm working on a local substitute, but don't have one yet. I might have enough left to make 120 bottles, but I'll need to check. After that, we're done until I can source additional raw materials."

"Can I place an order for 120 bottles now, or do I need to come see you?"

Again silence. I'm starting to get the impression Henry doesn't like giving bad news.

"I'm going to need payment in advance for these. The total will be 3,600 credits. I would normally give a discount for an order this large. But I can't since this is the last of my inventory."

Once again, it seems that I'm going to lose half a day running into Heroldstown to sign some documents.

"Any chance I could have my lawyer, or my banker, give you a check? I need the bottles, but I'm two hours away and don't want to spend four hours on the road just to make a payment."

"Do you bank at the Bank of Heroldstown?"

"Yes."

"I'm about 5 minutes away and can pick up the payment if you can arrange to have it waiting for me."

"Deal. Let me get that arranged, then I'll call you back, or have the bank call you back."

"Sounds good, and thanks for the business, Jared."

It's irritating that financial transactions in Heroldstown are as slow and in person as they are. But it is what it is, and a half hour later the matter is closed.

CENTRAL COMMAND

The next item on my list is contacting Admiral Tang at Confederation Central Command. I log into my secure messaging app and send the Admiral an update. The message is simple.

"We've been able to confirm that the aliens use space-time bubbles for both stealth mode and faster than light travel. We have reason to believe that these bubbles are not very stable. We speculate that a device that does the opposite of what the alien detectors do might be sufficient to drop a ship out of stealth or FTL. We've witnessed an uncontrolled drop, and it destroyed the ship.

"We've also learned that the aliens intend to slaughter and eat the residents of Taramoot. If the residents take my anti-DAGS supplement they will become toxic to the aliens. That may help them survive the encounter. But even if it doesn't, it may deter the aliens from pressing into the rest of the Confederation. If you have the means to provide the supplement to Taramoot, then you should."

WARDEN'S RESIDENCE

Just before the end of the workday, Summer came up to my office to tell me her mother invited us over for dinner. As daunting as the thought was, I was happy that I'd have the chance to spend some time with her parents. At least that's what I tried to tell myself.

Their home is just a few minutes' walk from my apartment. When we arrive, Summer opens the door, calling out, "Mom, I'm home." And we go in.

Her mother comes rushing out and gives Summer a deep hug that from my perspective they hold for an uncomfortably long time. When they release, I also get a big hug.

"Jared, I'm so happy you've come over."

"Wouldn't miss it, Mrs. Glenn."

"Oh, please call me June. Mrs. Glenn was my mother-in-law."

I can't help but chuckle. "Thank you, June."

The warden walks in and greets Summer with a kiss on the cheek. Then turns to me hand outstretched. "Jared, welcome to our home. Thanks for coming over."

I shake the outstretched hand. "My pleasure, sir."

I notice the look in June's eye. I think she wants the warden to tell me to address him in a less formal way. I can also see that's not going to happen.

Formalities over, June drags Summer away to the kitchen, leaving me with the boss. He turns and asks, "Why don't you join me in my study, Jared?"

I follow him to the far side of the house and enter one of the most beautiful rooms I've ever seen. At one end there's a built-in wooden bookshelf. It sits behind a large wooden desk. A pair of leather sitting chairs face the desk.

The other side is set up similarly with a generous sitting area in front of a bookshelf. The sitting area has a leather sofa, two more of the leather sitting chairs and a glass coffee table.

He indicates one of the sitting chairs, then seats himself on the sofa. I notice a small bar set-up on the coffee table.

"We don't allow alcohol in the camp, except for in this room, where I occasionally offer a guest a wee dram of some whisky, I

327

imported from New London years ago. They call it Irish Whisky, which is an old Earth reference, one I've never looked up.

He pulls a cork stopper out of the bottle and pours himself a small 50 ml taste. "Care to try it? Fair warning, it has quite the burn."

"Sure." I'm surprised by the room, whisky, and generosity. The only time Aaron took me out for a drink in Jaredstown, he'd pointed out a bottle of Irish Whisky on display behind the bar. He told me the bottle cost nearly a thousand credits. He also promised that if he ever made enough money, he'd have a shot of it.

The warden puts my glass down in front of me, then raises his. "Cheers. Start with just a drop of it on your tongue."

He takes a tiny sip and I try to copy his technique, but apparently suck it in too hard. The fumes light my sinuses on fire moments before the drops of liquid set my tongue ablaze. I cough so hard that I nearly spill the precious drink.

The warden chuckles. "The first sip is always the hardest."

I cough a little more, then set the glass down, while I catch my breath.

"What do you think of the whisky?"

"My brother Aaron once told me that he hoped to make enough money someday to get a taste of Irish Whisky. It's going to take a while for me to get used to it."

"That will probably happen faster than you think." He chuckles. "Your uncle Walter is quite the whisky connoisseur and collector. He shared some with Aaron and me one night. Aaron really savored it. Apparently the two of them went quite a bit heavier a couple nights later. They both looked a bit gray the next day."

He chuckles some more. "I decided that if I ever got back, I'd share a dram with you. Consider it a thank you for taking care of Summer while we were gone."

"Thank you, sir." I take another sip, more controlled this time, and enjoy the warmth as it spreads down my throat, then through my stomach.

"I hope you and Summer are getting along well."

This was my big fear in coming over here. Being pressed by her father over our relationship.

"I love your daughter, sir. I can no longer imagine life without her."

"Good to hear, but you're still in the honeymoon phase. That will eventually wear off. That's when you find out whether you really love someone."

The words strike me as overly pessimistic.

"I'm sure everyone says this, but I think our relationship is different. We have developed telepathy together, so are connected at a different level than most people.

"I think that's why our relationship matured so quickly. I truly fear any thought that I might lose her someday."

He looks at me critically but doesn't say anything for a few seconds.

"Again, I'm glad to hear that." Then a few moments later, "But I've been instructed not to interrogate you on the matter, so let me leave it at that. I don't think there's a better man for her on the planet. So, I trust her well-being into your hands."

With that, he taps his glass on the table and shoots the rest of his drink.

"Late this afternoon, I heard that you and Walter struck a deal on supplement supply to the north. Are you sure you can afford that?"

It's my turn to smile.

"It'll be tight for a couple months, but after that I'll have nearly unlimited funding."

"How so?"

"Jungle. They have manufacturing capability to make my supplement on 58 planets. It went up for sale this week on all 58. The sales forecast is stunning. That money will start making its way here in three months."

"How much do you expect to make?"

"I'm not comfortable talking about that. The forecasts are stunning, but they're forecasts. Until sales roll in, I don't want to speculate about how much I'll make."

"Prudent." He nods his head sagely, but I can tell he's not happy with that answer.

"I suspect the numbers will be remarkably high, which worries me. Are you really going to continue on at the camp once you have a million credits in the bank?"

I find the question curious. Given all the investments I've made in the camp and in emergency supplies, I'd have thought he'd have figured out that I already had a million credits in the bank. Or at least did at one point.

"We're a long way from the end of the DAGS crisis, so even if I wanted to move off planet, I couldn't. And there's no place on Jaredaan that I'd rather be than here."

There's a knock on the door frame. It's Summer.

"Dinner will be ready in a minute. Is the interrogation done yet?" The last part is said with a lot of humor.

The warden stands. "Guess it's time we go make ourselves useful."

...

Tonight's meal reminds me of the one Summer made for me. The big difference is that it's served with pasta. The juices from the beef permeate the pasta. Lenna doesn't serve a dish like this in the staff café. But if she did, it probably wouldn't be any better.

"So where do the two of you go when you venture out into the wilderness?"

I look at Summer, who indicates that I should answer her mother's question.

"So far, we've only explored to the East, not the north, south, or west. We've explored several paths that start at the end of the road."

"But why? What do you do?"

"Explore. Relax away from it all. Eat. We spend a lot of time riding in my truck, but an equal amount of time just hanging out, talking."

Although the questions were asked by June, I can see the warden isn't completely buying it.

"Jared, you're the most purpose-driven person I've ever met. I find it hard to believe you're just going out there to relax. Surely, there's something else you're looking for."

"Fair point. Initially, I wanted to check out the wells. It seemed that they had to be more than just abandoned wells. We now know that they're alien detectors. We also chased after a rumor that there were more wells downstream, but we haven't found any."

Maybe it's residual *profecia aumentar* in my system, but I can almost hear the warden thinking we're hiding something, and June thinking we're spending most of our time in bed as a young couple should.

Where the warden seems suspicious that we're up to something that will reflect poorly on the camp, June seems hopeful that we're in the process of making a grandchild.

INSIGHT

Last night's dinner with the Glenn's was... odd. I love Summer and she loves her parents, which puts the onus on me to figure out how to love them. It's something I want to do, but the mountain separating me from that place seems insurmountable. I toss and turn much of the night, then fall into a deep, deep sleep. My dreams bounce between the Glenn's, Admiral Tang, and the alien armada, strange bedfellows if ever there was such a thing.

But I awake in the morning deeply convicted to turn Admiral Tang to my side. And I think I know how to do it, at least how to learn to do it.

In the morning, I can't concentrate on anything in the office, so head out for a day in the zones. The first stop is in Zone 6 with supervisor Ashley Meyer.

Ashley has a checkered past. She was an inmate, who like me found peace here. When her sentence was fulfilled, she asked to stay on and eventually became a zone supervisor.

Like Vera Lopes in Zone 2, Ashley has a commanding presence I will never have. She is the master of everything within her scope and has the minimal required respect for things outside it. I catch up with her during breakfast service in the Zone 6 dining room.

I grab some breakfast and join her.

"Jared, to what do I owe the honor?"

The words are said tartly, but with a token of respect.

"It's been a while since I checked in with you. So, I thought I'd do it today."

"Sounds ominous. What's on your mind?"

Her words are so direct and sincere that it takes me off guard. So much so that my usual spiel sounds hollow in my ears before it even escapes my lips.

"What? Cat's got your tongue."

I chuckle. "Thank you. I've been wrestling with a problem. One I can't seem to make any progress on. Visiting the zones always seems to bring me clarity, so I decided to ditch the problem and come out. I think I've visited all the other zones since I was here last, so here I am."

"Jared, if you can't solve a problem, how could you possibly think I could help?"

"Don't sell yourself short, Ashley."

There's silence for a minute, then she says, "Out with it."

I look deeply in her eyes, then give in to the impulse. "Suppose you knew something of immense importance, but the person in power didn't believe you. What do you do to get them to listen?"

She looks at me oddly. "Jared, if this is some kind of perverse sex play, it won't work."

Now I'm the one that's baffled. "What?"

331

"Sorry. Lines like that have been used against me before. I know that's not who you are. Can we try that again?"

"I've learned about some Confederation things I'm not supposed to know about. I've found some solutions and offered them up but am not being taken seriously."

"Know that feeling," she shoots back. "Tell me."

...

An hour later, I leave Zone 6 knowing exactly what I need to do.

CENTRAL COMMAND

Tonight, Summer and I are going back to Confederation Central Command. But this time we're doing it differently. We're going to hide, watch, and observe. When we determine his briefing schedule, we will fast forward to each meeting and listen to what's reported. Everything new, we'll confirm. Then tomorrow or the next day, we will tell him everything of consequence that's going to happen in the next two weeks. That's the plan anyway.

We take our doses, which at this point are miniscule, then are off flying.

...

We arrive in an alcove that Summer had spotted on a previous visit. No one seems to notice us, so we settle in and listen. Summer senses that I'm not getting much, so takes my hand. It's like the earmuffs have come off.

"...we cannot verify everything this Daan fellow has told you sir. But the items we can find check out. The forward scouting force confirms that there are alien ships closing in on Taramoot. They are now 18 days out by our best estimate.

"Taramoot has a thulium mining operation. They are sitting on the largest deposit known to the Confederation.

"Some Confederation military scientists confirm that they are working on a thulium-based zero-point energy device. None of their work has been published. They were quite shocked that we'd heard of such a thing. They also confirmed that the power levels Daan reported are within the theoretical boundaries of their models.

"As to a reverse alien detector... This one is harder. They believe the basic theory put forward. If we could generate a chaotic alternating resonance in the layer of space time the aliens are using, it would in all likelihood destabilize their space-time bubble. They could use a variant of the detectors to determine the layer. But as of today, we do not have a power source large enough to build a transmitter with that much power.

"This kid is quite smart. Our scientists would like to interview him. But that specific proposal is beyond us.

"Next, it is true that a company he owns has a supplement that's available on Jungle. It's also true that it is in clinical trial for prescription use for DAGS. But we have no way to determine whether it's actually toxic to the aliens.

"That's what we've found at this time."

"Good work, Wilson. Anything else today?"

"No sir. But I think we'll have a few new items for tomorrow's briefing."

I hold Summer's hand tightly, then fast forward to tomorrow. Nothing of consequence comes up tomorrow, or the next day.

...

"Morning Admiral. We've established a sensor net of sorts along the path the aliens are taking. And we've made first contact. Unfortunately, the results were disastrous."

"Tell me," the admiral grunts.

"One of the reconnaissance squadrons came up with a method for tracking the alien's position. They determined that several alien ships would be passing through an area near them last night.

"We shared the idea about trying to knock the alien ships out of their space-time bubbles. One of the ships engineers jury-rigged a mine of some sort that would disrupt space time and hopefully trigger the aliens to drop back to normal space.

"It worked. Four alien ships dropped back. One was significantly damaged. The other three used their annihilation weapon to take out the entire squadron that had been sitting there waiting."

"We injured one alien ship at the cost of 12 of our reconnaissance ships!" The admiral looks like he's going to explode. "Where did this happen?"

I look at Summer, we need to get this data. She smiles and nods.

After a lot of back and forth, the Admiral laments. "If only we'd set some conventional explosives, maybe some antimatter mines, where the aliens fell back into space-time, then cleared our ships from the area." He shakes his head. "We cannot continue sustaining losses like this."

I nod to Summer and we return.

...

We've started putting notepads next to our easy chairs, so we can record information as soon as we get back.

Summer immediately starts scribbling. "I got the coordinates."

I do the same. "I've got the time and squadron ID."

Scribbling done, we look at each other.

"We need to check this out."

Summer looks at the clock. "It's midnight."

"But we have to do it. If we can get the squadron's perspective and the alien's perspective, we can turn this into a decisive win."

I can tell Summer is tired, and she looks like she wants to cry.

She puts her head back and closes her eyes. "I think I still have enough *profecia aumentar* in me. Lead the way."

...

It takes a few minutes, but I find the squadron. I skip forward in time a few minutes at a time until I see the event starting to unfold. Four alien ships shoot through the void like falling stars. One tumbles and a section of the ship falls away and breaks apart. The other three make the transition without incident.

The squadron ships start to scatter but are nowhere near fast enough. One of the alien ships spots them and flashes closer. It emits a streak of light that envelopes the squadron. Moments later, the squadron starts turning to dust. The dust spreads. Then there's nothing. Apparently one of the squadron ships was well separated from the main event. It must be the one that filed the report. It turns to run, but another of the alien ships streaks over to it, and moments later, the last squadron ship turns to dust, then disappears.

Apparently, the alien ship that tumbled out of its bubble is beyond repair. Escape pods come streaming out an make their way to the three remaining ships.

I skip ahead and skip ahead until all the escape pods are landed. Then what appears to be the lead ship uses the weapon on the broken ship. It decomposes to dust, then is gone.

Summer and I flash over to the lead ship. We hide in the alcove in engineering that she'd hidden in before.

There we hear the play by play as the aliens replay the logs trying to figure out exactly what happened.

We need to get this information into Admiral Tang's hands.

...

I wake in my easy chair. Enough light leaks in from outside that I can tell it's close to dawn. Summer stirs, then wakes. She looks exhausted.

When she sees it's 5:45, she starts crying.

I go over to give her a hug. "It's OK. Just call in sick. We accomplished something significant last night. Nothing you'd do at the camp is as important as what we just did."

She looks at me, but I can't read what she's thinking.

"Come on, let's get you to bed."

I help her up then go into the bedroom and help her get settled in.

"You going to join me?"

"No. I need to get this info to the Admiral."

She looks like she wants to argue but doesn't. "Tell them I'm not feeling well."

OFFICE

I head over to the office and am greeted by the watchman behind the desk in reception.

"You're in early this morning sir."

"Morning, Jasper. I've been at it all night. I have a report to file, then am going to go home to bed."

"Take care of yourself, sir. We need you well."

I head up to my office reflecting on the words just exchanged. Jasper was part of the team that brought me here two years ago. He was a nice guy then and is a nice guy now. But the exchange was a reminder of how much has changed. Two years ago, I was a scared kid, innocent to the ways of the world and as naïve as a person could be.

Now I'm the one that has the best chance of saving mankind. Crazy.

...

Once in the office, I light up the secure communication application and send a message to Admiral Tang.

Admiral Tang. In two days, one of your scouting squadrons is going to have an encounter with the aliens. They've apparently been able to triangulate the alien's position and are planning to plant a mine that will disrupt space time.

Unfortunately, the mine they create won't be large enough. The squadron plans to linger in the area to see if their mine works. A few alien ships will fall out of their space-time bubbles. Only one will suffer damage. The others will annihilate the squadron.

A better strategy will be to plant the mine, as many mines as they can make. Then to mine the area where the aliens will land with antimatter mines. As soon as the squadron has done this, they need to run.

Even at sub-light speeds, the alien ships are fast. And they will be angry as hornets. So, order your ships to evacuate the area as soon as the trap is set. And order them to scatter if they won't have time to get out of detection range.

Thank you for reading this, sir.

Jared Daan

I read through my message several times, then send it, hoping that advanced warning will hand the Central Command their first win of the new war. I send the message, then sit back in my chair awaiting confirmation of delivery.

I hear someone coming up the steps. It's the Warden. He stops in my doorway.

"Jasper says you were up all night. Is everything OK?"

"Yes. Summer and I had some urgent work to do for the Confederation Central Command. We finished about 6:00 AM. I came over to send in our report. Summer is in bed now. You probably won't see her today, at least not before noon.

"If it's OK with you, I'm going to head back and get some shut-eye."

"Is this for that Admiral Tang fellow?"

"Yes."

"You're working for him, too!"

"Sir, the aliens are only 38 light years away from us. Now that we have the treatment for DAGS and a solution for the food crisis, we need to start worrying about the pending alien attack."

He shakes his head. "Go take a nap. You're no good to the camp in your current condition." He heads off for his office, head still shaking.

WARDEN'S OFFICE

Something's going on, the warden thought. *All that time in the wilderness. Working for a Confederation Fleet admiral. It doesn't add up.*

Pressing the button on the intercom, he says. "Lillian, please ask Jack Johnson to stop over."

APARTMENT

I startle awake. My communicator is sounding. Looking at it, I see the call is from Henry Barros of the plastics company.

"Morning, Henry. What can I do for you?"

"Hi, Jared. You must be having a good day if you think it's still morning." He chuckles. "Just wanted to let you know your plastic bottles are ready to pick up. You'll need a big truck. These things don't weigh that much, but they take up a lot of space. So, you'll need something more spacious than your truck."

"OK. I'll get back to you with the arrangements."

"OK, but these need to go today or tomorrow. After that, I'll need to charge you storage."

I hop out of bed and go out into the kitchen. Unfortunately, the call woke Summer also. But it's probably for the best. It's nearly 2:00 p.m.

I put a call into Brock Newton to ask him if he can manage the pickup.

He says the timing's convenient. He has other items he was planning to bring over to the plant this afternoon. So could get the bottles on the way over.

I call Henry back to let him know, then put my head down on the kitchen table.

I hear footsteps, then Summer's voice. "What's the matter?"

"Nothing, just tired. That was Henry Barros. Our plastic bottles are ready. Brock was scheduled to bring some stuff over to the factory this afternoon, so he'll be handling the pickup."

"Want a bite to eat? I'm going to make myself something, then go over to the office."

A few minutes later, she puts a large plate on the table. It has an omelet that we're going to share.

"You got the message off to Admiral Tang?"

"I did. You going to be able to go back in tonight?"

"Maybe. Still planning to go back to Jaramor this weekend?"

"Yes. The aliens will be on Taramoot in two weeks. I think we need to work with the elders there if we're going to have a plan in time."

"That's a lot of travel time, for a little bit of working time."

"Think we could get a week off?"

She shakes her head. "How would you explain that to my father?"

"No idea."

We sit in silence for a minute.

"We have to go this weekend anyway. We need the raw materials. I could meet Jason at the end of the road again, but if I'm going that far anyway, it's worth the extra couple hours to spend a day in Jaramor.

"I'll tell your father that Walter wants me to look for the additional detectors."

"I don't like it when you lie to my father."

I nod my head in agreement. "I could call Aaron and ask him to ask Walter to call your father."

She looks at me skeptically. "Oh, and there's no way that plan could possibly go wrong." The sarcasm in the statement is so overplayed that we both laugh.

"Let's head out before dawn on Saturday, spend the entire day Sunday, then come back on Monday."

"Let me tell Dad. We've been pushing it too hard. We need a day off."

"Sounds like a plan. I'm going to head over to the plant this afternoon. I'll help Brock and Charlie unload the bottles, then put together a schedule for shipments north "

Summer smiles at me as she gets up to put the dishes in the sink.

ROAD TO NOWHERE

Surprisingly, Summer's father agrees with her. We've been pushing it too hard and deserve a day off. With the emergency order for seed placed and a delivery schedule for the supplement arranged, much of the camp administration, especially the warden, seems to be breathing more easily.

We go to bed early Friday night, opting to comfort each other rather than spending another night in the *mystery*, then get up and out two hours before dawn.

Strangely, I'm feeling a bit more paranoid about being followed this trip. But I see no lights following behind us. We reach the end of the road as the sky starts filling with pre-dawn light. I know the way to the upper trail well enough at this point that I turn off my headlights. It's still dark enough out that our lights could be spotted from the plant if you looked from the right place.

When we get to the trail, I stop and get out of the truck. The moaning of the alien detectors is uncomfortably loud, making it hard to focus my attention. Nonetheless, I use the binoculars that were part of the initial outfitting package to scan back the way we came. There are no lights, no signs of dust or other indicators of passage, except for the dust we kicked up at the end of the road.

After a second, more careful scan, I get back into the truck and proceed down the trail.

"Are you going to tell me what that was about?"

The noise from the alien detectors apparently woke Summer, who'd fallen asleep shortly after we left the apartment.

"I woke up paranoid this morning. Not sure why, but I've had this feeling that we're being followed."

"You have enough *profecia aumentar* in your system that you should pay attention to your feelings. Any clue as to what it could be?"

"No, just that someone's-looking-over-my-shoulder feeling."

"Then we should be on alert."

There's silence for a moment, then Summer asks, "Did you hear anything back from Admiral Tang? The attack happens sometime today or tonight. I'm hoping they're taking your warning seriously."

"Same here, but I think this is a one-way communication channel. We should work with the elders this afternoon and evening to see if we can determine what's happening. Then we need to start probing his briefings again. I think this is probably the best way we can help him."

We ride in silence for a while then come to the narrow spot along the trail. There's been a rockslide since the last time we were here. It's been cleared, but the crossing looks even narrower than it was before.

"Let me get out and guide you across," Summer volunteers.

She gets out and slowly walks across to the other side. She stops to check the stability of some rocks jutting out of the wall. Further along, she stops again to toe a spot along the cliffs edge. Seeing her that close to the edge induces a wave of vertigo that makes my head spin. She gets to the other side, then starts back.

"It's a little tighter than before. And there's a crumbly spot on the edge we'll want to avoid. But this should be easy. I'll walk ahead of you indicating your clearance from the wall. Just stick as close as you can. I'll let you know if you're too close or too far. Ready?"

I nod. This is the part of the trip I hate the most.

We proceed at a snail's pace. Summer does a great job of keeping me close to the wall. I get across in a few minutes, never feeling like I was about to go over the edge.

Summer pops back into the car and we speed down the trail. The plan is to meet Jason and the rangers at the watering hole halfway up the steep part. Their intention is to be there waiting for us by 10:00 AM. My sense is that we will beat them to it.

We arrive at the watering hole at 9:45. I can see the rangers just starting up the trail. I flash my lights and get an immediate reaction. Jason continues up the trail, but waves for us to start making our way down.

There's a funny thing about hover vehicles. They can move like lightening across flat level surfaces. And they climb hills easily. But going down is a much more cautious operation. Hover vehicles are slippery because they don't have ground contact. You have to watch your speed, or you won't have enough power to slow yourself.

We start the creep down, but I apparently am not paying enough attention to my speed.

"Jared, slow down," Summer calls out. "There's no place for the horses to get out of your way past the next pull over."

I apply maximum reverse thrust and finally come to a halt 10 or 20 meters past the pull over. The horses are still a kilometer away. But we would have been in big trouble if Summer hadn't called out the warning when she did. I creep forward toward a wide spot, then stop and let the truck settle. I'm a foot from the trail's edge, which leaves a wide enough gap between truck and wall for the horses to pass comfortably in single file.

Fifteen minutes later all but two of the horses have passed and are continuing up the hill. Jason pops down off his horse and comes over to talk.

"The other rangers are going up to monitor the trail. More are out scouting below. The elders sense that someone is following you. Have you been watching? Did you detect anything?"

"I've had the same feeling and have been watching. I even got out to look back, once we were up on the trail. But I didn't see anything. No lights. No dust clouds."

"OK. Glad to hear you were cautious. We've been instructed to bring you in, then we'll be heading back out. The elders are convinced something's wrong, so we've gone to high alert."

I offer our thanks, then start following them down.

"Strange." Summer offers.

She obviously has more to say, so I wait for it.

"You have a feeling. I'm guessing they've actually seen something. But none of us can put our finger on it. We must not be framing the problem right."

"What do you mean?"

"We're framing it as *being followed*. What if it's different than that? Could they have put a tracker on the truck? Or, maybe sent someone up on the peaks opposite to watch us? Is the space station in a place where they can watch today?"

"Interesting thought. Any idea who?"

"The likely candidates would be Walter or my father. Maybe even Admiral Tang."

"But why?"

Summer shakes her head as if the answer is screamingly obvious.

"Jared, you've become the center of attention on this planet. You've become rich. You pay for everything. You've developed the cure, staved off the famine, and are working with the Central Command to fight the aliens. Then every couple weeks, you disappear into the wilderness. Everyone in power wants to know what you're up to. What's out here that lets you do what you do?"

Her statement is made with passion.

"Well, the answer to at least one of those question should be obvious. You're the one that lets me do the things I do."

I get a harrumph, then a chuckle. "I think my mother agrees on that point. She seems to think your reason for taking me out into the wilderness is uninterrupted sex."

"What!"

"Don't worry. She likes you and is anxious for grandchildren."

JARAMOR

We arrive at the inn to a big welcome. The truck is unloaded for us, our stuff taken up to our room. Unlike other times, people on the street seem to know who we are. Several stop to greet us as if we were visiting royalty.

Inside the pub, it goes the same way. The place is unexpectedly crowded for 11:00 AM. Many of the people inside reach out with a kind word or a hand to shake as we make our way to the private room. There we find the elders already assembled. Jason must have alerted them of our early arrival.

Greetings are exchanged and Elder Aurora Simpson Lake gives us one of her very spiritual blessings. The experience is warm, like being home. But it's over the top, which worries me.

Aurora passes control of the meeting to Julian, who looks at me. "Something momentous has happened. I can feel your influence on it but cannot discern what you did."

Summer seems to understand what he's talking about, but I'm not getting it.

"Several momentous things happened over the last couple days. Which are you referring to?"

"The Confederation's massive victory over the aliens, of course."

I smile. "So it happened. One of our goals for the afternoon was to probe to find out what happened. Tell me."

"I know you don't like my grandmother's prophecies, but there were many of them. One of the ones about you was that your female companion would be the first to take the *profecia aumentar*. We assumed it would have happened before we met you, that we would not witness the event. Yet we did.

"Another of the prophecies was that you would set our ultimate victory in motion, but not learn of it until someone told you. Again, we expected that to be something different."

He pauses there as if taking in the moment. I sit there impatient to put the prophecy behind me.

"The two hundred ships in the alien advanced force fell out of their spacetime bubbles shortly after sunrise this morning. About half were destroyed by uncontrolled reentry into our space time. The other half fell into an antimatter mine field that had been set up to destroy them.

"Aurora and Jack report that the Confederation squadron that set the trap fled the scene last night but have now returned. All but two of the alien ships were reduced to rubble. But two severely damaged ships have been captured and a technology salvage operation is about to commence."

"Members of our scouting team report that the alien detectors fell silent shortly after dawn.

"How did you do it?"

"The idea was inspired by a conversation I had with one of our zone supervisors. The gist of it is simple. If someone doesn't believe you, do something that makes them.

"I've been feeding the Central Command information for several weeks now. I never hear anything back. The only direct conversation I had with them ended in threats.

342

"So, Summer and I started eavesdropping on the admiral's future briefing sessions. We found out that some enterprising squadron leaders had come up with a possible mechanism to knock some ships out of their space-time bubbles. They tried it and successfully forced four ships out of their bubbles. Three landed OK. One was damaged. But they quickly rallied themselves and destroyed the Confederation ships in the area that had set the trap.

"The admiral was devastated by the news, lamenting that they hadn't set a larger trap and hadn't mined the landing zone.

"In my next update, sent two days before the incident was going to take place, I told the admiral what was going to happen. He apparently verified that there were people planning to do what I told him they were going to do. He must have instructed them to set a bigger trap, mine the area where the ships would land, then leave the area until they knew what happened."

"Clever idea. Do you think the admiral is the one looking for you?"

"Don't know. I've had this deep feeling of foreboding since we started out this morning. But haven't been able to discern anything else."

"Do you have an agenda for us, Jared?"

"Yes. We need to determine two things. The first is to learn whether the entire advanced force has been destroyed. The second is to learn how the invasion force takes the news. Will they continue any way, without the thulium? Or will they turn back?

"There's a lot to search, so I'd propose a divide and conquer approach. Which of you had the most success studying the advance force?"

Aurora sheepishly raises her hand. "We mostly did that together. But I think Jack and I can find a remnant if there is one."

Clarissa follows suit. "Edson and I have been having some success reading the flagship of the alien fleet. We've found several good hiding spots where we can eavesdrop. Edson seems to have a knack for doing the things needed to get them thinking on topics relevant to our query.

Julian looks at me. "I assume you want to probe the Central Command?"

"Yes."

"Any chance we could come with you?

I nod.

"Shall we regroup at 5:00?"

The others agree, but I ask how they know when to return.

Julian pops up. "Give me one minute."

He exits the room and reappears a minute later.

"Here, put this on."

He hands me something that looks like a watch, which I strap around my wrist.

"Just set the time. It will tell you when to return."

I set the time, then moments later we're all off flying.

I take off slow, as I did the first time with Ethel and Norah, making sure Julian and his partner Sophia are tracking. Then move quickly toward Admiral Tang's conference room.

CENTRAL COMMAND

I stop well away from the building in which the admiral's conference room is located. I quickly confirm that Julian is with me, taking it on faith that Summer is with me and Clarissa is with Julian. Seeing that he's there, I scan the building to confirm the admiral is in his conference room. The admiral is there, and our hiding spot is empty.

We all flash in and I take Summer's hand in the hope of hearing more clearly.

" two squadrons are now on site. Four more are on their way. So far, we've been able to salvage several pieces of technology from the wreckage of the broken ships. Boarding parties are about to enter one of the two damaged ships that are still intact."

An image comes up on the admiral's holographic com device. It shows two smaller ships attached to the huge alien ship. A moment later, a vibration passes through the alien ship. Several moments after that, the scene changes. It's a live feed from a helmet camera. A human boarding party is entering the alien ship through the breach they've made in the ship's hull.

The boarding party has entered, apparently on one of the lower decks where the drones live. The scene is chaos, drones shuffling everywhere with no discernable purpose. A sighting reticule appears superimposed on the scaly chest of one of the drones. A stream of hot metal races away from the camera, hitting the alien exactly in the center of the reticule. Unfortunately, the slugs bounce off the scales. The drone turns toward the shooter and, filled with purpose now, starts marching toward the camera.

344

In the background, a voice is heard. "Switch to the capsule launcher!"

The reticule relocates to the drone's tiny, fleshy, face. A capsule flies toward the drone. It's moving at a much slower speed, the arc of its flight path clearly visible. The alien sees it coming in time to attempt evasion. But it is slow. The capsule hits the alien at the very edge of the fleshy area on his face. It ruptures, spraying out its liquid contents. Some hits the alien's flesh. Some lands on its scales. Some sprays onto the face of a nearby alien. And the reaction is immediate. The aliens shriek and writhe. The sprayed flesh begins to pucker, shrivel, then smoke. Within moments, both drones are down, and the rest run in panic.

Another command voice comes through the holographic projector. "Deploy the liquid cannons!"

A cannon-like device with a firehose nozzle comes into view. Its operator aims the cannon at the retreating alien drones, then releases a thick stream of liquid that soaks a hundred or more of the lagging aliens. They fall screaming to the floor. All movement stops moments later, and the air starts to fill with smoke.

An alien king emerges at the end of the long hallway and levels an energy projector towards the camera. Apparently, this was expected. A capsule hits the king's fleshy chest before it can fire. The capsule's entire contents discharge. The king falls screaming before getting off a single shot.

The command voice is heard again. "Deploy the misting system."

A cannon that looks similar to the previous one comes into view, then the video feed shifts. It is now coming from the front of the cannon. It starts spraying out a mist. The mist slowly obscures everything in the room.

Another door opens and more drones stream in, but they begin falling almost immediately. One falls close enough to the cannon that its shriveling face can be seen. Moments later, light smoke starts wafting out from beneath its scales.

The scene playing out on the holographic projector is mesmerizing, but the admiral has seen enough. He turns to an aide.

"The Daan kid's poison works. I want ship loads of it by the end of the week. I also want all the ships along the rim outfitted with the capsule launchers, hose and mist cannons immediately."

The aide runs off, then the feed on the holoprojector shifts again.

"Admiral Tang!"

"Captain?"

"We have recovered a functioning device that we believe to be a zero-point energy generator. We are searching for more."

"Congratulations, Captain. Send it back to New Beijing immediately via fast packet and continue the salvage operation. We want samples of all the enemy technology, as many samples as possible."

"Understood, sir."

The image disappears and moments later the timer on my arm buzzes.

PUB

I slowly come back to myself and see the others are back as well. The celebration out in the main part of the pub seems much louder than before.

I look at Julian and nod toward the door.

He smiles. "The news is better than we could have imagined. Some of that leaked out as we came back. It seems to have sent the celebration into overdrive."

Edson stands. Julian looks at him, then smiles. Edson takes his seat.

"My friend Edson suggests that we order a pitcher of ale to enjoy as we debrief. I agree, and just placed the order."

"Aurora, want to share what you've learned."

"Word of the advance force's destruction has reached the main invasion fleet. The current armada commander is worried, but still holding course. They are continuing to gather data from the advanced force and will convene a meeting tomorrow or the next day to discuss with the other captains."

She stops as if she's done, but her smile betrays her intent.

"And the good news?" Julian asks.

"The aliens go to great lengths to hide the location of their home world. Over the last couple weeks, we've put tremendous effort into finding the information. But no amount of probing their equipment or their minds has yielded anything.

"Today, when news of the advance force's demise became known, the armada captain actually spoke the location out loud as he established communication back to command headquarters.

"We now know where the alien home world is located!"

Julian looks at me. "You need to get the word to Admiral Tang as soon as possible."

The door opens and a waiter enters with a pitcher of ale. There's cheering in the bar as he heads back out.

As Edson starts pouring the glasses, Julian fills the others in on what they had observed.

Clarissa lifts her eyes to mine. "Jared, everything you've learned has been true. We struggled to discern what was going on in the Confederation for years. But in just a couple months, you've found the problems and the solutions.

"I propose a toast to Jared Daan, the true heir of our founder, the one who is fulfilling his dream."

I smile and clink glasses with everyone, but inside the toast smacks of the sixth son prophecy, something I resent. But then it occurs to me, the sixth son prophecy wasn't about the aliens. It wasn't about rising above them all either. It was about unifying our people. So, I may have attained my ancestor's dream. But I have not fulfilled the prophecy, at least not yet.

I snap back to the moment and see everyone staring at me.

"What have you discovered Jared?"

I lock eyes with Julian, who asked the question.

"I'd prefer to keep that to myself for the moment. It's personal, nothing of real consequence."

I can tell Julian's not buying it. None of the other elders seem to buy it either. But the tension of the moment is broken when Edson stands and points at the door, which opens.

Noise from the bar streams in as do several waiters. One carries a platter of beef. Another carries a basket of fresh baked bread. Its yeasty smell permeates the room. The third carries in two pitchers. He lifts the one saying, "Ale!" Then lifts the other saying, "Hard Cider from the first pressing."

BETRAYAL

The party atmosphere continues through the meal. Toasts are exchanged, congratulations offered. Then suddenly, the elders are all on alert and a commotion breaks out in the bar.

Anger overflows as the commotion approaches the door to the private room. Then the door bursts open. Several rangers flood in and throw a tightly bound man on the floor.

"We found the intruder!" Jason glares at the man on the floor. His anger and violence of spirit scream in my mind, amplified by the residual *profecia aumentar* in my system.

The man has been beaten. His clothes ripped in places. And he's bleeding. Jason goes to shove the man with his foot, but in a blinding flash of insight I know who it is before seeing the face. It's Jack Johnson, the head of camp security.

"Stop!" I shout. The room falls into silence, all eyes are on me now. I go over and kneel next to him. Taking his hand in mine, I search for a pulse and relief floods through me when I find it. I close my eyes and cast my mind out to understand what happened. The scene of the warden sending him to track us plays in my mind.

Summer sees who it is, sees what I just saw, and starts crying.

I point to the ranger closest to the door. "Bring me water and some towels so we can clean him up."

I look at Jason. "This is not your fault my friend. It's mine. Can you help me with him?"

The entire pub is silent. No noise penetrates from the street. It's undoubtedly the psychic power of the elders informing everyone in the area to be still.

"Who is it?" Julian asks.

"A friend of mine. His name is Jack Johnson. He's head of security at the prison camp. The warden sent him to track us. He's worried that there's more going on out here than we've been telling him. And he's afraid Summer and I aren't up to the task of taking care of ourselves."

Unexpectedly, Aurora speaks up. "And now the prophecy comes true."

CHAPTER 21: REUNIFICATION

Looking out the window, I notice the first rays of dawn's light flowing in over the Sea of Passion. It's beautiful. I've never seen sunrise over water before.

We brought Jack Johnson over to Jaramor's small hospital last night. I've been in the waiting room since. The doctors told me that they expected him to recover, but it would take some time before I'd be able to see him. I refused to leave and have been here since.

Summer is snuggled up on two chairs I pushed together so she could lay down. She's been asleep since midnight. She looks so innocent and sweet that it's hard for me to take my eyes off her.

Jason and Julian sat with me for the first hour after the doctors took Jack. Turns out Summer had guessed right about how we were being followed. When she asked her father for the extra day off, she told him when we were leaving. He had Jack go out the night before and head east along the north side of the river. There's an old utility road on that side that runs 40 kilometers east of the highway. From there a dirt road runs up the mountain that the river wraps around. There are many spots along that trail that provide excellent viewing of the entire area south of the river.

According to Jason, they caught a glint off Jack's binoculars near the peak of the cliff on the north side of the river. In that area, the terrain's too rugged for Jack's jeep, so he was on foot.

Jason called for a team of rangers on horseback to approach that peak from the East. An hour later, Jack found himself trying to outrun horses on rugged terrain. It was a short race.

Jack apparently put up a good fight. Two rangers ended up in the hospital with worse wounds than Jack.

...

"Mr. Daan." The voice and a gentle touch startle me from my sleep. "Mr. Johnson is awake. He would like to speak with you. Fair warning, he's agitated and in a lot of pain. We've had to restrain him."

I nod, then get up and stretch. Summer is still asleep.

"If she wakes up, would you bring her back?"

After a moment's deliberation, the nurse nods. "I'm not supposed to do that unless the patient asks me to. I think I can bend the rule a bit in this case."

I follow her back and hear Jack swearing as I approach the door. Jack's rant stops mid-sentence as soon as he sees me. We watch each other in silence as I walk over.

"Sorry to have put you in this situation." I start. "I was getting close to being able to tell the warden about this place, but some things needed to be settled first. They're mostly settled now. You probably could have come in peace in two or three more weeks."

"What is this place, Jared?"

"A settlement our founder set up in secret for his other wife and family."

"That was like 200 years ago. Why is it still secret?"

"His wife, the one on this side, had told her children to avoid contact with the other settlements until the sixth son of the sixth generation came or died. She made many prophecies about me and the things that would happen, if I was not the first to find them."

"I thought you hated the prophecy "

"I do. But it was important to him, and important to the settlement here. So, they remained hidden."

"No one from our side knew?" He says this in a way that suggests he doesn't think it's possible.

"A few. They've become collaborators."

"So, what next? I really hurt one or two of their men while I was trying to escape. I thought they were going to kill me. So, I acted in desperation."

"The entire situation is unfortunate. But when you're able to travel, you'll be free to return."

There's a knock on the door, then Summer comes in. She gives Jack a hug, fresh tears flowing. "I'm so sorry Jack. My father should not have sent you. But don't worry. You'll be well taken care of here."

There's another knock on the door and the doctor comes in.

"Mr. Johnson, I'm glad to see you're awake. I'm Dr. Astrid Simpson."

She turns to me. "Can I have a few minutes alone with my patient."

"It's OK if they stay." Jack says. "They're the closest thing I have to family."

"OK. I have mostly good news. You took a pretty good beating. You have numerous cuts and bruises. The only thing of real consequence is the concussion. Your brain became swollen, which is why you were unconscious so long. We went in to drain some fluid, and we also have you on an anti-inflammatory and mild pain killer. We can probably release you in a couple days, restricted to minimal activity. It'll be at least a week before you can safely travel. Longer, if you don't restrict your activity."

I see Jack wilt a bit. He looks at me.

"How's that going to work? They'll send a search party if I'm not back in the next two days."

I can see that Dr. Simpson is not happy about Jack asking me questions while she's talking with him.

"Do you have any questions for me before I go." She asks.

"Um, sorry. No. And thank you. I thought they were going to kill me and was pleasantly surprised to wake up in your comfortable facility here."

She smiles. "My pleasure, Mr. Johnson. Get better."

...

When the door closes, I ask Jack when he's expected back.

"I promised the warden that I'd keep an eye on you until you were back to civilization. We assumed that you would follow the road east from the distillery. So, the assumption was that I would keep an eye on you until you were back, which would be late Monday afternoon."

I ponder his words for a moment.

"OK. Unless I can come up with a better plan, Summer and I will head back on our own Monday morning. I can come get you to take you back when it's safe for you to travel."

"But that means, Summer and I will have to tell the warden what happened when we get home. Any thoughts on what we should say?"

Jack ponders the question for a while. I open my mind to him and can hear most of his thoughts. Some of them are not very charitable, which is understandable. His current situation is mostly the fault of others.

"I think his primary concern has been Summer's safety. His secondary concern is that you're up to something nefarious, something that'll reflect poorly on the camp or on Summer. But that's not who he thinks you are, so there's clear cognitive dissonance on that one."

He's quiet for a moment, then continues.

351

"I think you need to play this straight. Tell him about the settlement and assure him I'm in the hospital here and am on the path to a full recovery.

"That, of course, will open Pandora's box, so you might want to think through how much you're willing to tell him about Jaramor before you start."

DECISION

Confident that Jack is safe and will make a full recovery, I cast my mind to the problem of our return. I think Jack's advice was spot on. I also think Aurora called it right last night. Jaramor is about to lose the secrecy it's enjoyed for nearly 200 years. And it's up to me to make sure it happens in a way that preserves the *mystery*.

Summer and I return to the pub where the elders have already reassembled. Conversation stops when we walk in, but it's clear they're worried about the same things I am.

As usual, Julian is the first to speak.

"How is your friend?"

"Out of the woods. He's awake and they expect a full recovery. But it'll be at least a week before he can travel back."

"And how are you going to deal with that?"

"Summer and I will return as planned. We will have to tell the warden that Jack was injured and is being treated, which will raise the question, by whom?"

"And how will you answer that?"

"I don't know yet. I need to probe the *mystery* to find a solution."

"Would you like us to help?"

"In principle, yes. But I'm not sure how."

"May I make a suggestion?"

All eyes turn toward Aurora. I say to her, "Please."

"The Confederation is in a delicate place right now. Giving them insight should be our highest priority in the days and weeks ahead. Is there a way you could use your friend as an excuse to stay here longer?"

"I think there may be."

Julian slides a couple of tiny pieces of the *profecia aumentar* over to me. "Shall we reconnect at noon?"

Summer nods. She's already figured out what I want to try. She hands me the timer, which I put on. Then, moments later, we're away.

...

The plan is simple. I call the warden, tell him that we found Jack injured. We're taking care of him, but it'll be a few days before it's safe to bring him back. We're in an obscure location that would be difficult for rescuers to find. But we're comfortable and safe here, so will stay and nurse Jack back to health.

I fast forward to this evening, then initiate the call. The first several attempts are a complete disaster. But I rewind, trying different approaches each time and am close by the time my alarm goes off.

I come back to myself and see Summer looking at me unhappily.

"What?"

"I should do this, and we should include Jack in the call. OK, if I lead?"

We reset our timers for an hour, then Summer is away. I try to follow but can't. But I can hear her when I put my hand on hers. A half hour later, we know when to call and what to say.

As Summer comes out of it, I say, "You're good."

I notice the elders whispering to each other and assume that we have fulfilled yet another prophecy.

WARDEN'S RESIDENCE

Warden Archer Glenn is sitting at the desk in his study, reading through some reports that came in earlier in the day. He hated working on the weekends, but over time had formed the habit of checking his messages before dinner on Sundays.

"Archie, dinner's ready," June calls out.

Thankful to be rescued from the boring report, he gets up and heads into the dining room.

"I wish Summer were here." June says when she sees him. "We should start inviting them over on Sunday nights for dinner."

"That would be nice."

"I wonder what they're eating tonight. I hope they're safe." June muses as she scoops food onto her plate.

"I'm sure they are."

June's communicator sounds.

"Who could be calling at this hour?"

She picks it up.

"Oh, no. It's Jared!"

She accepts the connection, "Jared, what's the matter? Is Summer OK?"

"It's me, Mom. I hope I'm not disturbing your dinner."

"No, dear. We just sat down. Are you OK, sweetheart?"

"I'm actually calling to talk with Dad. My communicator is out of power. Jared's doesn't have dad's private number, but I remembered yours."

"What do you want to talk with your father about, dear?"

"Dad sent Jack Johnson to keep an eye on us."

"What!" June locks her eyes on her husband. "You sent Jack to spy on them while they're off on a romantic interlude! What were you thinking?"

While the warden sputters, Summer says, "Mom, it's OK. Jack managed to get himself hurt. It's all under control, but we'll be delayed getting home. Can I talk with Dad?"

June continues glaring at her husband as she hands the communicator over to him. "Start with an apology."

"Hi, Summer."

"Hi, Dad. We found Jack Johnson last night. He managed to hurt himself. We've patched him up, but it's going to be a couple days before we can bring him back."

"I'll send out a rescue party."

"No, Dad. We have it under control. We've found this obscure place that's quiet and private. We like it because there's only one easy way in and out. Jack tried to sneak up on us and took a nasty fall. We've got great first aid equipment. He's out of danger. But don't send others out. No sense getting someone else hurt."

"Can I talk to Jack?"

"Briefly. He needs rest and hurt his throat. Hold on."

"Evening, sir." Jack rasps, "Seems I'm the one that needs watching. They've found a beautiful little spot here with one easy approach. Good tactical thinking. I tried a different way and am paying the price."

"You sure you're OK? I'd like to send another team out to get you."

"Please don't do that, sir. Summer and Jared know what they're doing. I'm safe with them. But I'm going to need to heal a little before getting in Jared's truck." Jack coughs and Summer takes the communicator back.

"Can I talk with Mom?"

"Wait, I can't just leave you out there."

"Dad, if you hadn't sent someone to spy on us, we wouldn't be having this conversation. We have enough food for at least a week. When Jack is well enough to travel, we'll come back.

"Now, can I talk with Mom?"

Embarrassed to have been found out like this, the warden hands the communicator back to his wife.

"You're sure you're OK, dear?"

"Yes, Mom. I'd hoped to spend the night with Jared last night. Instead, we spent it caring for Jack. I think we've rigged up enough privacy now. But we aren't planning to rush back. I'm really upset with Dad."

"I understand dear. Enjoy yourself and come back when it's safe to do so. Maybe you can join us for dinner next Sunday."

"I'd like that Mom."

PRIVATE DINING ROOM, PUB

"Very impressive." Julian says as we leave the hospital and make our way back to the pub. "It's interesting to see children playing their parents so effectively. How much trouble are you going to be in when the truth comes out?"

"I think that framing this episode as dad spying on us, gives us the moral high ground. Which is a long way of saying, not much."

Julian chuckles.

"While you were buying yourselves more time today, the rest of us were keeping tabs on the Confederation and the aliens. By the way, the trick of hiding in the admiral's conference room and fast forwarding from briefing to briefing is quite productive.

"We learned enough today that it might be a good idea to send the admiral an update. There's something they've missed that they need. And on Tuesday, they're going to do something very unfortunate.

"We also have more information on the aliens, that he'll find useful. So, debrief over dinner?"

I look at Summer and see she agrees. "Sounds like a plan."

...

We arrive back in the private room and the debriefing begins.

Aurora goes first with an update on alien activities.

"The alien fleet has a strict hierarchy, possibly stricter than ours. But it operates differently. Their telepathy seems to reduce the difference in information between individuals. So, they might start divided, but usually by the time a decision needs to be made, they're all on the same page. The previous armada leader was apparently quite good at this, and the new one is learning quickly.

355

"In consultation with headquarters on the home world, they've decided to continue on toward human space. But there's an odd dissonance among them. They all agree they should continue on. Most seem to believe they will ultimately turn back.

"They know two of the advance force ships were captured. They have enough video coverage from within those ships to know that we are capturing technology and have a poison that kills on contact.

"This is what's driving the dissonance. Some think they must come and exterminate us, so we don't get more powerful. Others think we are a very distant threat, so don't see enough benefit to cover the cost of an attempted extermination.

"If they knew we had the coordinates of their home world, their calculus might be different."

"Thank you, Aurora." Julian replies, then asks the group, "Any questions?"

A few questions are tossed out, but little more is revealed. Then Julian passes the ball to Clarissa.

"Much of what Edson and I learned has been reported back to Admiral Tang, so our observations will probably overlap with Julian's.

"The fleet has been flooding ships into the salvage area. They successfully captured four King-Queen pairs and one or more of their associated drones. Unfortunately, all the drones died within hours of capture, but their bodies have been preserved for study.

"The pairs are deteriorating. Captivity seems to mess with their pheromones. But all eight individuals are still alive, though not cooperative.

"The zero-point energy recovery is going well. Half the units on the first ship have been removed and they've started on the second ship. Several other units have been recovered from destroyed ships.

"Unfortunately, the salvage teams have not been able to extract the propulsion systems or the space-time disruption weapon.

"I think the primary ways we might be able to help are to a.) help them find zero-point energy devices they're missing, and b.) help them figure out how to extract the propulsion and weapons systems."

Julian is usually the one to thank any of us when our report is done. But I jump the gun this time.

"Thank you, Clarissa. Julian, do you or Sophia have anything to add?"

Sophia answers. "I do. First, thank you, Jared, for teaching us how to probe. What we've been able to find in the few months since we first met exceeds everything we found in the years preceding."

She looks at Julian, who nods to her with a smile. My sense is that this is tonight's big insight, and Sophia was the one to observe it.

"None of what Aurora reported has found its way to Admiral Tang yet or will find its way there by other means for the next two weeks. So, I would advise you to forward that information.

"Admiral Tang is well briefed on the information Clarissa reported, so there's no need to send an update on that. But I agree with her analysis. It would be a significant help if we could find a way for them to extract the propulsion and weapons systems.

"We have two findings that need to be sent to the admiral. First, in two days the aliens will find a way to send a signal to the second ship being salvaged. The signal is just a spoof, but the salvage team will abandon the area for several days. There's no need, nothing happens.

"One week from today, the salvage team in the first ship will attempt to remove a zero-point energy device in the very center of the ship. It's extremely hard to get to. The salvage team wants to leave it, but they are ordered to take it. Unfortunately, this device is integral to the ship's self-destruct mechanism. In the process of extracting it, they blow up the ship, killing all Confederation forces aboard and damaging two Confederation ships nearby. They obviously need to be warned."

"Impressive." I reply. "Thank you. Anything else?"

"One item of concern. It's the same concern our founder had. The Confederation has taken a big interest in you. Admiral Tang is fixated on you. In the back of his mind, he's weighing three options: the status quo, defying the quarantine and coming to get you, or simply attempting to eliminate you.

"We should consider going quiet, and staying quiet, until we know for sure the aliens aren't turning back."

Clarissa's words stun me. I knew I'd be in trouble if I fed the admiral bad information. But it never occurred to me that he might try to silence me for sending him good information that saved his people.

NIGHT

Yesterday's meetings closed on a dark note. But now that I've had some time to think, I get it. I know and do things that the Confederation doesn't and cannot. Therefore, they see me as a threat.

Ironically, that's why our founder created this place. So that someone truly skilled in the *mystery* could practice their art in secrecy. I kind of blew that when I contacted the admiral, which puts the onus on me to figure out how to protect myself and Jaramor.

So last night, after Summer fell asleep, I started probing. I didn't take any of the *profecia aumentar*, as I really don't need to anymore. I only need it to journey with others. But it has changed me somehow and at this point I probe on my own without taking even a tiny dose. And unencumbered by others, I can do it fast.

Last night, scene after scene flashed through my mind; possibility after possibility was reviewed and refined. I'm no longer worried about Admiral Tang. I know his current priorities. I'm not one of them. I need to feed him a few more bits of information, then start weaning him off his dependence on me. That can be done in a couple weeks, at which point he will have no interest in me anymore.

I also think I know how to play the reunification. The next couple days are going to be crazy busy.

JARAMOR

Thankfully, the plan for today is to work separately in the morning. Summer didn't set an alarm, and we end up sleeping in past 9:00. Once up, we stop at the front desk to ask if there's a café we can walk to for breakfast. But the answer isn't as simple as I thought it would be. The streets aren't named and there are no addresses. In Jaramor, all navigation is done via landmarks. And, of course, we have no Jaramor currency.

But we're assured that isn't a problem. One of the porters, Tomás, will escort us and pay for the things we want.

"I know a place I think you'll like. It's a five-minute walk north. There's a little café that has real coffee and wonderful warm sweet buns. It also has outdoor seating with a view out over the sea. Interested?"

Fifteen minutes later, we're there and everything is as advertised.

"Are you having a successful visit sir? Everyone has heard about your defeat over the aliens and the unfortunate incident with your friend."

I see Summer sneak a smile at me. Tomás is about our age, maybe a year or two older. Yet he treats us like the elders.

"Yes. The events of the last year have been unprecedented. If not for the work we did in collaboration with your elders, we would be facing very difficult times ahead. At this point, I think we've avoided the worst of it."

"And will you be driving the reunification as the prophecy foretold?"

Possibly, for the first time in my life, mention of the prophecy does not upset me.

"Maybe. A path to reunification has been revealed to me. But it may not look like what you're expecting. I'm told that's been true of most of the prophecies so far."

"Why?"

"I'm not a puppet. I don't act out prophecies made by someone long ago. I use my gift to do what I think is best for my people. Your first elder, Mirella Padilla, got glimpses of the things I'm doing and recorded them to give our founder hope. But I don't do what she wrote. I do what needs to be done. She recorded some of those things, but that doesn't mean she recorded them accurately or with full understanding of the motivation or desired outcome."

"So, you don't believe the prophecies?"

"It's not as simple as believe or not believe. I do what I do because it's what the *mystery* guides me to. The prophecy doesn't cause me to do it. If anything, it's the opposite. The accuracy of the prophecy isn't about me executing a script properly. It's about the prophet having recorded my activities properly."

"Sounds like a lot of pressure, if you ask me," Tomás concludes.

Summer and I chuckle.

PRIVATE DINING ROOM, PUB

On past trips to Jaramor, I haven't brought my exo-net hub and tablet. This trip I did. And when we get back to the pub, I prepare a message for Admiral Tang. It includes three things: the coordinates of the alien home world, a warning about detonating the self-destruct mechanism, and a warning about the aliens surveilling their activities aboard the captured ships. I tack on speculation that the aliens will attempt to activate a minor ship system in the hope of scaring them away. But I reassure him the aliens have lost control of all major ship systems.

I ask Summer to read my report before I send it.

"Why are you so mealy-mouthed about Sophia's report of the alien spoofing?"

"The admiral has too much on his plate right now to come chase me. That will change in a couple weeks. I'll continue sending him stuff like the self-destruct. But over the next week, I only want to send him inconsequential stuff that is increasingly wrong. I want him to think the gift is transitory and waning, and I'm no longer of consequence."

"Do you think that'll work?"

"Yes. I'm confident it will."

She eyes me curiously but doesn't pursue the issue.

"And that brings me to the next issue."

"Which is?"

"I want to head into Heroldstown tomorrow."

"What?"

"I think Evelyn Fontes is one of Julian's sympathizers. I'm going to ask Julian about it this afternoon. If I'm right, I want to hand deliver a message to her tomorrow from Julian."

"What in the world for?"

"A lot of people know that we have something going on over here. Jack was the first, but he won't be the last intruder to come uninvited. I want to get ahead of it. I want knowledge of this place to leak slowly. And I want to provide a different context for our activities here.

"Word will eventually get out that our founder set up a secret settlement by the great sea. But if we can put enough legitimacy behind our presence in this area, no one will care when they find out about Jaramor's actual history."

I'm saved from further interrogation when my tablet beeps. It's a message from Jungle! But not just one message, dozens come flooding in. They're notifications of license grants from the various worlds. It takes a while for all the messages to be received. But when they are, I see that we've been granted sales licenses on all 58 worlds.

"What is it?" Summer asks.

"The supplement. It's been licensed for sale on all 58 planets where we applied."

"Does that mean it's up for sale there?"

"I think so. Let me check."

Summer moves around behind me to look over my shoulder.

My hand trembles as I flip to the sales page. The page loads, but there's so much on it that it's hard to read. After narrowing the display until it shows product totals only, I see that the first sales were on Wednesday last week. 5,102 bottles the first day. Over 10,000 the second, 20,000 the third. Yesterday, day 4, shows over 33,000. So far today, the same number as yesterday, which seems odd to me. Then I realize, demand has hit Jungle's production limit.

"Does that imply your making 33,000 credits a day?" Summer asks incredulously.

"No, that's the unit count."

"How much do you make per unit?"

"Depends on the type. Most of these are six and a half credits per bottle. Others are as high as 20."

"Your making 200,000 credits a day?"

"That's what it looks like. But we have to keep this quiet."

"Jared, you're the richest person on the planet, by a lot."

I shut my tablet and put my arms around her.

"Shush. We have to keep this quiet. It's not for me. It's for all of us. In 90 days when this starts paying out, we can order as much off world food, seed, and equipment as we want. But we can't let Walter find out how much money the company has. He will attempt to steal it all."

HEROLDSTOWN

I'm going to see Evelyn Fontes. Julian confirmed that she was one of his contacts. He gave me a note to give her explaining the purpose of my visit.

Today's journey is risky. In principle, I don't want anyone knowing I'm not in the wilderness. But as Audrey told me the day I bought it, my truck is very recognizable, and a lot of people know it's mine. So, the odds I'm seen and recognized are higher than I'd like.

It's also risky because of the length of the journey, six plus hours each way. I spent several hours probing the ways I could make this contact. This one was the best. I spent several hours probing the trip itself. Unless I screw up, the trip over should be safe. But I could find no probing trick to see the journey back. The decisions I make today apparently impact my return.

Summer isn't happy about what I'm doing. If she'd forbidden it, I wouldn't have come. She didn't, but still would have preferred a different approach. But this is the one the *mystery* revealed as working.

Jason sent an advance team to guide me across the narrow spot on the outbound. I crossed it a little after dawn. A different team will meet me there this afternoon.

I've come over without an appointment. If I'd made one, too many people would have found out I was in Heroldstown. But the *mystery* revealed that Evelyn will talk with me, if I arrive in the parking lot about the same time she does this morning. As I pull in, I see her car in my rearview mirror, coming around the bend in the road and turning into the parking lot.

I sit in my truck watching. I know the parking spot she'll take. As she approaches it, I screw up my courage and get out of the truck.

A minute later, we meet as we approach the main entrance.

"Jared? What a pleasant surprise. Do we have a meeting scheduled?"

"Good morning, Evelyn. No, we don't. Apologies for showing up unexpectedly, but I'm hoping you can give me a minute."

She looks at me critically. Based on the look, I'd be expecting to be turned away, if I didn't already know the way this was going to go.

And there it is. The glare morphs into a smile.

"Sure. Come in. I owe you for getting that seed shipment placed."

Her comment sounds very transactional. But I know from the emotions emanating from her it was an awkward expression of thanks, not begrudged payback.

As we walk up the steps, she points out another building, then points out some of the fields. When we enter, she introduces me to the receptionist, who hands me a visitor's badge. She also asks the receptionist to have a pot of coffee brought to her office.

Once in the office, she's all business and the expected question comes. "So, Jared. What can I do for you this morning?"

"I have a personal note to deliver. I'd like to discuss it with you once you've read it."

I hand her the note, which she takes and stares at for a moment.

"So, you've met Julian."

I'm surprised by her statement. It hadn't come out in any of the visions. I must already have done something different than planned.

"I can tell by the paper. They make their own in Jaramor. It's made from the local eucalyptus strain they grow north of the sea. There's no other paper like this on Jaredaan, and technically none that's identical on any other world."

She opens the envelope but doesn't unfold the page inside.

"I presume this note says that it's time for the sixth son to unite us."

"I'd be surprised if he used those words. But yes. It's time."

She unfolds the note, reads through it, then folds it and puts it back in the envelope.

362

"So, Archer sent his strong man to track you and he stumbled into a bee's nest." She sighs. "Typical. Archer's an honest and respectable man, but this isn't the first time he's done something without thinking through the consequences. It's hard to imagine a good outcome that could have come from it.

"But what's done is done. I presume you have a plan and a role in it for me."

"I do, but it's a bit of a deception. As I'm sure you know, our founder set up Jaramor as a place where the future could be probed in secret. He did that because every time a gifted seer emerged on New Brazil, the Confederation was quick to come in and scoop them up, never to be seen again.

"As the most gifted seer to emerge in hundreds of years, I have an interest in Jaramor retaining its secrecy. But I need a legitimate reason to go over there."

"I'm listening."

"Suppose we opened an agriculture operation by the great sea, a joint venture between your company and mine. I could claim that I've found a plentiful source of the raw materials I use to make the supplement. You could claim that the land I've found is better suited to crops than the land you have here, so you want to do your expansion there.

"If we set it up as a legitimate business, we could go back and forth without question. We could take supplies over; bring product back. It would even give us a pretext for taking some of our people over and bringing some of their people back. Over time, things would open up. But initially, little would change other than easier movement back and forth.

"Given the food shortage that's going to be with us for some time, I'd think this would be welcomed.

"The road is terrible, which will keep sightseers out. We could even put up an employee's only sign."

"Interesting idea. How would we finance it?"

"I'm short on money at the moment but have enough to get the paperwork set up. In about 10 weeks, I'll have unlimited funding. My supplement went live on 58 other worlds this week and we're already shipping at capacity."

"And what about the pending alien invasion?"

"We took down their entire advance force this weekend."

"What? How?"

"An enterprising squadron tried and failed to knock down some alien ships. I saw this three days before it happened and got word to them how they needed to change their plan. They did and it worked. They even captured two ships intact.

"The main armada that's about 2 years out hasn't turned around yet, but it will. I've seen it."

"Isn't Central Command going to be coming for you?"

"The quarantine is holding them back for now. But I have a plan that will make them lose interest in me."

Evelyn gives a harrumph.

"I doubt they're going to forget you quickly, but back to the immediate issue. What are you going to do about Jack Johnson?"

"He's been significantly injured. It will be a while before he can travel. He's switched sides, so will keep silent about Jaramor, but vouch for the viability of our plan to start an operation there."

"I'm in. What do you need me to do?"

"Several things. First, let's write up, sign and back date a letter of interest in exploring agricultural opportunities in the east. This will give us the cover we need for what follows.

"Next, I'd like you to call the warden. Ask him why he sent someone to spy on our planned joint venture. You can tell him I called you from the land we are looking at.

"Next, I'd like to start the process of drafting a joint venture agreement. I'm happy to take the lead on that, but you're welcome to if you'd like. Jaredaan Naturals uses Audrey Preston for legal matters."

She thinks for a minute.

"I should probably take the lead on that. I'll have my people loop with Audrey."

"I'll tell her to expect the call."

Evelyn stares at me for a bit.

"Have you even turned 18 yet?"

"Next month."

"Well, despite your age, you're by far the best businessperson on the planet. I'm glad I'm on your side."

"Thanks."

She extends her hand. "Deal?"

"Deal."

PRIVATE DINING ROOM, PUB

I arrive back safely in Jaramor earlier than expected. The return was more eventful than I would have liked. I know how I'll explain myself, but neither Summer or the warden are going to be happy.

I was spotted by Chief Santana as I was leaving Heroldstown. Then spotted by Charlie as I passed the plant. I arrived at the pass early, waited an hour, then crossed without escort, scraping my truck against the wall.

But despite being spotted and scraping the truck, today was a tremendous success. And I'm happy to be back.

The first person I see as I enter the private room is Julian. He immediately knows I have good news.

"So, Evelyn's on board?"

"Yes, she is. And she's moving quickly. On the way back, I called my lawyer while I was waiting for the rangers. Evelyn's lawyers had already contacted her and sent a draft framework for the agreement."

"Sophia and I have probed this path a bit. It's hard to see. We're probably not approaching it right. But all the possibilities we've seen suggest that you will be successful. It's a clever misdirection."

"Thank you. Have you been able to progress the other matter?"

"Yes. You were right on this one too. We have a list of minimally consequential discoveries for you to report to Admiral Tang. The positive items aren't worth his time. The false items are of zero consequence.

"Probing his reaction to these reports was interesting. At first, he's puzzled why you would send him such inconsequential stuff. He loses faith slowly, but after the second or third false report, he just drops you and stops reading your reports. About a month from now, he'll delete your secure channel."

I smile. It seems all the problems I set myself against are solved: the food crisis, the disease, the aliens, even a path to reunification. On top of that, I got Summer too. The weight of the world has been lifted, it's time to celebrate.

EPILOGUE

It's been three months since we returned from Jaramor. Our first stop on the return was the camp hospital, where Jack ended up staying another week.

We'd practiced our story enough before returning that no one doubts the version of events we gave. The warden was upset that we didn't tell him we were working a scheme with Evelyn to increase food production. He says that he wouldn't have sent Jack if he'd known we were up to something legitimate. I thought it was funny that the implied insult upset Summer more than it did me. And he's still in the doghouse as far as Summer and her mother are concerned.

I haven't taken any *profecia aumentar* since returning. Summer is relieved that we aren't spending every night in the *mystery*. What she doesn't know is that I spend hours probing the *mystery* every night once she's fallen asleep.

The aliens eventually did turn around and go home. The Confederation's Defense Research Agency has reverse engineered and improved on the alien's zero-point energy devices. Access to that much energy has allowed them to build a working jump drive and a working transporter. And, Admiral Tang is planning a mission to the alien home world, which he plans to drown in my supplement. I'm not sure the Confederation will authorize such a mission, but he's earnestly preparing for it.

As I predicted, Admiral Tang lost all interest in me once the prophecies dried up. He never really believed me, despite the victories I handed him. But that's good, because I can once again operate freely and unnoticed.

The preliminary read on the clinical trials for my supplement are overwhelmingly positive. It still hasn't been approved for clinical use. But Jungle has updated my product pages with links to the relevant reports and it has driven sales through the roof. We're now selling over a million bottles a week, which has driven costs down, allowing us to lower the price while taking a slightly higher profit. I'm now getting 7 credits a bottle.

I finally got my first big payday. The next day we released three emergency orders. One for the dry bulk, one for more seed, and one for a bottling machine and other equipment I need. Walter snuck in a few toys, but his term expires soon, and I will see to it that he does not get another.

Summer has been talking marriage and children. I really hadn't told her about my reproductive deficiencies before. The discussion ended in a series of unpleasant medical tests. The conclusion... my sperm count is low, borderline for natural conception. But more than high enough for *in vitro* fertilization. I'm looking forward to the extra work required to do it naturally.

And the new company is doing unexpectedly well. The water and soil along the southwestern shore of the great sea are perfect. We put in a new road south of the camp that goes directly to the new operation, bypassing Jaramor. In truth, you can't even see Jaramor from the new operation. It's allowed us to get more people involved while keeping Jaramor mostly secret.

And I finally came to an agreement with the camp board. I'm now a member of the board, for which I get a small stipend, not an employee anymore. I can keep my apartment for up to one year until Summer and I move into our new house, which we're building adjacent to the camp on the East, more or less next door to her parents. I still get to use camp medical services, spend time in the zones, and visit with Ethel and Norah. But the only time I have to be on site is for board meetings.

...

When I was sent here, two years ago, I thought my life was over. In retrospect, it's the best thing that ever happened to me. I found my beautiful fiancé, found purpose beyond keeping the lights on, and have come to understand the prophecy. It's what caused me to be sent here. It's what caused Julian to come find me. And it's given me a comfortable life.

Who could ask for more?

THE END

AFTERWORD

The idea for the Rise of Daan came from a chance meeting with an old friend. It had been years since we'd seen each other. He was delighted to hear I'd started writing science fiction and very curious about where the ideas came from. The next day, he sent me a message suggesting some historical texts that I could look to for story ideas. None seemed relevant to my interests, so I sent thanks, but didn't pursue it.

A couple days later, I bumped into one of his recommendations again and the ball started rolling. It led to a story of betrayal and loss, set on an isolated desert world, then the discovery of something of immense value. Who could resist?

CANE ECOSYSTEM

Although I've done some work in the sugar industry, I really didn't know that much about sugar cane until we moved to Hawaii. At one time it was grown throughout the state. Today, all that's left are the remnants of a long-lost industry.

On the Big Island, where we live, cane still grows wild on the northeast part of the island. It's warm and wet there, and cane grows along the edge of every road. There are some enterprising locals that still grow some and sell fresh crushed cane juice in the farmer's markets.

But the ecosystem that comes with cane is still prevalent throughout the island. Our home in Kohala is on the northwest side of the island in the rain shadow of Kohala mountain. It's basically desert here, but we still have cane toads, cane spiders and centipedes.

Cane toads are the oddest creatures. They are dark green and look a lot like a kosher pickle with legs. They avoid the sun but come out in the evenings to stare at the moon. On a typical evening, we'll have 10 or more of these things sitting out on the lawn. Every week or two, I'll find one in the swimming pool.

The ones we have are about 5 inches long from nose to stern. When they hop, the legs extend out another 5 inches. I didn't learn that they were poisonous until our pest control guys told us about a client of his that just lost his dog to one.

That got me researching them. Their skin is extremely poisonous, much like a puffer fish's skin is. They also secrete poison from glands on the head, behind the eyes. In some cultures, people have learned to skin and eat them, which I would not advise. Other cultures have used the skin and venom as poison. And a few cultures have learned to extract a hallucinogen from the venom.

To the best of my knowledge, there is no such thing as a cane viper. There are no poisonous snakes in Hawaii. The ones in the story are patterned after the North American water moccasin. But in many places on earth there are snakes of the viper class that live in environments where cane toads thrive. There are great video clips online of vipers attacking cane toads if you're interested. Those clips motivated some of the scenes in this story.

ION DRIVE

I first learned of the ion drive in a museum, not in a sci-fi book. If I'm not mistaken, it was at the Franklin Institute in Philadelphia while I was working on my master's degree in Electrical Engineering. At the time, the idea of shooting molecular particles out of an engine at high speed sounded interesting, but I was skeptical that such a scheme could generate enough thrust to be meaningful.

That was a long time ago. And since that time, many schemes to do this have sprung up: Hall effect thrusters, field-emission electric propulsion, pulsed inductive thrusters, magnetoplasmadynamic thrusters... All of which I sloppily put in the bucket labeled ion drive.

But for the scene in the pub, where Clarissa's giving the briefing on the alien's propulsion, I actually calculated out what the 'ion drive' needed to do. The answer... 16 thrusters, each putting out 1 kg of particles every second at 0.95 C is enough to accelerate a 50,000 metric ton ship at a little less than 10 G. Someone will undoubtedly double check this. When they do, I hope I'm close.

FIRST PERSON, PRESENT TENSE

My previous books were complex, dialog-driven, multi-threaded stories. Stories like these require a narrator to set up scenes and knit the pieces together. Something I do best in third person, past tense.

The Rise of Daan was different. It was conceived as a single thread presented from the main character's point of view, which in my mind required it to be first person. I'd never written a book that way before, but last year read the first several books in Craig Alanson's Expeditionary Force series. These were written first person, present tense, which really brought them to life. From the start, I knew I needed to go that way with the Rise of Daan.

You are the ultimate judge of whether it worked or not, but I enjoyed the writing experience.

COMING SOON

I have several books in the pipeline, three of which have at least one chapter drafted. The plan, as I sit here today, is to put out the next two books in the Chronicles of Daan series first. A sample follows this Afterword. It's drawn from scenes planned for the first chapter.

The book planned to follow those is entitled, Vergence. It will be the first book in a new series called Transcendence, which takes place in the same universe as my previous Ascendancy series. A sample drawn from the Prologue and first chapter also follows at the end.

I hope you enjoy the samples. If after reading them you have comments you'd like to share, please do using the email address below. I welcome all input from my readers.

...

Thank you for having read **The Rise of Daan**. There is great joy in writing a book like this, even more in knowing that someone read and enjoyed it. Please put some stars on a review and stay tuned for more to come.

If you have comments, suggestions, or just want to say 'Hi,' drop me a note. I do my best to answer every email. If you'd be interested in joining my pre-reader program, please contact me.

You can reach me at dw.cornell@kahakaicg.com.

COMING IN 2021

PROPHET
(CHRONICLES OF DAAN: Book 2)
By
D. Ward Cornell

104 Years Ago...
ELDERS CHAMBERS, JARAMOR

"Cedrick..." Senior Elder Mirella Padilla speaks the name compassionately. "We've probed to the south. Unfortunately, the only fertile land we've found is in forbidden areas where we will be exposed. That is why we search to the east."

Cedrick bows his head in respect, then lifts his eyes to the Senior Elder. "It's not for me to question your wisdom, or your ability to divine. But if not from the south, where did the soil come from?"

Mirella exhales sadly, shaking her head the way the teacher of a slow student might.

"Cedrick, the predominant winds come from the west. Yes, the soil on the southwest side of the sea is difficult to explain, but it is far enough north of the equator that the winds still come from the west."

Cedrick gives the senior elder, the protector of the *mystery*, a sad look. "If your theory were true, then there would be soil on the east side of the sea as well. But there isn't. And at this point we know the winds come from the east at the south end of the sea!"

In an instant, Cedrick knows his strident tone has done him in. He bows low. "I'm sorry Ma'am. That didn't come out the way it was intended."

There are several moments of silence, then the Senior Elder says, "I'm sorry Cedrick. Your application for a grant to explore down the west coast of the sea to the south is denied. Everything to the southwest of the sea has been forbidden to us by our founder."

In a fit of anger, Cedrick shouts. "That cannot be true. We are west of the sea. And he..." Cedrick points to Second Elder Julian, Marilla's grandson. "...has ventured there. That's why we know there is soil!"

"Enough!" Marilla snaps back. "The application is denied."

As Cedrick starts to protest, guards appear to escort him out. As he is dragged away from the petitioner's podium, he shouts, "Then I will go on my own!"

...

Cedrick is on his second ale when the familiar voice of his friend asks, "May I join you?"

Cedrick turns to the voice then looks away.

"I'll have what he's having," Julian says to the bar keep.

"Cedrick," Julian exhales heavily. "I told you I would get funding for your expedition. Why did you have to go against my grandmother? She lives in the *mystery*. She's rarely wrong. Why fight it?"

"Has she really probed the south!" The question Cedrick intended to ask, lands as a shout.

"That's your problem Cedrick. Instead of working your case slowly through the system, you demand immediate action from the highest levels without documenting the evidence that supports your claim."

Cedrick takes another sip of his ale, appearing to ignore Julian. After a full minute of silence, he whispers, "You are my evidence Julian, but you never support me."

More silence, then Julian says, "I'll get you half funding in three days. Trust me on this, Cedrick. But say nothing about it to anyone. If word gets back to my grandmother, you will face banishment.

"I have personal funds sufficient to get you south of the sea. Meet me on the shore, thirty kilometers south of town. I'll have supplies waiting.

101 Years Ago...
JARAMOR

"I believe that completes the business scheduled for today. Do we agree to adjourn?" Senior Elder Mirella Padilla asks.

One-by-one, she meets the eyes of each of the elders, then says, "Meeting adjourned."

Everyone stands, then Mirella heads for the exit at the far corner of the room. Elder Aston Jardim calls after her, "A word if I may?"

She nods and says, "Walk with me."

He catches up, then the two of them, already locked in conversation, make their way toward the exit.

From the opposite corner, Julian's aide, Edson Jardim (Aston's son), slips quickly into the room and comes up to Julian. He whispers softly, "Julian, you must come."

Marella, who is almost to her exit, stops in her tracks, locked in a trance the way the elders sometimes do.

Without a word, she turns and looks at Julian, then says in full voice. "Cedrick Frazer has returned. He has made a great discovery but is near death."

She comes back to herself and shouts, "Julian, you must find him and bring him back!"

...

As the two younger men exit the building, Edson takes off running. "This way, Julian."

Two of the rangers stationed at town hall, Andre and Clark, see the Second Elder and his assistant run by. They mount their horses to follow. Andre, the one in the lead, shouts, "Can we help you, Second Elder?"

Julian stops, as does Edson. Then Edson says, "There's a stranger about a quarter kilometer south of town, walking alone by the shoreline. He's clearly out of his mind. He appears to be possessed, shouting nonsense, and periodically calling Julian's name. But he swings his case at anyone that approaches."

Andre extends his hand down toward Julian.

"Let me give you a lift, sir. We can get you there in a few minutes."

Julian extends his hand and is hoisted up onto the horse. Andre's partner, Clark, does the same for Edson, then the four of them take off at a gallop.

...

As they get close, Julian points. "There he is. Stop here. I want to approach on foot."

Only fifteen meters away, they hear the man's cracked voice say, "Away beasts... ...no steal..." He waves an arm, then falls over, clinging to an old leather map case.

Julian slides off the horse and approaches slowly. The old man, agitated, but too weak to offer any serious resistance, glares at Julian.

Julian continues his slow approach. As he gets closer, the man's expression softens.

"Julian, is that you?"

373

"Cedrick?"

With great effort, Cedrick pushes the map case towards Julian.

"This is... It has..." Cedrick's voice trails away, then he goes limp.

Julian runs over and takes Cedrick's emaciated hand, then checks for a pulse.

"Come help me!" Julian shouts out. "He's still alive."

Julian looks up at the rangers and sees Andre in a trance. *"He must have taken a little of the profecia aumentar, so he could call for help."*

A moment later, Andre is back, and the horses trot over. Edson, and the rangers, dismount. Clark goes immediately for Cedrick. As he lifts him, Clark shakes his head.

"This guy can't weigh over 45 kilos. There's nothing to him."

Andre comes out of his trance and shouts, "Jackson and three others are on their way to help, maybe five minutes out."

"I don't want to wait," Julian replies. "We need to get Cedric to the hospital."

Andre and Clark eye each other, then Andre says. "We can take him, but only one of you."

Edson is quick to reply, "Julian, you go. I'll start walking back. It won't take long, but I'll take a ride with Jackson and his team if they come." He points down. "Bad shoes for walking on the shore."

Clark mounts his horse, then Andre passes Cedrick's limp body up. They professionally strap him in place in front of Clark.

"Secure," Clark announces. Moments later they trot away toward the hospital with Cedrick's map case over Julian's shoulder.

...

Edson wheels himself into the Conference Room on the hospital's top floor. Through the windows, he sees the sea, its gentle waves periodically splashing up against the rocks along the shoreline.

Julian is hunched over papers laid out on the table. Having heard the door open, he straightens and turns.

"What happened to you?" Julian asks in surprise.

"The rangers found me, but another crisis came up. Jackson offered to have one of his men bring me back anyway, but I volunteered to walk so they could deal with their other problem."

Julian points at the wheelchair.

"Did you fall down or something?"

"Shoes," Edson says with embarrassment. "They were new. They got totally trashed on the walk through the muddy area, so the guards at the entrance made me take them off.

374

"When I did, there was blood everywhere. I mean, my feet hurt like crazy, but I didn't realize they were rubbed so raw they were bloody.

"You can probably guess from there. They wheeled me to emergency, cleaned up my feet, wrapped them, then brought me up."

"I was wondering what took you so long."

"Any word on Cedrick?" Edson asks.

"He's in a bad way. The doctors say it's less than 50-50 he'll make it."

"Sad to hear that." Edson pauses. "How are you taking it, Julian?"

"He was assumed to be dead. There's a five year wait, so he hadn't been declared yet. But no one here thought we'd see him again. His parting was less than cordial, and he never checked in, despite the tin of *profecia aumentar* I gave him.

"Now he's back, but he's not expected to survive."

"Sorry to hear that," Edson says with the compassion of a good friend. He points to the table. "What are you looking at."

Julian lets out a chuckle. "Did you know Cedrick at all? You were young when he left."

Edson shakes his head no. "I knew of him, of course. He was already a legend because of his discoveries in the north. He was included in the list of explorers we learned about in school.

"But, no, I never knew him personally. Just the legend and an occasional glimpse of him entering the pub the year before he left."

"Cedrick was a master surveyor. Come look at what was in his case. It's a map. It shows a southern river."

"He speculated there would be one, didn't he?"

Julian chuckles. "Yes, He made a big deal about his theory that there was one. Apparently, he found it.

"It runs over 300 kilometers down to Mount Jaramor, as he speculated. But look at the detail in the map. He has the locations of all the peaks and ridgelines. There's a second tall peak that we can't see from here. He's taken the liberty of naming it for himself, Mount Frazer.

"And check this out, the river meanders north from its headwaters near Mount Jaramor all the way to the great sea, detouring around this massive ridgeline that runs east from his self-named mountain.

"And check out the detail. Fields of something he's marked 'bitter fruit.' And this, a cave he's marked as Scale Cave. The annotation says it's filled with huge scales and thick bones."

Edson shudders. "Sounds like the aliens."

Julian chuckles, "That's a good one."

"You know..." Edson starts. "We should name this for him."

"Name what?"

"The river and valley. Call it the Frazer River and the Frazer River Valley."

"My grandmother will make us wait until he dies before she'll even consider it," Julian cautions. "But I think you're right. He discovered it. He surveyed it."

After a moment's reflection, Edson asks, "Why didn't we know about this? Surely it can be seen from the space station.

"My grandfather forbade it. There's a large area that runs from about 200 kilometers north of the great sea to 400 kilometers south of it, down past Mt. Jaramor. And from ten kilometers east of the sea to 500 kilometers west. He built interlocks into the space station's scanners that prevent that area from being scanned. He even made it a crime to bypass them. This is a restriction that the elders in Jaredstown have strictly enforced."

"Why?"

"In time, my friend. In time. There are many secrets the elders keep, and good reasons why we do. You will eventually find out. The *mystery* runs strong in you."

Present day...

EASTERN REGION AGRICULTURAL

I'm standing atop a short hill with my business partner, Evelyn Fontes. The hill is located at the northwest corner of Eastern Agricultural's property. From here we have a view of our entire domain, east to the great sea and south to the foothills of Mount Jaramor. Immediately in front of us is our new wheat field, planted several months back. It's not to the amber-waves-of-grain stage, but it will be in a month or so. It's the first time Evelyn's been over to see this particular field.

"Beautiful, isn't it?" I ask.

Evelyn nods her head. "Agreed. Millions of stalks swaying in the gentle breeze. You've done an incredible job with this Jared. I'm really impressed."

"Thanks, but most of the credit goes to Declan and Vera."

"I know. It's all Declan's talked about for weeks." Evelyn sighs. "But you, Jared, are the force behind this." She spreads her arms indicating the entire field.

...

Five years ago, Evelyn and I launched this joint venture to solve a problem. Our world was under quarantine, and it didn't produce enough food to feed everyone.

At that time, I was the assistant warden at our planet's only real prison—a sugar cane plantation operated as a prison camp. Evelyn was, and still is, the president of the largest agricultural concern on our world. Between us, we controlled most of our world's arable land. The crisis was that we didn't have enough land to grow enough food.

We live on a desert world, one that was believed to be devoid of life when first colonized. Over the previous hundred years, our founders terraformed enough land to significantly reduce our dependence on imported food. But when the disease and quarantine hit, we were in trouble.

About the same time the quarantine hit, I found another settlement on our world, one our founder had set up in secret. They had enough arable land to feed themselves and knew of arable land to the south. That's where Evelyn and I set up our joint venture.

...

Evelyn motions at the broad swath of land in front of us.

"I'm still surprised how fertile this land is. Have you been able to determine how deep the soil goes?"

"It varies." I point to the left, toward the sea. "In the east, closer to the sea, it's less than a meter." I turn and point toward the mountains in the distance to our right. "About ten km in, it's all regolith. No soil at all, just dust and rock.

"But here where the wheat is, there's at least two meters. In some places a lot more. It's perfect for growing wheat."

"But where did it come from? This much soil couldn't have been carried here by the wind from our properties in just 100 years."

I smile. "A few of our geologists disagree on that assessment. But I'm with you. There's too much soil here to have come just from our fields." I point south toward Mount Frazer. "In the Frazer River Valley, there's even more. In some places more than 20 meters deep. My hypothesis is that the soil came from there."

"What?"

"You haven't read the background data we sent you on the Frazer River Valley?"

"Apparently not."

377

"The Jaramor Elders added it to their version of the official planetary survey about 100 years ago." I explain. "As part of our expansions south, we did our own survey about four years ago.

"We now know that extensive plant life has thrived in this valley for a long time. We don't know its origin. But some of this plant life does not exist in the Confederation's database of known plant DNA.

"Three years ago, we commissioned the development of orchards and vineyards in the Frazer River Valley. The leader of our survey team, Aldo Peres, whom I've not met in person yet, is now the chief horticulturist for our operations there."

...

On returning from the brief trip to the wheat field, we pull into the parking lot at headquarters and see Ayla, the headquarters receptionist, walking toward the building. She sees us and comes over toward the jeep we borrowed.

"Sorry I wasn't here to greet you when you arrived this morning. Declan had me out running errands. He's so excited about the peaches." She stretches out the 'so' in emphasis. "Thanks for coming by so he can tell you about it in person."

Declan Fontes is the General Manager of Eastern Region Agriculture. He's Evelyn's second son. He married Ayla the year before I met Evelyn. I didn't know Declan prior to the establishment of the joint venture. In truth, I was less than impressed the first time we met. But Evelyn insisted he was the right person for the job, so I went with it and am happy I did. He's done a fabulous job and built our world's largest, by head count, business in only five years.

The headquarters building is beautiful. It's a two-story timber frame log building constructed from Jaramor eucalyptus. The interior and exterior are made of squared off logs with natural wood finishes. I love it.

Ayla shows us to the conference room, which has already been prepped with water, Jaramor coffee, and some baked goods. As she's about to exit, she turns to us. "Declan will be with you in a minute."

I help myself to a cup of coffee as Evelyn takes a seat.

"Can I get you something?"

"Thanks, Jared. A cup of coffee?"

As I pour, she asks, "Are you as excited about peaches as they are?"

I ponder the question a moment.

"I don't think it's possible for anyone else to be as excited about peaches as they are. That said, I'm pleased at how well this operation is going. It's making a huge difference. And I'm glad we're bringing new foods to our world."

Evelyn chuckles. "Same here."

The door opens and I see Declan and Aldo walk in.

"Hi, Mom." Declan gives Evelyn a hug and kiss on the cheek, then turns to me.

"Jared, welcome. You know Aldo, right?

I put my hand out. "Aldo, a pleasure to finally meet you in person."

As the greetings go around the room, I open my mind to Aldo. He's nervous to meet me and Evelyn in person for the first time, but obviously excited about what they've accomplished. I sense it's more than just peaches, which piques my curiosity.

Once seated, Declan starts.

"Jared, I want to thank you again for funding the expansion to the south. Aldo and I both thought the climate there would allow us to introduce some new crops. What we've found, and been able to build out, is astonishing.

"Give me a second to tie in our orchard manager and we can start the virtual tour."

The two-way holoprojection comes to life at the end of the table. It reveals a man I haven't met before standing near a river with rows of trees behind him and a snow-capped mountain in the background.

The orchards in question are a couple hundred kilometers south in the foothills of Mount Jaramor.

"Jared, this is Cameron Ward, Orchard Manager of our southern-most operation. As I'm sure you know, my mother's company has a small orchard in the mountains west of Lake Herold. Cam ran that orchard. She sent him to us when Aldo found this land.

"Cam, meet Jared Daan."

Cam smiles, then quickly responds.

"Jared, it's a pleasure to meet you."

He nods his head toward Evelyn. "Ms. Fontes. Good to see you again ma'am."

After a bit more back and forth, Declan starts in.

"The orchard is at the far end of the Frazer River Valley about 300 kilometers south of here. The valley stretches all the way from the great sea to the headwaters of the Frazer River in the foothills of Mount Jaramor.

"This orchard is at an altitude of about 1,000 meters. The river is well formed here and has a strong flow year-round. Except for a couple weeks in the winter, this section of the valley sees few clouds and little rain. The year-round sun and cold winter nights are perfect for cold weather fruits. The best varieties of fruit such as apples, apricots, cherries, peach, pear, plum and nectarine all require 100 to 1,000 hours below 10°C to bud.

"Jaramor found places like that north of the sea. Aldo discovered nearly a thousand hectares in the foothills of Mount Jaramor that are perfect. This was part of the Southern expansion you authorized three years ago."

I nod my head in understanding.

The trees behind Mac look beautiful.

"As you can see, the trees on the uphill side of the river have budded."

Cam apparently has a portable version of our holoprojection system. From his current vantage point, we can see the preponderance of buds. There's something organically beautiful about them. The image zooms in on a twig that Cam gently holds between two fingers.

"The buds are still fragile, so I need to be careful, but what you see here will grow to become a white peach."

He turns and points up the hill. "A little further up the slope where its cooler, we're seeing the first buds of our yellow peaches. And, in the orchard a little further up," he points, "the first apricot buds will appear in a couple weeks."

"Next season, we hope to add pears, cherries, and plums on the slopes opposite." Cam points to the eastern slope, his hand rising with each fruit named. Then he turns and points to the next slope south. "The following season we plan to put in nectarines and apples."

I smile at the hand motions. Cam seems to know exactly where he wants everything.

Cam's been walking up the hill as he's been speaking. Now he turns around, revealing the vast Frazer River Valley stretching out below. In the distance, he points out vineyards, strung row after row across a ridge.

...

The virtual tour is done and Declan's down to the last section of his briefing.

"Jared, I know you're always interested in knowing about problems on the horizon. So, I'd like to spend a minute on the things we'll need to address before too much longer.

"The biggest issue will be the bounty from this season's harvest. It will be far bigger than our world can consume before it rots. We have adequate storage for things like onions, potatoes, and corn. But we have virtually no storage for fruit. I've contacted the food packaging operation in Heroldstown. They can take maybe five percent of our harvest. We might be able to sell five to ten percent fresh. The rest will need to be processed."

Declan plops a document on the table.

"I've developed a plan for your consideration to build a food processing facility here. It will have multiple preservation methods: drying, canning, jam and jelly packaging, etc. If we can put this in motion within the next month, we can have enough of it online by harvest to preserve half or more of this year's crop. That which we can't preserve will be composted."

I ponder the words spoken. I'd like to think I'd have thought through the harvest problem far earlier. But how could anyone who operated without insights derived from the *mystery* have known the fruit yield would be so bountiful?

"Will the preservation facility be large enough to handle next year's harvest and the expansions you've planned?"

"Yes. The target capacity is sufficient to handle next year's crop and the planned expansions over the next five years."

"Good. I'll review the proposal this week and get back to you if I have any questions."

ATMOSPHERIC SHUTTLE

Last year, I finally broke down and purchased an atmospheric shuttle. The constant travel between Heroldstown, the distillery, Jaramor, and Eastern Agricultural was taking too heavy a toll on my time and on my body.

The shuttle I ended up buying is a beauty. Its primary propulsion is grav drive. Its power plant is anti-matter. But unlike the grav drive used in hovercraft vehicles like my truck, this one has power.

The shuttle has retractable wings that allow it to take off and land vertically, then deploy in the air for normal atmospheric flight. It can make the flight from home to our estate in Jaramor in less than an hour.

Given the quarantine, the only way to get it delivered was to find a pilot willing to emigrate to Jaredaan. After a month of advertising for a commercial pilot and getting no applicants, I changed gears and started looking for pilots that had lost their licenses. There were a shocking number of them. Most probably should have lost their licenses. In the crowded space that comprises the Confederation, these folks were a hazard. But on a world like Jaredaan, where there are no other atmospheric shuttles, I found dozens of pilots that would do.

One rose to the top of the list, an ex-military pilot named Dylan O'Malley, who was also a certified technician for this class of shuttle. He'd lost his license because of repeated paperwork errors. I read through the transcript of his suspension hearing and thought it was a bit harsh. But, in a place like Jaredaan where there is no aviation infrastructure whatsoever, someone with impeccable flying and maintenance qualifications is all that actually matters. Dylan was my first choice.

RETURN

Evelyn and I exit the building and see the shuttle sitting in the space reserved for it at the end of the parking lot. As we make our way toward it, the shuttle door opens, and Dylan comes out to greet us.

"Successful meeting?"

He reaches out to take Evelyn's overstuffed briefcase, which she gratefully hands to him.

"Thanks. I think I need to get one of those briefcases with anti-grav assist." She visibly relaxes as Dylan takes the load. "The meetings went great."

Once aboard, Dylan and I head toward the cockpit. I've started taking flying lessons, so sit up here with him on almost every flight. Evelyn takes a seat in the first row. The shuttle interior is relatively open. There's a short wall that separates the cockpit from the passenger section. The two pilot's seats are set a little lower than the ones in the main cabin, giving the passengers a good view out the front. The passenger seats are organized as three rows of two seats. The seats in each row are separated by a wide aisle in the middle.

Dylan runs through his take-off check list. I'm in the co-pilot's seat, running through mine, checking gauges and clicking switches. Once the shuttle starts moving, I'm not allowed to touch any of the controls since there's a passenger aboard.

In truth, there are no rules on Jaredaan, so in principle, I can do whatever I want. But Dylan has made it clear. The cockpit of any aircraft he captains will abide by Confederation military flight rules. Any violators will be written up the first time and thrown out the back the second. I like the discipline.

"By the way," I start. "There's a small change of plan for the return. I want to run down through the Frazer River Valley to get an aerial view of the vineyards and orchards."

"Not a problem. Are we just taking a fly over? Or do you want to go in lower and hover?"

"Low and slow, I think."

"You got it boss."

I see Dylan's smile. One of the things I love about him is his willingness to fly. Any mission. Any time. He's always on for it.

...

We enter the valley at an altitude just higher than the mountain tops on either side. The view ahead is spectacular. Less than a kilometer in the vegetation starts. When we were growing up, we were told our planet was devoid of life. Yet here, plants unknown to the Confederation grow. Another couple minutes and the vineyards come into view.

The vineyards are beautiful. They're planted in curving rows that span the mountainside and an adjacent ridge that juts out into the valley. Row after row descend the curved slopes. The vines are lush. A few clusters of buds are still visible.

In the distance, beyond the ridgeline, the orchards are visible as are the headwaters of the Frazer River. The river runs from south to north along the twisting floor of the valley. It twists around the ridgeline ahead, then continues flowing north into the sea.

"Still good at this altitude? Or would you like me to go in lower?"

I turn to look at Evelyn.

"Want to go lower?"

She smiles. "Sure. But no thrill rides, OK?"

I see a devilish glint in Dylan's eye.

"Let's drop to 100 meters and cut speed in half."

The glint fades as Dylan replies, "Got it, boss."

Dylan expertly brings us lower and slower. I know the shuttle well enough at this point to feel the grav drives take more of the load as the aerodynamic lift on the wings falls away. Dylan adjusts the controls, nosing the shuttle down a little to get a better view.

"We can't go very fast with the nose down like this," Dylan says in his flight-instructor voice. "With the nose down, aerodynamic pressure to descend increases. We offset it by increasing thrust from the grav generators. But that puts a lot of stress on the wings."

Dylan takes us in closer to the mountain, which is starting to look really close on our right. Then he turns to the left and follows the curve of the vineyard. From this vantage point it's easy to see how well maintained the vines are.

Ahead at the far end of the ridge, I see someone on horseback wave. The long dark hair running down the riders back gives away her identity. It's Vera Lopes, the vineyard manager. I became good friends with Vera while at the camp. She ran Zone Four for many years, then jumped at the opportunity to organize the camp's new food zone. That operation went so smoothly, I knew I wanted her to lead this part of Eastern Agricultural's expansion.

As we pass the end of the vineyard, Dylan levels out then takes us up as we continue south. Ahead are the orchards, which look as beautiful live as they did in the holoprojection.

...

After dropping Evelyn off at her company, Dylan lets me fly the shuttle back to headquarters. I have none of Dylan's finesse, but I'm becoming increasingly confident in my ability to fly the shuttle while the sun is up and the sky is clear. The shuttle makes little noise, but we still make the journey 1,000 meters above Lake Herold to pass civilization as quietly as possible.

The trip goes smoothly, as does the landing... Well, mostly anyway.

CHANGES

Shortly after the warden's return from Jaredstown five years ago, it became clear I needed to resign from the camp. Uncle Walter was the chairman of the camp's board at the time. He wanted me either fully in or fully out, which was impossible.

The warden and the remainder of the camp's board were terrified of losing me. They successfully pressured Walter to continue with the status quo. But once the food shortage and Doffenplod Acquired Genetic-disorder Syndrome (DAGS) crises were brought under control, we needed a new arrangement.

I agreed to resign my position as Assistant Warden. They offered me a seat on the camp's board. In lieu of other compensation for board service, they gave me a one-year fully-paid lease on my apartment, and continued use of camp facilities like the staff café, staff gym, and the camp hospital.

It ended up being a good deal for everyone. The camp is doing better than ever before. We now produce about 10% of our planet's food, about twice what we need to feed the camp. Cane output has nearly doubled, allowing the ethanol plant to run at capacity. And our population is by far the healthiest on the planet.

The deal allowed me to stay involved at the couple-hours-a-week level, while building my businesses. I now have five businesses:
- My original personal power pack business with Jungle
- Jaredaan Natural Supplements
- Jaredaan Pharmaceuticals
- Eastern Region Agricultural, joint venture with Evelyn
- Jaramor Science Institute.

Of the various businesses, the Institute is the one I want to focus on the most. But that goal has been elusive.

Across the businesses, I employ about 1,000 people. The preponderance of them are with the joint venture and under Declan's management. But I have about 100 in the supplements business, over 200 in the pharmaceutical business, and am slowly building out the staff for the institute.

Summer still works in reception at the camp. I wish she would go full time with the Institute, but I haven't been able to make that sell yet.

HEADQUARTERS, JAREDAAN NATURAL SUPPLEMENTS

Jaredaan Natural's headquarters are located on the property that came with the old distillery. The new office building is a hundred meters east of the distillery, the shuttle's hanger is another hundred meters beyond that. The old chain link fence is gone, replaced by a more substantial steel fence that's four meters high. The road in has been replaced with a new one that is smooth and wide, designed to handle the daily traffic volume an operation like this generates.

As I come in through the front door, I'm greeted by our receptionist, Helen.

"Good morning, Jared. I hope you had a productive trip."

"I did. Anything come in while I was out?"

She laughs. It's a joke of sorts between us. A ton of stuff comes in every day, far more than I can sort through.

"You'll have to ask Brenda about that, but I do know two calls came in from Elder Board members."

"Great," I groan.

She laughs some more.

I head up the steps, wondering what Brenda has waiting for me. I met Brenda at the camp about five years ago. She'd been bit by a cane viper and was quite literally on death's doorstep when she got to me. I got her help in time for her to make a full recovery. It was one of those bonding experiences that lasts. When her sentence was up two years ago, she came to work at the company as my assistant.

The door to the outer office is open as it usually is. As I approach, I hear Brenda talking with someone over the phone. From the context of what I hear, I can tell it's Cousin Kinsley, the mayor of Jaredstown and a member of the Elder Board.

"He just arrived, ma'am. Let me see if he can talk."

She hits the mute button, then greets me.

"Welcome back, Jared. Things are buzzing here today. It's Kinsley, something about the vaccination program."

"Put her through."

I enter my office, take a seat at the conference table, then accept the light blinking on the virtual conference room controller. The image of Kinsley appears, sitting on the other side of the table.

"Jared, I was hoping to have received your progress report on vaccination percentages at Eastern Agricultural by now."

I have to chuckle. No greeting, just 'where's the report?'

"Good morning, Kinsley. Good to see you this morning. I hope you're having a good day."

"I'd be having a better one if I had that report."

Now I really laugh. "Well, I have mixed news for you. Everyone in the company has been vaccinated at this point. But I still do not have the numbers from Jaramor."

"Nothing?"

"I'm told things are proceeding well there. But I don't have any numbers."

There's silence on the other side of the table. But I can tell Kinsley's not very happy with me. The problem regards the disease and quarantine.

Jaredaan has been under quarantine for about five and a half years at this point. We were put under quarantine when DAGS spread here.

DAGS is a bioweapon left behind at the end of the Great Alien War (GAW). The bioweapon consists of two parts: a) a virus that spreads a weaponized gene, and b) problems created by the malign gene once it's inserted into the human system.

I made my fortune by finding a treatment that shuts down most of the effects of the bad gene. Recently, a vaccine and treatment for the virus were found. Between them, they are more or less 100% effective at eliminating the virus.

Quarantines will be lifted from planets that can prove the entire population has been vaccinated and everyone is virus free. Four of the five major population centers on Jaredaan have that proof now. Only Jaramor is showing less than 100%.

I look back up at Kinsley. "Let me call Julian. He's the mayor of Jaramor. I'm sure they're mostly done. The problem, if there is one, will be in their agricultural operation north of the great sea."

...

This is one of the problems with Jaramor's current status. The reunification is nowhere near complete. It's barely started. They've been purposefully hidden from the Confederation, but for edicts like this, they must be compliant. Most of that burden falls to me. Kinsley and the Elder Board know of Jaramor, but they have no connection with it. At some point I'll need to address this issue. For now, I need to manage it personally.

NOTICE

Once off the line with Kinsley, I start working through the items Brenda has prioritized for me. At the top of the list is an urgent call from Uncle Asher. He's the head of the planetary Elder Board this year—the *Prime Elder*. I initiate connection and moments later Uncle Asher is sitting across the table from me. He doesn't look particularly happy and, like Kinsley, just plows in without greeting.

"Jared, I just got a notification from the Confederation saying that our status as a Protected World is being revoked. They are giving us 30 days to cure the problems with our current charter, apply for membership in the Confederation, or declare ourselves as non-aligned.

"Apparently this has something to do with the alien detectors. As you are our resident expert, I'm forwarding this to you. I want you to brief the Elder Board at the meeting on Friday, explaining the problem and our options."

I'm shocked by the news, then equally shocked when he drops the line connecting our virtual conference rooms. What's going on up north today?

COMING IN 2022

VERGENCE
(Transcendence: Book 1)
By
D. Ward Cornell

[Sixty Years Ago] CRYOGENICS INSTITUTE

Emma Schuler picked up the pen, her hand trembling. This was the final release. She was committed to this course, but the finality of the moment was not lost on her.

Emma was sick, her condition uncurable. She'd fought it, fought it hard. Her family's wealth made that possible. But at this point, she knew the disease was going to win.

If she were older, finished with her work, maybe she'd give in, slip into the darkness peacefully as she'd seen her parents do. Near the end, her mother had told Emma not to mourn for her, she'd lived a full and good life, and was ready for whatever was coming next.

But Emma couldn't do that. She was young, talented, the descendent of a royal family. It was so unfair. But not because of her age, wealth, or social status... because of her work.

Emma was a physicist. And she was close, right at the threshold of finding the means to penetrate the multiverse, of probing the layers of space-time and finding their secrets.

But the disease was not going to allow that. It was going to steal her away unless she took the last escape open to her, cryogenics.

She'd been told that the process would kill her. Maybe it was the certainty that the disease would irreversibly do the same, that made this seem like the better option. So, she bought the best plan she could afford. The rest of her estate would be held in trust. Hopefully enough would be left if she ever woke again to resume her research.

Determination restored, she signed the last document, then laid her head back. "You can start the drip, when you're ready."

[One Year Ago] TEMPLE OF THE ANCIENTS

David flashed into existence on the planet, Pa'Hoya'Don. Though he'd been here many times, he hadn't learned the planet's name until recently. The name meant *Ancient Garden of Rest*.

The huge red crystal in front of him began its rhythmic pulsing as soon as he arrived. Moments later, a sentinel appeared.

"David Washington. Human. Compatible species. Transformed. First of your kind. You are welcome to enter the temple and stay as long as you desire."

Having completed its duty, the sentinel disappeared.

David smiled at the rigidity of the sentinel's greeting. The sentinel was an artificial intelligence, a construct of the Ancients. It was designed to be their protector. It had extreme intelligence, extreme logic, and all the power of the Ancients. But it had little personality. Its sole reason for living was to protect the temple, this temple.

The crystal's pulsing filled David with energy.

The Ancients were what the name implied, an ancient species whose origins reached back hundreds of millions of years. Their technology was vast, magical to the uninitiated. Only one member of the original ancient species could still take corporeal form. His name was So'Gen La'Hoya. David knew him as James. James was David's mentor.

The Ancients' greatest achievement was mastering the technology to exist as pure energy. It functionally gave them immortality. When the sentinel announced David, it identified him as being human, which he was. It also declared him to be of a compatible species, meaning a species capable of existing as energy. And lastly, it declared him as transformed, meaning a person that had undergone the changes required to exist as energy.

David was born in 1995 in inner city Baltimore. But he was also the first human to be gifted by the Ancients with the training to convert into energy and back at will.

It's time, he thought, then flashed into energy and entered the crystal.

David was greeted by many as he made his way in. But this was not a social visit. He'd been summoned by the Judge's collective, the most senior and respected of the ancients living in this temple. They'd given no reason for the summons, but David could tell they needed him for something important.

...

David felt the immense antiquity of the Judges as he approached. Although not a member of their collective, David was a judge, one who had performed well in previous missions. As he got closer, David could sense their good will. He could also feel their anxiety.

"*David Washington. Thank you for coming to meet with us.*"

The image of a galaxy appeared in David's mind. Moments later, the human designation for the galaxy did also, Messier 81 (M81). More facts and images raced his way. It was 13 million light years from Earth. There was a temple in M81.

M81 also hosted a Confederation of Planets founded by the Ancients. But its confederation was smaller than the one Earth joined 15 years ago, and less technologically developed as well.

"*David, a vergence is occurring in M81. It was first reported to us by the Temple in that galaxy. We can observe it from here.*

"*It's already grown to the point where it disrupts communications and we recently lost contact with the temple there. It is at risk, as is this portion of the Milky Way.*"

"*What is a vergence?*"

The collective seemed to struggle to answer this question. David perceived disagreement within the collective, which was extremely unusual.

"*It could be described as a folding, or focusing, or even as a crossing of spacetime. A disruption in the normal flow of matter, energy, and time. From this distance we cannot discern the cause, only its existence. This type of event has been observed before. It is not naturally occurring and, if allowed to continue, it will consume M81 and possibly this portion of the Milky Way as well.*"

"*How do I stop it?*"

"*Until the cause is known, the answer cannot be.*"

"*Do you know how much time we have?*"

"*Years, possibly tens of years. But certainly not hundreds or thousands.*"

There were several moments of silence.

"*David, the Confederation must assemble an armada of capital ships and go to M81. They need to find the source of the vergence and stop it. You need to go with them. This is not something you can do on your own, and it's not something the Confederation will succeed in doing without you.*"

Daniel Porter stood by the window in the observation lounge. Outside was the immense ship that would soon become his flagship.

From bow to stern, it measured 5,000 meters, from top to bottom 250. He viewed the ship from its port side, so didn't have the angle to get a sense of its width. But he knew it was a full kilometer from port to starboard.

Daniel was an admiral in the Confederation Fleet. The Confederation, whose full name was the Intergalactic Confederation of Planets, was composed of over 1 million worlds in three galaxies with members from over 10,000 species. Fifteen years ago, the Confederation had revealed itself to Earth, which was granted membership later that year.

The Fleet operated ten armadas in the three galaxies it controlled: five in Andromeda, three in the Milky Way, and two in Triangulum. The ship in front of him would lead a new armada, the eleventh. Its mission would be to secure the galaxy M81 from the vergence threatening civilization there. No one really knew what the vergence was, but it was clearly visible from Earth. The Confederation had higher quality images, but even the images produced by the Webb Space telescope showed the odd folding taking place in M81.

Behind him, he heard someone approach. Turning, he saw that it was Dr. Kelly Williamson, winner of two Nobel Prizes and the developer of the technology used to build his ship.

"Admiral Porter." Kelly put her hand out to shake Daniel's.

"Dr. Williamson. A pleasure to see you as always." He shook the hand offered.

Kelly motioned toward the ship. "Beautiful, isn't it?"

"I never thought I'd see a ship so large."

The observation deck was part of the permanent space station located near Sun-Earth Lagrange Four (SEL4). The ship in front of them was centered over the Lagrange point itself. This location had gone into production nine years ago. It had been selected because of the low microgravity and relative stability of this Lagrange point. Low microgravity was important for the construction of spaceships this large. The keel, superstructure and hull were grown as a single crystal. The source material was derived from metals extracted from Earth's molten core.

The space station had been added five years ago, as were the two space garages hovering above and below the ship in front of them.

The garages housed the thousands of bots and replicators used to build the ship.

Out of sight behind the ship were two others just like it. Their hulls had been completed earlier. They were in the final stages of interior build out but were not going to be part of the new armada. They'd been configured as colony ships, destined for missions elsewhere in the Confederation.

"It's quite an achievement," Kelly said. "A lot of new technology went into its design. It's not just a bigger version of our other ships."

"Really? It looks similar and the interior layout seems to be the same, just more spacious."

Kelly smiled. "Good, that's what we were trying for. But we had to make quite a few changes to the hull design in order to accommodate vibration and gravitational shear. We also had to change the way we distribute power to the propulsion field emitters."

"Really? Why?"

"For a ship this large, field propagation from any single source is too inconsistent. Previous Confederation designs addressed this problem using delay lines to equalize distribution. But that technique is inefficient and subject to failure. More than one ship was lost because the stern dropped from jump a hundred milliseconds before the bow did.

"We beat the problem using a distributed power and field generation system, controlled via quantum-entangled communication links. None of our existing ships can transition to warp or jump as smoothly as this one can. You'll feel the difference the first time you take her out."

"Truly amazing." Daniel chuckled, shaking his head. "Are you spending much time up here?"

"I pop up now and again. I have access to all the instrumentation from my lab on Earth, but some things I like to see with my own eyes."

"Same for me. When we're out on mission, it's easy to spend all my time on the command deck. So, I purposefully walk the ship at least once a week to get a feel for it and the crew.

"Is Dr. Xu working with you on this project?"

"He contributed yes. But he's been away on Ardessa most of the last year."

Dr. Eugene Xu had been Kelly's research partner for the last 10 years. The two shared the Nobel Prizes they'd won. Eugene's wife,

Nelly, was on temporary assignment in Ardessa, the most populous Confederation planet in the Milky Way.

"Eugene did most of the work on the new power sources, distribution and field emitters. Most everything else I handled with Nadia and the rest of the AI team."

Nadia was the third member of their research team. She was an AI and was also named as a corecipient of the second Nobel Prize the team won.

"I heard the ship's going to be commissioned today."

Daniel smiled. "Yes, I'll be getting the command codes later this morning, then going aboard this afternoon. The mission will commence a few days later."

"Well, I hope the ship serves you well."

ABOUT THE AUTHOR

D. Ward Cornell lives on the Kohala Coast of the Big Island of Hawaii. His work as an engineer, consultant and entrepreneur has taken him all over the world. Many of those places are featured in his writings. Although still dabbling in those fields, his passion now is bringing stories to life.

OTHER BOOKS by D. WARD CORNELL

Ascendancy
    Book 1: Revelation
    Book 2: The Institute
    Book 3: Emergence
    Book 4: Alliance
    Book 5: Return of the Ancients

Chronicles of Daan
    Book 1: The Rise of Daan
    Book 2: Prophet   (Coming in 2021)
    Book 3: Liberation   (Coming in 2021)

Transcendence
    Book 1: Vergence   (Coming in 2022)

Made in the USA
Middletown, DE
21 June 2023

33096946R10223